Then Came October

Then Came October

L. E. USHER

Harbour

First published in paperback original by Harbour in 2008
Harbour Books Ltd, 20 Castlegate, York YO1 9RP
publicity@harbourbooks.co.uk
www.harbourbooks.co.uk

UK and Ireland sales by Signature
20 Castlegate, York YO1 9RP
Tel 01904 633633   Fax 01904 675445
sales@signaturebooks.co.uk

A catalogue record for this book is
available from the British Library.

ISBN   978 1 905128 13 6

Typeset by Antony Gray
Printed and bound in Finland by WS Bookwell

To my parents

Winifred Maxwell Usher (1941–1987)

Francis R. Usher (1940–2007)

Author's Note
This novel is based on a true story. Names, dates and locations are drawn from the known facts of Edith Carew's life. However, all interpretation of events is the work of the author's imagination.

Acknowledgements
The final draft of this work was assisted by a New Work Award from the Literature Board of the Australia Council, Sydney.

Thank you to the Authors' Foundation, the Society of Authors, London, for an award that allowed me writing time at the Wordsworth Trust, Grasmere, Cumbria.

Molly Whittington-Egan's *Murder on the Bluff: The Carew Poisoning Case* (1996), a detailed presentation of the Carew trial, was consulted during research for this novel.

Contents

Cwm-yr-Eglwys, Pembrokeshire

October 1934

October 1st   It is now October & the wind will pillage the trees of their leaves & strew them upon the river & in Berry Hill Wood the rambling hogs will fatten from eating the acorns & the field-hare will stand still & be caught by the hunter's gun & the wild-fowl shall be shot from their flight patterns & fall on to the mossy moors that lie beyond Brynberian & the fox will flee the hounds & the mice will sleep in their mouse-holes & the last of the chimney swallows will soon be gone & the robins & blue-tits & blackbirds will hide in the hollows of hedges & tree-trunks & the rooks will become garrulous & the crows will circle the Carn in the lessening dusk-light, & though it will blow wet on more days than not, I shall gather the wild rosehips & the haw of the hawthorn & the sloe of the blackthorn & the remaining apples & pears from the orchard & at night I shall sit close to the fire, reading. And this I know. This I know, because it has been written before & will go on being written.

Later. She has been & gone already. And she will attempt to goad me, as if she hasn't learned by now. But it is almost as if she cannot help herself. I no longer mind that she comes, following me around like a stray dog for an hour or two. She likes it here, I can tell. Yet even so, she never offers a hand to help. She is bone idle, I do believe. However, this afternoon she poked and prodded & refused to take no for an answer & so I walked away from her. The stupid child, when will she ever learn? But she will come back, of that I'm certain, not tomorrow, or Wednesday, but the day after, perhaps.

Her mother stands.

Mardie watches, before prompting, and then?

And then nothing, she answers, walking to the window, signalling that for now their conversation is finished. Mardie too stands, although she wants to continue. She is being dismissed and will acquiesce, will bend and bow and scrape to her mother's will, thinking, Bitch, bloody bitch, while smiling with her mouth.

Slamming the car door, she stares through a windscreen slimed by an invisible rain. The dampness enveloped her, seeped into her skin, her innards shrivelling at the contact. Depression tickles the base of her brain and suddenly she is nauseous. She needs a drink. She wants to obliterate this place from her mind.

She drives too quickly, winding roads that are hardly more than tracks, hand hitting the horn at each blind corner, tyres greased with mud are sluiced clean at fords. She switches on the headlights although it is only early afternoon. I will hit something if I don't slow down, she thinks, but doesn't really care.

At home she pours herself a drink, downing it in one gulp, breath hissing through clenched teeth as the whisky burns her throat. And then another. It is the wrong time of day for this but that has long ceased to matter. She lights a cigarette and draws mingled smoke and whisky fumes into her lungs. She smiles then catches sight of herself in the mirror to see that she isn't smiling, after all. Yes, her teeth are bared and wetly catch the light, but her lips are not smiling. She watches herself drain the glass and smack her unsmiling lips together and pour another measure before raising the glass in a silent toast to her Mardie-mirror-self.

I really am the spitting image of father, she says, not for the first time, except for his 'tash, of course, then laughs, an off-key sound that doesn't know that it is meant to be a laugh. I always was daddy's girl, wasn't I, and I'm your age now. I'm forty-three, the same age you were when you left me. I'm not a little girl any more, she adds, but her eyes return her stare, unbelievingly. She lights another cigarette, mouth muttering around its shape as she takes her glass and the bottle to settle by the fire. She tilts her head to listen as the clock strikes three. At this rate I'll be tight by four if I'm not careful, and we can't have that, now can we? The forgotten cigarette burns her fingers and she puts them into her mouth, sucking soothingly, watching through the window as the pouring rain pounds the sea into submission.

She moves her hand to the books on the side-table, fingers hovering, hesitating, withdrawing. These are her mother's diaries; taken without her knowledge. They will tell the truth of her father's death, surely. Mardie can still recall her grandfather's voice, overheard on an afternoon more than thirty years ago, calmly saying, But, my dear, as if a woman who may have murdered her husband would stick to telling the truth. And her grandmother's furious reply, How can you say it, how can you even think it? Mardie and her brother Ben eavesdropping. Ben's elbow sharp in her ribs as he hissed, You see, you see, he thinks mother did it.

Again she moves her hand to the books on the side-table, fingers brushing the spines. Yes, she says aloud, I will find out what happened, mother, even if you won't tell me.

Glastonbury, Somerset

1878–1885

1878

April 30th   Tomorrow is my 10th birthday and Mama has given me an early present. It is a diary. She says that I should write here every day, just as she does in her diary. Mama says that if I have nothing to write of, then I should describe what I see, such as people and places. She says this is good mental exercise, doing for my mind what walking and riding Owl do for my body, which is give it fresh air. Mama says that just because I am a girl does not mean my mind should not have airings. I am not to tell Papa about my diary. It is to be our little secret. Mama's and mine. And since I like secrets very much I have crossed my heart and promised not to tell.

May 1st   Mama has been in to brush my hair. She says that I am her fairest maid and it will always be so, that I am her maiden May. I am wearing my blue dress and later I will have cake and presents and then we will look at the May Pole which Mama says is just for me because it is May's Day.

May 2nd   Yesterday my presents were a musical box from Papa and a pink-satin-lined box from Nile for keeping my handker-chiefs. Mama says the boys are still too small to give me presents so I must wait two or three years until they are bigger. But even though they are small they ate a huge portion of my birthday cake. After cake, we went to see the May Pole and the dancing and singing. All the girls had ribbons and flowers and were dressed very pretty. Even the big boys were washed-up nicely. And the horses and the oxen and the cows and even the pigs had nosegays. And it didn't rain once although the clouds came and pretended that they would open at any moment.

Right at this very minute Mama is smiling because I am writing in my birthday diary. I like it when Mama smiles especially because of me.

May 3rd   Yesterday after lunch Gregory drove Mama and me into Wells and I had my photograph taken twice, once on my own, then once with Mama. And then we went to the cathedral and looked and looked for hours, as we always do, mostly at the tombs, and then we went for tea and I had three small cakes, one with thick pink icing, and then the clouds came and Gregory drove us home before they decided to rain.

May 7th   Mama is cross with me. I used a not-nice word for my seat. She said she doesn't expect me of all the people who live in Glastonbury to use such a word. Not you Edith May, she said. She only calls me Edith May when she is cross. When she is very cross she calls me Edith May Porch. Just as when she is upset she will call Papa, Mr Porch or Your Father, not Johnnie or Papa, as she normally does. Usually it is because he has done or said something that is not-nice. Then he will look embarrassed, sometimes he'll even squirm, and say, Now, now, Daisy, because that is Mama's name. Although her True Christian name is Margaret everyone calls her Daisy, except for those who call her Ma'am or Mrs Porch, and the boys and I who call her Mama. At other times when she is in a bad temper, only for no reason that anyone can understand, she will lock herself in her morning room and not speak to anyone for hours.

May 8th   There have been words between Mama and Papa because Papa took me out on Bayard and we jumped hedges and rode through puddles and there was a lot of mud even on my face and in my hair. Papa and I were sent to our rooms to think over the dangers of a little girl on a big horse. When I said, but it was fun, Mama cried and so I cried and promised I wouldn't do it again even though I want to. Mama said I will fall and crack my skull just as I did when I was almost five when Dr Bought came and sewed my head back together. I don't remember this happening but Mama remembers even though she wasn't there because Cecil was in her tummy and she was at home with her feet up. Mama says that it was Papa's fault then for putting me on a fast pony and if she had been there it wouldn't have happened.

Sometimes she will have tears about what she would do if something happened to me. And then I'll cry too because I don't know what I would do if something happened to me and Mama was not there.

May 9th I have had the cold chills and been in bed all day. Mama says it was all the splashing mud from yesterday and that it is Your Father's fault. I have had a lot of beef broth which is my very favourite.

May 10th Papa says that I am to have Bayard for my very own. Mama is not happy at all. She has said, I think not, Mr Porch, more than a hundred dozen times. But Papa winked at me and said, Edie May's not a little girl any more, she has to have a suitable mount or she will get left behind at the hunt, and we can't have that, now can we. He said that I will probably take two or three tumbles before I get the knack of hanging on, and that there is nothing wrong with a tumble or two so long as I'm the sort who bounces when I hit the ground. Then he laughed and laughed but Mama looked cross and asked me to leave the room so that she could have private words with Papa.

And today Nile came back from visiting with her friend for six whole weeks in the Lakes. Mama told her that we had hardly noticed she had gone because we have been so busy and it is true.

May 11th Mama and I are in London for three days and are staying with Cousin May. We took the fast train which was very fast and exciting. Mama told Papa that we are doing Spring Shopping and we are but we are also not. We are going to see Mrs Lurgashall in Bloomsbury so that Mama can talk to Albert. Although this has not happened yet Mama believes it will. She says Albert might be in a part of heaven where little boys are not yet allowed to speak to their mamas. In Bloomsbury, Mama said, they sit at a table and hold hands and Mrs Lurgashall calls each person's name and waits for them to come and speak. Sometimes they don't want to come and she has to call their name again and again before they answer. Mama says that there is nothing at all to be frightened of and when I am 12 I may come with her and try to talk to Albert. But I'm not sure what I will say as I don't remember him at all. I was only 1 year and 5 months when God took him to be an Angel.

May 12th   London is not-nice, Mama and I both agree. We saw a fist-fight between two street urchins and there was blood and they had to be dragged apart. Although we have only been out shopping for a short while, our dresses and gloves have nasty black marks on them.

May 13th   Today is our last day in London. In the morning we finished our shopping in Bond Street and Mama bought three summer shawls because she couldn't choose between them. After luncheon we went to the Regent's Park where a band was playing. We walked and walked around the pond and then we bumped into Mr Kingsley who is a friend of Mama. I don't like him. He made Mama's face go red and she fanned herself quickly as if she were cross, but when I asked if she was she told me not to be a big silly.

May 19th   At church we sang for St Dunstan. He lived nearby and pulled off ladies noses if he thought they were being not-nice. He did this with tongs that were baked red-hot in the black-smith's fire. When I asked why the ladies didn't run away, Mama said she would tell me when I was bigger.

May 20th   Last night I picked a bunch of lilac and burned it in the fireplace. Jane helped me and promised she wouldn't ever tell. Then she helped me to put some of the ashes in an old handker-chief to place beneath my pillow. Mama does this twice a year and then writes down her dreams. She has said that I must not do it yet, that I must wait until three or four years when I will be a young woman. I had no dreams at all so perhaps she is right.

May 25th   Mama and Papa have gone to a ball. I was allowed to stay up to watch them leave. Mama wore a rose-pink gown and had flowers in her hair. She looked like a Fairy-Tale Princess and Papa kissed her on the hand and they waltzed so that I might see what they would look like dancing at the ball.

May 26th   I have not seen Mama all day because she danced so much last night that her head aches. Nile says if I am very good and very quiet then tomorrow we will have a picnic day by the sea.

June 1st   Papa and I are to ride together every afternoon so that I am used to being on Bayard when the hunt starts.

June 9th   Last night I saw him again. I was suddenly awake as if he had called my name and I tiptoed to my window and I saw him standing near where he is buried. When he saw me at the window he raised his sword to me. I am one of his chosen Knights. When Mama finally takes me to see Mrs Lurgashall I am going to ask her to call King Arthur's name so that he can tell me what I might do to help him. He stood there a long time before he disappeared, just as he always does.

June 30th   Mama is disappointed with me because I do not write here any more. She says she knew that I would lose interest. But I don't have anything to write. Now that it is summer all my days are the same. In the mornings I do lessons with Nile and in the afternoons I ride Bayard and go swimming. When I said this to Mama, she said nonsense, every day is very different. Then she kissed me on the forehead and sighed, you're still a little girl, go and play, then she turned away. But I don't want to play. I'm ten, I'm big. I want to be grown-up and have different sentences to write every day just as Mama does.

July 1st   Although the sun is shining I am not outside but sitting with Mama. We are both writing in our books. She has promised that this afternoon, after riding, we shall pick flowers to press for my book of flowers. I did not know what to write so Mama has suggested that I describe her today, then Papa tomorrow, until I have described everyone who lives in our house in Chilkwell Street.

Mama first. Today she is dressed in green which is also the colour of her eyes. Her hair is dark brown and plaited in a fat coil around her head. When her hair is not up it is very long, down to her legs, and sometimes she will let me stand on a chair and brush it. She has a wide smile and sticky-out teeth at the top, just like me. She is big and has a fast walk.

Mama is also Mama to Cecil who is 5 years and 5 months, Robert who is 3 years and 3 months and Reggie who is 1 year and 6 months. And Albert who is in heaven. Mama loves Albert and me the most, she told me so. She says I am her maiden May. Sometimes Mama and I will take a bath together. This is one of our little secrets and only happens when Papa is away. Although we are the same, she is a lady, and has hairs where I have none and bosoms. She says when I get old enough to be a young woman I too will grow hairs and bosoms. When we bathe together I sit between her legs and she soaps my back. She likes the water boiling hot so that when we get out of the tub our skins are very pink. Sometimes I am allowed to sleep in her bed which upsets Papa. He will slam doors and say I am spoilt and that it is all Mama's fault.

July 2nd   Papa is married to Mama. He is on the Town Council and is always very busy and not to be bothered unless it can't be helped. He does not like a lot of noise or running in the house. He has whiskers on his face which are scratchy but which Mama likes. She says that when my brothers are bigger they will have whiskers too, because just as cats have kittens, boys have whiskers. He especially likes horses and dogs.

July 3rd   Nile is Mama's cousin's cousin. She lives with us to teach my lessons. Her True Christian name is Alexandria Nile Quaintance and she is named after a town and a river in Egypt which I can find in the atlas. Papa says it is a silly name and just typical of the Bagehot's. Mama named me after her Aunt Edith Stuckey and Cousin May Stuckey. Papa says he would have called me Maud if he had had his way in the matter.

July 4th   Cecil, Robert and Reggie are my brothers. They are boys and not very nice most of the time but Mama says that boys will be boys and it can't be helped.

July 5th   Our servants are Tizzy who looked after me when I was a baby and now takes care of the boys, Jane who is our maid, and who Mama says is the laziest girl in Somerset and possibly all of England, Woodsie who is our cook and Gregory who looks after the horses, including my Bayard, and Papa's guns. And that is all of us who live at the Abbey House in Chilkwell Street in Glastonbury in the Shire of Somerset which is in England, and ruled by Her Majesty the Queen Victoria.

July 8th   Today Cecil and I saw a snake slither into King Arthur's tomb through a crack in the side. We both crossed our hearts and promised not to tell but Cecil told anyway so I punched him.

July 13th   We are out all of the days because the weather is sunny and not to be missed.

July 17th   There have been tears. Cecil broke his last unbroken toy. Mama said that he is the most horrid little boy it has ever been her misfortune to know and that she will not speak to him again until he is nicer. Cecil cried until he was in fits but Mama would not budge. Nile had to give him some laudanum to calm him down.

July 18th   Mama is speaking to Cecil again. But, she has told him, he is not allowed to have any more toys ever ever ever again. Even Papa agreed. Cecil had another fit of tears and had to be put to bed with a dose of laudanum.

July 21st   I am playing with Cecil because he has no toys. Today we played Funerals. Since there were only two of us I had to do everything. I was the vicar and the crying mother and I picked flowers and chose the spot where he was buried. Cecil was a very good dead boy, he didn't giggle once.

July 23rd Mama and I have been asked to visit her friends at Woody Bay. Mama says there will be the sea and walks and ancient burial places to see and we are to stay for almost six whole weeks. Only I am to go with her, Papa and Nile and the boys have to stay here. Nile is upset that she is not invited but Mama says Nile will recover in time and that there are worse things in the world than being left behind.

August 3rd It is already our third day at Woody Bay. Mama's friend Mrs Woodford has a daughter called Harriet and we have become best friends. She is two years older than me and has eight older brothers. She says I must call her Hetty and so I do. We are sharing a room which is the best fun of all. Her favourite thing is talking.

August 8th Today Mama and Mrs Woodford and Hetty and I went into Lynmouth. Mama wanted to find the house where Mr Shelley wrote poems. She says that if she could have lived at the time of Mr Shelley she would have been the happiest woman in all of England. In Lynmouth, Mama asked all the very old fishermen if they could remember where Mr Shelley had lived but not one of them could, which she said was most disappointing. On the way back to the house Mama recited *Queen Mab* which she knows off by heart.

August 10th Today Hetty and I went to the Valley of the Rocks on our own. I did not like it. I thought the rocks might fall on us at any moment. So we left and walked in the woods which had spidery webs everywhere but no spiders. It was horrid so we ran to the sea and collected specimens from the rock pools.

August 12th Hetty likes to play at Funerals and is very good at dying which she says is more fun than being dead and having to lie still all the time. Yesterday I pretended to be drowned at sea from a shipwreck and then washed up on the shore. Hetty buried me under seaweed and sand which tickled in all my underclothes.

August 14th Hetty and I have fallen out. It took her an hour to die of wasting away and then it truly seemed as if she was not breathing so I ran screaming for our mamas to come. Mrs Woodford said that Hetty is not-nice for frightening me in such a way. She said when she was young she knew a girl who was very good at holding her breath, just as Hetty does, and one time when the girl's mama was away everyone thought that the girl had died and so they buried her in the churchyard. When her mama returned two days later she insisted that the grave be dug up and the coffin opened but it was much too late. The girl's hair was white from fright and her fingernails were all bloody and broken from trying to claw her way out of the coffin. Mrs Woodford said, just imagine being buried alive. Then she added that she suspected that one day Hetty will have a similar narrow squeak if she is not more careful and mending of her ways.

August 15th Hetty and I have made up. She has shown me how to hold my breath until I faint but I don't want to play that game.

August 18th It has rained and rained for two whole days long. Mama says she has never seen so much water in all her life. We have had charades and play-acting and tea parties and singing and games and it has been great fun. I wish Hetty was my sister and we could live together for ever.

August 21st Yesterday we went up on to the moors. There was nothing there at all but grass. I didn't like it. It made inside my head hurt. But Mama said it is a most romanticated place.

August 22nd We are going to take a boat to Lundy Island and look at the castle and the birds. Mama's friend Mr Kingsley is staying there with the Heaven family, who are the owners of the island and the castle.

August 25th We are back from Lundy. Mama and I are leaving tomorrow. Something scareful has happened and I am not to tell anyone. Mama has made me cross my heart and hope to die should I say a peep. Mr Kingsley attacked Mama. I rescued her by hitting him with my fists. Mama says it was only an accident. He was holding her tightly and biting her neck and she was crying. He only stopped when I began to hit him. Mama says I must forget what happened. She says if anyone knows they will be upset for weeks if not for ever. Especially Papa.

August 26th We are not to leave after all. Mama made me promise again not to breathe a peep to anyone. It must be our little secret. Mama's and mine.

1879

January 7th   We are home from Grandmother's house. Mama says she is much too tired from the hurly-burliness of Christmas and the New Year and very pleased to be home. We visited Cousin Walter Bagehot's graveside where he has been for almost two years. We also went to visit the place where King Alfred burnt cakes hundreds of centuries ago. It is nice not to be in Langport. Grandmother was cross for almost all of the days that we were there.

January 18th   I ride Bayard every day even though the weather is raining.

February 17th   Mama has another baby in her tummy. This means we cannot go ice-skating. I can, but Mama is not allowed to. She says I might go with Nile but I do not want to. It is no fun without Mama. She is good at skating and can run and spin and hold my hands so that I never fall. And if there is a mistake and I do fall she is there to make it better, just like when I hurt my wrist four winters ago and it had to be strapped in a sling.

Mama has to be careful all day long. That's what everyone says to her. Even when we go out Mama is not allowed to drive the trap, Gregory must, and he has to take the horse at a walk. Mama likes to go at a gallop so that the wind makes tears run from her eyes. It irritates Mama when Gregory goes slowly so she stays indoors all day and sits by the fire reading and sewing. Sometimes she plays the piano and sings. Sometimes she walks around the house checking on Jane, but she walks very slowly so I can get to Jane first to tell her that Mama is on her trail. A lot of the time Mama goes to the kitchen and asks Woodsie to make something special for the baby, who seems most to like potatoes mashed with onions. Mama sleeps a lot as well and this is dull and makes me bored.

I hate being indoors for all of the day and it makes my legs swing so that Mama says, That's enough, Edith, run along and play. But I don't want to. I want to be with Mama. I don't believe we need another baby but Tizzy says that there can never be too many babies in the world. She remembers when I was in Mama's tummy and says that no one will ever take my place in Mama's affections. Tizzy says that I am spoilt and that I rule the roost. If this were true Mama would change her mind about the baby and take it back but she will not.

February 24th   All the snow is gone and now there are mud puddles. This morning I did my atlas and got all the capital cities right which made Nile happy. This afternoon I did my practice at the piano for two hours. I am being extra good because yesterday I pushed Cecil and he fell and there was blood. He howled and screamed and Gregory had to hold him steady. Everyone was cross with me. I only did it because he kicked me but Mama says that he is only 6 and does not know any better.

February 27th   Both Tizzy and Woodsie have said that when I grow up I too will have babies in my tummy. When I said I shan't, they laughed at me as if I am a big silly. This made my head hurt and I shouted that I would not have babies because I hate babies. Then I ran out of the room and cried on my bed hoping that Mama would come but she did not. I prayed to God not to make me have babies. Nile does not have any. She says that babies are dirty and nasty and that they are not little angels but little devils which is why they have to be baptised as quickly as possible. She says that boy babies are the worst because they are born from passions while girl babies are born from love. When I said I did not understand she said that I will soon enough.

March 4th   Gregory is teaching me to shoot flying objects. Papa thinks this is a very good idea. Mama would prefer me to learn my French lessons. Papa says that if I am any good with my aim then he will take me shooting in August. He let me hold some of his guns which were very heavy.

March 6th   Today it rained and everyone had to stay indoors. Mama let me cut pictures out of her *London Illustrated News* for my scrapbook while Nile read aloud to us from Mr Tennyson's poems about King Arthur and All of His Knights.

March 8th   Mama has been crying and Tizzy says it is because the moon shone through the window on to her sleeping head as her curtains were not closed properly and that this is all Jane's fault.

March 11th   Mama is still crying more often than not even though her curtains are closed every night.

March 14th   Gregory has left and it is my fault. It is all because I have been practising shooting and not been doing my lessons and this has upset Mama and Nile, but especially Mama who has been in floods. She said if I refuse to do my lessons I will be sent away to school. Then Papa put his nose in and said that there was no chance of that happening under his roof. He said that no woman in his family had ever been taught in such a manner and that I was not going to be the first. He said education in a woman is unattractive. Then he said Mama's problem was that she had read too many books for her own good and that if he had not come along she would have been left on the shelf, just like Nile was, who had to live on his charity, teaching his daughter who knows what useless nonsense. Mama started to shout horrible things at him and I put my hands over my ears. Gregory ran in with Nile and Tizzy and they dragged Mama away while Gregory tried to calm Papa. Papa hit Gregory so hard he fell down, then Papa left the house. By the time Papa came home Gregory had packed his bag and gone.

Nile says it is my fault and she is right. I wish I had done all my lessons twice over. She says that if I do not do all my lessons I will end up married and having babies all the time.

March 17th   Mama and Papa are still not talking. The house is very quiet. Gregory has not come back. When I asked Papa where he had gone, he said to the devil for all that he cared. I miss him and so do Nile and Tizzy and Woodsie and Jane. He has been here for all of my life. I am doing my lessons to make everyone happy, but especially Mama.

March 18th   Mama and Papa have had arguing words again. Papa came into Mama's morning room without knocking and I was excused. I listened at the door and heard their raised voices although I could not understand what they said. After a long time Papa opened the door and said to Mama, Madam, you are my wife and you will do as I say. Then he shut the door and walked down the hallway. He did not look cross. He looked like the normal Papa. I went straight in and Mama was writing at her desk as she usually does. When I came to sit beside her she took my hand in hers but said nothing. When she finished writing she put away her ink and papers and led me to the settee. She was very calm and said that I was a big girl now and should know certain things. She said if I do not do my lessons that I will be useless for anything but getting married sooner rather than later. I told her that Nile had said that it was books or babies and Mama squeezed my hand until it hurt. She said Nile had been jilted because she was not as clever as she liked to think she was and that her fiancé had married someone who was truly clever. When I asked what was jilted, she said she would tell me when I was bigger. Then Mama said that when she married she believed that she could have both books and babies and it had not taken long for her to realise her error. Papa had not wanted her to continue with books, and because she had wanted him to be happy she stopped. She said that it would be a too awful thing for the same to happen to me.

March 24th   Barrow is here. He is to take Gregory's place. Nobody likes him because he is not Gregory.

March 26th   Mama is only speaking to Papa when she has to, she says. She calls him Your Father or Mr Porch. I am working very hard at my lessons. Tomorrow Papa is to go to London for nearly three weeks.

March 27th   As soon as Papa left everyone sighed in big relief. Even Barrow does not seem as awful. He was not careful when he drove out with Mama and me. The horses did not gallop but they went at a fast trot and Mama smiled and enjoyed herself.

March 28th   Barrow accompanies Cecil and me when we go riding. Since he does not know the land or the lanes I am allowed to lead the way. He let me gallop ahead. He says I have the makings of a fine horsewoman.

April 1st   There are one million daffodils and Nile and I picked half of them for our bedrooms. Mama said she thought they were much prettier left in the wild and quoted from Mr Wordsworth's poem about lonely daffodils wandering up and down the hills near a lake in the north of Cumberland.

April 3rd   Today Mama talked about how nice it was without Papa here and Nile agreed. It was very cold and Tizzy says that it is going to snow. She says she can feel it in her waters.

April 7th   Tizzy's waters were right and it has snowed. Because it is too cold to be outdoors, Mama let me copy the title pages from some of her books; she says it is good practice at developing a neat hand. I copied from Mr Mellor's *History of Glastonbury*. Mama and Nile laughed at him. Mama said that one time he climbed into the sacred well with a candle and bucket to clean it out. Mama and Nile saw him and said that he was so dirty and muddy that he looked like a common farmhand which was disgraceful. I think Mama and Nile were not-nice. I think Mr Mellor must be very clever to have written a book. He is a good friend of Grandfather Porch. Perhaps I will meet him someday.

Mama has let me bring Mr Mellor's book to my room so that I can copy the title into this book as well. He has signed it with his very own name on the first page, so I must be careful with it, Mama says.

GLASTONBURY AND GLASTONBURY ABBEY

GIVING THE PARTICULARS OF

THE LANDING OF SAINT JOSEPH AND

HIS ELEVEN COMPANIONS A.D. 30; THE BUILDING OF THE

FIRST CHRISTIAN CHURCH EVER ERECTED IN BRITAIN A.D. 60,

made of the trunks of trees set edgeways in the ground,
wattled willows and clay, being thatched with rushes
from a neighbouring swamp;

SAINT JOSEPH'S CHAPEL

ITS HISTORY AND PROPOSED RESTORATION

Some account of its many tales and traditions;
together with a list of its mitred abbots; ancient burials
in the abbey grounds; the miraculous holy flowering thorn,
still growing on Weary-all Hill;

RUINS OF SAINT MICHAEL'S CHURCH ON THE TOR

Erected A.D. 160

THE CELL OF ST DUNSTAN, AND HIS FORGE AND BELLOWS

The surrounding marshes and peat beds which supply
the inhabitants of the lowlands with fuel; walks in the vicinity;
the old tribunal; Sharpham Park; the Abbot's Fish-ponds;

KING ALFRED'S SAXON PALACE AT MUDGELEY

WELLS CATHEDRAL WITH ITS TOMBS AND MONUMENTS

BY

JOHN MELLOR

Antiquary and Saxon Historian

ILLUSTRATED WITH NUMEROUS ENGRAVINGS
INCLUDING THE GENERAL ANTIQUITIES OF THE
TOWN AND NEIGHBOURHOOD

BEING A USEFUL GUIDE FOR THE TOURIST & OTHERS

Containing much new additional material.

Just to think I know all these places and they are written about in a book.

April 9th Mama says that if I am very good and only if, then this afternoon we will go to the Porter's Lodge so that I may look at the Rod of Holy Thorn that was found in St Joseph's grave. Mama says that St Joseph knew Jesus and that they had long talks about where to build the First Church in England and finally decided on Glastonbury. She says they came in a boat, first landing in Wales, but they didn't like it there, so they walked until they came to Glastonbury, which looked very pretty because all the roses were in bloom and the summer sun was shining, and so they decided to stay. More than anything it was the roses that decided them because it reminded them of Jesus's Mother Mary, who always smelled of rosewater. After they finished building the church, St Joseph and Jesus went back to Wales, found their boat where they had left it, and sailed home. But when Jesus died on the Cross, St Joseph decided to come back to Glastonbury and brought with him the Holy Grail which held all of Jesus's Blood that had dripped from the Cross. Mama says that somewhere near to Glastonbury the Holy Grail is buried but that it is too sacred and holy to be found and not even King Arthur or His Twelve Knights could find it although they tried very hard indeed.

April 10th Yesterday we went to the Porter's Lodge to see St Joseph's Holy Rod but it was very disappointing. It just looked like an old stick full of worm holes and was broken in the middle. Mama said this is because it is hundreds of years old. I was not allowed to touch it but Mama and Nile were which was not fair.

April 16th Papa brought back late Easter presents for us. I have been given a blue summer coat and a big globe of the world to help with my lessons. He looked at Mama when he gave me this and asked her what she thought. She said her opinion was unimportant as it was my present not hers. He gave Mama ear-rings with red ruby stones, toys and games to the boys, and a shawl to Nile. I was the only one who got two presents.

April 17th   Mama is unwell and has rested in bed now for two whole days. She says it is because of the baby. I see her in the morning and then again just before I get ready for bed.

May 1st   Today I am 11. I am very grown-up compared to last year when I was only 10. I had breakfast with Mama in her room, lunch with Papa and Nile, and cake with my brothers. It is the first birthday when I have not spent all of the day with Mama and it did not feel like my birthday at all. This morning she spoke of what we will do together when the baby is finally here. She squeezed my hand very hard and promised that there would be no more babies after this one. She has given me a book called *The Ingoldsby Legends* which she would like me to read to her each day. Nile gave me some red and blue beads to thread to make a necklace and Papa gave me a musical box, just like last year, only the music is different.

May 9th   Today Mama came downstairs for the first time in many days. She mostly lay on the sofa. We were all very quiet and tiptoed so as not to disturb her. Even Reggie didn't make a lot of noise which is unusual for him, as everyone agrees he is the noisiest boy ever to be born.

May 12th   Grandmother has come to stay. She will be here for ten days. She has had words with Papa and given him an eight-page list of chores to be done before Mama's baby arrives. She went through each room with a fine-tooth comb which took two days. Then she said this house is a disgrace and Papa should be ashamed of keeping her daughter and grandchildren living in a word I don't know but which Nile says means pig-pen. Barrow and Jane are busy doing chores and extra people are coming to help them. Papa is out all day, sometimes even for dinner. Grandmother also had words with Nile about my lessons. She said it is a terrible shame that I obviously don't have the Bagehot brains, but at least it was not like in her day when you either had to be quick-witted or a beauty because if it was she was uncertain where that would leave me.

May 15th   Today I rode out with Grandmother in the victoria. She called me child all the time as if she could not remember my name. She makes me frightened. When I said this to Mama she told me not to be a big silly.

May 16th   I am in my room because I was smacked with the wooden spoon. It happened at teatime when we were running. I was chasing Cecil who was chasing Robert who was chasing Reggie, we were having fun and all the grown-ups were laughing at us. But then Reggie fell and Robert and Cecil and some tea-cups were broken and it is all my fault because I am 11 and should know better. Grandmother insisted that Nile smack me with the wooden spoon. Mama tried to stop it but gave up when Grandmother said, Daisy, your children are unlikeable little savages without a single grace between them. Nile was told to smack my hand three times but she only did it once, and not hard, so Grandmother did it three times. It is only four more days until Grandmother goes home to Langport.

May 17th   Papa and Grandmother have had words over my being given the wooden spoon. Three days until Grandmother leaves.

May 18th   There have been more words because Grandmother found Barrow in the kitchen with Woodsie and Jane. She said Barrow is a very lazy fellow. Papa had his angry face on but didn't shout at Barrow. Two days until Grandmother leaves.

May 19th   Grandmother sat with Mama all day long. Everyone else kept as busy as could be. I did my lessons and then Nile and I walked a long way near to Sharpham Manor and back again. We collected flowers which we will spend this evening pressing. When they are pressed we will make bookmarkers with them. My feet hurt from walking so far. Grandmother is leaving tomorrow.

May 20th   When Grandmother left, Mama wept and begged her to stay. This made me sad and I cried as well.

May 23rd Mama is very fat and expecting her baby to be here any day now. She cannot stand-up from sitting without someone to help her, or walk up stairs.

May 30th Mama sleeps most of the time. Her stomach is as enormous as a barrel. Tizzy says that maybe there are two babies in there and wouldn't that be nice.

June 1st Mama's best cousin, Louisa Maude Bean from Hertfordshire, has come to help. Papa says the more girls there are in the house the merrier.

June 2nd Mama cried on and off all day. I went out on Bayard with Barrow and we rode as far as Godney Moor. It was very hot and my face has got sunburn and freckles. When Mama saw this she cried even more.

June 5th Papa is never here. He says he has a lot of work to do because he is the Mayor this year. Nile says that just for once he is being sensible and staying out of the way.

June 6th Today we thought the baby was going to be here for supper but it didn't arrive after all. Mama now has to stay in her room all the time in case it changes its mind.

June 7th I am not allowed to see Mama. She has to have rest and quiet.

June 18th I have not seen Mama for eleven whole days. Dr Bought comes twice a day to see her. Nile says there is nothing to worry or fret about. But I heard Louisa say that they might have to cut open Mama's tummy if the baby does not pop out soon.

June 20th I have been allowed to see Mama because she insisted on speaking to me. Her room was very hot and the fire was lit and the windows were closed. Her face is puffy and her eyes are very small. She held my hand but not tightly and made everyone leave the room, but Louisa wouldn't so Mama whispered to me. She said she is about to die because this baby is too big for her stomach. She said it is squashing her lungs so she cannot breathe and that when it moves its arms and legs they bruise her heart so that it is hurting very much. Mama says that when she is dead and buried I must go to Mrs Lurgashall in Bloomsbury so that we can speak to each other because there are things that she must tell me. It is very important that I contact her in the next world and that if I do not she will come back to find me. She started to cry and said I must always remember that I am her maiden May, and I started to cry and Louisa made me leave.

I have come to sit in my room. I feel hot and sick in the back of my head. Where would Mama come back to find me? Here in my room? Or at her grave? How will I know? Nile says that ghosts are the unhappy dead and to be feared because they want to get inside your body and be alive again. When Mama dies I will have to get to London to visit Mrs Lurgashall. Maybe Nile will help me. She would not want Mama to be an unhappy dead ghost, would she?

June 21st   I was awake for most of the night waiting for some-one to come and say that Mama is dead. I have three ideas about how to get to London. All I have to do is convince Nile.

June 22nd   The baby is coming. Nile keeps saying your poor Mama and holding me tight. But I do not feel afraid.

June 23rd   There is good news and bad news. Mama has not died but I have yet another brother whose name is Edward.

June 30th   I have been allowed to see Mama for two minutes. I'm not sure she knew I was Edie. I whispered that I was her maiden May and kissed her cheek and crept out. Louisa and Tizzy are looking after her. Grandmother is here.

July 2nd   I saw Mama again for two more minutes. I heard Louisa say that she could go on like this for months and that the poor soul would be better off slipping away.

July 3rd   I was not allowed to see Mama today.

July 4th   Louisa said black is not going to suit me at all, because I do not have the colour for it.

July 5th   I was allowed to see Mama for one minute. She was asleep.

July 6th   Nile said Louisa is like a crow flying from sickbed to sickbed because it gives her life a purpose.

July 7th   Nile slapped Louisa very hard and refused to apologise. Louisa said because she is a Christian she will turn the other cheek. Nile said, If you do I shall slap that even harder.

July 8th   Papa and Grandmother have had a shouting argument. He said, Madam, I would ask you to remember that you are in my house. I asked Nile what this meant and she said that Grandmother had nerves and forgot where she was. But I do not understand. This is the Abbey House in Chilkwell Street, how could it be anywhere else?

July 9th   Papa has red itchiness on his hands. He said it is because he is writing too many Mayor's Letters. Nile said it was because of nerves. She said all of us are having nerves except for Louisa.

July 15th   I have not seen Mama now for ten days.

July 20th   Grandmother has taken the boys to her house in Langport. Everyone is happy that Baby Edward hardly ever cries. Papa is never here but in the Town Hall writing the Mayor's Letters. I spend all my time with Nile and after lessons we swim and ride and walk. I cannot remember when I last saw Mama. Nile says that it is for the best.

July 22nd   Cousin May has arrived. Nile and I are going to stay with her at her summer house on the Island of Wight. If Mama is no better by September we will go to stay with her in London. When Nile told me this I understood that Mama will not die until I am in London and can visit Mrs Lurgashall easily.

July 23rd   I have told Cousin May what Mama wants. She says that if Mama passes over we will visit Mrs Lurgashall to speak to her. She let me sit on her lap and stroked my hair. She says that I am very brave.

July 24th   I have been allowed to say goodbye to Mama. She hardly even looked like my Mama; her head was swollen big with bones. But I think she smiled a little when I whispered that I will be in London in September and we will be able to speak together when she has died.

1880

April 27th We are home. Everyone has made big fusses over me. Woodsie made my favourite food for supper and Tizzy cried so hard that Mama had to take Baby Edward from her. Jane said I looked very grown-up. Barrow said, Hello, miss. Bayard's certainly looking forward to seeing you. And the boys ran round and round in circles being shouty until Papa got annoyed and said, For goodness sake, Daisy, control the children can't you. But even he was pleased to see us, although Nile later said he hid it rather well. He kissed both Nile and me on the cheek and then went off to his room because he had work to do. Mama linked arms with Nile and me and said she wanted to hear everything we had done during our time away. First of all she unwrapped all the presents we had brought for her and then we talked for hours and hours and I told her all the sights I had seen in London. Especially the museums. Mama said I am become quite the young miss about town.

Afterwards I went to see Bayard. At first he ignored me and swished his tail and pretended that I did not exist. So I stroked his neck just the way I know he likes, pressing the tips of my fingers into his sleek coat and whispering in his ear. After ever such a long time he turned and nuzzled my hair and I kissed his nose and he shook his head yes, meaning more, more, more, and when I asked him if he forgave me for going away for so many months he stamped his hoof twice for yes.

May 1st Today I am 12. This morning Mama came into my room with a vase of flowers for my dressing-table. She said that from today I am no longer such a little girl. She told me that when she was 12 she had her first kiss on the cheek from a boy. Then she brushed my hair for one hundred strokes with the pretty hairbrush that she has given me. It is gold around the edges and has flowers on the back and a matching hand-mirror. This afternoon I will wear my new dress which is white with pink and yellow flowers embroidered all over.

May 2nd I am out of sorts because last night I was allowed to stay up very late past my bedtime. I was given some very nice presents. The best is a puppy from Papa, whom I have called Merry. He is two months old. I hugged and kissed Papa and he pretended to be annoyed but he did not push me off his neck as he normally does. I also received games and ribbons and bracelets and red stockings and too many books which will give me a headache if I have to read them all. We had tea and cake and sandwiches and played charades. Afterwards we went to see the May-Pole and everyone was dressed very pretty with a lot of flowers in their hair.

When it got dark Barrow lit a bonfire that he had built from the wood and sticks of nine different trees and all the bigger boys took turns in leaping over it. Cecil burst into tears because he wasn't allowed to leap and ran off to his room. When Barrow jumped everyone clapped because he went higher than anyone else. Then everyone went home except Grandmother who is staying for one whole week.

May 3rd Grandmother insisted that I play the piano for her. Because I am still tired from my birthday day I did not play very well. She said to Mama that I do not practise enough and am a lazy girl. Mama kissed me on the head and said she quite liked my playing. When I had finished she and Nile clapped very loudly and Grandmother said neither of you is doing the child a kindness by encouraging her lack of talent. I felt very choky but did not cry. When I came up to bed I had to kiss her cheek, and as if accidentally I stepped on her toes very hard. She looked at me but did not say anything because I made a pretend apology.

May 10th Grandmother has gone home today. She is a horrible old witch. I do not believe she is Mama's mama at all.

May 12th Today Barrow let me drive the trap. He and I went alone. Afterwards I could not tell whether Mama was cross or not. She says that sometimes I behave more like a boy than any girl that she has ever known. When I was out with Barrow he stopped and picked some wild flowers. He said that Jane had asked him to pick them for her and made me promise not to tell. But when we drove into the yard Jane was outside and he hid them so that she could not see and said that he would give them to her later. Then he winked at me and laughed.

May 17th   Raining, raining, raining. We can only be indoors.

May 22nd   Today we had a picnic with our cousins. They kept disappearing and hiding from me. When I found them they said I could not be in their adventures any more because I was a girl. When I told Mama she patted the cushions beside her and said now that I am bigger I really should not be running and shouting and climbing trees, instead I could do needlework or read a book, just as she does. I said I do not want to be bigger if it means sitting around for all of the day and Mama told me not to be a big silly. I shouted I'm not, and ran off to be on my own. I sulked for a long time but no one came after me, so I fell asleep. Merry woke me up by licking my face and Nile was with him. Nile said I should be more careful where I fall asleep because oftentimes the fairies carry off what they find beneath trees. I started to cry and said I wanted to be carried off by the fairies because they might play with me since no one else would. Nile said that I was a big silly to need boys because they are horrid little devils. She said that we could be friends if I would like and held my hand as we walked back to the picnic. There we sat and she braided flowers into my hair. Mama said I looked very pretty indeed. I think Nile is right about boys.

June 14th   Today I was forced to play with Cecil because Nile was busy with grown-up things. She and I are becoming like sisters. She has let me try on her brooches and bracelets and necklaces and shawls and bonnets. We whisper secrets to one another that I am not allowed to write down or tell to Mama. Nile has made me promise. I told her about King Arthur and she said that once she had known someone whom she had believed was one of King Arthur's Knights, but this had been her big mistake. Then she would not say any more.

June 17th   Cecil has had a thrashing from Papa. He threw a stone at Mrs Monaghan that hit one of her sheep, making it panic and run off with the other sheep following. When Cecil tried to help gather them she shook her stick at him so he ran away. Then, Mrs Monaghan came to tell Papa what happened and Cecil was called into his study. It was quiet for a long time before we heard him wailing from being given the strap. Afterwards Papa called me into his study and said it is a girl's duty to set a good and proper example to her brothers in how to behave and I am failing in my duties. He said, Your Mother and I are very disappointed in you, Edith May. Cecil told Papa it is my fault that he threw the stone because I had said Mrs Monaghan was a frightful old witch who had no hair under her bonnet. Papa told me that such words are just not acceptable in a young lady. I have been sent to my room to think about ways to improve my behaviour. I have to stay here for the rest of the day.

June 18th   Today I punched Cecil in the belly. I told him I will never play with him again because he is a tell-tale. He has not told anyone about me punching him. But Nile guessed that something had happened and told me that she would not be my friend any more if my behaviour is not more becoming and proper for a young lady. I hate being a girl. It's not any fun.

July 3rd   Today Mama and Papa have gone to Scotland for two months to fish and shoot and walk. Baby Eddie and Reggie and Tizzy have gone with them. Robert and Cecil have gone to Langport to stay with Grandmother and our cousins. Only Nile and Woodsie and Jane and Barrow and I are staying here at Chilkwell Street. Nile says she will take me to the sea if I am good. I am to learn to play tennis with Amelia Street who is one year older than me. Her mama is friends with my mama and they have decided that Amelia and I will be friends as well. Amelia is pretty and never runs and shouts like I do. She prefers to sit quietly with her needlework or her book. And she plays the piano very well and does watercolourings. Mama says that Amelia and her three sisters are her idea of perfect little girls. But Nile says that Amelia is a bit too pink and white for her liking.

July 18th Barrow is upset. He said that while he was exercising the horses up near Kennards Moor, he saw a girl-child who was crying. He thought she might be lost so dismounted but she hid from him. When he called and tried to find her but could not, he continued on his way. A little farther along he could hear crying again and when he rounded the bend she was standing in the middle of the path with her arms held out towards him. The horses screamed and reared and Barrow was nearly thrown. By the time he had managed to control the horses the girl had disappeared and he galloped back to raise the alarm. Woodsie said there was no point because he had seen someone long dead and buried and that no good would come of it. She said it is Mary Thrush who died in 1852 when she was 9. A big branch fell and cracked her back in two while she was wood-gathering with her father. She died three days later without once opening her eyes. Just after she had passed over her father took the lamp from her bedside and went up to Kennards Moor. Mary Thrush's spirit followed the light and then could not find her way back to her body, and she still wanders there looking for a way to get back to her home.

Nile says that I may sleep with her tonight for the company.

July 20th I asked Nile if we could ride to Kennards Moor to see Mary Thrush's ghost, but she said not, because ghosts do not like to be stared at as if they were in the circus.

September 5th Everyone is at home again. Baby Eddie can walk and Reggie is noisier than ever. I had to explain to Mama why I have not become friends with Amelia Street. I said Amelia didn't like it when Merry licked her hand or jumped on her skirt. Mama said most little girls would not. Then she said I must try harder to be friends. But I don't want to.

September 14th This morning we went mushrooming on Muncombe Hill. Cecil is not speaking to me. He says he does not talk to girls any more. Everyone thinks it is very funny. Mama says that he will grow out of it because all boys do.

September 17th   Yesterday Mama discovered Jane sitting on Barrow's knee. In one month they will be married. Mama says it is a terrible shame and the waste of a good man. Nile says that Mama does not like Jane because Papa does. Papa is pleased for them both.

October 16th   This afternoon Jane and Barrow will be married. I am allowed to go and watch. Nile has given Jane a pair of her very own lace gloves to wear.

It is later now. The wedding was most pretty. Jane cried and so did her five sisters. Nile cried as well and when we arrived home she went straight to her bed. Mama said it must be very hard for her realising that her moment for such things has passed. This made Papa cross. He said it is cruel to say such a thing. Then Mama said, Nile is 28, after all, which while hardly being old is certainly not young. And Papa said, Perhaps, Mrs Porch, you would do well to remember that you did not marry until you were almost 28. Mama's face went very red. Then Papa said, It is just as well I did not think you too old, isn't it, my dear? Mama didn't answer. But I agree with her, 28 is very old.

Jane and Barrow will be away for eight days. They have gone to Shropshire for Jane to meet Barrow's family. Mama says it is not at all convenient but what else can be done. Jane's sister Kitty is going to help while Jane is off visiting.

October 21st   Mama and I are going to London at the end of the month for a shopping visit. We will also visit Mrs Lurgashall. I am allowed to go now that I am 12. Mama says that we will try to reach Albert. I'm going to ask to speak to King Arthur and find out why he doesn't come any more. I want to know if it is because I am a girl. If it is I am going to ask him to put me to the test so that I can show that I am as good as any boy.

October 25th   Jane and Barrow are back from Shropshire. I helped Tizzy and Woodsie to decorate their room with flowers.

October 29th   Today we are going to London although Papa thinks it is unwise of us to do so. It is very windy and the leaves are being tossed in the air and the sky is boiling with gloomy clouds. As well, I have a running nose and Papa says I should not go, but Mama says we will.

October 30th There is a very thick fog and it is difficult to see even with the street lamps. Cousin May thinks that we should not go to Mrs Lurgashall because I still have a running nose but Mama insists we shall.

November 1st Mama keeps stroking my face and saying I have a special gift. I cannot remember what happened although I can remember very clearly; both at the same time. Mama says we must never tell Papa, never, ever, ever. It is our secret. Mama's and mine and Cousin May's and Mrs Lurgashall's. At Mrs Lurgashall's house we sat around a big dining-table and held hands and closed our eyes. Mrs Lurgashall called out people's names so that they could come and speak to their loved one. Sometimes there was a reply, sometimes not. I felt very fidgety and could not sit still. I opened my eyes and everyone else's were closed. Then I noticed a boy standing in the corner and I said Albert's here. Even when I heard Mama cry out I did not look at her but at Albert. I said, I thought you were a little baby. He looked cross and said, boys do grow up in heaven, you know. When I asked why he was cross he said because I am most tired of singing all day every day. Then he looked at me. Straight into my eyes and I felt warm and cosy and comfortable as if I were in bed snuggled under the covers. I know who you are, he said, I came and took your doll. I said, You threw her out of the window and broke her neck and her head fell off and Mama and Papa and Nile all blamed me and told me nobody likes little girls who tell lies about breaking their toys. I asked him why he had done it and he said because his throat hurts all the time from singing. Then I turned to look at Mama to see if she had heard that I had not lied about my doll but I could not see anyone else at the table, they had all disappeared.

I don't remember the next bit but Mama says I cried out and then vomited and then fell into a deep sleep. Mama brought me home to Cousin May and her doctor came to look at me and said that apart from my running nose I am as fit as two fiddles. Yesterday I spent resting by the fire and telling Mama and Cousin May what happened over and over again. I described Albert and Mama wants to know who he most looks like, her or Papa. But I can't decide. Sometimes when I talk about him she cries, at others she laughs. She said he is a very naughty boy for breaking my doll and letting me take all the blame.

Mama is sleeping with me so that I am not frightened, but I don't feel frightened at all.

November 2nd Mrs Lurgashall has been to tea. She held my hand and said I have the rare and very special gift of being able to see beyond the here and now. She asked me to tell her very clearly what I had seen. She wanted to know if anything like this had ever happened before and I told her about King Arthur. Mama was very shocked and hurt that I had kept such a secret from her, so I didn't say I had told Nile. Mrs Lurgashall read my palm and said that my gift is not extensive. She said, sometimes I will know people before they know me. Mama asked when we might try to see Albert again. Mrs Lurgashall wants to wait three months or so. She says that it is best not to rush a young gift.

In four days we will go home. I am to have special treats every day while we are here.

1881

January 1st   I have been crying and crying. Mama and Papa have said that we are to leave Chilkwell Street and move to Edgarley House. I don't want to. I will never see King Arthur again. Edgarley was Papa's home until he married Mama. He says he liked being a boy there because there is more room for horses and dogs and there are big gardens for growing more vegetables. And, he said, last year hot-water pipes were put in so we shall always have hot water and be warm in the wintertime. Mama said it will be most pleasant not being so near to town. And Nile is happy because she will have an extra room all to herself. She will be able to bring more of her books from where they are being kept at Cousin May's house. Mama says Nile is very lucky that Papa is so generous. Everyone is happy except for me.

January 2nd   For all of the day everyone has been talking and talking about moving to Edgarley. I had no choice but to listen because it is too slippery for me to be out of doors.

January 3rd   After dinner Papa told ghost stories. I was allowed to stay but Cecil had to go to bed. It wasn't very scareful yet Nile jumped twice when Papa did sound effects. I wanted to tell them both that some ghosts are cruel and mean and horrible because they do not much like being in heaven, just like Albert when he broke my doll. I think Mama guessed what words were on the tip of my tongue because she gave me two of her looks to make sure I bit my tongue and didn't speak.

January 4th   Tonight Papa told us about the common spooks that each country town of England is likely to have. He said every street in Glastonbury has its very own ghost and ghost story, about such things as vulgar sprites that like to frighten boys of all ages mostly in the wintertime, and milkmaids who accidentally catch trains driven by fairies and are never seen again, and carriages pulled by headless horses so that the carriage crashes and everyone's limbs are torn asunder and flung through the air to land in other people's gardens, and night-roaming ghosts with saucer-sized eyeballs that can see inside one's head. Then Papa said that even though it's all mysterising nonsense it's jolly good fun, unless the ghosts and goblins get into your tummy and give you tummy-ache, and he hoped that was not going to happen to me, because there is nothing worse than spooks in the middle of the night keeping one awake with their ramblings around one's tum.

January 5th   Today Mama stayed in her room. Nile said it was not because of spooks giving her nerves but because sometimes ladies need to rest and be alone away from their husbands and children and households. When I asked why, Nile said she would tell me when I was bigger.

January 9th   Mama is taking a tonic that Tizzy has made for her because she is being delicate. She has to drink it three times a day. I was allowed to have a little sip and it is not very nice. For most of the day she rests by the fire on the chaise longue and reads the books that the Reverend has lent to her. Mama said Reverend Arnold was on one of God's Very Own Missions in India and escaped with his life only by a very narrow squeak before he came to live in Glastonbury. She said, brave people go to India and many of them never ever ever come back.

January 10th   When Mama is not left in peace to doze and think and read about the Native Hindoos she is in a very bad mood. Today she shouted three times in one hour and when Papa said, Daisy, what in earth is the matter, she shouted, Nothing, and then burst into tears and had to go to bed from crying.

January 12th   Mama has gone to London on her own although Papa said it was not at all advisable because she has nerves. She has taken the train because the roads are too miry for the carriage. After she had left we played hide and seek and made lots of noise and for once Papa did not mind.

January 21st   Mama is back with presents for us all. She is very pale and quiet and says that this is because the train stopped and started all the way back. She said she shared a compartment with two older ladies who would not stop talking about their younger years as if she were not even there. Mama said she cannot think what the world is coming to when even people who should have the manners to know better discuss their private lives for the rest of the world to hear.

January 22nd   This afternoon I accidentally overheard a conversation between Mama and Nile. Mama was crying and I heard her say what on earth was she to do now that Mr Kingsley is gone to the Hindoos. She said she was resigned to the life she had although it was not the one she wanted. She cried very hard and Nile tried to comfort her. I crept away and went to find Merry. I took him to my room and we curled up on the bed together and I read to him from the *Fairy Tales* of the Misters Grimm who are also Brothers. Merry pretended to be asleep but every time I stopped reading he thumped his tail on the bed until I began again.

This evening Mama took a dinner tray in her room because she is under the weather and has nerves again. Papa said he is not surprised but that he is not going to say I told you so, at least not to Mama. At dinner it was only Papa and Nile and I and Papa's dog Bertram. Berters is very old and Mama does not like him because he makes smells. Papa gave him tidbits from his plate which he is forbidden to do when Mama is at table. Nile was very quiet. Even Papa noticed. He said, You're being very mysterious, Nile, is it something you'd care to share with Edie May and me? But Nile said she wasn't being the least bit mysterious and that he had a very fanciable imagination indeed. After dinner Nile went to sit with Mama and Papa went to his study. I did not know what to do with myself so I have come back to my room with Merry. Perhaps if I long for King Arthur enough he will come and rescue me and then I won't have to move to Edgarley.

February 2nd   Mama and I are going to stay with a friend of hers for two or three weeks in the hope that it will make Mama's nerves less jangly. It is a very long way in Wales on a Broken Shire Coast. Mama said if it were any farther west it would be all the way into Ireland and then we would have to take a boat as well as the train.

Later. Nile has shown me on the map. It is called Pembroken Shire and the town is called Near Nevern.

February 6th   We are in Wales with Mama's most best friend, Mrs Vateson. I have been here twice before when I was a very little girl of three and then five and a half, but I don't remember. We drove over a bridge to get to the house and the sun shone on all the frosty ice so that it seemed as if the bridge were a rainbow. It was very pretty, even Mama agreed. The house has a Welsh name which I can't write. Mr and Mrs Vateson have twelve children and in four or five months there will be one more. One of the boys is named Crantock. He is simple and I am not allowed to stare at him. He hardly speaks except sometimes to himself. He is very beautiful and everyone agrees that he looks just like an angel with his big blue eyes and golden curls. He has to be with his Mama all the time otherwise he gets upset. My mama said it must be a terrible trial and goodness knows what would become of Crantock should anything befall his mama.

February 7th   Bad news came with the mail that a friend of Mama's Cousin Walter has passed on to the next world. Mama said she just knew something had happened when she dreamed of an owl near her window. She said that Cousin Walter's friend is almost the last of his kind and that soon there will be no great thinkers and writers left. And then she and Mrs Vateson talked about all the dead people they have known, which took up all of the day.

February 8th   All the children here speak Welsh so it is hard to play with them. There is a girl almost my age whose name is Adwen but she is always busy with her horse whose name is

Radish. I tried to make friends and tell her about Bayard but she didn't listen. She is very huffy and not-nice. And there is another girl Ninnon who is younger than me but she will only talk to one of her brothers, not even her mama or papa, or other brothers and sisters, which I think is silly. I'm bored. I hope we can go home soon.

February 9th Crantock is very taken with me, his mama says so. When I am near by he rocks to and fro and murmurs over and over. His mama says that this means he likes me very much and that I must not be afeared of him because he is gentleness itself. Mama and Mrs Vateson talked about more of their dead friends.

February 10th Today it snowed a little so we played Mr Brown of Brighton's Spectropia. Even Mama and Mrs Vateson played. There were enough of us to be one ghostie each. We fixed a white linen sheet to the wall and then took turns to stare at a different picture-plate and then stare at the sheet and describe the ghost we saw appear there. From each description everyone had to make a drawing. Neither Mama nor I have played ghosties before but all the Vatesons are very good, even Winnow who is only 2. His favourite thing is jumping. He even tried to jump up and down while he drew his pictures. Crantock sat near to his mama with his eyes tightly closed shaking his head from side to side muttering, No.

When it was my turn I had the picture of the red witch that became a green ghostie when I stared at the linen sheet. When I described what I saw Crantock was most upset and began to shake, saying, Not like this, loudly and then loudlier. When his Mama took hold of his hand and said, Shhh, my sweet angel, he became very still and looked straight into my eyes. I felt very warm and shivery, both at the same time. Then, just before fainting, he said, Edith, you know they are not like this. His words were loud and clear but no one else heard what he said except for me, not even my mama or his mama.

February 11th Today I didn't see Crantock at all. He is ill with a fever. He often gets fevers after he gets excited. I asked if I might see him but his mama and my mama said not. When I begged and pleaded and almost started to cry they said, Yes, but only for a little minute. Crantock was awake but even when I stood directly in front of him it was as if I was not there. I did not know what to do so I put one of my hands on his and squeezed very hard, but he didn't respond so I tipping-toed away.

February 15th We have come home early because Crantock is very ill. Four nights ago he tried to climb out of his bedroom window and would have been successful if his brother Rhun-Owen had not been there and held him and shouted, Help. If he had fallen he would have died. Mama said that is what the poor troubled soul intended. But I said not. Crantock would never commit a sin because he is one of God's Very Special Angels. Mama said perhaps I am right, but only perhaps.

February 16th We are settled back at Chilkwell Street as if we had never been away. Today it rained so much that even the puddles flooded and joined together.

February 17th No rain but a very gloomy sky for nearly all of the day. The clouds broke apart only the once. Tizzy spotted the break and said there was enough blue to make a pair of sailor's trousers. When Mama, Nile and I went to the window to look, Mama said he would have to be a very small sailor, indeed, for such a small patch of blue to be enough for a pair of trousers.

February 21st We have had a letter from Mrs Vateson. Crantock is still ill. She writes that when he is like this there is nothing to be done but wait for the illness to pass. I include him in my prayers every night, which Mama says is very good and kind of me.

March 1st Everyone is busy with the move to Edgarley House. I have been there with Mama and Nile and it is very big. I do not think we need so many rooms and I said so. I don't want to leave. I have lived here for all of my life. Please, God, let Mama and

Papa change their minds. I promise to never ask for anything ever again and always to be good and kind, even to Cecil, if we can only stay at here at the Abbey House.

March 21st I have been having tummy-aches. Nile says it is nerves because of moving, Papa says maybe it is ghosts, and Mama says it is wind bubbles because I do not chew each mouthful forty times before swallowing. I think Nile is right. When we leave here it will be for ever and that is a very long time. For the rest of my life I will have to sleep in another bedroom. How will King Arthur know where to find me? I don't want to move to Edgarley. Please, God, don't make me. It is going to be awful and then even more awful, I just know it.

April 9th We are moved to Edgarley. Papa is cross and Mama has been crying. There are at least one million boxes and Nile is in charge of them. I am helping as much as I can but whatever I do seems to be the wrong thing.

April 19th Today Nile took me to a secret place of hers that is near to the Tor. We walked awhile and then scrambled through some bushes and then we were in a dell full of primroses. Nile says it is Special and called Paradise. She said that one time when she was there she fell into a dream and saw a Knight and a Lady standing side by side and that the Lady held her heart in her hands and it was stuck all over with pins like a cushion. Nile said she didn't know what this meant. Then she said she wanted me to stop being sad and sulking about living at Edgarley, because from every room we can see the Tor, and the Tor is very sacred. She told me that the Tor is dedicated to St Michael who killed bad dragons but not the good ones. She wants me to find one nice thing about Edgarley every day for one whole week and if I do then we will go to the top of the Tor and she will tell me a secret.

April 20th One nice thing is that my room is next door to Nile's.

April 21st The second nice thing is that Nile is right and I can see the Tor from my bedroom windows. I can also see two old towering horse-chestnut trees and a sundial.

April 22nd   The third nice thing is that Bayard and Merry like being here. And so do Tizzy and Woodsie and Barrow, but not Jane who says it is too big for one girl to clean and she needs help or she will leave and Barrow will too, because they are married and he has to do what Jane wants.

April 23rd   The fourth nice thing is that Jane and Barrow are not going to leave because Mama has said there will be two more girls to help Jane.

April 24th   The fifth nice thing is that my room is very big and an armchair can be fitted in near the fireplace.

April 25th   The sixth nice thing is that there are a lot of places for me to hide from my brothers, especially Cecil, so that they can never find me.

April 26th   The seventh nice thing is that hot water is better on the mornings when it is very cold. I have told Nile my seven things and she says that soon we will go to the top of the Tor.

May 1st   Today I became 13 years of age. I had some presents but not as many as last year. I did not have a nice day at all. Everyone is in tempers because we are still settling into the house and too many things are unfindable in boxes.

May 3rd   Nile and I have been to the top of the Tor. We could see Wells and she said a blue line in the far-off distance was the Welsh Mountains where Crantock lives. Nile told me that in ancient days the Tor was an island and that all of Glastonbury was under the sea, even the Abbey House and King Arthur's Grave. Then one day the tide went out and forgot to come back, but left behind rivers and streams and lakes and a dragon. When the land had dried out, flowers and plants and trees began to grow, then animals and people came, but they didn't like the dragon and the dragon didn't like them so it came to live on the Tor. When St Joseph came with Jesus they asked St Michael to kill the dragon because it had started to eat people. And St Michael did this and the Church was built on the very same spot and the Tower is all that remains. But while they were building the Church they found an underground passage-way that led down hundreds of steps to a big cave. In the cave was a pond with water-lilies so huge that the water was completely covered. A bridge crossed this pond from one side to the other, and on the other side was another cave with a pond with pelicans and herons and swans and ducks, and there was a bridge over this pond too, to yet another cave where there was a pond with fishes of all shapes and colours as well as turtles. This place of three caves is where the Angels live who are the Guardians of the Holy Grail. When the builders of the Church left the caves the earth closed behind them and they couldn't find the doorway in again, and since then no one has ever found the way. Not even King Arthur although all the Knights from the Round Table helped him to search.

Nile says we are truly blessed to live in such a sacred place.

May 6th I look at the Tor every morning when I get up and every night before I go to sleep.

May 15th Yesterday, Mama, Nile and I had a day out in the countryside, sightseeing at houses and walking. We went to the cottage that Mr and Mrs Coleridge lived in while he wrote The Mariner's Rhyming Poem and then we walked to All Foxes Park where Mr Wordsworth and his sister Miss Wordsworth lived. We walked in the woods and had a picnic and Mama read from her book of poems. Mama's grandmother, who was from Stogursey, met the Coleridges and the Wordsworths when she was out walking one day. She said to them, How d'you do? and they said the same to her. The very first time Mama came here was with her grandmother who read from the same book of poems. Mama cried because she was happy.

May 17th Mama is to have her portrait painted. It is Papa's surprise late birthday present for last year. The artist is Miss Jane Winford Burns and she will be here in two days.

May 19th Jane Winford Burns is here and we are all to call her Win. She has an accent from Scotland but lives in London. She has dark frizzing hair and bright green eyes that run all over people's faces when she is staring at them. She is very lively and smiles all of the time. When she laughs she tips her head back and yelps, just like Merry does if you tread on his paw. The first time she did this Mama and Nile looked at each other and fanned themselves very quickly to hide their smiles.

All afternoon Mama played dress-ups in her favourite dresses to see which one she looked best in. Papa said the one with the yellow-and-white-striped-corset bodice and white silk gauze-ruffle skirt. Mama said she thought it a trifle too young for her these days. But Papa said, what nonsense, it reminded him of their wedding day and Mama hasn't changed one jot since then.

May 20th It is as if Win had been here for ever, not just one day. Last night at dinner she and Papa argued about politics and Papa got huffy and went off to his study. Mama and Nile were very quiet.

May 21st This afternoon I took Win to the top of the Tor. She threw herself on the grass and turned her face up to the sun and dozed, and afterwards she did watercolouring. I wanted to tell Nile's secret about the Tor but didn't. Win talked all the time and told me stories about all the places she has travelled. She asked a lot of questions about Mama and Nile and Papa and the boys. At first I felt very shy. She only became huffy with me once when I tried to look over her shoulder at her watercolouring. She said, nobody likes a snooping girl. I went red in the face and wanted to die. Perhaps she won't want to be my friend.

May 24th Nile is upset. She says that I have ignored her for three whole days and moved my affections to Win. Nile calls

Win, Miss Burns, and Win calls Nile, Miss Quaintance. At dinner Win always tries to draw everyone into the conversation, even me, but Nile won't join in. With Win, our dinners have become very noisy. She and Papa never agree, but Papa doesn't do sulks any more, instead he gets loud and shouty. And Mama will say, Mr Porch please, not even Reggie shouts so much. Nile says that it is all become unbearable and that she will take a tray in her room if it continues.

May 25th Win is working on Mama in the new summerhouse. Nile and I were doing my lessons in the garden and every time we heard Win laugh, Nile stopped speaking. Twice she said, Miss Burns is rather common and vulgar, don't you think, and looked very annoyed.

May 28th We have had a letter from Mrs Vateson. She has two new baby girls who are named Kew and Keyne. When Papa said they are the silliest names ever, Mama shushed him and said that they are taken from ancient saints. Papa said his favourite name is Maud and why aren't girls called Maud any more? Win has a lot of names, Jane Kathryn Anne Elizabeth. She said Edith May was very pretty, and Nile's name was both marvellous and strange because she could not imagine what it must be like being named after a river.

May 29th Nile and Win have fallen out. Papa says Nile must apologise but Nile says she will not under any circumstances. It happened when we were in the garden. Mrs Street and Amelia and her sisters came to tea. Nile tripped when Merry ran under her skirts and Win put out a hand to steady her. Nile was horrid. She said, Don't touch me, your hands are filthy. Everyone fell silent. Win held her hands up and looked at them and then said, You are quite correct, Miss Quaintance, my hands are filthy, do forgive me. Then she turned away and started talking to Mrs Street as if nothing had happened. Papa was furious. I heard him shouting at Nile in his study.

May 30th Win is being very polite to Nile and Nile is being very polite to Win. It's too awful. It makes my head hurt on the inside. I don't want to have to choose between them.

May 31st I have apologised to Win for Nile. I said it was very unlike Nile to say such a thing. She didn't seem to mind and said that one can't always be liked by everyone. But everyone does like her. Even when Merry jumped on her skirts with wet paws she didn't get shouty, she laughed and pulled Merry's ears. She said that she must get on with Mama's portrait so that she can go home to London. When I said I would be very sad when she left, she told me that I could come to visit her whenever I liked.

June 2nd It has been storming for two whole days and we are stuck indoors. Win is keeping us amused by making drawings and cutting and pasting pictures for our scrapbooks. She managed to get Reggie to sit still for more than five minutes which even Nile agreed is something of an achievement, because everyone knows that Reggie has had ants since he was born.

June 3rd This afternoon there was an almost argument between Nile and Win. It was too hot and the clouds boiled for hours before deciding to rain. When the drops started we were in the garden and had to gather everything quickly and run. Nile asked Win would she carry her parasol because her arms were too full and Win said she'd best not as her hands were rather dirty. Nile's lips trembled but she pressed them together and said nothing and managed to carry her parasol herself.

June 4th Win is ill and stayed in her room all day. It was Nile's idea that we take her a posy from the garden. Win smiled when we gave it to her. We offered to read to her but she was too sleepy so we did not.

June 5th Win is still unwell. Nile surprised everyone by carrying her lunch tray. Nile says she is trying very hard to be kind to someone whom she finds most difficult.

June 6th Win is still unwell so Nile is keeping her company. When Papa said, I can't think what you girls would have to talk about, Nile replied, We are comparing impressions of the Cathedrals of France and Italy.

June 8th Win is up and about again and working on Mama's portrait. She and Nile are being very shy as they are still becoming friends. This evening Win and Nile and I looked at Nile's travel sketchbooks of the Cathedrals of France from her visits there with Cousin May.

June 11th Win is now working on two pictures, Mama in the morning, and Nile after lunch. She is doing a pastel of Nile reading by the window.

June 13th Now that Win and Nile are friends they are too busy to bother with me. No one noticed that I was in my room for three hours this afternoon. I waited and waited for someone to come but no one did. When I came down they all behaved as if I'd been there all the time. They didn't miss me at all.

June 21st Today was Win's last day. Nile and I helped her to pack. She has given me two small watercolours, one of Bayard and the other of myself and Merry. She has asked if I will give her one of my drawings but I am too embarrassed as they are not very good. At dinner, Papa gave a speech and made a toast to Miss Jane Kathryn Anne Elizabeth Winford Burns and we all clapped. Win spoke of her next project which is to paint a series of murals based on Mr Homer's *Odyssey* in the house of a Viscount who lives in Herefordshire. She said that she is looking for an assistant should Papa or Mama hear of someone they think would be suitable. A woman with an interest in art, free to travel, and not afraid to get her hands dirty, Win said. Papa said, Well that leaves you out, Nile, as we all know your feelings about grubby hands. Nile burst into tears and ran from the room. Win looked very cross and said it was cruel of Papa to remind Nile of her comment before they had become friends, and then she left the table and went after Nile. Mama said, Mr Porch, really! and she tutted and tsked for some time until Papa got huffy and went to his study.

June 22nd   We all waved Win off. Last night when I was supposed to be in bed I crept downstairs because I could see Win and Nile sitting on the steps. They were holding hands and talking quietly. Through the open window I heard Nile say, You'll forget me, I know you'll forget me. But Win promised she never would. Then she took all the pins out of Nile's hair and arranged it around her shoulders and said, One day I'll paint you like this. Nile started to cry and said, You won't, you'll go away and forget me. I climbed through the window and ran out and when they heard me they both held their arms open. I cried because Win is going away but also because Nile loves Win more than she loves me. When Nile and I had stopped crying, they both kissed me and said it was time for me to go back to bed. Nile stood up to take me but Win kept hold of her hand and kissed it on the palm and held it to her cheek and Nile cried again and so did I.

June 29th   Aside from lessons, Nile doesn't have much time to be with me. She writes to Win twice a day. I can't imagine what she would have to write so much about. Whenever I ask her to do something with me she is too busy. Today I told Mama that Nile doesn't want to be my friend any more, since she loves Win more than me. Mama said I was being a big silly because it is natural for Win and Nile to be friends as they are nearly the same age. She said that I will understand in two or three years when I am a young woman. She wants me to make better friends with some of the girls of my age who live in Glastonbury and Wells. But I don't want to. None of them likes galloping on their horse the way I do with Bayard. Or dogs. Or running. They like playing at tea parties and being grown-up which I find dull.

July 14th   Tomorrow we are off to London. Mama is very excited and has written me a list of questions to ask Albert. But what if I can't see him? What if he doesn't come? Mama will be upset.

July 17th   It happened just as it did last time. I was sick and fainted and had to rest. Mrs Lurgashall says that this is because I am still not experienced, but eventually the sickness will pass. Mama is very happy even though Albert wouldn't answer her questions. She says he is a very naughty boy and I must tell him his Mama says so. She is keeping a separate journal of his conversations with me for her own private record, but this time there was nothing because he wouldn't speak. Mama has asked Mrs Lurgashall if she might try to capture Albert's likeness with a camera and Mrs Lurgashall has agreed. She has a friend who is an expert in capturing the likenesses of the departed.

July 18th   We went to Win's house so that she could do the finishing touches to Mama's portrait and there was trouble.

Her house is not like any that I have seen before. It was very untidy with paintings stacked everywhere. Outside it was very pretty and overlooks a square at the front. We had tea in the small garden and her three cats made a lot of noise until they were given a saucer of milk to share. Win and Nile were very shy with each other so Mama did all the talking. We all looked at Win's studio which is at the very top of the house with windows in the roof to let in the light. While Win did Mama's picture, Nile and I explored. We only got as far as Win's bedroom. There were dresses everywhere. Nile and I decided to tidy them away for her which was a big mistake. She was very angry when she saw what we had done and shouted until she was red in the face and said horrid things to Nile about not being married. Nile went very pale and her lips trembled but she pressed them together and didn't cry. She waited for Win to stop being shouty and then she asked if Win had finished. When Win didn't answer, Nile left the room and then the house and stood outside on the steps. Mama and I quickly gathered our things and left as well.

All evening we have been very quiet. Mama and Cousin May played card games. I pretended to read my book. Nile did her needlework. Whenever Mama looked at her she pretended not to notice.

July 20th We were still at breakfast when Win arrived. At first Nile refused to see her but Mama and Cousin May took sides and persuaded her to. It took almost three hours before Win and Nile came out of the drawing-room and said that they were friends again. Win has taken Nile home to her house to visit overnight. I wanted to go as well but Win didn't ask me.

July 21st Win and Nile sent a note asking Mama's permission if I might join them at Dorset Square for a few days. Mama has said that I may go, but only until July 30th when I must come back so that we can go home.

July 26th I wish I could live at Dorset Square for ever. I am allowed to sleep in in the morning and stay up at night. Every day we have an adventure. With dinner I am allowed a very small glass of wine, and I have promised not to tell Mama. After dinner we sit in the garden and look at the stars. Last night I crept into Win's room and squeezed in between them and they let me stay.

July 29th Today is my last day at Dorset Square. It has been the best time ever in my life.

1882

January 5th We have been ice-skating and there has been an accident. Mama and Nile and I were skating very fast when my skate caught Nile's and her leg skidded beneath her. She came down on her left ankle and we heard the bone crack. I stayed and held her hand while Mama ran to get help. Papa and Barrow came to carry Nile to the carriage. She didn't cry out or make any sound at all but she bit her lip until it bled. Dr Bought came and she is not allowed to walk on it for four whole months if not longer. Nile has asked for Win to be sent for. At present she is sleeping because she has been given an extra strong dose of laudanum.

January 7th Win has arrived. She didn't say hello to anyone or even stop to remove her coat which was dripping with mud. She ran upstairs to Nile's room and slammed the door after her. I wanted to go in but Mama said not. She said that Nile and Win would want to be alone.

January 9th Win is always at Nile's bedside. She even sleeps in her room to tend her in the night. She has barely spoken to any of us. Today I walked with Merry from here to the Abbey House and back again and no one even noticed that I had gone. All the puddles were frozen solid and I jumped up and down on the edges to crackle them. Some of the slabs of ice were thicker than my wrist.

January 12th There has been shouting and crying all day and the house is in an upheaval. Papa ordered Win to leave and has forbidden her ever to speak to or see Nile again. When Nile heard this she began screaming and didn't stop until Dr Bought came and gave her a big dose of laudanum. Mama keeps crying and Papa is slamming doors. No one will tell me what has happened. Tizzy and Jane and Woodsie and Barrow know but they refuse to say. Whenever I am near by, Tizzy shushes everyone, although I did hear her say that little pictures had big ears. Is this a clue?

January 13th   It was a clue. Papa has removed Win's portrait of Mama and given it to Barrow who is to make a bonfire and burn it to ashes! It has to be because of the way Win has painted Mama's ears, from what I overheard Tizzy say. Everyone is walking on tipping-toes. Nile is still asleep.

January 14th   I heard Papa say to Mama that Win should be flogged within an inch of her life. Nile is still sleeping.

January 15th   Dr Bought has been again and he agrees with Papa that Nile needs to be somewhere very quiet until she is well. When I asked Mama where Nile will go, she said to a very nice house in the country where she can rest with other invalids.

January 16th   Papa said to Mama that when Nile is well he is going to arrange a marriage for her. Mama cried. She has asked me a lot of questions about last summer at Dorset Square but I could tell her nothing more that I did before.

January 17th   The carriage came to take Nile away. She was still deeply asleep. Mama says that it is all for the best. When I asked if we might visit her, Mama said not. Nile must have complete rest. No visitors. No letters. I think Nile will be very bored but Mama did not agree.

January 18th   Mama and Jane and Tizzy have packed away all of Nile's clothes and books and knick-knacks. This is because Nile won't be returning to Edgarley. When she is well she will have a husband and a home of her own to go to.

January 26th   It isn't the same without Nile. I asked Mama if she had had news from her but she said not. From next week I am to take my lessons with Amelia Street and her sisters and their governess.

February 2nd   I have had tears. Jane and Barrow are going away for ever. They are going to live in Australia, which is all the way on the other side of the earth. It is so far that they will never ever come back. Barrow has two brothers who live there on a sheep farm in the outback. Barrow said that the outback is in the middle of nowhere and not even on the map. Barrow's parents are going, and so are Jane's sisters Kitty and Milly.

February 5th Mama is interviewing for more servants.

February 10th I hate being with girls all day. Amelia and her sisters give me a headache because all they do is talk and giggle. I've asked Mama to please, please, please, not make me go, but she says I must. Their governess Miss Lett-Jennings was the governess to Lady Bigbury when she was still Miss Rose Piney. And Miss Lett-Jennings's very own sister is married to an Honourable. Mama says that Miss Lett-Jennings has connections that I will appreciate when I am a young woman in two or three years and deciding on a husband. When I said that I'm not going to get married, not ever, Mama got shouty, saying, All nice young ladies want to get married including you, Miss Edith May Porch.

February 13th From next week there will be four new servants here. Fisher, a footman; and Adah, Elizabeth and Emma, who will help in the house. Adah will also help me in the mornings. Mama says now that we are at Edgarley it is important that we have the right help. She is pleased that Jane is going but not Barrow. She says that Barrow is a great loss.

February 15th It isn't the same here without Nile. I have no one to talk to. Mama is always busy. And the Street girls are dreary and dull. All they ever speak of is clothes and hair and connections. They like listening to Miss L.-J. tell stories about all the weddings she has been to in her time and what the bride was wearing. Most of the time I sit and stare through the window, imagining that I am out on Bayard.

February 22nd Today Jane and Barrow left. Tizzy and Woodsie and I cried and cried. Jane gave me a big hug and said, Oh, Miss

Edie, just to think I will never see you again. Barrow shook my hand and said to make sure I look after Bayard and Merry and I have promised that I will. I watched until they had driven out of sight.

March 3rd I am very sad and moping. Nile and Jane have gone away and I have no one to talk to any more. Mama and Papa and Tizzy and Woodsie are always too busy. Adah and Elizabeth and Emma are not the same. They are just servants and not like a part of the family. Jane knew me from when I was a baby, which is almost fourteen whole years.

March 28th Mama has said that I am at the beginnings of becoming a young woman. This was because I told her that I had swellings on my chest that are very painful. When I said this she touched her own chest where her bosoms are and asked did I mean there. I said yes, and she went very pink. Then she rang for Emma to bring us some tea. After Emma had gone, Mama held my hand and said that during the two to three years during which a girl is becoming a young woman some not-nice things will happen that at first I will mind very much, but as time passes I will not mind so very much. She said I must take very special care of my body. No one must ever see it, not even Mama. When I said what about Adah, because she helps me to dress, she said, Adah does not count, as she is a maid. And then she cried and talked about when I was a baby and a little girl and how quickly the years had gone by since then.

April 5th I have been most careful for too many days. I have walked carefully and slowly, and sat carefully and slowly, and stood carefully and slowly, because it is what Mama said I must do. But today when I was with Merry, as soon as I was hidden from the house, I ran until I could not run any more and had a stitching pain in each of my sides. Merry ran with me and when I stopped he barked and ran in circles around me. My head was hurting from too much slowness but now I feel better.

April 8th   Early this morning before Adah came to light my fire, I took my nightdress off to look at myself in the looking glass. My bosoms are hardly bosoms at all. They are like boils and very sore. I remember from bathing with Mama that hers were large and soft. I wonder if mine will get to be that big. It just doesn't seem possible. But just in case, I have been watching Mama to see what she does with her bosoms, although she doesn't seem to notice that they are sticking out in the way.

May 1st   Today was my 14th birthday. Despite the sopping weather the Street girls came over. It was Mama's idea, not mine. It did not feel like other years. My presents were awful. I am much too big to be bothered with birthdays anymore. After everyone had left, I sat in the stable with Bayard and Merry and listened to the rain. I have no idea what I would do without Bayard and Merry. Life at Edgarley is so very different. I don't like it here as much as I did at the Abbey House. It still seems strange that someone else sleeps there in my bedroom. I wonder if King Arthur visits them. And I miss Nile and Jane and Barrow very much. Nile has not written, not even once. I suppose she has forgotten me.

May 2nd   Mama has given me a secret present, Mrs Catherine Crowe's *The Night Side of Nature*, which is about spirits and hauntings and the Other Side. Together, we are to read a dozen pages or so each day. But reading is so dreary, even if it is about ghosts. I'd much rather be out with Bayard and Merry.

May 13th   Mama's friend Mrs Vateson is coming to visit with Crantock and his two older brothers. They have to be in London and will come to us on their way home to Wales.

May 23rd   Mama and I ride together in the mornings and after lunch I have lessons with the Street girls. In the evenings Mama and I read a few pages of Mrs Crowe.

May 25th   Mrs Vateson and Crantock and the two eldest boys are here.

May 31st I'm often left on my own with Crantock. Mama doesn't mind, she says he is a Harmless Soul. I think he likes me although he never looks at me but only at the floor. Today I played with his hands, nibbling at his fingers and pretending I was going to eat them up. Tizzy did this when I was little and it always made me laugh. Crantock didn't laugh but he rocked faster and said Edith, over and again. His brothers, Nectan and Rhun-Owen, never speak to anyone except their mama and Crantock in their own Welsh language.

June 1st I overheard Papa being horrid about our guests to Mama. He said that Crantock was an Idiot and an Imbecile and that his two brothers were just as Feeble-Minded and that it as well that they lived in the depths of Wales and didn't care to show their faces in Society because Society would turn its back on them. Mama shushed him, saying, Some things are best left unsaid. I think he is hateful.

June 2nd I'm not talking to Papa although he hasn't noticed.

June 4th Today poor dear Crantock had one of his moments. He started moaning and rocking very fast and hitting his head with his hands. Nothing I said would make him stop. I started to cry because he was hurting himself. When he saw that I was most upset he took my hand and started to lick it and then he put my fingers in his mouth and sucked them very hard. He put his head in my lap, just like Merry does at times, and fell fast asleep. Our mamas found us like that and he was carried off to bed still asleep.

June 7th A telegram came for Mrs Vateson. Adwen was in a riding accident. Her leg was impaled on a gate-spike when her horse made a bad jump. They all left for Wales immediately. Mama offered to go with her but Mrs Vateson said not.

June 13th We have had a letter. Adwen is being very brave and has asked if she might have a small cart and pony to pull it, so that she can get around until her leg is working again. Her mama writes that she is mending very well and seems not in too much pain at all.

July 4th We have had an awful letter. Last Thursday Adwen Vateson didn't wake up. Mama cried until she was sick and her eyes almost swelled shut. She says that although Adwen's mama has thirteen other children to love, the loss of even one is a Great Blow, especially a young life such as Adwen's. Mama said that God obviously needs Adwen in Heaven much more than her Mama and Papa and brothers and sisters need her at home.

Mrs Vateson wrote that Adwen's Going to Rest was most beautiful and peaceful. She wore a white gown embroidered around the hem with roses and a green vine. Her golden brown curls were circled with a crown of roses to match those on her dress. In her hands she held a bouquet of fifteen different flowers from their own garden, one for each of the children and her mama and papa, and tied with her favourite velvet hairbow. After taking her to the churchyard they went on her favourite walk. While Mama read this, she held my hand and kept breaking into tears, saying. My Poor Darling Azenor. She will wear black for three weeks for Adwen's mama.

July 11th Mama stays in her room most of the time. She says she has the lows for Adwen's mama. Papa says that she must pull herself together or she will be ill.

July 27th It is one month since Adwen's Going to Rest. A card came, edged with black ivy:

In the Most Loving Remembrance
of
ADWEN DAISY VATESON
In the 15th Year of Her Age
Gone to Take Her Place
Among the Angels and Saints
June 27th 1882

In the centre is a photographic portrait of Adwen that was taken on her last birthday. Her middle name was after Mama because Mama was there when she was born, the spring before Mama was married to Papa. Papa said, How was I supposed to know? Then Mama said, Because you never ever ever listen to what I say, and then cried again until she was sick and had to be put to bed.

August 1st Mama still has the Lows and is taking Tizzy's tonic. We are all to go to the sea near Kilton so that Mama can rest and get fresh air. Grandmother will come and Cousins May and Louisa. I am allowed to take Bayard and Merry. The big hurrah is that Cecil isn't coming because he is going away to school in September and must be prepared. Cousin May says that he and Papa will just have to manage with Woodsie and Fisher and Elizabeth and Emma.

August 28th It is almost the best summer ever. When I am not out on Bayard, or swimming, Cousin May, Merry and I are making a collection of nature specimens, of plants and stones and shells. Grandmother and Louisa are with Mama, Tizzy and Adah look after the boys. Robert and Reggie are always up to some mischief or other. Reggie is the ringleader, and he is naughty really, but it is impossible not to laugh. And Baby Edward is very sweet and placid and likes to sing nursery rhymes all day.

September 14th Cecil has gone to school. He was very excited and ran up and down the stairs at least a dozen times shouting for Papa to hurry or they'd miss the train. Mama looked a little choky when he left but didn't cry.

September 19th For the past two nights I've dreamt of Crantock. In the dream I am at the Abbey House and I can hear him calling my name but no matter how hard I look I can't find him. Sometimes the dream changes and I can see him in the garden but the window won't open and he can't hear me knocking on the glass to draw his attention. Both times I've woken up crying.

September 30th   In one week there is to be a ball for Adelaide Street's 17th birthday. Mama says that she believes that Adelaide's engagement to James Merridge will be announced. She says that although the Merridges are New Money, this isn't to be sniffed at.

October 8th   Last night was the dance. Everyone was most surprised that James Merridge wasn't there. I danced with Alexander Pightley four times. It was my very first dance with a boy who isn't Papa or one of my cousins. I didn't let him stand too close but his hand was hot and sticky in mine and he held my waist too tight. I tried to imagine sucking his fingers but they looked hairy and not-nice. While we danced I closed my eyes and pretended that he was Crantock. This made me feel happy, but when I opened my eyes and saw that it was only Alexander Pightley, I felt annoyed. I'm sure he thought I was being dreamy for him. He asked if he might write to me while he is away at school and I answered that I must ask Mama.

This morning when I asked her she smiled and said yes. She said Alexander's Papa owns a goodly portion of Lincolnshire.

October 14th   Today my first letter arrived from Alexander Pightley. It was two pages. He wrote about his horse called Juniper and his friends at school. He is three years older than I am.

October 21st   Alexander writes one week and I write the next in return. I have told him about Bayard and Merry and what I am doing in my lessons.

October 23rd   Mama was very excited and happy today because Papa had lunch with the celebrated novelist Mr Anthony Trollope. Mama's Cousin Walter knew Mr Trollope and Mama has met him twice. Mama said that Mr Trollope said that Barset is Somerset, which she considers the greatest compliment an English county might have. Mr Trollope was visiting Glastonbury with his friend Mr Freeman, from Wells, whom Papa doesn't like at all. Mr Freeman is against riding to hounds and Papa is not, and nor is Mr Trollope. Papa said if a Great Novelist can take luncheon with Mr Freeman and not argue about the hunt, then so can Papa, and so he did. Papa has invited Mr Trollope to join Our Hunt whenever he wishes to. Mr Freeman believes that before the end of the century hunting will be outlawed. Papa said, What nonsense the man speaks. If Mr Fox can't outwit Mr Hound then he deserves to ripped to bits. Papa said that Mr Freeman's deficiency was that he obviously didn't know how to enjoy himself because no one could deny that riding to hounds was jolly good fun. I agree with Papa and Mr Trollope.

October 25th   We are going to stay with Cousin May so that we might visit Mrs Lurgashall.

October 30th   Today is Albert's 13th birthday. When we called him he didn't come. Mama was most disappointed and said he must be very busy in Heaven with his birthday celebrations if he could not spare time for his Mama.

November 18th   We have been to see Mrs Lurgashall every other day but Albert still won't come when he is called. Mama has had tears and said I have lost my gift of being able to see him. Mrs Lurgashall said, What nonsense. Those on the other side do as they please, if Albert doesn't want to come, then he won't, and we must wait for him to be in a better humour. I asked Mama if we might try and call Adwen Vateson but she said not under any circumstances.

November 25th   We took afternoon tea with Alexander and his mama, Mrs Pightley. They have a very grand house in Belgravia. Mama was most impressed. Mrs Pightley says that Alexander is going to be a Bishop just like his grandfather and two uncles and two great-uncles. She says that in her family there is a tradition of Great and Influential Bishops. She and Mama got on very well. On the way back to Cousin May's, Mama said she could just imagine me as a Bishop's Wife.

December 7th   Yesterday Mr Trollope died. He had been ill for one month. Papa and I are agreed that it is a great shame that we did not have the chance to have him join us riding to hounds.

1883

January 8th It is just too awful to write about but I must, Adelaide Street has been jilted and James Merridge is now engaged to Cressa Creighton who is shockingly rich and has dozens of titles in her family tree. We are all forbidden to gossip. Mama and Papa have argued over it and are not speaking. Mama said, What is the poor girl to do? Her life is ruined, how will she go about in public? And Papa said, It is Augusta Street's fault for encouraging her daughter to believe a harmless flirtation would lead to a marriage proposal. Mama tsked a great many times, sounding more cross each time. Then she said, Mr Merridge was hardly conducting a harmless flirtation, Mr Porch, everyone witnessed that young man pursuing Adelaide. Papa replied, Every young chap has a great number of impulsive but meaningless flirtations – James Merridge's behaviour was promoted into something of more importance by the girl's mother. Let us be quite frank, Papa said, Augusta Street is a flibbertigibbet with little thought in her head beyond what to wear to her next social engagement and she encourages her daughters to be the same. If Adelaide has had an embarrassment then the blame lies with her mother. And I hope that you, Madam, take it as a lesson in how to behave with your own daughter when such situations arise. Mama was almost apoplectic. She walked out the room and slammed the door after her.

January 10th Today Adah told me that Fisher had told her that James Merridge jilted Adelaide because he discovered that the Streets' estate is heavily mortgaged. Fisher heard from a footman who heard from one of the housemaids who heard Mrs Street's housekeeper talking with Miss Lett-Jennings. When I told Mama she pursed her mouth and was very sharp with me, saying that I must not gossip with the servants. She said that when we were at the Abbey House they were more a part of the family but now they are not, so we must keep a proper distance. She said that obviously it is different with Tizzy and Woodsie but that one must be very careful because tittle-tattle can be a dangerous thing. Mama doesn't believe for a single moment that the Streets' estate is in any danger at all because they would not live the way they do and always be dressed in the most current fashions if it were so.

January 14th   Adelaide has gone with her mama to visit with her cousins in France. No one mentions James Merridge, not even Miss Lett-Jennings. Adah told me that he and Cressa Creighton will marry in March.

January 17th   Alexander still writes to me every week although his letters are somewhat dull reading. In the autumn he will take up a place at Oxford.

January 28th   Hunted to hounds this morning despite the rain. Bayard took me over four places which were very high. Papa was most impressed. I was covered in mud from top to toe. It was all rather splendid. When we got in, Papa and I stood steaming by the fire, drinking our tea. What a telling-off Mama gave us both! She can be such a spoilsport these days.

February 13th   Gallop out every morning on Bayard no matter what the weather. Then lessons in the afternoon with the Lett-Jennings, whose voice gives me a sick headache.

February 14th   Had a very narrow squeak this morning – took a tumble and just missed having Bayard come down on top of me. Landed hard on my right side which has come out in a blackery-blue such as I've never seen before. I was quite worried about dear old B, but he picked himself up and on we rode. I've told no one. They'll only make a fuss.

February 15th   A very gentle walk for B. & me today. We're both stiff and cranky.

February 27th   A weekend in Bath with Mama. She bought a lot of books about India and I chose a blanket for Bayard, a drinking bowl for Merry, and five pairs of riding gloves for me. And I bought a bangle with my very own money that has a horse charm hanging from it.

February 28th Mama has given me a surprise treat from Bath. They are china bookends in the shape of horses' heads. I have put them here on my little desk so that I see them when I sit to write.

March 14th What we all tried to avoid speaking about today was James Merridge getting married. We all pretended to have forgotten, even the Lett-J., which is not like her at all. At one point, Mama said, At least the weather is dismal, and Papa shouted, Madam, enough! Then Mama said, Well, we must be charitable and wish them a very long life together, and be grateful that they are not spoiling another couple. At this Papa told me to leave the room immediately, which I did, and even though I tried to listen through the door, I couldn't hear what happened next.

April 12th Tizzy is ill. As she is not contagious I am helping to look after her. Papa said he didn't think it proper that I do so, but I put my foot down and insisted. He looked most surprised. He is not accustomed to my putting my foot down. I am allowed to sit with her in the late afternoons.

April 19th Tizzy is slowly on the way to recovery and telling me all manner of stories! She remembers Mama from when she was a little baby.

May 1st Today is my 15th birthday. I feel very grown-up. After breakfast Papa and I shall ride together and this afternoon the Street girls will come for a tea party.

May 2nd I received many lovely presents yesterday and spent half of this morning writing thank-you notes. The best present was a book about horses in art which Mama gave to me. It has a great many plates of paintings and drawings and watercolours and sculptures. It reminded me of Win. I wonder how she is. I still have her drawings of Bayard and Merry. And Nile, I miss her terribly. I wonder if they write to each other. It's fairly obvious that they've forgotten me.

May 3rd   This morning I said to Mama, Nile has forgotten us, and she replied that Nile is very much occupied with her new husband. I was too shocked to speak. Mama heard from Nile and did not even tell me! She has said that she will find Nile's letter for me to read. But why didn't Nile send me her news? I thought Nile loved me.

May 7th   I've secretly written to Win. I need to know if she is in touch with Nile. I enclosed the letter with one to Alexander and asked him to forward it.

May 16th   Alexander has returned the letter which was returned to him. Win is no longer at Dorset Square and there is no forwarding address.

May 29th   Out all the time with Bayard and Merry, at least they both love me, there is no doubt about that at all.

June 16th   The dreary summer round of tennis and picnics and excursions has begun. I hate dressing-up and afternoon tea parties in the garden, or the summerhouse if it's raining, as it often is, and have told Mama so.

June 24th   I'm in trouble every day because I go out early with Bayard and Merry and don't get back until luncheon. Mama is in fits. She says if I don't mend my ways I shall be locked in my room every night and only allowed out in the morning when I'm suitably attired.

June 25th   Papa has taken Mama's side against me. It's just too awful to be believed. I've been in tears until I was almost sick. I will die if I can't go out on Bayard every day, I just know it.

September 2nd   It was a wonderful summer after all. I've been much too busy to write. The biggest news of all is that Alexander Pightley loves Amelia Street and not me and only we three are in on the secret. It is almost too exciting having such a secret. I guessed about their love, neither of them told me. Each time Alexander and I were together, Amelia was included, at his suggestion. And whenever he was near her, he was always accidentally bumping against her, like a dozy old cat. And there were at least one hundred other signs. We were on a picnic when I pointed this out to him and he went so white I thought he might faint. He bravely admitted to me that it is Amelia whom he adores, even though he was terrified that I would be upset. But I was not, which confused him a little. When Amelia was told that I knew and was not upset she cried with happiness. They have both sworn me to keep their secret. They realised that they loved each other when Alexander was 10 and Amelia was 8, which is eight whole years ago. On Alexander's 12th birthday they made a vow to be married when they grew up. It was a secret vow and it is important that it remains so, especially now as both their mamas have fallen out over the ghastly James Merridge.

Alexander says that James Merridge is not a gentleman despite speaking French and Latin and being able to hunt to hounds and shoot. Alexander said New Money might buy learning but it cannot buy manners which can only be learnt from one's family. James Merridge has told vile stories about Adelaide to anyone who will listen. He said that Adelaide has fits and rolls on the floor, foaming at the mouth, and that she did this before his very own eyes. He even said this to Alexander's mama who said that she was not surprised that there was Bad Blood in the Street girls. Alexander says that if he ever has the opportunity he will very happily horsewhip James Merridge and if there isn't a horsewhip to hand he will box him on his nose until it is very bloody indeed.

Alexander is pretending to do as his Mama wishes until he comes of age and obtains his portion of his inheritance, upon which he intends to marry Amelia. He sincerely begged my pardon for writing to me as he had done, but it was so that his mama did not suspect his feelings for Amelia. He is most taken aback that I am not green with envy and upset. But I am not. Amelia will be a much better Bishop's Wife than I could ever be. From now on, when Alexander writes to me, he will include a letter for Amelia, and when she replies I am to forward it. This will be our secret until we are older and they can marry. It made the summer great fun, having a Romantic Secret, even Mama has guessed that something is up. She said she suspected that I had secrets from her now and that this was all a part of being a young woman. I am sure she thinks Alexander and I have a secret agreement. Dear Mama. If only she knew the truth.

September 15th   Today Cecil returned to school and Robert has gone as well. Poor little fellow. He clung to Mama and cried as if his heart was breaking. All she could do was try and push him away saying he must be brave. Cecil laughed at him, the horrid beast. Papa refused to shake his hand goodbye until he stopped crying. But he didn't stop, not even when Papa walked away. Everyone on the platform watched as he was put on the train kicking and screaming. I felt very choky but managed not to cry. Even Reggie was quiet and solemn, which is most unusual.

September 20th   Poor Robbity writes every day. He cannot eat or sleep and is going to throw himself over the banisters if he cannot come home. Mama is often in tears.

September 25th   Robbity is ill but Papa has refused to allow Mama to go to him. Poor Mama – it is just too awful.

September 28th   It's worse than awful, much worse. Papa has been sent for because Robbity was pretending to be ill. Mama has taken to her bed.

September 30th   Papa is home. Mama is still in bed.

October 2nd   Out as much as I can be. Bayard in the mornings, lessons with Amelia in the afternoon. Papa is still slamming doors and barking orders at everyone. He even shouted at Berters whom he has had since he was a tiny puppy, nearly nineteen years now. Dear old Berters, the expression on his face, it was too awful. I got incredibly choky but managed not to cry. Imagine shouting at Berters. What was Papa thinking of?

October 3rd Berters is ignoring Papa. It would be funny if it didn't make me feel so choky.

October 4th Papa is doing his best to wheedle his way back into Berters' affections but Berters won't have it. But I do hope they make it up soon, it's almost worse than when Mama and Papa aren't speaking.

October 7th Mama and I have been in London since yesterday. It is so nice to be away from Papa and perhaps he and Berters will make it up while we are away. Even Mama looks a little better. We are here to see Mrs Lurgashall. I'm very worried that Albert shan't come when he is called. Mama will be very upset if he doesn't and I don't think I can take too much more of Mama's tears.

October 8th Much relief to all of us that Albert came. His Psychic Photograph was taken. Mrs Lurgashall insisted that we ask his permission before the attempt was made, otherwise he might be frightened off. The photographer was Mr McKibbin who is an Expert in the Photographing of Angels in Country Churches and Churchyards. He was very amusing and chatted to Albert as if he could see him, although he later admitted that he could not. He took two photographs and we waited a long time for them to be developed. After seeing them Mama was taken ill. She was unable to move or speak and we had to return to Cousin May's so she could rest.

In one photograph was Albert's face, floating without a body. The other showed his whole body. He had his hands resting on the chair that Mrs Lurghashall leaves empty for the departed to sit down on and rest, should they need to. It was obvious even to me that Albert resembles Papa. Tomorrow Mr McKibbin will come with copies of the photographs for Mama to keep.

October 17th Mama has spent the last week in bed. Cousin May and I have been out gadding every day to concerts and lectures and galleries and shops. There is too much to see and do. It is nice to visit but I would not want to live here, London is too busy and noisy for me. Tomorrow, if Mama is up to it, we will go back to Mrs Lurgashall.

October 30th I have seen Albert nine times in the past days and not been sick once. Albert was very late every day. We would call him in the morning and after luncheon but he only came when called after tea. He was cross and annoyed that we had kept calling. He said that he does not have a lot of free time as a Song-Uttering Chorister Angel, especially at this time of year when the Celestial Composers are busy preparing new works to celebrate the Coming to Earth of Jesus, exactly one thousand eight hundred and eighty three years ago. He would only stay for five minutes.

November 2nd Home to Bayard and Merry, and weren't my dear ones both pleased to see me!

November 14th Mama and Papa are to host a Ball for New Year's Eve. Alexander will attend, which has made Amelia very happy. Some of the Vatesons are to come and stay. I wonder if Crantock remembers me at all. I'm to have a new dress. How very exciting it is.

December 3rd Busy helping Mama with the umpteen preparations for the Ball, hardly time to draw breath, but I still manage to go out on Bayard for a couple of hours every morning.

December 14th Cecil and Robbity are home from school. Poor dear Robbity still has a mark on his leg from where Papa thrashed him. It's just too awful. He's thinking of running away to sea and has made me promise not to tell if he does. I've made him promise to wait until after the Ball at least.

December 24th Christmas Eve. Today Mama and I had a very long conversation about Albert. We both tried to imagine how busy he must be in Heaven at this time of year. We'd both quite like it to snow for Christmas only it might delay people's arriving for the New Year Ball, which would be a terrible shame given all our hard work.

1884

January 2nd   Everyone is still recovering from the Ball. It went on until the morning and then, because so many people remained, Mama and Papa put on breakfast. Afterwards people still wouldn't order their carriages, but sat chatting and yawning and drinking tea. Mama gave up and went to bed and no one noticed!!! Reverend Cox suggested a walk, some of the ladies did not want to go, but in all nearly thirty of us set off. It was a glorious morning, a slight frost on the trees, but mild with sunshine and a blue sky. We all agreed when the Reverend commented that it was as if God were smiling upon us. I walked arm in arm with Alexander and Amelia. After our walk we were allowed a hot toddy and told we must go to bed. The three of us kissed and swore our undying friendship. They have become my dearest friends and to think I used to find them dreary and dull. Afterwards, I was much too happy to sleep. Instead, I lay snuggled under the bedclothes, watching the flames of my fire with Merry snoozing nearby. Eventually I did drift off because when I awoke the fire was out and I could see stars in the sky.

January 3rd   All today I have had a nervous feeling in my stomach. I think – no, I believe that this year I will meet the man who will become my husband. It was hard not to think about Adelaide being jilted this time last year. What if the person I want to marry does not want to marry me? What if I too were jilted? How awful that would be. Poor Adelaide is still in France.

And it seems that I've hurt Crantock's feelings because he is ignoring me. Only he and his mama have come to stay for the Ball. What a strange family they are, none of the others wanted to come, not even Mr Vateson, they wanted to stay at home in Wales. Mama was much surprised and a tad peeved. However, Crantock was allowed to be at the Ball to watch the dancing. I neglected him, I suppose. But what else could I do? He does not dance. He does not even make conversation. He just sits at his mama's side, rocking to and fro. I think it was very good of Mama to invite them in the first place. When I told her so, she shushed me saying it was the very least she could do as it must be quite trying for Mrs Vateson to live with her sullen unsociable family who never want to peep out of their own Welsh doorway.

January 4th   Crantock is still ignoring me. When I try to talk to him he closes his eyes and hums very loudly over my voice. Mrs Vateson says I must not take it to heart, because he is only having a stormy spell. But I think Mama is right. Crantock is a dear, sweet, simple boy and that was fine when I was still a little girl, but now that I am becoming a young woman it is very different. Crantock will never become a young man. He will always be as he is. Just imagine, he is four years older than me, but still like a little boy.

January 8th   Crantock and his mama have finally gone. When he took my hand in front of everyone I did not dare resist, not even though he was hurting me by digging his fingernails into the palm of my hand. When I thought I could bear it no longer he finally let go. When I looked, he had broken the skin on my palm.

January 9th   Yet another bad start to a day. Cecil and Robert have returned to school and Robbity had tears again at the station. Papa has decided that he is not to be allowed home until he has become less girlish is his behaviour. At Eastertime he will stay at school and in the summer he will be sent to Scotland. This means we will not see him until next Christmas! It beggars belief. Mama and Papa argued all the way home. Papa said, It will be the worse for everyone if Robert's Womanish Sensitivity is not nipped in the bud at this stage. Mama was furious. She said, It must be a most curious thing, Mr Porch, to be so insensitive as to be unable to appreciate that a little boy might be sad and unhappy at the idea of being away from his mama and papa and sister and brothers for weeks on end. Papa replied, That is too ridiculous a comment to warrant a response and, my dear, entirely typical of Your Sex. The child needs to learn to be rational about his feelings, not hysterical. Why? Mama shouted, so that he grows up to be like you, a man with no interests beyond horses and dogs and men's pursuits and no ability to appreciate poetry or music or art? Is that what you would prefer? When Papa said, Yes, Mama burst into tears. Then Papa said, My dear, you must calm down, you are upsetting the children and yourself unnecessarily.

Poor Mama. I do not know how they ever came to be married. It can't have been for Love. Mama is Sensitive and Papa is not. He is the same day after day. Although he is just a little right when he says that she is prone to tears. Sometimes she will cry just to have her own way, which even I find infuriating, and not something I would ever do.

January 10th   Mama insisted I go to the dentist. No teeth were snatched, thank goodness. I have an awful headache from it though.

January 11th   I have a cold. I'm sure it's the teeth snatchers fault for picking and prodding into my teeth. Mama says it's because I do not wear enough layers.

January 13th   Mama is reading me *The Woman in White*, which makes me very shivery and goose-pimply. Imagine if it were true and not a story.

January 14th   Still sneezing and dripping and oozing, too disgusting. *The Woman in White* all day. Thank goodness it ended happily. It would have been unbearable otherwise. Mama and I both cried in relief. Although I did say to Mama that I thought Mr Hartwright should have married Marian, she seems much more interesting than Laura Fairlie, and Mama agreed. I wonder what will happen to Marian next; surely she doesn't stay in Cumberland with them as a governess to their children? Mama said she imagined Marian might write a novel or two out of her experiences and be very happy without either husband or children.

January 15th Mama started reading *Desperate Remedies*. We are both agreed that Mr Hardy it is not quite as accomplished a storyteller as Mr Collins.

January 16th Today Mama and I had the longest ever conversation about Husbands and how on earth one might recognise an Aeneas Manston if one were to meet him. She said one cannot, because Love makes one blind and then one is married and it is too late. She looked so very sad. I don't think Mama is very happy, but at least Papa is not a murderer or a lunatic.

January 18th I have decided that I will never marry. It would just be too awful to marry the wrong person and be unhappy for the rest of my life. I'd much rather stay at Edgarley and ride Bayard every day, with Merry running beside us. I can keep Mama company when she is old.

February 7th I'm much affected by the weather these days. When the sun is out I feel as if my heart will burst from happiness. When it is grey like today, I want to hide beneath the bedclothes and never come out.

February 16th It has been raining without stopping for four days and all I have done is to sit by the window, watching it fall and create enormous puddles and mires. Mama says I am being too melancholy and has suggested a trip to Bristol to cheer me. But I don't want to go.

February 18th My lower back aches all the time and I am too tired and sluggish to do anything at all. I keep bursting into tears for no reason at all. I have made Mama promise that I don't have to get married, and she has, but she says that she is sure I will change my mind.

February 20th Today I became a young woman. Mama sat with me and stroked my brow. We both cried. All day yesterday I had a crooked pain in my stomach and this morning it was worse. I have been given some drops in my tea to help with the pain. Mama said that the first time is the very worst of all.

February 21st   It is all too painful and hideous. Today my bed-linen was changed four times. Tizzy has given me two heating pans, one for my feet and one for my lower back. Mama read to me from *Pride and Prejudice* which has always been one of my favourite books. But I think of Lizzie and her sisters differently now. How can I not? They are young women just as I am. What would Mr Darcy think if he knew? He would be revolted and never speak to Lizzie again. I wonder if Papa knows about these things. I certainly hope not.

February 22nd   Amelia has been to visit me. She brought flowers and chocolates and a bookmark that she has embroidered with my name. We did not talk about my sickness but she kept squeezing my hand in sympathy. I cried until I had a headache.

February 24th   Today I had no pain and was allowed out of bed to sit by the fire in a big armchair that Mama has moved into my room. It is from Papa's study and he suggested I might like it since I was very very unwell.

February 25th   It has ended. When I looked in the mirror I looked different, pale and weak, which is not like me at all. Tizzy is to keep a calendar for me so that we know when It is about to happen again. I will be sick once a month until I am old like Mama and Tizzy. Mama says it is just something that one has to learn to live with.

March 7th   I am changed. I don't even want to ride Bayard. My bones ache and my skin hurts.

March 22nd   I have been sick again but this time only for two days. I am never going to write of this again. I cannot.

March 23rd   Out on Bayard for the first time in weeks. We rode very slowly. He kept turning his head to look at me as if asking, Can we gallop now? Perhaps I shall never want to gallop again.

April 16th   I have received a letter from Nile. I don't know how to write, my hand is shaking so. The letter came to me through Agatha Penrose, the milliner in Wells to whom we occasionally go. Miss Penrose received the letter before Christmas so it is many months old, but Nile requested that it be put directly into my hand by Agatha herself. It is just as well I decided to go with Mama to have her summer hats retrimmed or it might have been many more months before I received the news.

While Mama was examining trimmings with Agnes Penrose, Agatha took me aside on the excuse of showing me some silken flowers. I must admit I was rather cold and unfriendly and when she attempted to press Nile's letter into my hand I pushed her away. She was very awkward and embarrassed and whispered something about a friend's long travels on the Nile River in Egypt. I looked at her blankly. I honestly thought she had gone terrifically mad. She then knocked a box of roses on to the floor and begged my assistance in picking them up. By now I was becoming angry, thinking her nothing more than a thoroughly stupid woman, yet I did assist her, during which time she said Miss Quaintance has written and slipped the letter into my hand. I was too shocked and spilt the roses again.

The rest of the day's shopping was drawn out and painful, and the afternoon seemed to last an entire year. Finally at home, I told Mama I needed to rest and came here to read Nile's letter. It is so brief! She says so little! She says that she is living in Suffolk with Win, whom she considers as her husband! I felt faint and dizzy. Indeed, I think I did faint, before reading this line one hundred times at least. She and Win Love each other! She wrote, 'One day I hope we will meet again. Although I miss you with all my heart, I am happier than in all my life. I love and am loved in return. For you, my dearest Edith, I wish a similar blessing.'

I have been crying. There is no address for me to contact her directly. If I wish to write I must do so care of Agatha Penrose. I am too confused to know what to think.

April 17th I have realised that Mama lied to me. She said that Nile had written to her, telling of her marriage to a doctor. Or perhaps Nile did write such a letter? I do not know. I do not know what to think. I wish I could talk to Mama about this, but that is impossible.

April 18th I have spent the entire day trying to compose a letter to Nile but haven't an idea what to say.

April 21st Life suddenly seems much too complicated. I want things to be the way they used to be.

April 28th We are come to London for my birthday. Amelia has come as well, more because she wants to see Alexander than because she wishes to be with me. We're staying with Cousin May, who is always so serene. Goodness knows what she thinks of life.

May 1st My 16th birthday, for what it is worth.

May 6th Days filled with all the usual London events – galleries and concerts and talks and shopping. No Mrs Lurgashall because Amelia is with us. I am unable to enjoy any of it. I just want to be at home with Bayard and Merry.

May 14th Finally back at home. London is so dirty and nasty; goodness knows why anyone would want to live there.

May 30th There has been Trouble. A friend of Mrs Pightley saw Alexander alone with Amelia when he was supposed to be visiting with us at Edgarley. Mrs Pightley wrote informing Mother and Father. Father has railed at Mother and me for days on end. According to him, it is All Mother's Fault. I am not allowed to see either of them, and poor, poor Alexander has been forbidden to see Amelia ever, ever again. All Mother keeps saying is, Edith, how could you? Father has instructed her to open all my letters which is most humiliating. The beastly Lett-Jennings has resigned her position at the Streets'. She had the audacity to say to Mother and Father, and in front of me, that Amelia Street was aiming above her station in trying to snare Alexander Pightley, given her family's Bad Blood, not to mention the extensive mortgages on their Estate. I wanted to scratch her ghastly face. I am too furious to write any more at the moment.

June 16th   Mother suggested that I might go with Cousin May to the Cumbrian Lakes for the summer but Father said not under any circumstances am I to be trusted out of Mother's sight.

June 18th   Today Cecil arrived home from school. Poor Robbity has been banished to Scotland, as Father said he would be. Cecil has to be the most hideous boy ever to be born. He follows Father around like a silly little dog. The only words he seems to know are Yes, Sir, and No, Sir. He shows off terribly all the time. I am determined to make him thoroughly miserable all summer long.

July 2nd   Life is too dreary to be believed. There is an endless round of games and parties and picnics and dances. I am never on my own even for a minute. Cousin Louisa has come to stay and she accompanies me everywhere, even when I am out on Bayard. It isn't even possible for me to play tricks on Cecil, so closely am I watched. It is all hateful and I wish I were dead.

July 17th   The most amazing ructions during the past couple of days. Mother has fled to Cousin May and goodness knows when she will be back. It all started when she said she was going to Scotland to see Robbity, whether Father liked it or not. They argued for days about it. I have never known such arguments. It all came to a head when Mother actually struck Father in front of Louisa and me – I still can't believe I saw it happen – and Father looked murderous with rage and responded by seizing Mother and shaking her. Louisa was squawking like a dozen hens and I was in tears and Mother was shouting, Murder! Murder! and all the servants came running in and Tizzy managed to bundle

Mother from the room. The very next thing Mother was in the carriage heading for London with Tizzy. Letters have gone to and fro at the rate of a half dozen a day, but Mother has refused to return until she has been to see Robert. Goodness knows what the gossip among the servants is like. By now we must be the talk of every house in Somerset.

July 25th   What if Mother doesn't return? What if I am trapped with Father and Louisa until I find someone to marry?

August 1st   Sick with nervous headaches. Even Louisa is having upset stomachs.

August 21st   Mother is returned with Tizzy. I cried until I was sick and had to be put to bed. She came and sat with me and said that Robbity is putting on a very brave face for such a small chap. Most days he goes fishing or shooting or riding or walking. I did not dare ask what about her and Papa and would they ever speak again and when will life return to normal.

September 15th   Edgarley is as quiet as the grave. Cecil has gone back to school and Reggie has gone as well. Dear little Reggie, he is such a silly, always mimicking someone. He does Father wonderfully and Louisa, too. It's impossible not to laugh. Now there is only Mother and Father – who are still not speaking – Louisa and myself. Edward hardly counts because he is still in the Nursery. I go out on Bayard as often I can.

October 1st   I would like to know how Mother had such appalling taste as to marry a man like Father. I will never marry – NEVER!

November 2nd   We have been in London for one week. For three days we have tried to reach Albert but he will not come. Mrs Lurgashall took Mother aside and they spoke together for some time. Then Mrs Lurgashall spoke with me. She told me that sometimes a girl's psychic energy wanes when she becomes a young woman, because all the energy is being directed to Other Parts. My monthly illness has stolen my gift. After I was told I cried until I was sick and had to be put to bed. Mother is wearing a brave face but I can tell she is sour and very down in the dumps about it.

November 10th There has been more Trouble but at least this time I could truthfully say I knew nothing and was not involved. The Good News is that Amelia and Alexander have eloped! And no one knows where they are. The Bad News is I am mortally wounded and offended. How could they go without telling me? How could they? I thought we were friends. I thought we shared secrets.

December 28th Only three more days left of this hateful year. I hate everyone and everything except for Bayard and Merry. I particularly hate Louisa whose face I could easily scratch to pieces. I wish they would all die so that I could live at Edgarley on my own.

1885

January 6th Mother is unwell so I am trapped with only Louisa for company. There seems to be nothing but the endless drone of her voice mixed in with the rain. I have tried playing the piano but she talks over me. I've tried reading aloud to her while she does her needlework but every paragraph – or two, if I am lucky – she interrupts to voice her opinion, as if the characters were real people. It is too maddening. She delights in provoking me, I know it. I will go mad if I am cooped up in this house for too many more days. Please, God, why can't someone rescue me?

February 7th I ride, I walk, I eat, I sleep, and I see people in whom I am not in the least interested because Mother insists upon it.

February 27th Today I told Louisa that if she died no one would care and no one would miss her. She just smiled and said, But you would miss me, Edith, because then you would have no one to whom to be horrible.

March 8th The only time I feel alive is when I am out on Bayard, with Merry running alongside. I love them both more than any-one else in the world.

March 26th Shocking news. Mrs James Merridge – Cressa Creighton – has died of a fever after childbirth. Mother was very cold about it all, saying, It serves her right for taking someone else's intended husband. James Merridge is now a very wealthy young widower. I will never forget Alexander saying how he wanted to box J. M.'s nose until it fell off. Adelaide is still in France. I wonder if Cressa Creighton's death will help her get over being jilted.

April 1st   I am entirely alone except for Bayard and Merry. If I died no one would notice or care.

April 11th   Mrs Merridge's baby went to join his Mother.

May 1st   It is my 17th birthday. I refuse to celebrate. Mother says I have become the most horrid young woman ever to draw breath and that no one, particularly young men, are going to be at all interested in someone who spends her days sulking. As if I care. None of the young men around here are of the slightest interest to me. They are all too much like Father.

May 5th   Mother says no, I may not put my hair up one year early.

May 9th   Day after day the same round of social engagements with the same dull people. I will suffocate to death, I am certain of it. Am I really to endure this tedium with ladylike resignation until I meet the man I am to marry? Must I pretend an interest in other people's lives while waiting patiently for that person? But what if I never meet him? I never do seem to meet interesting young men. I must be the only girl in Somerset who has never been the smallest bit in love with anyone. What if I am here with Mother and Father and Louisa for years to come? Just the thought gives me a sick headache.

September 12th   I have lacked the heart to write anything for months. It's finally autumn again. The summer was bearable because Reggie was home. What a wag he is, so jolly and full of life. After only one year he already has the reputation as the naughtiest boy in the school because he is always up to some prank or other. Cecil has grown very tall and pompous and says he will never marry. Robbity is very bookish and unsociable. He hardly spoke to anyone the entire time he was here, and just kept his nose in his Latin and Greek. Edgarley is deadly quiet now that they have gone. Even Louisa's prattling inanities are preferable to the silence.

October 1st We are not to go to Mrs Lurgashall this year. Mother said she could see no point. She had on her awful, sour, disappointed face. It is all too unbearable. I will have to marry the very first man who asks me just to get away from Edgarley, even if he is utterly penniless.

November 1st A letter has finally arrived from Amelia. She is now Mrs Alexander Pightley and the mother of a small daughter, Alexandra Pightley. They are living in Paris where Alexander has taken a position as an English teacher in a private school. She writes that though they have little money to speak of, they are a very happy little family. Aside from this she tells nothing of where or how they became married. At only two pages long, I found it a most unsatisfactory letter. I am so annoyed I have a mind not to reply at all. She should have written to me months ago.

November 3rd I have relented and written to Amelia after all. How exciting it was addressing the envelope to Mrs Alexander Pightley. I have begged for more details of the wedding and a photograph of little Alexandra.

December 1st Soon the boys will be home from school. At least the house will be lively again.

December 25th I have been given the most wonderful present for Christmas. Next year I am to do the London Season. Mama and I will stay those months with Cousin May. We will take Bayard and Merry and I am to have an entirely new wardrobe. Mama says by this time next year I will very probably be married and have a home of my own. I am so excited that I have been sick and have come to bed.

Cwm-yr-Eglwys, Pembrokeshire
October 1934

We have so much in common, mother and I, don't we, Mardie says to an empty room. I too grew up at Edgarley. I too grew up with Daisy as my mother because you were not there. Mardie's top lip quivers around the nostrils like a dog's muzzle before a snarl. She looks out of the kitchen window and is able to see nothing beyond the soft folds of the sea mist, but can hear the conkers shamble through leaves before hitting the ground. She sighs, lights a cigarette and then pours herself a coffee, half a cup, as black and as thick as tar, gentling it with whisky up to the brim. She gulps it despite the heat, feeling the colour rush to her cheeks, then pours herself the same again, or almost the same, a little less coffee, perhaps.

Daisy. Her mother's mother. Mardie's grandmother. Those early memories are blurred, but she had only been five – no, just turned six, or thereabouts – when she and her brother had been taken to live with her grandparents at Edgarley. And those first memories were of Grand's smile, of her buck teeth which remind Mardie of her mother. And Grand's gentle voice saying, Well here she is, as Mardie comes into the room without knocking, to stop and stand and stare, her little voice demanding, I want Uncle Reggie. And Grand shaking her head no, saying, But, my dear child, Uncle Reggie is gone, a long way over the sea to – to where? Mardie can't remember. But she can vividly recall that room with its long sloping view over pasture and fields. Her grandmother's room, full of books and chairs, a sofa and a *chaise-longue*, and plants and cats and cluttered with clutter. Over the years that room would become an extension of her own self, as she fought with the cats for a space in which to curl up and read, while Grand sat at her desk writing.

Edgarley House – all those roomy rooms with just her grand-parents and herself and her brother Ben to fill them up, not including the servants because they have their own rooms. Tizzy and Woodsie and Adah and, God, she can't remember the names of the others, but cannot really be bothered to. They had not seemed part of her life, merely on the sidelines, tending to her needs and giving her someone to complain to. Tizzy and Woodsie, for example, who had known her mother as a baby and yet never spoke of her. Speaking instead of Uncle Reggie, gone off to who knew where until the next letter arrived to explain, and Uncle Eddie in India, and sometimes Uncles Cecil and Robert, but never Mardie's mother Edith. And they hadn't liked Mardie, she could tell, such that she hadn't been sorry when Tizzy died and Woodsie retired with her annuity. But Grand had been very despondent and shed quite a few tears on the quiet. Dear old Grand, such a softie beneath her Victorian manners and morals and fuddy-duddy formalities.

Her death four years ago had seemed sudden and unexpected, although she was nearly ninety. Both she and Mardie had thought she would reach her centenary, and had talked about it often, and the less they had believed in her death, all the time the closer it had been coming. One August afternoon she had gone to take her nap and not woken up. It had been as simple and as peaceful as that. Realising what had happened, Mardie had sat and taken her already cool hand, lifting it, kissing it, holding it against her cheek. She hadn't cried, not then, not for months. It was more than a year before she had realised that her grandmother was gone and she was entirely alone.

She was here by then, here in the cottage, and one afternoon had opened the front door and looked out at the sea swelling in the sunshine and along to the ruined churchyard whose head-stones tip-tilted. So picturesque, so romantic, this view from her own front door, a scene worthy of – she scoured her mind for an appropriate artist – well, of any of those early-nineteenth-century painters and watercolourists that Grand so loved. And for the first time Mardie had realised that Grand would never see it or have it described to her because she was dead. Quietly she had closed the door and gone into the sitting-room and poured herself a stiff whisky and then another, and another, until the whisky released the tears and she could cry herself to sleep on the sofa.

On that night she awoke, mouth rust-filled, head thumping, to the sound of Uncle Eddie's voice reprimanding her, *Now, Mardie, how many times must I tell you that you have a home with your* aunt and I in Calcutta, should you wish. His colonel's voice brisk, brooking no opposition. But oppose him she did and would continue to, saying into the dark, yes, I know, I know. I came to Pembrokeshire because I wanted to and I have stayed because I wanted to. No one made me. No one asked me. It's not like she wants me here. She wouldn't even notice if I left. After all those years did I think she would be interested in me just because she is my mother?

Three years had passed since that night. Three years of drinking a little more as each day passed. Three years of regularly driving the fifteen or so miles to see her mother, and of attempting to communicate, of the endless bickering and roundabout conversations in which nothing was ever said. Trying to learn more of her father and his death; trying to learn more of her mother and her life. Three years of this, only to have it fall into her lap on Monday when she asked her mother if she might borrow a handful of novels to read and her mother indifferently waved her hand in the direction of a stack of books left higgledy-piggledy in a corner.

Mardie had browsed through the spines, sneezing at the dust she was throwing up, the pads of her fingertips becoming blackened. Dickens, Dickens, and more bloody Dickens, and ditto Mrs Braddon, Wilkie Collins, Thomas Hardy, Bulwer Lytton, Mrs Oliphant, George Eliot, Amelia Edwards, Rhoda Broughton, and dear god, who would want to read Mrs Henry Wood. And so on and so on and – oh my, oh my my my my my – look at this, just look at all this Trollope. Shivering with pleasure she ran her fingers along the spines, smiling as she thought, Well, this will keep me quiet for a while. How many years is it since Grand read me the Barsetshire novels? I really dread to think. Trollope, whom no one cared to read any more; he was too Victorian, too out of fashion. But they reminded Mardie of her grandmother; of the sound of her voice, reading aloud.

After making a separate pile of books to take with her, Mardie had delved into those that lay hidden behind, opening one after another. She crouched, her heart battering her chest and jolting her entire body, and looked over her shoulder to make sure her mother had not reappeared. Her mother must have forgotten these were there, Mardie thought, because these books had not been touched for years. She quickly took as many as she could carry and put them in the cardboard box near her, and then did the same again, starting at every noise.

When her mother appeared in the doorway Mardie felt a sharp pain in her stomach. She breathed shallowly, and her voice sounded too high and grating as she said, I'm just taking the Trollope, mother, if you don't mind. She didn't dare look her mother's way as she casually placed the Trollope on top of the other books, trying to make her actions seem natural. But when she stood and turned it was to find that she was alone. Grunting she picked up the box and left, without finding her mother to say goodbye.

Walking to where she had parked the motor, she put the box containing her mother's diaries on the back seat, and stood for a moment, her mind entirely blank. Then, without crashing the gears as she tended to, she started the engine and drove carefully, slowly, along the driveway that is bordered by massive horse-chestnut trees. Turning right through the gates on to the main road, glancing up to Carn Ingli to find it obscured by low cloud, and then the opposite way, down to Newport Sands, to see that the tide was neither in or out. Driving onward she thought, the leaves haven't even started to change yet, but it won't be long now, won't be long at all. And on she drove, slowly, carefully, as she hadn't driven for years, so that she was well able to brake in time for the twenty or so donkeys ambling down the road ahead of her, led by a bandy-legged fellow in a shiny clean suit who, using thick gobbets of Welsh, parted the donkeys so that she was able to drive through and past them and again onward. Not too much farther along she took a sharp turn inland on to a sunken road which crossed the first of the fords, a mere trickle really and hardly worth the name of water, and took her through the woods and Cwm Dyffryn and past Soar Hill until suddenly visible on the left was the sea. Then she inched the motor through the last of the fords to reach Cwm-yr-Eglwys and her small white cottage.

It is here she has sat sipping whisky, reading and rereading her mother's childhood diaries. Diaries that would sometimes end abruptly, for no apparent rhyme or reason, leaving weeks and months unrecorded and only to be guessed at. At first, Mardie had thought to read the diary for the year of her father's death immediately. Yet she had not done so. It was cowardice, she knew that. As much as she wanted to know, she was afraid to know. The truth of his death had eluded her for well over thirty years – did another few days matter? Instead, she had decided to start with the earliest diary, drawn by the idea of her mother as a little girl, growing up first at the Abbey House and then at Edgarley.

Stillness. The unattended sound of wood shifting in the fire-place. The damp smell of the sea mist slinking through the cracks of the window frames. Mardie lights a cigarette, enjoying the sting of the smoke in her eyes, and lifts her fingers lipward to pick away tobacco. My mother, Mardie says aloud, then adds, but what does that word mean to me? What does the word mean to her?

Mardie hears the noise of geese carried faintly through the fog, a signal that Mrs Palmer is on her way down the road. She would rather not be here when she arrives. Normally, as soon as lunch is eaten, she is out walking, but in the close mist this is not possible. So there must be the basic pleasantries, Mrs Palmer, how are you today? I'm very well, Miss Carew. And yourself? And is there any especial job you'd like me doing this afternoon? And that is all. Mardie has never known how to talk to the servants, a fact that always bemused her grandmother, although Mrs Palmer could hardly be called a servant, or certainly not as Mardie had known them at Edgarley. Mrs Palmer was what was now called the Help; such a nasty term Mardie always thought, because it made her sound as if she was the poor one, and she was hardly that. She simply did not want the responsibility of servants, who were a chore in themselves. Even Grand had admitted that. And the things servants knew about one's life, the power of their gossip. Not that Mrs Palmer was any different in that respect. Did she gossip? Mardie wondered. Had word got out how much Miss

Carew liked her drink? Mrs Palmer had been with her from the first year here, silently dealing with the empty bottles. And when Mardie was occasionally bedridden with a hangover, both were in agreement that it could only have been caused by something she had eaten. But it was some time since Mardie had succeeded in laying herself out with drink; instead, she had reached a point where the more steadily she drank the more sober she felt. It was as if the whisky steadied her.

For the rest of that day she sits in the front room, feeding the fire, sipping whisky. She says good-evening to Mrs Palmer as she leaves, watching the darkness mingle with the fog and slowly steal its shape, before switching on the lamps. In the late afternoon Ben comes. Standing there, looking at her in that serious way he has, much too serious for a thirteen-year-old. But then he always was grave – such a grave little fellow, everyone would say, wise beyond his years. And Mardie, his older sister by eighteen months, could only agree. Ben always did seem the elder, somehow understanding what needed to be explained to Mardie, understanding that she relied on him to be there, just at the right moment.

Even when you were dying you came to me, she murmurs unconsciously. She had been at her lessons on that raw April day and seen him through the window looking in her direction. When she stood up at her desk thinking, Ben, what on earth – ? he had turned and begun to walk away from her down the path and through the trees, until out of sight. Twenty-eight years later she can still remember the shock, her sickened fear-filled thought: Ben is leaving me. The following morning when news had reached Edgarley of his sudden death from meningitis, Mardie had nearly said, Yes, I know, I saw him walk away from me. Instead, she had comforted her grandparents, surprising them with her forbearance.

During the years that followed she saw Ben regularly. Anywhere. Everywhere. Sometimes only catching a brief glimpse of him from the corner of her eye. At other times he would come and stand close by and she could talk to him and he would listen. Gradually his visits grew less frequent, although she continued to look for him, and often waited for him to come. Now, he rarely came, although she sometimes heard his voice telling her that something was about to happen. Last week, for example, she had suddenly heard the words, 'Very soon you'll know,' and a few days later Mardie had uncovered her mother's diaries.

Mardie had never spoken of Ben with anyone, not even with Grand. Although her grandmother must have suspected, sometimes asking who it was that Mardie talked to in the middle of the night, Mardie always replied, Did I? Was I? I must have been talking in my sleep. Ghosts, her grandmother had said to her, are the unhappy dead; very often they do not even know that they are dead. She had shown Mardie the McKibbon Psychic Photographs taken of Albert on that long-ago October afternoon of 1883.

But Mardie did not believe it. She didn't believe in ghosts or vampires or werewolves or fairies or the McKibbon Collection of Psychic Photographs that comprised over one hundred thousand Angel photographs alone. But she did believe in Ben. She believed that she saw him and spoke with him, and he with her, while at the same time knowing and accepting that he was dead.

Mardie awakes not knowing where she is. The room is so still that her breath seems harsh and nervous. She sits up in bed, dislodging the books beside her so that they fall to the floor. She coughs: she can hear her breath whistling in her nostrils' hair. She puts her hands to her face and coughs again. She is tired. She wants a drink. The sharp morning light edges around the curtains. She doesn't need the lamplight to see to reach the bottles on the bedside table. A finger of whisky in last night's dirty glass softened with water and guzzled. And then another. She catches sight of herself in the mirror, eyes focusing on a middle-aged boozer's face, puffy and creased from sleep. Her father's head and face on her own shoulders. A sensation of strangeness swamps her. She is reading her mother's diaries and will discover things she both does and does not want to know. I want to know the truth, she says, as she switches on the wireless, and the voice lulls her temporarily.

After coffee and whisky and coffee and whisky she heads out of the door to walk around the headland, around to Dinas Sands. She follows the trail, soft and slippy underfoot, looking out at the empty sea, observing the flight patterns of the gulls, listening to the wind and the surge and break and ebb of the waves on the rocks below. At Pen-y-Fan she stops. Her heart and mind are steady. This weather cannot last, she says to herself, scanning the sky for confirmation of her words. At Dinas Sands she turns inland, picking a pathway that leads past the cove to a fishermen's shack. As she opens the door every face turns towards her, then away. Not one of the men offer any sign of acknowledgement, yet neither are they surprised by her presence. She sits in her regular corner, lights a cigarette, murmurs thank you as a bottle and a glass and a jug of water are placed on the table, and then stares out of the window at the slipway, at the sea-swell and at the fishing boats. She hesitates to look around the room, constrained by the knowledge that while these men are fishermen they are certainly smugglers too. It is an unspoken rule that if she does not appear too curious her intrusion will be tolerated. Despite the greasy surface, she eats the stew placed in front of her. It is what she wants; it is why she has come here. The blubbery, coarse meat will settle her stomach. Her mind is deliberately blank, allowing the men's burred prattle and patter to scratch at her eardrums, Welsh and Gaelic, Irish and Scots. As she stands to leave she knows they are watching, assessing her, tall and full-fleshed in a fattish but sturdy fashion, and she continues to feel their eyes upon her until she closes the door. Outside she doesn't linger, the wind is pushing clouds towards her. I knew this morning's mildness couldn't last, she mutters. Well, it is October, after all. But even though she takes the short cut that leads from Dinas Sands straight across to the seaside Cwm, by the time she reaches home, a Pembrokeshire drizzle drapes her.

She goes up to change, leaving her wet clothes where they fall for Mrs Palmer to tidy away. Downstairs, she prods the fire into flame and pours a stiff whisky before standing at the window, head cocked to one side, listening to the noiseless noise of the view. Does the longing to relive a mishandled moment never end?

Of course it does. It becomes less and less until it is only a memory of longing, which is not the same thing at all. She tips her head back to pour the contents of the glass down her throat. Mrs Palmer's voice makes her jump. Miss Carew, did you call? Mardie turns from the window. Mrs Palmer, good-afternoon, no, I said nothing, I require nothing, thank you, thank you, that's all, Mrs Palmer. Mrs Palmer nods and retreats and Mardie mutters a string of filthy words, adding, Bloody snoop, I'll sack you, knowing that she will not because finding someone to replace her will be impossible. She sloshes more whisky into her glass and throws herself into the chair.

Mardie has not had another drink all afternoon. She doesn't want one. She wants – she would like – to go back. But she is not sure to where exactly. She wants to be herself in a place that she remembers, one of those long lunches at Edgarley or being teased by Ben in a game or out driving with Grand. Anywhere. Anywhere but here. She can feel her earlier selves inside her, their movements are familiar, comforting, it is she who is a stranger to them.

She shifts her head to look through the window. The rain has stopped. The sea is the colour of dead fish, so is the sky. It is impossible to tell where one begins and the other ends. There might be nothing out there at all, yet the sight makes her eyeballs ache. She is cold, she needs to stoke the fire but doesn't have the energy to lean forward and lift the poker and prod until the embers catch alight on a fresh piece of wood. It is too much to expect of her. If only Mrs Palmer would come in and see to it.

If only. Two words that crop up too often in her life. If only her father had not died. If only her mother had not had to go away. If only Ben had not died. Or Uncle Reggie. Or her grandmother.

She sits shivering, thinking of all the dead she has known. For each of them she tried to be what they wanted – brave, strong, dependable. And with each one there had come a moment when she was meant to reach out but could not, not even when they had reached for her first to leave the taste of their lips on her own.

No, I don't want this, she says now, getting to her feet, looking at Ben where he stands. I don't want it, she says to him, and watches him nod, agreeing. She begins to cry. Ben, she says, Ben stay, don't leave me on my own. Desperately in need of a drink, she grabs at the bottle and sucks on it, drinking too much so that she chokes and coughs and the whisky dribbles down her chin. She cries harder, louder, but when Mrs Palmer appears in the doorway, Mardie immediately reduces her bawl to a snivel and lifts one hand to her lower face to wipe away snot and saliva and whisky. I want my mother, she says. Why isn't she here? I want her, do you hear me? Why isn't she here?

Mrs Palmer looks at Mardie with uncurious eyes and smiles an economical smile, saying, Why, Miss Carew, you've let the fire go out and it's been so cold all day, you'll catch your death. I'll run you a nice hot bath, shall I? – and afterwards some soup on a tray in bed, and then a dram of something to help you sleep.

Mardie lets the words wash over her. She lets Mrs Palmer take the bottle of whisky and put it to one side. As she is led away for a bath, she hears her own voice, plaintive and pathetic even to her own ears, Would you be so kind as to read to me for a little while, Mrs Palmer? I will of course pay you for your extra time.

Penfeidr, Pembrokeshire

1886–1888

1886

January 2nd   I feel quite unlike myself. As if my body no longer fits me properly. I tried to speak with Mama about it but she insists that I am merely suffering early nerves concerning our forthcoming trip to London. I began to feel irritable and tired on New Year's Eve and not at all in the mood to celebrate. Being with people made me fidgety so I left early and went to bed, but was unable to sleep. I tossed and tossed again and every time I thought I was about to nod off I imagined someone had entered the room and said my name. So convinced was I that four times I sat up and asked, Who is there? Poor Merry was most disturbed by my behaviour.

Since then I have felt awkward in myself and hardly slept at all. Almost certainly Mama is right – I am over-excited. Just to think, by the end of this year my life will be entirely different. I will probably be married, with my very own home. How unimaginable not to live at Edgarley. As well as exciting, of course.

January 5th   Even more peculiar in my head. It is almost as if I do not exist. I look at my hands and the blue veins threading beneath the skin and do not recognise them as mine. I am sure that if I were to look in the mirror at this very moment it would be empty. Yet at the same time I am definitely here in this room with the fire sparking and the clock ticking and Merry snoring. I am at a loss to say what this is. Perhaps I am coming down with a fever or a chill.

January 6th   I am lost, somehow. I keep repeating to myself: I am Edith May Porch. I was born on the 1st May 1868. I live at Edgarley House, near to Glastonbury, with my Mama and Papa. I have four younger brothers, a horse named Bayard and a dog called Merry. Tizzy and Woodsie live here too and have known me all my life. Through my bedroom window I can see the Tor.

January 7th   Merry is asleep across my feet. My very own Merry-Hound, the most faithful of dogs. If only I were like you. How easy it must be to love everyone and to be loved in return, to sleep so peacefully and moan just a little when my hand caresses your head and ears, and to look at me with such devoted sleepy eyes. My dear, dear dog. My truest friend apart from Bayard.

January 8th   I have been in tears. Even Mama says she knows not why. She was stitching and I was reading to her from the *Cornhill*, when Edward came rushing in. He had found an old skipping-rope hidden away and asked if he might skip with it, not knowing whose it was. But it was mine and I thought it lost a long time ago. And I saw myself as a young girl, skipping the paths of the Abbey House, up and down to where King Arthur lies. Yes, I saw myself as I was then, with all my sweet dreams and games and it felt a long time past and I felt such sorrow sweep over me that a huge pain burst open in my heart, and it was from this pain that I wept.

January 9th   Today my heart ached and shook and trembled as if I had been running. My whole body shuddered with its vibration. I could hear the swish and swill of my blood as if it were the sea pounding. And my breath came so fast. Something is wrong. I am ill. Perhaps I am dying. Yet I don't feel at all afraid.

January 10th   Am I still alive? Perhaps I died in the night and no one has noticed. Perhaps it is my ghost that everyone sees.

January 11th   How they will mourn me when I am gone. Mama will go to Mrs Lurgashall and I will come to speak to her, or I suppose I shall, for I will have no reason not to do so. And they will love me even more and regret all the times they were cross and shouted. They will wish that they had appreciated me when they had the chance to do so. How sorry they will be when I am not here.

January 12th   I have been up on the Tor, although I am unsteady on my legs. I was certain that I could hear ringing bells from the Tower. But no, it was only an imagining.

January 13th Out on Bayard full tilt, despite my delicate condition. How I shall miss such moments. Of course, Mama said, Don't blame me, Edith, if you return full of sniffles. I could hardly say that it didn't matter, that I am on my way sniffles or no. It would only upset her.

January 14th I have the slightest of sniffles, so of course Mama had to say I told you so. The Very Reverend Ash is visiting and talks ceaselessly about weeds and their different types. And Mama does humour him so. She says weeds are one of his especial subjects aside from sermons.

January 15th I have taken to my bed. Anything to get away from the V. R. A. and his weeds and sermons and Mama's humouring of him.

January 16th Sudden and sharp pains in my head on and off all day long. I have a feeling that my time is not too far off.

January 17th Still more pains all over my body.

February 15th I am still alive, but only just, and much too weak to write at length. I am confined to bed because I cannot eat without my stomach rebelling. Occasionally I am able to take a little broth, so I have not yet wasted away entirely. I like the lightness that I feel in my body. I am so light I could float away. Everyone is very concerned, of course, except for me, I feel very calm. I don't mind dying at all.

February 17th My bed has been placed near to the window so that I might see outside and up to the Tor.

February 20th So much rain that the garden is almost a lake. Edgarley will be washed away. Edgarley will be drowned up to the rooftop. I have tried to say so. I try to tell them. I need to be safe from the raining water, but they won't listen, they won't listen to a word I say. They think I am upset, but I am not.

February 23rd   These daffodils will kill me, their tight heads like lances waiting to stab and stab me, I don't want them, not here, please listen to me, please Mama.

February 25th   Badly infested with daffodils

Undated

– stinging nettles and stinging on my legs, I want my stockings

– old dog skin, my Merry, soft, oh soft on my face

– something sneaking past the window in large quantities

– a truce between the daffodils and me because they've crept along the garden path and in here and in and in and they know that I know but no one else does

– I snapped off the daffodil heads, the sound of breaking, oh the joy of twisting, such a big task, but I had patience

– don't, just don't touch me whatever you do

– He is in the corner. His face is pale. With large blue eyes that are like looking into an endless summer sky. He is my husband-to-be.

– He is here every day. He comes. He sits. He is waiting for me. Sometimes I hear him say my name. So soft. A whisper. Edith, he says.

– His smile is like sunlight. Warm. On my face. Edith, he says, Edith, be well.

– You and only you.

– Love. Wait.

April 23rd   Every time I awoke today Papa was there at my bedside and every time he could see that I was awakened he held my hand and kissed my forehead.

April 24th I have asked Mama who he is that comes to me and she says that he is my very own Guardian Angel sent to keep me safe.

April 30th Each day for the past few days I have managed to eat a little more. Dr Gersham has decided that I need to rest somewhere in the countryside. I overheard Papa say, But Edgarley is in the countryside and Mama shushed him.

May 1st Today was my 18th birthday. Mama brushed my hair and put it up. We all had supper in my room. It was lovely. I couldn't have had a more special evening. But, oh, how it has tired me.

May 2nd Mama has written to Azenor Vateson asking if I might come to them in Wales. I said, But what if she says yes? I would be in the Welsh wilderness for months on end. Mama said I would be very happy there, she knows it.

May 3rd I have lost all feeling in my left hand. It is so heavy and numb that I can barely lift it. Sometimes I have terrible stabbing pains along my ring finger.

May 8th I walk a little farther each day but still have no feeling in my hand. Although I am eating a little more my skin is still baggy on my bones. But I want to be well.

May 14th Everyone is pleased with the daily small improvements I am making. Next week Mrs Vateson will come to take me to Nevern for the summer and early autumn. Dr Gersham has decided that it is best if Mama does not travel with me. But I am allowed to take the Merry-dog.

May 19th Mrs Vateson is here with her eldest son, Nectan, and eldest daughter, Corth. I will admit that I am dreading going. What if Crantock still hates me? I will be trapped. I must not think about it.

May 24th Tomorrow we leave. I do not want to go. I want to stay at Edgarley. Mama wept and said I must go so that I will be well again.

May 25th Waiting to leave. I have never been away from home for so long. At least the Merry-dog will be with me, but not Bayard, so I have left strict instructions concerning his exercise. When I awoke I heard my Guardian Angel say, Edith, so near to me that I turned thinking to see his face. He wants me to go, to be well, and so I will.

Penfeidr

May 29th Yesterday we arrived at the house and I was put to bed straight away. It was such a long journey. I cried all night and upset the Merry-dog. I want to go home. I want Bayard and Mama and Papa. I want to be in my very own bedroom, not here.

June 1st Mrs Vateson came in while I was crying. She was not nice to me. In fact she was perfectly horrible. She said, What a spoilt patient you are, Miss Edith Porch. It will do you the world of good to be with other children. When I cried even harder she patted my hand and left. Why has Mama sent me here to be with such a heartless woman? How can Mama even think that Mrs Vateson is her friend when she speaks to me so unkind?

June 4th Each day has the same routine. In the morning I go to the long library where a day-bed has been placed for me. From here I can see over the gardens and orchards on one side, and to the river and Nevern in the distance. It is a very lovely landscape, and when I am better, I am sure I shall enjoy walking a little. However, every two hours I am given something to eat, a boiled egg, or some soup, or a portion of meat, or vegetables. Even if I am not hungry I am made to eat. I have a cordial to sip all day, which is to help rebuild my strength. Mrs Vateson made it herself from her own secret recipe.

Although there are many Vatesons, I don't see anyone until the early afternoon when one of the older girls, Corth or Tybie, will come to keep me company, often with Mrs Vateson. Then I am read to and allowed to walk for a while. They all seem much occupied with their own lives. I haven't seen Crantock once, not even a glimpse, or Mr Vateson. Although everyone else has peeped around the door to greet me, even the little ones. I retire to bed in the early evening, by which time I am exhausted, and sleep for at least fourteen hours, if not more, until morning. And then the day begins again.

I am lonely, much more so than at Edgarley, and bored unto death with staring out of the window and dozing, but I am trapped into this dreariness until I am well. Even the Merry-dog has abandoned me to be out in the sunshine. Although I still have no feeling at all in my left hand, I am beginning to fill out my skin and my bones seem less boney.

June 5th   In the mornings I like to watch the view from my own window. I can see to a hill in the distance that seems to have a rocky top. When I am well I shall go there.

June 6th   Today I spied Crantock in the garden with Mr Vateson. He is much changed, but I cannot say how. He appears much taller and stood laughing and talking with his papa almost as if he were a normal young man. He would, I suppose, be 21 or 22 years old now. He was dressed like a woodcutter in a smock and trousers. It is how all the Vateson men dress during the day. I was most shocked at first – what would Mama say if she knew that they did not dress as gentlemen should? Even Mrs Vateson and the girls dress very simply.

June 7th   I hate Mrs Vateson. I overheard her say to Corth & Tybie that Miss Edith May Porch enjoys too much being the invalid. I am to be left to my own devices more often so that I become wearied of my own moodings and wish to seek out company a little more. If only Mrs Vateson knew how exceedingly dull I find each and every one of them. Just what would Mama say if she knew I was being treated in such a fashion? I shudder to think. I do not doubt that she would come immediately to take me home.

June 8th   Being left to my own devices I decided to make a small exploration of the house. It is very old and although it is dated 1620 they call it the New House. The Old House, which still stands near to the river, is from the 1200s. The estate itself is called Penfeidr. All the furnishings are of heavy and ancient wood, with drapes that are beautifully embroidered. It is most unlike Edgarley where so much is new. Here everything is worn and slightly shabby. Every room is wainscoted with lovely carvings. Many of the ceilings are beamed with texts painted on each side in ancient Welsh. Yet the house does not seem dark as it is lit from the many windows in every room. It seems strange to think that I have been here before because I have so few memories. It is truly lovely, but such a shame that it is in the middle of the Welsh wilderness. Imagine having such a house in Somerset. Just think how wonderful that would be. The weekend house-parties and dinners and balls one could have. There are seventeen bedrooms here alone! And, oh, it is all so wasted on the Vatesons.

June 9th   Today I discovered where the Merry-dog slips off to when I found the three smallest Vatesons – Winnow, Kew and Keyne – decorating him with flowers to pull their cart! He seemed not to mind their proddings at all, but rather stood there wagging his tail, with the silliest big smile on his face, thrilled to be the centre of so much attention. No wonder I never see him these days. Winnow is a sweet little boy with the most endearing pointy little face. He must be about 6 or 7, I imagine. The twin girls are very shy. I think I remember Mama being informed of their birth, perhaps four or five years ago.

June 10th   Tonight I am to join the family for dinner whether I wish to or not.

June 11th   What an excessively boorish family. Last night was nothing more than tedious or dull. There was not much conversation and the meal consisted solely of vegetables! The Vatesons consider meat unnecessary during the summer months, from June to September, unless one is in poor health, as I am, when it is taken at luncheon. Goodness, the meal seemed to drag on for hours, but I was relieved to see that they take more care with their appearance in the evening. Afterwards, neither Mr Vateson nor the boys went off, as Papa always does; everyone remained together, which seemed quite queer. Crantock sat near Mrs Vateson with his head held to one side, humming and rocking occasionally, just as I have seen him do before. Three times he said, Look, Edith's here, but didn't as much as glance my way. I felt most awkward, I was quite unsure of where to sit, or how to fit, and my attempts at conversation were met with very little response. But I must have fallen asleep because when I awoke I was in my bed and it was this morning.

June 12th   How on earth am I going to get through the next months until I am well enough to leave? Already I am bored almost to expiration, as Mama would say. I am trying to walk a little farther every day, although I become fatigued very quickly. I still have no feeling at all in my left hand, but have become adept at doing things with just the one.

Later. Another endless dinner. Lettuce soup this time, which I refused to take. Imagine drinking something green, how truly revolting. And followed by dish after dish of vegetables!

June 13th   And another thing – none of them attends Church. Mr Vateson says that one does not need to because God knows what is in our hearts and souls. However, should I wish to attend I will be taken to St Brynach in Nevern, both on Sunday morning and in the evening.

June 14th   I am completely ignored by everyone during the day and expected to entertain myself. Papa is right, the Welsh are horrible. I've written to Mama saying that I wish to come home immediately.

June 15th   Until Mama comes for me, I have decided to fill my time by exploring the nooks and crannies of the gardens and grounds. I must say I had not quite realised how extensive Penfeidr is. If I were staying it would take me weeks to see every corner. There is a series of orchards with fruit trees by the dozen and of every sort, vegetable and herb gardens, as well as flowers. They keep sheep and geese and ducks and hens and stable a great many horses. This afternoon I whiled away a good two or three hours chatting to the horses. If only my Bayard were here, I would not feel so neglected. I have not yet been to see the Old House, which, I am told, is moated and has a private chapel near by and the Vateson burial-ground.

It is all very lovely at this time of year. It is just a terrific shame that the ghastly Vatesons live here.

June 16th   Every evening is the same. Not one of them has anything of interest to say, but then how can they when they never go out and no one ever calls to visit. Nevern is only one mile away but there is little of interest there except the church. The nearest thing to civilisation, if it might be called such, is St David's, which is some miles away.

June 17th   This evening I refused to go down for dinner. They are all hateful. Today I thought to walk to Nevern but only got as far as the main gates. The drive alone wound for almost two miles, much longer than I thought, and I thoroughly exhausted myself. As I rested beneath one of the massive horse-chestnuts that line the drive in the prettiest way, Nectan and Rhun-Owen, who are the two eldest boys, rode past me, nodding as they did so, not even having the minimum amount of courtesy to enquire as to whether I needed their assistance in returning to the house. So, when I had rested and regained my little energy and managed to make my way back, I sought Mrs Vateson and made a complaint to her concerning their discourtesy. She said, and these are her exact words: Fiddlesticks, you need to take more exercise if you are to be well. I said nothing. What could I possibly say in response to such coldness? I have come to my room and here I have stayed. How on earth did Mama become friends with such a woman as Mrs Vateson?

June 18th   I am ignoring them and they are ignoring me.

June 19th   I have been in tears until I was almost sick and taken to my bed. Mama's letter arrived this morning. She says that I must stay here until the early autumn as originally planned.

June 20th   I insisted on being taken to church this morning and sat in the family pew with Miss Corth Vateson, whose sour expression showed how much she enjoyed accompanying me. The service was in Welsh, which seemed rather ridiculous. How is one supposed to follow the service? Is there any point in going at all? I must enquire of Mama whether my church-going is entirely necessary.

Afterwards, I insisted on looking at the churchyard which has some old stones, but most fascinating are the ancient yews that line the pathway, one of which actually bleeds, oozing a red sap from the bark where a branch was removed in the 1840s. How terrifically strange and mysterious!

June 21st   I dine with them because I must eat, but as soon as we are finished I retire to my room. I have made it quite clear that I am as little interested in them as they are in me.

June 22nd   Every morning one of them reads from an ancient book called *Breton's Prognostications*. No more than a sentence each day; this morning it was something such as: 'The roses and sweet herbs put the distiller to his cunning.' Goodness knows what it is supposed to mean, or if it even has any meaning at all.

June 23rd   I manage to walk a little farther each day. Anything to get away from the Vatesons. I go on my own since the Merry-dog has abandoned me for the children.

June 27th   Today is the 4th anniversary of Adwen's Resting. They have invited me to go with them this afternoon to visit her grave. I felt terrifically awkward but unable to refuse.

June 29th   I have been resting in my room for the past two days during which I have had such stabbing pains in my left hand that they cause me to cry out. Mrs Vateson says that it is the blood beginning to flow again and that I must not be fearful because the pain will pass. For all of yesterday and today she has sat with me for twenty minutes every hour rubbing a lotion into my hand and arm all the way up to the shoulder and stretching my fingers in every direction. It is a lotion that she has prepared herself with many warming herbs, including ginger all the way from Western Africa. It is to assist the blood's circulation of my hand.

The pain began on Sunday evening. During the afternoon we went to Adwen's grave, in their private burial-ground, near to the chapel. Beneath the chapel is a crypt where the early Vatesons are buried. One passes through a hedge of fuchsia to gain access to the burial-ground, on the other side of which the river rushes by hidden by a thicket of purple and white lilac. In between the headstones wildflowers grow where they wish to. The oldest headstone is from 1679 and belongs to Brychan Vateson who built the New House. The current Mr Vateson is also named Brychan.

I watched as they decorated Adwen's grave with garden flowers; then, from the youngest Vateson to the eldest, each told of their favourite memory from the past year, when they had last stood there. Some were stories almost, and took a little time. Even the smallest children had something to tell. Winnow surprised me by saying that his favourite thing had been my coming to stay because I had brought with me the Merry-dog who has become his friend and great companion. Near to the end they all joined hands, circling her grave, and sang a song, this time in their own Welsh language. Crantock's voice rose larger and louder than all the others. He sang with head tipped backwards straight up into the sky. Then, when the song had ended, he stood at the foot of her grave and struck strange poses, with his arms and body formed like a young tree shifting in the wind, and when he stopped it was all of a sudden, to go down on to his knees and rest his head on the flowers at the foot of her grave. At this I began to weep, although I was the only one to do so. They all smiled and kissed each other. Mrs Vateson said to me, There is no need for tears, for while Adwen is in our hearts she is with us still. But I wept all the way back to the house and went straight to my bed and cried until I slept from exhaustion.

The pain in my hand woke me and gradually became worse, although today it is a little better.

June 30th My hand is almost as it used to be except for an ache very deep in every finger-bone. Mrs Vateson has requested that I assist her with some of her tasks. She says that I will be well even more quickly if my mind and hands are occupied. If I am at all fatigued I am to stop at once. I have not been given a choice in the matter. How bossy she is.

July 1st I am exhausted and have come to bed. The morning started badly with boring Mr Breton's prognostication: 'It is now July,' read by Mr Vateson. I mean truly, the simplicity of this family beggars belief! And, then I worked all day – like a maid – with only a break for tea in the morning, luncheon, and then tea in the afternoon. I assisted in rearranging the pickle and preserve stores. This is done thrice a year and consists of moving every single jar – and there are dozens – so that those to be used in the coming months are brought forward, and space is made for the newly bottled. There was everything one could imagine, much of it produced on Vateson land. My task was to write and date the labels. Although I did not have to lift and carry, my entire body aches as if I had done so, such that I can barely sit upright to write this.

July 2nd This afternoon I was given a simple task, still being very tired from my exertions yesterday. I sat in the garden stitching and have stitched myself into a bleeding blister. I am sure Mama will be horrified to learn that I am doing the Vateson mending.

July 3rd A different task again. I helped Mrs Vateson, Corth and Tybie to pick strawberries and their leaves. She intends to make a cordial from the fruit, while the leaves will be boiled to make a concoction to rub on everyone's gums because it strengthens them, or so Mrs Vateson says. We left early, in a cart as ancient as the hills. I have not seen the likes of it before. It is so rustic it could only be Welsh, but pulled by two sweet, shy drays. We drove for some miles, along barely marked tracks, deep into the countryside before finally stopping. And there, right before me, lay a hollow covered with wild strawberries. I was given a large straw hat, and a pair of very aged and worn kid gloves to protect my hands, and a small very low stool on which to sit and pick. We passed what was left of the morning upon our task, then rested for lunch in the shade of the cart, and then began again. We did not get back until just past five, so it was a long day of almost nine hours. It was not difficult to be in their company for we were silent for the most part, although occasionally Tybie would sing what, she told me, were local songs, and in Welsh of course.

At the end of dinner we had some of the strawberries with wine and sugar and they were most delicious. Everyone congratulated us on picking the nicest strawberries to be found.

July 4th   I have woken stiff in every bone from yesterday. I can barely sit up in bed, let alone walk.

July 5th   Still aching but today I managed to assist Mrs Vateson with her strawberry preparations. I was taken to her very own cottage, down near the copse, where she does these tasks. When we arrived a dozen or so cats came running from every corner to greet her, all of them black with little white paws. They don't have individual names but are all called the Mims. Every now and then, throughout the day, she would ask in a loud voice, where are the Mims got to? and two or three would always appear and she would have a long conversation with them. They mewed as if they too were conversing with her.

She showed me her small cottage which has two rooms on each of two floors and a big stone stairway at the centre. The left downstairs room is packed with crocks and glass jars and bottles of all shapes and sizes and colours. The other downstairs room is a kitchen with a table and a press and pots and pans and funnels and three sets of scales. Upstairs, the left-side room has bottles and jars filled with all manner of plants and liquids and from the ceiling are hung dried flowers and herbs. The last room is filled with books, a comfortable chair and a writing-desk. It is a very peaceful place, very private and tucked away behind shrubs and trees.

Firstly, we made the gum strengthener because it was the easiest to do. We boiled the leaves, but not to a mulch, and then wrapped them in wet calico to keep them damp, and then placed these in pots. The remaining leaves we tied into bunches and hung upstairs to dry. Mrs Vateson uses them to make tea. Finally we made the cordial, or began to, because it must steep for five whole days.

July 6th   I am free to do as I please today but I cannot imagine what to do, except go walking.

July 9th   The last four afternoons I have spent in the orchards helping to put the cherry-clacks on all the fruit trees to frighten the birds off. On the plums and nectarines we tied small jars of cider mixed with honey which draws the wasps and flies away from the fruit. It was most enjoyable, although I still tire very quickly and had to rest regularly.

I am, however, beginning to be treated with much less coldness by them all. And such a very curious family they are. Truly, they never see anyone. The Vatesons never visit, nor are visited. Though they are certainly not poor, they actually appear to enjoy working in the gardens. Even the Smallies – which is what the little ones are called – do chores when they are not at their schooling.

Most mornings Mr Vateson goes off with Crantock to the Old House, which I have still not seen. This is where Mr Vateson writes and conducts his researches, in which, I am told, Crantock assists him, though goodness knows how, as he can barely read or write. Mrs Vateson is either at her cottage or busy in the garden. She seems to have very little to do with organising the house. I think it is Corth who directs the servants. The two eldest boys, Nectan who is 27 and Rhun-Owen who is 25, both studied at Cambridge. Neither of them likes England at all and can be very rude about the English. During the day they take turns to give lessons to the Smallies. The eldest girls are Corth, 24, Tybie, 23, and Elined, 21. Corth and Tybie seem quite content to be old maids, but Elined is very bad-tempered, she is always in the throes of a temper over something or other. She prefers to be in her room, where she likes to make things from wood. She hasn't spoken to me even once. Then there are Cleer and Ninnon, who are 16 and 15, but no one seems to remember which way around. They are inseparable and might even be twins, they look so alike. But Mrs Vateson says not, one definitely came before the other. They are making a study of the local springs for Mr Vateson and have found eighty-three so far. They are mapping them, measuring them and collecting water samples. The Smallies are Rhawin who is 9, Haran, 8, Winnow, 7, and Kew & Keyne, 4, who really are twins.

All the family look the same, very pale and slender with big blue eyes and birdie-brown hair. They all have very large noses, which are fine on the boys but a terrible shame on the girls. Only Crantock is a little bit different, his hair being golden instead of brown. When they are not speaking in their own Welsh language they have a lilting accent which at times I find difficult to understand. For the most part, they are silent, although it sometimes seems as if they are nevertheless communicating.

July 10th Today Mrs Vateson and I made twelve pints of strawberry cordial. She and I had the first glass each and it was divine. I have written to Mama saying that I am learning to do things that will definitely please my eventual Husband.

July 11th This afternoon I managed to find the chapel again. It was not as easy to do as I had thought. It is such a peaceful, tucked-away spot. This time I went inside and was taken aback to see all four walls covered in paintings of biblical scenes. I've never seen such a church interior. There is no furniture save for an old font and two carved effigies – one of a knight, the other a lady. They must be the almost-first Vatesons. I spent some time in the graveyard reading the many headstones.

I think it is my favourite place at Penfeidr.

July 12th   A ferocious thunderstorm this afternoon with lightning that covered the sky.

July 13th   Today I received a letter from Mama asking if I am sad not to be in London as we had planned. But, if I am to be honest, I have hardly thought of London in recent days. My first weeks here of illness seem such a long time past, although it is not even two months since my arrival. I am not as unhappy as I then was. I hope Mama will not be too disappointed that I do not mind remaining for now, rather than going to London for the Season.

July 14th   I am in a thoroughly terrible temper. Everything has been spoiled. This afternoon we went for a picnic down near the river. It was only we girls, except for Ninnon who had gone off collecting water-specimens with Cleer. It was very hot and still and everyone swam. Only I did not. There had been no plan to swim and the Vateson girls, including Mrs Vateson, removed their clothing and swam 'as God made them', in Mrs Vateson's description. I was shocked and embarrassed and revolted and pretended to nap so that I might not witness their making such a spectacle of themselves. On the way back I walked behind everyone else and Mrs Vateson dropped back to walk with me. She squeezed my hand and said, I fear you disapprove of us. You have the look of your dear Mama when she is most displeased. She did not await my reply but instead walked on ahead.

Of course I disapprove. How could I not? Their behaviour is utterly disgraceful and unnatural.

July 15th   Somewhat troubled dreams of which I do not care to write. Today I will walk a long way on my own and find a quiet corner in which to sit and think.

July 16th More troubling dreams. Perhaps I can go home now that I am no longer unwell.

Later. I have spoken with Mrs Vateson about leaving. She said that if it is what I wish then she will arrange it. She said she is most sorry that I am not happy here and that it would be sad if I were to leave and miss the best part of summer. What am I to do? She will be offended. I wish I could ask Mama, but I can hardly tell her what happened for she would be too dismayed.

Later again. But perhaps Mama would not be shocked. Perhaps she knows they do this – this manner of thing. I mean, after all, she has been friends with Mrs Vateson for many years and has often visited. Perhaps even Mama has gone swimming 'as God made her'. I must not think of such things, I shall only upset myself again.

July 17th Last night I sat in the garden watching the full moon. I could have sat there until moonset. The sky is so clear here, with thousands of stars. I have decided that I will stay until the autumn as was the original plan. Mrs Vateson is pleased, but I am uncertain if I have made the right decision. I have asked for a regular task so that I might organise my days as the others do.

Later. This afternoon we walked all the way to Newport Sands. Newport itself consists of little more than a few cottages. The Sands are where the river, the Afon Nyfer that borders Penfeidr on one side, runs down to the sea. And the sea was calmness itself, unruffled by any breeze at all. It is all very lovely, very isolated.

July 19th Yesterday we picnicked, walking across country to Carn Ingli, the hill I can see from my bedroom window. On the way we splashed through fords and drank from springs because the weather was so warm. Mr Vateson says that Carn Ingli is known as the Place of the Sleeping Angel. It is where St Brynach communed with angels thirteen hundred years ago. From the top I could see all the way down to Newport Sands and far out to sea and my chest ached with the beauty of it all.

We ate our picnic and then napped in the shade of the stones. Afterwards, everyone except Crantock spoke of their dreams, each trying to outdo the other in tall dream tales. Many times I laughed, although I was the only one to do so. Mr Vateson wrote each dream down in a special dream book that he keeps. When he asked what I had dreamt, I said I had not. But he did not believe me, saying, Everyone dreams at Carn Ingli. But truly, I did not. Then we all, even the smallest of the Smallies, clambered to the top again. But when I looked out to the view it seemed too bright, the sunlight hurt my eyes and made everything splinter and swirl around me. I fainted a little and when I came to myself, I was still on my feet, supported by Mr Vateson. Crantock had tight hold of my other hand and swung my arm from side to side. He was most excited and words tumbled from his mouth. He said, Edith look. Blue sky. And blue sea. Look. And grass and stones. Here Edith. And here. And he pointed in every direction. Then he looked at me, directly into my eyes, as he has never done before, and began to cry. At this he dropped my hand and his mama took him in her arms and led him down off the Carn.

I felt near to tears myself. What had I done? Mr Vateson too was most perplexed and looked at me with a very furrowed brow but remained silent. A few minutes later, when the rest of us clambered down, I found Crantock fast asleep with his head in his mama's lap. He looked like an angel with the sun on his hair. It was almost as if he wore a halo. He does have such a lovely, sweet face.

I do not know what to make of what has happened. Today, I have not seen Crantock at all, which is not unusual. Everyone behaves as if nothing untoward has happened. Perhaps it is so for them, but it is not for me!

July 20th   Crantock and Mr Vateson will sleep up at Carn Ingli for one whole week. Apparently they do this every summer.

July 22nd   The house is curiously quiet without Crantock and his father.

July 24th   Today we drove to a very special place called Dinas Head and picnicked looking out to sea with the sea breeze to keep us fresh. On our return journey we came to a small village named Cwm-yr-Eglwys, which in English means the Valley of the Church. It has its very own ruined church, dedicated to St Brynach, just as Nevern's church is. A storm washed the church out to sea in 1859. Mrs Vateson remembers it well as it was her first year here as a bride. There are many springs and fords and streams – everywhere the cooling sound of water. It is most unlike Glastonbury. It feels secret and hidden and it is just too Romantic for me to describe. It is almost like a painting by Mr Turner, so full is it of mysterising light.

I think I am almost glad that I have decided to stay.

July 25th   Today I am sad and low. This happens on some days since my illness. It is as if I have mislaid something, but do not know what. I have noticed that it will often occur after I have had an especially happy day such as yesterday.

Later. Mr Vateson and Crantock have sent word that they will stay on the Carn for another week.

July 28th   I have had a somewhat cross letter from Mama. She says that I am neglecting her and not writing often enough, and it is true. There is so much to do here and so little time. I am often tired by the end of the day and it is nice to rest and gaze at the stars and listen to someone reading a story. Mama just does not understand that here unlike at Edgarley we do a great many things for ourselves and do not sit around simply waiting for time to pass.

July 29th   Earlier this evening Crantock and Mr Vateson came home unannounced. It was very curious. Just as we were finishing dinner Crantock burst through the door shouting my name! He came straight to my side and started to take stones from a bag he was carrying, saying, Edith look, in that excited way he has. And there was no keeping the small children in their bed once they had heard that Crantock and their papa were returned.

July 30th   It is one month since the feeling returned to my hand – it seems like a lifetime ago, so well have I settled here since then. And just to think how unhappy I was at the beginning. Occasionally I still have a very deep ache in the bones of my thumb, but not too often.

August 1st Such an afternoon! All of us rode to the sea at Newport Sands and then the men took the horses in, not just into the shallows but out so that the horses swam, while they rode them bareback. I have been told this is a Vateson family tradition, and a more magnificent sight I have rarely seen. Even Crantock rode out, and Winnow too. They went together – sixteen horses in all – and stayed out for fifteen minutes, if not more. The dogs accompanied them, including my own Merry-Hound who was very much pleased with himself afterwards. When they returned to the shore they rubbed the horses dry and then we ate together, even the stablemen, who held themselves only a little way apart.

By the time we returned here it was very late. Despite my tiredness I have taken the time to write to Mama while today is still fresh in my memory.

August 2nd Very deep sleep last night, awake early. All the holly-hocks are out and how happy they look. It is much too hot to do anything but to take turns to do the watering and to laze in the shade.

August 3rd Another shocking event – why do these things seem to happen when I am at my happiest here? We girls were in the garden when Crantock suddenly appeared. I cannot write of what I saw for my hand is still trembling from the shock. He was – I cannot write it. No, I cannot. I was hot with shame and blushed red to the roots of my hair. I was too horrified to make a sound. Mrs Vateson noticed my distress and stood in front of me so that I might not be further mortified. She said to me Crantock gains great pleasure in being 'as God has made him' and she believes that in Heaven we all walk so.

What would Mama say to such baseness? She would be disgusted and rightly so. What I saw is a beastliness, an ugliness beyond belief, beyond imagining. What if I had been alone? What would I have done? Even the thought makes me feel sick and faint and I am going to have to lie down.

August 5th And again today, just as he behaved yesterday! How can I not be revolted? Such behaviour can only be entirely unnatural.

August 6th I have spent most of the day in my room. I am sick to my stomach.

Later. Tomorrow we are to go to Dinas Sands for a picnic. I do not wish to go – I cannot. He will make me ill with his behaviour.

August 7th I must go. Mrs Vateson has insisted, saying that if I do not then no one will and we will picnic another day. I feel awful – I want to go home. I want Mama to be here.

August 8th I know not how to write of yesterday. My life is changed for ever. How? Oh how did I come to be in this place!?

Later. It was a perfect day, sea breeze, lunch beneath parasols, paddling in the shallows, and then, and then, how –

Later again. I have been staring out of the window, up to the Carn. All I can do is write down exactly what occurred. We were playing at tossing the ball, chasing one another. I was desperately trying to avoid being near Crantock because he – because I – I held the ball – and then somehow he grabbed me at the waist, trying to take the ball from me. His touch repulsed me and I was fighting to be free of him. I was angry, almost in tears. The strength of his hands was so surprising. He just seemed to grip me more tightly, with me struggling to get away. Then I felt his breath on my neck and every hair on my body lifted and I tingled with great goose-pimples on my flesh. I cried out, I do not want this, and then I felt his next breath and it was as if the world had slowed its motion. I could see the waves, and such an age it took them to lift and move towards the shore, but they had no sound. And around me I could see laughing faces but hear no laughter. It was as if I were deaf. But I was not deaf, because I could hear whispering and I turned toward Crantock and this simple action seemed to take me an hour or more, so slowly did my limbs move. I turned to look full into his face, into his eyes, and I felt his breath on my cheeks. I opened my mouth to say again, I do not want this, but could not, and took his breath into my mouth, and felt as if I would fall if it were not for his hands at my waist holding me steady and close to him. I shifted my eyes trying to focus on his right eye and on doing so saw reflected there the sun, a blazing disc of golden fire. And when I looked to his left eye I saw there the moon, full, fat and waxen. Then I clearly heard the words 'the destruction of the harvest', and I repeated them and Crantock nodded once, saying, 'And also of travellers,' to which I replied, 'Yes.' Still, I was able to feel his breath on my lips and I said, 'Fire,' at the very same moment as I saw flames burn in his eyes. And then I fainted and later came to myself with my head resting in Mrs Vateson's lap, and many faces around me.

I have spent the better part of today with Mr Vateson going over and over what happened. He has asked me a dozen questions and then asked them again about every tiny detail. We would reach the end, where I came to on the sands, and then we would return to the beginning. He has written every word, as if what I am telling him is of the utmost importance. He is both believing and unbelieving. The first time I spoke of Crantock's words his face was livid. He said, do you expect me to believe he told you, just like that, for no reason at all? My dear, it took me three entire months before I managed to obtain those sentences. Three months of recording and deciphering his dreams. And you expect me to believe that he told you in the space of a handful of minutes? All I could answer was, Yes.

I am too tired to write any further tonight. But, what in Heaven's name is this Vateson eccentricity I have stumbled upon now? What has happened between that idiot boy and me? God forgive me! I did not mean to write that. He is not an idiot. What a terrible thing for me to write. I am just too tired – too tired to think.

August 9th Continued from yesterday. I awoke at daybreak. The house is so quiet, so peaceful. I am different. I know and feel it inside myself. I do not know how, but it is so.

Yesterday Mr Vateson asked me about the sun I saw in Crantock's right eye, and in particular the landscape upon which it shone. I could recall no landscape, just the bright rays of a golden sun lighting the world. Yes, he said, the Sun is at the heart of all things, it is at the precise point of intersection of the two periods of light and darkness. Then he consulted a map. It seemed to be of Nevern and had a great many triangular lines drawn over it connecting in a sixteen-pointed star. He spoke again, almost as if to himself, saying, The Sun sits on His throne and guides His children, His golden hair fluttering to provide us with warmth on Our journey.

And the Moon, he asked me, what then of the Moon? The moon, I told him, was full and waxen in a velvet sky. And the Stars? No stars, I said, as my mind recalled my vision in Crantock's eye. I watched him write the words I spoke, hearing the scratch of nib on paper. Then I remembered and said, Wait, yes, there were stars, three stars. He lifted his eyes from the page and in his look, in the look that passed between us in that moment, I felt a small amount of trust begin to kindle. Then he said to me, there are twenty-eight phases of the Moon and in each phase there is a Mansion which has a Name, an Image, Strength and Virtues. He spoke of a separate key to each Mansion which when found would be smelted together with the others to create another key. A master key, I believe he said, but cannot be sure, for his words were complex and lost me in their intricacies.

Next, he asked me of the Fire, which I described as a steady burning glow. And that was all he had to say. He stood and walked to the window, remaining there as if he had entirely forgotten me. In the heat of the afternoon the windows were flung wide and I watched the dust motes and sprites drift and dance around him. When finally he turned to me the clock-hands had completed a revolution and then a little more. He stared at me until I felt the colour burn in my cheeks, but I would not look away. Eventually he spoke, saying, The art lies in the discovery of the fire, the lightest most pure element. And Crantock has chosen you to see it.

He hesitated, paced a little, and then confided to me the following which I shall attempt to record as exactly as possible: When Crantock entered the world he was all in a rush, so fast did it happen that I was midwife. From the beginning he was different. Not once did he cry. Not in hunger, or pain. Nor, as he grew older, did he speak, although he definitely heard and responded to our voices. He was a silent child, unsmiling, content to be on his own, but not withdrawn. He had no interest in reading but loved to be read to. On his fifth birthday, to coincide with the hour of his birth, I took him to Carn Ingli to invoke Our Lord's Blessing and the protection of the Angels, just as I have done with all my children. Nectan, our first, on his first birthday, Rhun-Owen on his second, Corth on her third, and so on, down to Kew and Keyne whom I shall take on their thirteenth birthday. It is a Vateson family tradition. This year, it is Rhawin's turn to be taken.

So, Mr Vateson continued, on the 19th of April 1869 we went to the Carn. It was the most pure and clear of days, I could see to every horizon. On my knees, with eyes closed, I summoned the Angels and asked that they walk with Crantock and keep him from darkness. When I opened my eyes Crantock was gone and a mist had descended obscuring even my own hand in front of my face. But I heard laughter, followed by a high sweet singing. Instinctively I knew it to be Crantock, although he had never made a sound in all his five years. I turned in the direction of the sound, slipped on the mist-wet stones and fell, and when I opened my eyes again the sky had cleared. Crantock ran towards me and he was smiling, the first time I had ever seen him do so. A smile like sunlight, so bright and shining was it. And he stood beside me, my dear small, slender boy, saying, Papa, look, hawthorn, Papa. And he held towards me a branch of hawthorn that in its shape resembled a cross. He rocked himself to and fro, as he had often done before, but he was humming, and when I asked him where he had found this, he smiled and said the Lady had given it to him, but would say no more.

I brought him home to his mama and how she wept at his smile and the sound of his laughter and his humming. But it was to be another six days before he spoke again, this time to say, No, which rapidly became one of his favourite words.

In the months and years that followed it was as if there had never been those five years of silence. We learned to take him as we found him on any given day. We became used to his simple pleasures, such as being unclothed even in the dankest winter weather. We learned to forgive his temper which could be cruel and spite-filled. He has no sense of his own strength or that he is causing pain. And I watched him, waiting for another sign, watching and waiting for another seven years before it finally occurred. Again it was his birthday, his twelfth, on the 19th of April 1876. We were in the garden when suddenly the sky blackened as if it were night. The heavens were silent. There was no thunder on that day. But as the sharp lightning flashes began I managed to get everyone inside. Or, at least, I believed I had, but found Crantock was not with us. I hurriedly lit a lamp, but as I reached the door the heavens opened and hailstones as large as fists fell as if to smash the world to pieces. The storm barely lasted five minutes, although it seemed five days had passed before the clouds cleared as abruptly as they had gathered and the sun glinted on the hailstones that covered the ground like snow. Amidst all this stood Crantock. And while every tree and shrub and flower surrounding him had been martyred, he was untouched, unbruised, unshivering. But he was weeping, the first tears he ever shed.

That night, I sat beside his bed and did so for the next forty nights. During those nights I recorded the words he spoke in his sleep, just as I have done ever since. Whole conversations he will have, with himself so it seems. At other times a fragment, a word or two, and I piece together the information he gives me. And – At this moment he stopped and patted my hand. But that is enough for one day, he said. You are tired. Tomorrow we will continue.

And so that is where his story was left. But what is all this, what is it that Crantock is telling him?

And I?

What is Crantock to me or I to him?

Later. I have been out for a walk with Mrs Vateson. This afternoon I am to be told some great family secret by Mr Vateson. It is just too mysterising and exciting and – and – I need to lie down. No, of course I do not. I need to write everything here while I can still remember.

We took a path to the river from where we could see along the estuary to Newport Sands. This, Mrs Vateson told me, was a favourite place of Adwen's, and here they have placed a bench on which to sit and take in the view. For some short while we sat silently together before she took my hand in hers. Then she said to me that because of the love she has for Mama, I am as a daughter to her. And yet as much as she loves Mama she knows there are aspects of her life of which Mama does not approve and due to this she would never ask me to go against Mama's wishes. Mrs Vateson said, Your dear Mama finds our way of life eccentric and strange to say the least. If only she knew how restrained we must become when she visits, how shocked she would be otherwise; and you are her child, her only daughter, and I have seen her disapproval in your face at times.

I made to protest, but she shushed me, saying, It is only natural that you do not understand our ways. She continued by saying that this afternoon Mr Vateson will tell me more of their life here at Penfeidr and she has requested that what he tells me should remain private. I have been asked to keep whatever I am to be told a secret from Mama. She said no more. I too was silent, knowing not what to say, but feeling ill-at-ease and chilled despite the sunshine. We walked back to the house and before we parted she said, You must not be afraid of your shadow, Edith, because the shadow is the Queen of all colours. Quite what this is supposed to mean is beyond me.

So here I am, waiting for Mr Vateson to send for me. I will admit that I am a little afraid. What has Mama said of this place? I know of her love for Mrs Vateson, but I also know that she thinks herself the superior. She is always kind when speaking of Mrs Vateson but too kind, almost. I have heard her say to Papa, dear Azenor took the first offer that came along. And as for Mr Vateson, I have seen her be most cold and disdainful to his face, and behind his back make a mimic of him in a spiteful manner. I have heard her say that the Vatesons live in the Welsh wilderness in such a state that one would think them poor. And it is just a little true, for their furniture is shabby and Mrs Vateson's hands are quite ruined from gardening without gloves, and none of the girls are anywhere near married. And yet it is so lovely here, so peaceful, and not at all a wilderness, but very old-fashioned and full of nooks and crannies and hidden dells. It is almost what I imagine Somerset to have been like when Mama was a girl, before it was covered with railway lines and thoroughfares. I think –

Oh dear, I am sent for by Mr Vateson. I am all a bundle of nerves.

Much, much, much later. It is very late and I am most astounded. I must think and think and then I must think some more. I wish I could talk to Mama but I cannot. I feel very alone and uncertain and it really is just too much for one girl on her own to have to think about.

August 10th I have thought for all the night and still I do not know what to think or to believe. I will try to write clearly and keep to the facts, which, I will own, have become all of a jumble inside my head. I hope I have remembered rightly.

Mr Vateson believes that there is a Fragment of the True and Holy Cross upon which Jesus died buried on or near to Penfeidr! It was, he says, brought here by the Empress Helena, the Mother of Constantine the Great. After her return from Jerusalem she travelled far and wide, showing the Fragment to the Holy Men of England. Then on the first anniversary of finding the Fragment, as she was on her way to St Davids, she stopped to rest at Carn Ingli. Here she received a visitation from an Angel who told her to found a village nearby and to name it Constantinople in honour of her son. The village was to be built mid-point between Pentre Ifan and Carn Ingli. Near by – and here Mr Vateson went into a great many geometrical details which I did not comprehend and cannot even begin to recall – the Fragment of the True and Holy

Cross was to be buried. The secret of the hiding place was entrusted to the Empress's twelve most valiant Knights.

Centuries passed, and the line of each of these Knights passed into extinction, due in no small part to their heroism in battle. Thus, the secret of the hiding place was lost. In 540, in an attempt to find it, St Brynach the Irishman crossed the sea and spent three years camped on Carn Ingli communing only with Angels. They ordered him, so it seems, to build three churches, one at Nevern, one at Cwm-yr-Eglwys and one at Pontfaen. But still, said Mr Vateson, the secret hiding-place of the Fragment was not to be revealed.

He told me that these stories have been told in his family for generations, passed down and down. But that he has learned more from Crantock than from his own father or his father before him! These communications began with the visitation Crantock had on his fifth birthday. Crantock is special. He sees and hears things that the rest of us do not. At Carn Ingli the Angels come to him, and he tells Mr Vateson of what they speak. Crantock, he believes, is leading him to the place where the Fragment of the True Cross lies buried. So far they have been at work for ten whole years.

As he spoke, I sat in silence not knowing what to think. Then he said that he wished to see if Crantock and I are able to replicate what happened between us before. He would like to find out if there is a true bond between us.

I felt I should share with him a little of my own personal history and so told him of my sightings of King Arthur at the Abbey House, and of my visits to Mrs Lurgashall. I concluded by saying that I have been considered Sensitive in such matters. Mr Vateson appeared somewhat taken aback, replying that he had thought my mother too sensible to hold dialogues with ghosts and suchlike. His response greatly surprised me given he had been speaking of Angels and Messages and Messengers. Obviously this showed upon my face for he said that the difference is between 'seance' and 'science'. Crantock, he told me, communes with Angels not with the dead, he is of a mystical and spiritual nature and is not a psychic.

However, I have agreed to see if we might replicate what occurred on Dinas Sands. I have also promised my silence on this matter. I have been taken into their confidence and I shall not betray it. I have given my word. Mama would only laugh and think it nonsense, so I do not feel I am betraying her trust in any way at all.

August 11th   Last evening was different from the others. For the past months dinner has been formal and polite, but last night everyone was a little more relaxed and friendly towards me. Previously they put on a show of manners for my sake and lapsed into awkward silences because there were other subjects of which they preferred to speak. Now they were quite different, each of them. And to think I had found them all so dreary and dull and boorish and Welsh! And they are, it is true, but not nearly as much as I first thought. I sense that they do not trust me yet. But I can do nothing to win them over, I am only myself. I can pretend at nothing.

Later. Mr Vateson and Crantock have gone away for two days and I am too restless and agitated to settle to anything. I must write to Mama, but I cannot think of a single word to say. Twice I have burst into tears for no reason at all.

August 12th   A long day. Every hour dragging. Tears again. It must be the heat.

August 13th   More tears. Tiredness. Heat. Haze.

August 14th   They are returned. In the early hours of the morning while we slept. But I knew, nevertheless, waking and thinking at once, Crantock is here. At breakfast there he was, humming and rocking, as if he had never been away.

Later. Tomorrow I am to go to the Old House and learn more of their work together.

August 15th   Jangly nerves in every part of my body, especially my head. Heaven knows what I will discover today!

August 16th Last night I was too exhausted to do anything but go to bed, so overwhelmed was I with all that I had seen. There is absolutely no question now that I will not assist in attempting a new communication with Crantock. I feel strangely at peace, as if all my life has been leading me to this moment.

Later. I don't quite know how or where to begin in describing what I saw – but if I think too much I shall not write it all down. So I shall do my best.

The Old House, Old Penfeidr, was where the Vatesons first lived in the 1200s. It was built by a Knight at the Court of Henry III, and his French wife, who came in search of the Fragment of the True Cross. It is their effigies that lie in the chapel. This was my first visit to the Old House, and tucked away it certainly is, at the end of a spidery track about a mile from the New House. There is something serene about this track, just wide enough for a cart, and edged on both sides by ancient trees whose branches hook together, their leaves providing a curious green light in the air. We walked this wending path where I could never see too far ahead. It ended abruptly at a stream, quite thick flowing, an offshoot of the river I am told. The Old House is almost an island, being surrounded as it is by a ring of water, with the moat on one side, and the river on the other. We passed a stone gateway, crossed a bridge, then advanced through a gatehouse and across a great expanse of lawn. There was Old Penfeidr itself. I don't know if it might be properly described as a house at all, as it is comprised of a Hall and a Tower. It was the most perfect light in which to see the place, such golden sunlight on the walls. As we crossed the lawn, a man – the shortest I have ever seen in my life though not a dwarf – came towards us and spoke to Mr Vateson in Welsh. I was later told that he is called Wymp and that he is caretaker of the Old House. His family have been with the Vatesons for generations. He and his wife only speak Welsh, but their son speaks English, and I was told that should I need anything when I am at the Old House, I am to speak to him.

I was shown over the entire house, right to the very top of the Tower, to a beautiful room that has windows on all sides allowing a perfect view in every direction – up to Carn Ingli, down along the river to the sea at Newport Sands, over the tree-tops to the chimneys of the New House and inland to Nevern's church tower and the countryside beyond.

The Great Hall, is sparsely furnished as if from another age, with wall hangings and heavy oaken furniture that was made more than six hundred years ago. Off the Great Hall are three rooms, each containing a desk covered with piles of books and papers in almost-tumbling stacks. The floors were similarly encumbered. There was a kitchen, spare and simple, and at whose table sat Wymp's wife. She too was tiny and ignored me just as her husband had done. Her smile was for Crantock who kissed her cheek and spoke to her in Welsh.

We went up an ancient stone stairway, worn smooth from centuries of feet, and here I must write slowly, think carefully – there I saw their work rooms. They are, I was told, each devoted to a different Mansion of the moon. Some of the larger rooms are divided by heavy curtains into two, three or four spaces, depending on their size. So far only three are used, and the remainder are empty. But I can hardly begin to describe what those resplendent, yet curious, rooms contained, so much was there to see. In one there was the statue of a man made of black wax; in another a woman made of silver and exquisitely clothed in an embroidered dress; in another a life-size horse made of wood; and in yet another was the sickening smell of amber. In every room I saw strange words painted upon the wall, and so much else that it all seems a jumble and confusion in my mind.

During my visit Mr Vateson spoke little, if at all. He merely declared the Mansion's number as he opened each door or held the curtain to one side, allowing me to look in silence, to think my own thoughts. I had one thousand and more questions clamouring to be answered, but I too remained silent.

Crantock always followed me. Twice I stepped on his toes, so close did he stand. He was quiet, in a most un-Crantock-like fashion. Not humming or rocking, but wearing a dear, sweet face, and his eyes watching my every expression. Indeed, never in my entire life have I been more intensely scrutinised than I was by both Mr Vateson and Crantock all afternoon. More than once did their stares bring the colour to my face.

When we returned downstairs, Mr Vateson spoke of many complex things concerning geometry and the stars, and the waxing and waning of the moon, and how each Mansion somehow represents one day of the moon's cycle. For the most part this astrological talk was far beyond me. But Crantock seemed to listen to every word and when I wondered how much of this he really understood, it was as if Mr Vateson had read my mind, for he said that there was little that Crantock does not know of these matters. Indeed he knows a great many things of which we know not.

Today I must decide if I wish to proceed in assisting them. How could I possibly say no? I am very much intrigued by what they are doing, though I am not yet certain whether I believe any of it. I will gladly admit that I am full of nerves and somewhat baffled.

August 17th   We are to begin straightaway. Mr Vateson is delighted with my decision. I will admit that my stomach is thoroughly churning with nerves.

Later. Nothing happened! We stood in the tower room trying again and again, looking towards Carn Ingli. Crantock's breath was on my ear and neck. But there was nothing, nothing at all. Everyone's face showed their disappointment. Mr Vateson tried hard to raise our spirits, and repeatedly said that we shall try again tomorrow.

August 18th   Another failure. Mr Vateson says I must not be despondent, but it is very hard not to be. Only Crantock seems unaware that we are failing.

August 19th   I feel so very unworthy of them. Of their life, their great quest, their trust in me. What happened on Dinas Sands was – must have been – an accident. What am I doing here? I am not in the least bit special – it was a mistake, after all. I am just an ordinary girl – Edith May Porch of Glastonbury.

August 20th I could hardly bear to sit with them at breakfast. Mr Vateson and Crantock have gone to the Old House alone. There is a pain in my chest so sharp and deep that I cannot even cry. Every time I breathe it worsens. I so wanted – I wanted to be special.

Later. I want to go home. I do not wish to be here a moment longer. I want Bayard and my very own bedroom and the Tor. I want to look out of my bedroom window and see the Tor, and not Carn Ingli. I want Mama and Papa and my annoying brothers and Tizzy and Woodsie.

August 21st I am exhausted though I have slept all afternoon. How to write of what has happened? How – ?

I must put it down honestly. Write the truth. That is all that matters.

This morning Crantock had a fit of rage. Never have I witnessed anything more fearsome in all my life. It descended from nowhere, just as we were finishing breakfast – I had hardly been able to eat, so preoccupied was I with how exactly to communicate to Mr and Mrs Vateson my wish to leave. Just I was on the point of speaking, Crantock suddenly shouted, No! and stood, sweeping to the floor everything on the table that he could reach. Mr Vateson and the older boys surrounded him and soothing words were spoken, though these did no good at all. Crantock stood there swaying, black in the face with rage. Still I remained seated, fearful now of moving, and as I watched he seemed physically to change, shrinking into his clothes, smaller, like a child. Only when he grabbed a knife and began to cut his hand did I stand. Where my words came from I do not know, but I spoke to him softly. Crantock, I said, Crantock. Look, fork. I held up the fork with a trembling hand, then, pointing at the knife which he held, I said, Knife. And I dug the fork into my own hand, not hard, but in pretence, copying his action. As I did so Crantock made a noise which rang in my ears. It was like the cry of a fox – that dreadful sound so like the wail of a lost dead child. It came from him again and again. But he had stopped hurting himself and ran to my side and looked at me with the horrific cry still issuing from his mouth. Taking his hand, I pressed my handkerchief there to stem the flow of blood and as soon as I did this the hideous cry stopped and he began to weep, while also reaching for me the way a small child reaches for his mother. I opened my arms to him, but as he is not a boy but a grown man, his weight threw us both to the floor. He held me tight, tears pouring on to my neck, soaking my dress. There we lay on the floor, with Crantock weeping until from exhaustion he finally slept. Only then did Nectan and Rhun-Owen carefully lift him up and carry him to his bed, leaving me where I lay, too stunned and confused to move.

I was left in the care of the girls and was helped to the bathroom. There I was undressed, as if I too was a child, and put into a steaming bath. I was too exhausted to be embarrassed. As I soaked, Elined removed the pins from my hair and brushed it slowly, soothingly, then fashioned it into two plaits and coiled them atop my head. When finally I was warmed through and through I stood, and many hands towelled me dry and dressed me in a gown and took me to my own bed where I fell instantly asleep.

When I awoke the sun was setting and I watched the lessening light before rising and dressing. I am still able to smell the perfumed bathwater on my skin and have redressed my hair in coils just as Elined fashioned it.

Crantock, poor dear Crantock, he suffers so.

Later. Nothing is different and yet everything is changed. It is almost as if I am accepted as part of the family. At dinner Mr Vateson spoke of the events of this morning. Twice, sometimes thrice a year, he said, a raging fit will descend on Crantock and he will attempt to harm himself. When this occurs, force is used to restrain him, and he is tied to his bed until the fit has passed. At these times, the only person who ever came close to soothing him was Adwen and since her passing his rages have become more violent.

After dinner I looked in on Crantock briefly. Nectan sat by his side and was most courteous, calling me Miss Edith, whereas normally he declines to address me. Crantock slept like an angel, his damaged hand thickly bandaged and resting on the cover. I will admit I entered his room with racing heart, afraid to find him tied down to his bed. I am told he will sleep now for two days or so in order to recover his energy.

August 23rd One heat-lazy day follows another in a similar fashion. In the morning I tend the garden for a couple of hours, then we take an early lunch and rest. In the afternoon we swim, boys and girls separately. My embarrassment and awkwardness of some weeks back is forgotten, and I too swim with the others 'as God made me'. I cannot now find any harm in doing so.

I try to write to Mama every day, although I find I am constrained. What can I possibly say about the situation without feeling that I am telling untruths. So far, I have merely told her that I am indispensable in assisting Mr Vateson with his researches, without saying exactly what they are. I tell her of the house and the children and the garden, topics I know she will enjoy reading of.

August 24th This morning Mr Vateson and I walked together in the orchard. He reminded me that Dr Gersham will arrive in a week to assess my health. I am well, of course, and told him so, and he agreed that he could see that this was the case. He further reminded me that I had come to Penfeidr to regain my health and that my parents would expect me to return to them when this was achieved. We walked together in silence. I knew not what to say. Finally I answered that I was sure that if I explained to Mama and Papa that his researches were at some crucial point and that my continued assistance was essential to keeping his papers in order, then they would understand and allow me to stay for a short while longer. He agreed. Eventually I realised that there was something further on his mind. How I knew this, I know not and when I asked him if this was so, he looked surprised, as if I had read his mind. We have not succeeded in what we hoped for, he said to me. I could only agree but added that we must go on trying. He nodded and made it quite clear to me that I am welcome at Penfeidr for as long as I wish to stay.

So, I am to stay. Should Mama be agreeable, that is.

Have I made the right decision? And yet, as soon as I write those words, I know there is no real decision to be made. At Edgarley I would merely fall into a round of pointless socialising, with day after day the same faces and places and conversations. If I were to go to London, well, there at least the socialising would have the higher purpose of finding me a husband. But surely that can wait a little longer, can it not? I am only eighteen, after all. I shall begin to worry if I am not married by twenty or twenty-one at the latest.

Later. Crantock joined us briefly after dinner. His dear sweet boy's face. It is almost as if he were my own child, so tender do I feel towards him. He stayed only a short while before retiring.

August 25th I have written to Mama asking that I might stay on until early next spring. Mrs Vateson has written asking her to come here for a long visit, as soon as is possible, so that we might see each other.

August 26th Crantock is up and about again and has resumed his work with his papa. I am to join them when the heat is a little less stifling. I said I did not mind, but Mr Vateson felt it best to wait.

August 27th The early arrival of Dr Gersham surprised us all. He is three days before expected and will only stay overnight. He has come on his way to holidaying in North Wales. He was delighted to find me blooming given my condition three months past, and with all feeling returned to my hand. He said it did seem the Welsh waters greatly agree with me. But he believes there to be another reason for the colour in my cheeks and had the effrontery to quiz Nectan and Rhun-Owen as to their prospects as potential husbands. I was mortified and horrified and blushed more than once on their account. Dr Gersham took some convincing that neither of them had such aspirations for my hand and then shouted, Why on earth not?! Luckily everyone chose to be amused, including Nectan and Rhun-Owen, neither of whom I had credited with any sense of humour at all.

I cannot say that Dr Gersham has endeared himself to me. In

fact, I am very cross indeed. When Crantock joined us, Dr Gersham said, So this is 'The Boy', and appraised him as if he were a freak in a sideshow. I intend to tell Mama that I find his manners greatly insensitive and offensive. Quite what the Vatesons thought, I cannot imagine. I have known Dr Gersham all my life and only now realise what a pomposity he is. I am sorry to say, there is something in him that reminds me of Papa, though I would hate to think that Papa could ever be quite so tactless and boorish.

August 28th   Dr Gersham is gone. I've written to Mama to ask Papa to take him to task for his rudeness concerning Crantock. I also stated that I think an apology would not be amiss.

August 29th   I have come over all sad in every part of my body. Today when I heard the church bells ring I wept for no reason at all.

August 30th   A letter from Mama. She is delighted that I am well and happy at Penfeidr. She has written me at great length and detail of the death of her friend Mr Kingsley in India, and of how she is determined to have his papers on the Native Hindoos published. When I first read this I was quite shocked that she would go to so much trouble for a man who had so horribly attacked her. But then I remembered her kindness to him at the time, and of how she forbade me to tell Papa. Perhaps Mr Kingsley suffered from an illness that occasionally caused him to act with such ill-manners, just as Crantock does.

I am learning much from my time here, particularly that sometimes it is easy to be too judgemental. Mama also said I should not be too harsh with Dr Gersham as it is a part of his 'scientific nature' to treat all humans as if they were specimens. She added that she hopes to visit in mid-September. When I read this my heart sank. It will not be the same when she is here. I confess I wish she were not coming at all.

Later. Of course I do not mean what I wrote earlier. I cannot wait to see Mama again! It has been three whole months. We shall have so much news to catch up on. And it was so lovely to have such a long letter from her, especially with news of Papa, who never writes to me but always adds a message for her to send, and also of my brothers' doings and dabblings, of course.

August 31st   I have been to the Carn on my own. I sat there for some time admiring the view. It is so different to that from the top of the Tor. The countryside of Glastonbury is so gentle, so delightfully English, while there is something half-wild and other-worldly about this place. I could only just make out the chimney-tops of the Old House, so hidden are they by trees. But I caught a glimpse of the swoops of the river and the outlines of the orchards and gardens and was able to imagine my dear Vatesons at their various tasks. In my musings I felt at peace with myself as I have not done since Mama's letter bringing news of her visit. I am not her little Edie May any more. I am changed. I am becoming the young woman she said I would be. I feel it happening, and only in coming here has that been made possible. This peacefulness I have found through the inexplicable and curious bond that I seem to have achieved with Crantock. Will Mama understand this? The thought of Edgarley and the endless round of social engagements fills me with dread.

September 1st   Rain all day – but still hot and close and steamy and sticky. Crantock ran in the rain 'as God made him' for quite some time before he was coaxed indoors. Although I made sure I was busy elsewhere, I can no longer see any harm in such be-haviour. He is as a child, and is as dear to me as if he were my very own brother.

September 2nd   I have entered Crantock's world again, for that is the only way I can think of to describe what has happened. We were in the garden of the Old House. He stood close to me as he sometimes does, and I could feel his breath on my neck in a ticklish way that is not unpleasant. I very clearly heard him say, Edith. As I turned, the entire world seemed to slow in front of my eyes. I could see each blade of grass as if it were singular. I looked into dear Crantock's eyes. No words passed between us, but I felt such warmth as if I were atop Carn Ingli gazing into an endless blue sky. How long we stood so, I know not, but it was I who looked away. And what I saw was most extraordinary – a magical-looking bird that was walking away from us with a most stately gait towards a golden chalice, where it stopped to drink. When it had drunk its fill, its tail feathers lifted and opened like a fan to display what seemed to be every colour of the rainbow, and in the feathers were dotted black-green eyes. I stared into one of these eyes and there I could see reflected a church on whose roof stood another such bird.

I do not know how long afterwards it was that I awoke to find myself lying on the grass with Mr Vateson beside me and my dear Crantock in tears. I was assisted indoors and made to rest although I felt no need to do so. Mr Vateson sat beside me and asked me to relate what I had seen, writing down every detail. He asked if I could draw the church on which the peacock stood – for those were the birds I saw – and I have agreed to try. He is pleased. Most pleased, in fact. He believes that this is a breakthrough. He now declares that the bond between Crantock and I must not be forced but allowed to happen of its own accord. He says that Crantock and I must be in each other's company as much is as possible without exhausting us.

September 3rd   I have achieved a pictorial resemblance of the church that Crantock showed to me. This was not done without difficulty. After a thoroughly wasted morning Elined came to help me express my vision on paper. At first she did this with pencil drawings and then with watercolouring. She was most adept and asked me one thousand more questions and so we obtained the finer details of the bird, the building and the landscape. But just as we thought ourselves finished I remembered an additional important detail, and I said to Elined, the church is on a promontory, it is near to the sea. So she began again and added the sea into her picture until there was an image with which I was satisfied. There are now three watercolours that come very close to a resemblance of what I saw. Unfortunately, it appears that they do not depict any nearby church that Mr Vateson knows of.

September 4th   Mr Vateson has sent to London for three dozen peacock feathers. For most of the day we were at the Old House examining maps of the Welsh coast, seeking places where there are churches by the sea. He said it is possible that the church is on Bardsey Island and told me something of the island's history. As we studied the maps, I could hear Crantock singing in Welsh. When I asked Mr Vateson what it was he sang, he replied it was not a song at all, just words that he had strung together.

September 5th   Mama has arrived one week earlier than expected, but I cannot be annoyed because she has brought with her my very own Bayard. I could not see for my tears for quite some time. Bayard was overjoyed to be reunited with me – in his usual restrained fashion, of course. It was the Merry-dog who insisted on making a thorough spectacle of himself, chasing his tail, jumping on everyone and generally showing off in his excitement.

How lovely it is to see Mama's face. She is much the same as ever and yet changed in some most subtle way. There is sadness in her, I think, a heaviness and slowness, almost an oldness that I do not remember at all. Over lunch she spoke at length of her friend Mr Kingsley. She is to be here only for a little over a week and is going on to London to seek a publisher for his writings on India and the Native Hindoos. Indeed, not much else was spoken of except Mr Kingsley. Mrs Vateson too spoke highly of him. Obviously Mama has not told her of the time he attacked her.

This afternoon I rode out on Bayard – what joy and bliss my B is – I galloped him to the top of the Carn and showed him the sights of his new home landscape. I do believe he approves.

September 9th   Each day passes much the same. In the mornings Mama and I ride together, and in the afternoon we sit in the garden with Mrs Vateson. Their conversation travels the past, and I do feel as if I am intruding, but when I attempt to excuse myself, they beg me stay. Today they talked ceaselessly of when they were girls of ten; at one point Mama laughed, and I realised that it is the first time I have heard her do so since she arrived.

We only see Mr Vateson and Crantock at dinner which, due to

Mama's presence, is more formal. There are an additional four girls from Nevern helping while she is here – and it is true, she does seem to make a great deal of extra work even though she is only one person.

September 10th Mama has asked me to show her my most favourite place so that when she is in London and returned to Edgarley she might imagine me there. What a hard decision! The chapel and graveyard, or the sea at Dinas Head, or Cwm-yr-Eglwys's romantic ruin, or Carn Ingli, or Newport Sands – there is so much here that I love.

Later. After much dithering I chose the Carn. We rode out late and watched the sun descend before returning in the last light. Mama sighed many times over the view, but otherwise was content to sit in silence. When she finally spoke it was not as if she spoke to me at all but rather to herself, so low and soft was her voice. You are much changed, she said. You are become a young woman, and so quick it has happened, almost as if your illness was a series of growing-up pains. You are well and happy here, I can see it, and it is all thanks to dear Azenor. She has become like a second mother to me and this pleases Mama greatly. She is the best of women, Mama said to me. She is loving and true, and has remained so even when Mama has not treated her so kind.

Mama said, Azenor married for Love, some of us are not so lucky. Some of us meet our Love when it is too late for it ever to be anything but idle dreamings and then one can only hope that in the next life one will find a place in Heaven beside one's Beloved. She was silent and from her expression I could tell that her mind had wandered to some place from which I was excluded. When eventually she continued, it was to say, And you, my dear Child, who is not a Child any longer, when the time comes I wish for you too to follow your heart.

After dinner when we had retired, Mama came and brushed my hair, just as she used to do when I was a Smallie. Then she tucked me into bed and kissed my forehead, saying, I wish happiness such as Azenor's on you, my maiden May. Dear old Mama. Why is she so unhappy? Why so melancholy? I hope she is not ill.

I could not bear it if anything happened to her. And she has passed her sadness on to me and now I cannot sleep. I too hope for Mrs Vateson's happiness. She has an almost perfect life here. But what if it does not happen? What if no one loves me? What if I am always to be alone?

September 11th   Mama is her usual self once more. There is something faintly judgemental in her air and she is once again sparring with Mr Vateson. Tomorrow she will leave for London and I may not see her again for some months.

September 12th   I accompanied Mama as far as Dinas Cross. We shed no tears as we parted but through the carriage window, she held tight to my hands, as we said our goodbyes. As I write this she is on her way to London. It is a beautiful day for a journey, the leaves are just beginning to change, and the sunlight is sharper. I almost wish I were going with her. I feel quite a pain in my heart, I love Mama so. But she is right, I am not a little girl any more. I must have a life of my own.
     Later. I feel very lonely tonight – for Edgarley, for Mama and Papa, and my own noisy brothers. I wonder if they miss me too sometimes.

September 13th   In a little over one week we will harvest the fruit trees. I have been given the especial task of pruning them. It will be quite a thing to achieve as there are at least six dozen trees. Rhun-Owen will give me instruction on how and where to cut the branches and, given my inexperience, I have been told it should take me three to four weeks to finish. Three to four weeks! Penfeidr time is different from any other I have experienced.

September 14th   Dark day, the rain set in yesterday. Everyone agrees that by spring I shall be very used to the Welsh drizzling days. It is Rhawin's 10th birthday and despite the weather he and Mr Vateson have gone to the Carn. This afternoon there will be a tea party and then games.

September 15th The peacock feathers have arrived. They are so soft and beautiful with their dark eyes set amidst jewelled colours. Crantock was in raptures, brushing the tips along his own face and then his mama's. Regrettably his manner with me is as it was when I first arrived. He hums and rocks when I am near by but no longer says, Edith, look, and I must admit to missing it. However, he is silent with everyone at the moment. Last night when the Smallies were over-excited and noisesome, he pressed his hands to his ears and screwed his face up in the ugliest fashion until Mrs Vateson insisted they stop their racketing.

September 16th Even more rain. For the first time I assisted Corth in bathing Winnow, Kew and Keyne. How they loved it! From the great water-plashing they set up it is hard to say who was the more wet, them or us. We dried them by the fire and afterwards Corth washed my hair, scrubbing my scalp raw, so it felt, but somehow it was a delicious agony. My hair is the longest it has ever been, down to my hips almost, and smells delightful from the soap that Mrs Vateson makes from July-flowers. I had not at first realised that this was the smell of sweetness wafting from all the Vatesons. There really is very little that they do not provide for themselves. Theirs is an entire world unto itself.

September 17th Crantock is very in the downs. He sat in a corner on his own and whistled to himself, rocking to and fro. Sometimes he stopped, closed his eyes, and grimaced in the ugly way he has. Mr Vateson noticed my concerned glances and patted my hand, saying, Even Crantock has his downs, just as the rest of us do. He is whistling the wind to sweep clear the cobwebs from his mind. I must have looked bemused because Mr Vateson said I might try it sometime for it works wonders. He does say the most curious things. As if a lady would ever whistle!

September 18th Crantock is still not quite himself. And the weather remains wet although Mr Vateson says that by this time tomorrow the sun will be out. He can tell from the shape of the clouds over the Carn. Despite the rain I ride every day, exploring new pathways on my dear Bayard, my big-hearted one.

September 19th A clear day, just as Mr Vateson predicted. Crantock is almost himself again. After tea, he curled up on the chaise-longue like a tired old dog and soon fell to snoring. We did our best not to disturb him as he has not been sleeping well at all and has lavender bruises beneath his eyes to show for it.

September 20th Up at dawn to pick fruit. It is heavy and hard work, not least because the sun is favouring us with its presence again. Everyone helps, even the Smallies, and Wymp's family and people from Nevern and Newport and Dinas. There was quite a gathering. Crantock is most definitely returned from the downs, he ran all around, shedding his clothes as he went, with two village girls chasing him. They all disappeared to goodness knows where. I pretended not to notice.

September 21st Up at dawn to continue the fruit harvest. At present I am resting because tonight we will go to the Carn and sleep there. I am too excited for words. I have never slept under the stars before.

September 22nd I will remember last night for the rest of my life. We arrived at the Carn to watch the setting sun and, oh, the heavenliness of the clouds at moonrise, before we settled to sleep! My eyes did not reopen until first light this morning. As soon as I awoke I wrote down my dreams, as we all did, the Smallies doing it with the assistance of their parents. Mr Vateson shall read them later. We then had a little to eat and walked back to Penfeidr, Nectan singing us along our way, with Tybie and Elined occasionally joining in. Then we sat down to a large breakfast that lasted until lunchtime.

My dream was very simple: I was walking along an unfamiliar path and the seasons came and went and came again and still onwards I walked. Finally I came to the land's end and before me spread the sea. Yet the path continued into the sea and I followed it down and down beneath the waves, until I was walking on the seabed, the sea water silken against my face. Eventually the path began to climb upwards again, and I walked into an enormous cavern with giant sea shells covering the walls. This cavern led into another cavern and yet another – fourteen in all – and after I had passed through each one I stepped into a garden filled with lilies and lavender and lilac. Crantock was there. Near by, I could see a lion striding towards him, and the wider I opened my mouth to warn of the danger, the faster the lion approached, finally leaping and knocking Crantock to the ground. But the lion did not bite. Instead it licked Crantock's face, and he laughed and laughed and stroked the lion's ribs and belly until its purring was so tremendous in my ears that the sound woke me and I found myself on the Carn surrounded by sleeping Vatesons.

How happy I am here. Such peacefulness I feel. As if it was my true home.

September 23rd   The entire afternoon was spent at the Old House with Mr Vateson discussing my dream. Crantock too had dreamt of a lion that licked his face. Mr Vateson thinks we are approaching some revelation, but he is not quite sure what.

September 25th   More rain and wind – like the sound of the sea in the chimneys. It has been so dark that we have had the lamps lit all day. I have not seen Crantock for an age. Apparently there are times when he stays at the Old House with Wymp and his family.

September 26th   A sodden world. And the walk to the Old House through more mud than I have ever seen before. Mrs Vateson has given me a pair of boy's thick sturdy boots. They are incredibly heavy and even heavier when caked with mud. But there was something heavenly in not having to mind where I put my feet. In fact, I will admit that my feet so much enjoyed not having to mind the pathway that they seemed to find the muddiest stretches to mulch through, leaving my poor skirts in a terrible condition.

September 29th   I am under the weather. This morning I was convinced that I might die from the pounding in my head and sickness in my stomach. Now, although I am still in bed, I feel a little more alive. Last night we celebrated the last of the fruit harvest with an impromptu dance. After dinner Mr Vateson suggested we taste last years cider for the first time, and delicious it was, light and sweet. We all became most jolly. Nectan took out a violin and Rhun-Owen a flute, and Tybie and Elined sang. Then Crantock appeared from nowhere after many days absence and began to make his elegant dancing postures. The Smallies weren't to be left out, and Haran, Winnow, Kew and Keyne began a four-sided dance, and soon we were all dancing, myself included, partnered first by Rhawin and then Corth. The evening went on for hours before we finally found our beds. But this morning my brain knocked so hard inside my head that I was convinced that it would split into two halves. I had a light lunch on a tray in bed – Mrs Vateson insisted I have a small glass of wine to settle my stomach, which I wasn't sure I could drink at all, but she said that when one has danced too much one needs a hairy dog, which is what this wine is called, for some very curious reason. I must admit I felt a little more myself afterwards, and have been able to read and daydream out of the window.

September 30th In the downs all day. When I was in the garden of the Old House I heard the distant clang of St Brynach's bells and began to weep. I felt I was in mourning, but for what, I know not. I am not tired but I think I will go to bed.

Later. Such a loss inside me all day – I tried reading Miss Rossetti's poems, but each and every one sent me into a storm of tears.

October 1st Two dreams. The first of birds and floodwater – two dark birds flying over an endless expanse of water. Are they looking for a place to land? And the second of Crantock – he is holding my hand saying, Edith, be well. When I awoke I could still feel the warmth of his hand in mine. At breakfast, I stared and stared. What sort of bond is there between us? I watched his hands, a man's hands despite there slenderness. I remember their strength holding my waist, that day at Dinas Sands.

Later. The first properly cold day of the year with the fires burning, the musk of wood-smoke at the back of my throat and in my hair. Dear October – I do love this time of year, the light, the colours, the calm moist air. How can I possibly be unhappy here?

October 2nd   This afternoon Crantock and I had one of our moments of special connexion. It was different from the previous occasions in that he was standing nowhere near to me but rather was engaged in play with Haran and Winnow. I could hear his voice – a song-lilt that carries far. Suddenly, I had a vivid flash of remembrance of his breath on my neck and the world slowed, just as it has done before. It was as if I was in the midst of a pine forest. I could feel the soft needles underfoot. High above the trees a white-faced falcon hovered and I watched it swoop and pierce a small hare with its claws, before carrying it in the direction of Carn Ingli. When I came to myself I was lying on the grass with Mr Vateson beside me. After I had rested and taken a small glass of wine to revive my blood, I spoke with him about what had occurred. He seemed delighted and tells me we are making immense progress. Quite how, I know not. He saw my disbelief and smiled at me gently, patting my arm in that way he has, and asked whether I trusted him or no. I said yes. And I do, it is true. Although I do not understand into what he is leading me.

But what does this all mean to Mr Vateson? Is he just continuing his family's tradition of the search, which has now gone on for so many centuries that it is impossible to stop? Or does it have a deeper meaning for him?

October 3rd   Very early – I kept waking thinking I could hear two crows calling. No one else is up yet – such peace and silence – as if the house itself were sleeping.

October 4th   Last night I cried myself to sleep and have awoken in tears. I cannot write of what is inside me because I know not what to write.

October 6th   Every night the same dream – Crantock sitting on a chair, staring at me.

October 7th   Haran's birthday – a special afternoon tea and then we played at the ghosties, his very own choice.

October 9th   I am tired. I will take a tray in bed for dinner. This afternoon I rode out on Bayard, full tilt to Dinas Sands where Crantock and I made our first connexion. I sat on the sand for hours remembering that moment of turning to look into his dear sweet face so near to mine. So very near. While I sat a sea-mist rolled in, damping me, chilling me, but still I sat, until sea and sand were invisible. Then I whispered to Bayard, telling him of Crantock, explaining what had happened, and he nodded, understanding every word, pawing the sand. I kissed his neck over and over again and he nuzzled my fingers, licking them, tickling them. And such joy swept over me as I have never experienced before in my entire life. Such joy that I laughed until I began to cry, as if my heart was breaking into many pieces, and I could not stand but fell to my knees. When I had cried my fill, I managed to mount Bayard, and despite the mist he brought us safely home. I walked in, a most bedraggled soaked-through sight, and was rubbed dry by the fire and put straight to bed. And so here I am.

Here I am – can I know anything with certainty ever again?

October 10th   I am trying to continue as if nothing is changed. And nothing has, except inside me.

October 11th   Rhun-Owen has given me two books to read concerning the pruning of fruit trees, a task I will begin, with Cleer and Ninnnon to assist me, in two or three weeks' time.

October 12th   Today I was sitting in the sunshine, discovering a great deal about the keeping of plum and pear and apple and cherry trees, when I saw Mr Vateson and Crantock walking towards the house. From the sight of their dear faces I felt all of a sudden lightheaded and lighthearted. To think, I am here, knowing such happiness.

October 13th Every morning I wake early and imagine seeing my dearest at breakfast. By the time I go down my stomach aches with knots of nerves and I am not able to eat very much. Then I go through the day preoccupied with thoughts of him, his dear face.

October 14th I must be more careful – I speak too much of him. I am caught staring at him – someone will suspect.

October 15th We girls have been down to Newport Sands collecting sea kale, the wind singing a chilly note or two.

October 16th The same again, but this time in a sharp sunshine cutting at our eyeballs.

October 17th We shall pick the last of the pears while the sun holds.

Later. One of my strangenesses. I was picking pears while listening to Cleer and Ninnon, who almost remind me of two garrulous crows, for they don't say words, but chitter noises which only the other understands. All of a sudden it was as if a door opened in my mind and I could see my dear one curled up in pain, rocking to and fro, saying my name. I closed my eyes and willed him to sense me near to him, to allow me to ease his pain. But when I reached out to touch him I found my way barred by four Angels. I stepped back, shocked at the velvet softness of their wings to my fingers and felt myself begin to fall.

I opened my eyes to find Ninnon knelt beside me, crooning her curious language. Cleer had gone to find Mr Vateson. I sat up despite Ninnon's protestations, insisting that I felt perfectly well. Upon Mr Vateson's arrival my first question was to ask of Crantock's well-being. His face clouded, so I asked if he was troubled today. He nodded yes. Then I told him of my vision, and when I came to describe the Angels I said that they were four, that they had the faces of eagles and their wings were stretched upwards and two wings of every one were joined one to another. Where these words came from I know not, but I spoke them. Afterwards Mr Vateson assisted me to the house so that I might rest. Although I felt it unnecessary, for his peace of mind I acquiesced.

Later again – My dear one did not join us for dinner. I have retired early to read awhile.

Early morning. It is Monday, but I write under yesterday's date. I woke a little while past to the thought that Crantock was calling me, and so sure was I of this that I left my room and went to his bedroom door. I could hear his weeping, such sobbing as to break my heart. I could also hear Mr Vateson murmuring as he attempted to soothe my dear one's sorrow. If only I could go to him, but I cannot. But it shall not stop me from loving him. I will love him better than a mother and nurture him as much as I am able. No none will know of my deep tenderness for him and it will be all the more precious for being unknown and secret and hidden.

There – it is written – I have written it.

October 29th   A long week of mourning. Still it is hard to write of this. One week ago today my dearest Bayard was put to sleep. He was all of a sudden sick, unable to eat, or even to stand. An old horseman the family knows came to see him and said my brave one had an almighty lump in his belly near to his right back leg and that it would be a kindness to send him to his Maker so as to keep him from further suffering. I wept. Oh, how I wept. And then I asked to be left alone to prepare him. Gently I did so, brushing his coat until it shone, plaiting his tail with ribbons, whispering to him all the while, crooning his favourite words, weaving a story of the place to which he was going – my Bayard, such a beautiful place. I stayed with him as the gunshot rang out. Only when I was certain he had passed over did I kiss him one final time. Then I thanked the old horseman for his gentleness and walked up to Carn Ingli. I cried every step of the way because I have lost my dearest truest friend. All our adventures over the years, my Bayard, all the secrets I shared with you. There will never again exist a being in whom I can confide everything. From the top of the Carn I sat and watched the smoke rise from your pyre, and in this smoke I believe I saw you rise up into the heavens. I watched as the clouds cleared to allow the sun to stream through lighting your path.

Today I have spent in walking. I have wanted to be alone although the Merry-dog consented to keep me company, sensing my sadness somehow. I so rarely see him any more as he has abandoned me for the Smallies. Only when they exhaust him with their larkings does he seek me out, looking for a hiding place to sleep and recover his energy. I have told him of you, Bayard, of the very first time I saw you and the special bond there was between us. But I'm not sure he understood, or not the way you always did.

This afternoon when I returned to the house, tired from my wanderings, there was a horse in my room – not a real horse, but a wooden one, as large as a rocking horse, and with your colouring Bayard, and a tail and a mane made from your very own tail and mane. And in the side of this horse's belly is a door, and inside a wooden box with your name carved on it, and inside the box are some of your ashes. It was made for me by Elined.

I have thought much of leaving Penfeidr during the past days. But to do what? Return to Edgarley? Go to London for the Season? How can I possibly leave when I know that my heart is here?

Later. I have not spoken a word to Elined of her present, but after we retired for the evening I knocked on her door. I have not entered her bedroom before, and hardly can it be called by such a name so cluttered is it with paints and wood and tools. It is like – I hardly know how to describe it – no girl's room I have ever seen. There is a slender single bed and very little furniture. The walls are covered with murals – three of them represent different fruit trees, a plum, a pear and a cherry, with flowers and vines twining and winding and birds nesting in branches laden with fruit. They remind me of the fruit trees in the orchard, while also being entirely different. They are Elined's own work, of course. I asked if I might brush her hair, and although her face rebelled – she truly is the prickliest creature of a girl ever – she permitted me. So I brushed her hair just as Mama used to brush mine and then plaited it over her shoulder. We did not speak at all, not one word passed between us the entire time. As I left I squeezed her hand and to my surprise she returned the pressure.

October 31st   All Hallows – there will be a bonfire in Nevern this evening.

November 1st   There was much noise and the blowing of horns and running and jumping over the fire. My heart was not in it. I am quite in the downs.

November 2nd   A cold clear day. We are to walk inland along the river to the pine-tree copse near Llwyngoras to collect the branches and needles and cones that are fallen. Mr Vateson needs their scent.

November 3rd   Still tired. Drained. But at least I have some strength to write, unlike last night when I was carried upstairs to my bed – then I could not have walked to save my life.

Yesterday we briefly lost Crantock. When it came time to return home from Llwyngoras he could not be found. We could hear him singing somewhere among the trees, but he would not come when called, and could not be found, despite the fact that we split into groups to search. It was beginning to get dark and even colder. Then one of my strangenesses descended. I was all of a sudden leaden in my limbs so I could not stand. I fell down and could smell pine and taste its rancidness in my mouth. I heard myself say, Crantock, and as soon as I spoke, I saw him. But I knew he could not see anything, not that he was blind, rather he could not see his way to where we were waiting for him. He was lost and it was up to me to guide him. Again I whispered, Crantock, and he turned to face me, and I felt my body become heavy and cold and sink into the earth as if it might swallow me. With my mind I guided him, not to where we were but to Penfeidr, and as soon as he arrived there at the gates my mind became dark, and I vomited the taste of pine needles from my mouth, and came back to myself. I was too weak to walk and Rhawin went home to fetch help. Halfway there he was met by Mr Vateson and

Nectan who said that Crantock had arrived home shouting, Edith lost. And so they had come to look for me, Rhawin leading them, and they made a chair with their arms to carry me back.

November 4th   Tired and of little use – still resting in bed. I have had a letter from Mama. She is sad that we are not together, and that I seem not to miss her or Edgarley. I have written that I do miss her, and do miss Edgarley, and think of them every day, but feel that Mr Vateson relies on my assistance with his paperwork. I have explained that I am good with the Smallies, and much needed here, while also implying that I am almost desperate with homesickness. It is only a little lie to save her feelings, because although I do think of Mama every day, I rarely think of Edgarley.

November 5th   I have not seen Crantock for days – it is almost as if he does not want to see me.

November 6th   A glorious day of cold sunshine, ideal for pruning. The first tree – a pear – took the longest time. I kept referring to the book in order to know how and where to make each cut. Both Cleer and Ninnon were most annoyed, whittering at each other like two very cross blackbirds. They held the ladder and collected the branches to tie into bundles, which later shall be taken to an old woman who weaves them into baskets. I only achieved the pruning of four trees, and as there are some seven dozen it is going to take me days to finish.

November 7th   Ten trees today – I surprised myself as well as Cleer and Ninnon.

November 8th   And another ten trees.

November 9th   I have had the cave dream again, the same, but not – I am walking a path that leads beneath the sea and then up into a series of caverns. One cavern was lit by candles, thick and tall, and so many of them that it was as bright as day. The ground was scattered with pine needles whose smell infused my head to a sickening degree, and there were a great many goats with bells at their necks which chimed one after the other, as a clock chiming the hour. In the very last cavern was Crantock, laid out as if he were dead, wrapped as a corpse in a white shroud. Over him stood a tall fair Angel holding a vase in each hand – one vase red, the other blue – and pouring liquid from one to the other. From this drops fell on to the shroud, slowly changing its colour from white to violet, and when it had entirely changed colour, Crantock stood and the cloth fell away from him, scattering as violet flowers, their delicate sweetness perfuming the air. He stood dressed as a knight in armour, brightly shining. He walked towards me and went down on bended knee, taking both my hands and pressing them to his lips. We remained thus until the sound of cockcrow, when I awoke.

November 10th I have told Mr Vateson of my dream – I lied and said that it was from last night because I could not bring myself to speak of it yesterday.

November 14th The pruning is finished. Cleer, Ninnon and I celebrated with a picnic lunch beneath trimmed branches. We rugged ourselves warm and had small bowls of broth and sand-wiches. For the very first time I noticed how very cold the weather has become. They gave me a gift of one of their treasures – a bird's nest – which was offered with much ceremony and speaking of each other's words. They are the most curious brother and sister – I don't believe that I have ever seen them separate from each other. Not even in the summer, as Ninnon would never swim with us.

November 15th My heart is heavy – in every Vateson face I see my dear one's face. I have promised myself that there are things I will not write of here, and so I shall not.

December 13th The winter weather is set in – it rains most days and even when it does not there are dense mists that do not lift at all. I ride down to the Old House, so bad is the weather, and spend my mornings with Mr Vateson. In the late afternoon the Smallies are in my care for a short while. Such bundles of energy are they that by teatime I am thoroughly exhausted. It quite amuses Mrs Vateson to see me with them. She says I must be more firm, otherwise I shall be creating untold miseries for myself. They do not mean to be naughty but they seem quite unable to help it. Winnow particularly is a rascal, but I can never be cross with him for more than two minutes. He has just discovered handstands and cartwheels and standing on his head while propped against the wall. And if I can get him to sit still to listen to a story all he does is ask, Why this? Why that? so that it takes an hour to read a paragraph. However, he is very liberal with his kisses and likes to hold my hand and sit on my lap for the brief seconds he can remain still. I must admit he is my very own favourite.

December 15th   I have come to my room pleading a headache. I am in the lowest of lows. I promised I would not write about this, but I must. Why have I been allowed to feel such an attachment to someone for whom I can never be more than a sister? It is unbearable to me.

December 16th   Sometimes I am sure there is the spark of something more there – the sudden intense way he will look at me and the many ways in which he draws my attention to him. And even as I write this I know I am just dreaming – he is a little boy in a man's body. It will always be so.

December 17th   Mr Jack Frost is about – and all of his family, so it does seem.

December 19th   Dear Corth has noticed that I have lost a little weight and that my skirts hang loosely at the waist. She is such a lovely woman, so gentle, so calm. If only I could be more like her.

December 20th   At breakfast I burst into tears in front of everyone and wept until my eyes were almost swelled shut. Mrs Vateson put me to bed, dabbing my temples with lavender water, crooning to me, as she does with the Smallies. She believes I am homesick because it is almost Christmas and entirely blames herself for not thinking either to send me home or to invite Mama and Papa to be here. I awoke some hours later to find three Smallies in my room trying their very hardest to be quiet but not really succeeding. They had their colouring pencils with them and were engaged, I later found, in making me a drawing to help me feel in better spirits. Mrs Vateson sat by the fire embroidering and shushing them when their squabblings grew just a little too loud. For the next couple of hours, while I pretended to doze, every single Vateson put their head around the door to ask after me, including my own dear one with his papa.

December 21st I have assured Mr and Mrs Vateson that I am perfectly happy to be here for Christmas and that I am not in need of Mama or Papa or Edgarley. This evening we are to go up to the Carn to salute the solstice.

Later. It is late now, almost midnight. Earlier we rode to the Carn in the lowering light. Other people had gathered, some from as far afield as St Davids. Three enormous bonfires were lit that must have been visible for miles. We all took a place by the Carn and Mr Vateson gave to each of us a stick, cut to our own individual height, with feathers tied to the end – mine were peacock feathers, but everyone's were different. We pushed our sticks into the ground, and as the wind fluttered the feathers we said silent prayers, reflecting on the past year and the year to come. Mr Vateson explained that the fluttering feathers wafted our prayers upward, heavenward, where they could be more clearly heard. After this we had a hot toddy, which was most welcome in the bitter damp. We stayed until the fires died down before returning to Penfeidr, our cheeks ruddy from fire, wind and hot brandy, to take a simple supper of soup and bread and cheese. Our feather-prayer-sticks will remain where they are until the 12th of January, which is the local feast for New Year, on which day we shall go and reclaim them.

December 31st How different my life is compared to one year ago. Who would have thought I would find such beauty and happiness as I have found here? And all due to my dreadful illness. Blessings in disguise, as Mama would say.

1887

January 1st It is now January, according to Mr Breton's *Prognostications*, and we have not had a good beginning to the year – rough-and-tumble winds felling chimney-pots and tree-limbs.

January 6th Blessed with a snowfall on Epiphany – we've been out snowballing before breakfast. Later we are to go sledding up near the Carn.

Early evening. What an afternoon!! All the Vatesons wore trousers and I do mean all of them, including Aunt Azenor! My eyes almost popped straight out from my head! I've never seen women dressed so and it did seem most strange and unnatural. I was shocked and I cannot say that I approve. Despite their many eccentricities surely this is going too far, even for a Vateson. However, the sledding itself from almost atop the Carn was wonderfully daring.

After dinner we shall have cake and wine and continue playing at Shipwrecks, which we have been at now since New Year's Day. Every evening we start again and are taking turns in choosing where exactly the shipwreck takes place – it is very great and jolly fun. Last night it was Haran's turn and he insisted on being a Man-Eating Native of a South Sea Island. We all pretended to be washed ashore in the night-time – it's much better if the shipwreck occurs in the dark – and then he had to bite each of us – not too hard – and decide whether we were man or woman, because as a Man-Eating Native he would only eat men, leaving the women alive to do the cooking. Crantock fell asleep as has become usual and snored through the entire evening despite the shrieking and shouting, which came especially from Winnow, who insisted on being cooked first, then stood on his head and refused to be eaten saying instead he had to be a ghostie helping to cook everyone else!

January 7th More snow in the night, so we will be out again today. It is like a dream-world. Complete silence except for the crackling of branches beneath their white load. And so beautiful it makes my heart ache. I've asked Nectan to fix a better horse for me than the poor old mare I was given yesterday. As I said to my Uncle Vateson, I would like at least to keep up. It is too humiliating when even Kew and Keyne are outpacing me.

Late. I almost fell asleep by the fire, so content and tired am I. We are all much too weary for Shipwrecks. Everyone wore trousers again, but I have determined not to be judgemental. It is one of my New Year's Resolutions. We rode farther today, across snowy country to the coast, where there is a waterfall called Pen Pistyll that tips into the sea. Sluggish it was, thick with ice. We crossed the stream that feeds the waterfall to follow a path leading to a cairn. Below are caves, hidden in the cliff-face, that apparently no one has ever entered. The sun was so sharp and clear that we could see as far as Dinas Head to the outline of the ruined church at Cwm-yr-Eglwys. The boys built a fire and we cooked sausages, eating them with buttered bread washed down with hot tea. Oh and what a feast it did seem. Our return was more sedate because the wind picked up seaward and bitterly lashed our faces.

And now – my bedroom, a dying fire, a going-to-sleep house. My family, for that is what they have become, are all around me. I never thought to experience such contentment. Every day is happier than the last.

January 8th   We skated along the river a short way, to Glendwr and back again. Crantock stayed by the bridge with Aunt Azenor. I thought a great many thoughts of Nile, remembering the dreadful time she hurt her ankle. I so much wish I could write to her, to hear of her life with Win. I can only hope that she is happy, that they are happy together. However, we arrived back at the bridge to find Crantock in a snowball fight with village children, some of whom are hardly children at all. One girl in particular was teasing him, pelting him with snowballs which he pitched back with great relish. She teased him terribly until he chased her, making such a dreadful display of himself that Aunt Azenor should have put her foot down and stopped it. I was so angry that I walked back on my own and hardly had I got to my room than I burst into tears.

January 9th I've had an awful night's sleep. How can I possibly be so fond of someone who would chase such a silly peasant girl? It is unimaginable!

January 10th More snowball fights. I rolled one ball as large as my fist and threw it hard to hit Crantock, and when it did he only shook his head and laughed and continued to tumble with the Smallies. He is such a – a little boy.

January 12th Crantock has sensed my distance from him. He is being especially sweet and bringing me little gifts of feathers and stones which I accept before throwing them out. This afternoon we will go to the Carn to collect our feather-prayer-sticks.

Very late. We arrived on the Carn at dusk, and ferociously cold it was. I could hardly walk for being thickly layered in clothes. Our feather-prayer-sticks looked pretty in the darkening against the snow. As before, there were three huge bonfires and in the distance the glow of other fires could be seen in all directions. We prayed as we did last time, and then returned home to a dinner, a feast that lasted for hours.

January 13th I dreamt of Crantock as I have often done before, only it is not now as I should wish. I have been left with a bitter taste in my mouth. In the dream I push him away with all my might, shouting No, I do not want this. I woke to find my heart racing and tears on my face.

January 14th The first lambs have been born.

January 15th For the past two days Crantock has been in the downs and kept his own company in his room.

January 16th Last night I dreamt of the cave – I walked along the path until I came to the sea and went beneath as I have done before. But this time the water went on and on and I realised I was lost. I opened my mouth to call for help and began to choke on the sea water and then woke myself crying out. I did not sleep for the rest of the night and lit two candles and lay and watched their flickering.

Late morning. Crantock came down to breakfast this morning for the first time in days. He stood near to me and said, Edith lost. He would not look at me and I said, but I am here. He shook his head no, and then he turned and went to take his seat. He looked tired. There are bruises under his eyes as if he too had not slept.

I must think of leaving here. It will be hard – I have become so attached to them all. They are a second family to me. Mr Vateson will be so very disappointed. Perhaps I should write to Mama asking that she send for me on some pretext or other, at least then it will not seem as if I want to leave.

January 20th Too shivery to sleep, too many ghost stories read this evening. It is, I am told, Cwn Annwn, when the Welsh Hounds of Hell roam roads and pathways – though if they are doing so, then they shall surely be sucked into the sea of mud surrounding us, never to be seen again. Even the Merry-dog is nervous and has come to me for comfort. I am pleased to have him beside me, despite his snores.

January 21st For the first time in weeks I have experienced a connexion with Crantock. It happened as we gathered for lunch. I heard a log in the fireplace crack, showering sparks into the air, and turned to find Crantock staring at me intently. I could not look away. I watched his head turn slowly from me and heard the sound of my own breathing loud in my ears. Then the room seemed to plunge suddenly into a darkness that lasted an age but at length there was the sound of a door swinging open. Through this door, I went into a room and saw I was in a church. I walked down the aisle towards the altar, and there I stopped. To my left I saw Crantock seated in a pew. He was dressed as God made him, and as I stepped forward I could see scratches on his face oozing blood, and his hands were open by his sides and dripped blood to the floor, a dripping that seemed to echo throughout the church. I heard myself say, Oh, my dear heart, my darling Crantock, what has happened? I opened the pew door and could see that his legs were crossed at his feet in a most awkward pose and also covered with blood. I heard his voice whisper, Edith lost, although his mouth did not move. I took out my handkerchief and tried to stop the blood of his wounds, but could not, and began to weep because I knew that he was dying. He lifted his head weakly to look at me, hissing, No, I do not want this. I recoiled, not from his words, but from his blackened rotting teeth and the foul stench of his breath which made me retch and I came to myself vomiting into a cloth which Aunt Azenor held to my mouth.

I have rested all afternoon – still able to recall that noisome smell as if it were caught in my nostrils. Mr Vateson said that we must wait to speak of what has happened. Crantock has been given a strong dose of laudanum and put to bed. I am told he began to scream, Edith lost, attempting to hurt himself by clawing his face before he could be restrained.

January 22nd   Crantock is still confined to his room. I am full of the weeps. I keep hearing these words running through my mind: if you give your heart to someone you cannot take it back.

January 23rd   Tomorrow I am to view the Ninth Room which has been completed much in advance of the others, due to my connexions with Crantock.

Evening. I am nervous about what tomorrow will bring. Crantock joined us for dinner – a trifle paler than usual, and afterwards insisted on sitting beside me and holding my hand, like a small lost child. It is impossible not to love him when I and only I know how much he suffers. If you give your heart to someone you cannot take it back.

January 24th   The Ninth Room – I do not know what to write, so I shall just describe what I saw.

The room was cold enough to see our gusts of breath. Painted on the wall was the word 'Archaam' and beneath this, painted again, the head of a lion with one eye only. On another wall were two peacocks their fanned tails made of real feathers. In the middle of the room was a round piece of lead, the size of a carriage wheel, and engraved upon it the figure of a man who held his hands over his eyes so that he might not see. Covering the floor were pine needles that perfumed the room. This room seemed more heavily decorated than the others I had seen. Crantock seemed most serene and occasionally spoke, saying, Edith, look, and touching things to draw my attention to them.

I did not know what to say – I just nodded my approval. I stood near the window looking out, down to the moat, all ice at the moment, and I wondered if anyone had ever skated all the way around Old Penfeidr, going in circles, again and again, a daughter of the house, or a wife, and for some reason tears burned my eyes at the thought.

Downstairs Uncle Vateson went through the notes he has taken of my visions. I cannot quibble as he has drawn upon what I have been allowed to see. As usual, every Vateson has had a hand in the making of the room – Elined in particular. When I asked how he knew the room was complete, he drew triangles on a plan of the room to show to me that there is a sacred geometricity to the filling of the space. But that is all so baffling, so beyond me.

Now we are to begin again. There are another nineteen rooms to complete before he has every key to the twenty-eight mansions. It is just over five months since our first connexion. So if it takes five months for each room, then that means eight years. By then I shall be an old maid of 27 and Crantock will be 31. We shall be growing old together.

Is this to be my fate?

January 25th   A special day – it is my Aunt and Uncle's 29th wedding anniversary. It is also St Dwyn's Day who, I am told, is the Welsh equivalent of St Valentine.

We had an afternoon feast in the Great Hall of the Old House and then they danced together as they had done on their wedding day. An old dance, courtly, such as I have never seen before. Imagine being as happy as they are together.

February 1st   I am riven with guilt – I must write here of what I did yesterday. While we all rested before dinner, I stole into the sewing-room and borrowed a pair of trousers and back in my room I tried them on. They were most uncomfortable, tight, and shaping the outlines of my upper legs in the most embarrassingly ugly manner. I pushed my hands in the pockets and walked to and fro in front of the mirror, stepping large as the boys do. Then, very early this morning I crept out while the house still slept and walked more quickly than I have ever done. I ran and leapt puddles as I have seen boys do until my heart thudded and my skin prickled from heat. Despite their tightness, I felt light and free and could have stayed out all day, but instead I crept back inside and now am dressed in my usual skirts.

What on earth would Mama say? She would certainly be ashamed of me, just as I must be of myself. What I have done is beyond vulgarity. It is obscene. I am becoming loose and irresponsible. No decent young lady should act in such a manner. Just because the Vateson girls do so, does not give me permission.

February 2nd   Candlemas – a most moving hallowing of the candles held in the chapel, crammed with all the estate workers, including Wymp and his family. Every one of us held a small candle lit from the large one. Then a prayer was spoken in Welsh, which Aunt Azenor wrote out for me in English, but it was not one with which I am familiar. Afterwards, a large breakfast was served at the Old House and everyone joined, including many aged faces that I have never seen before, but who have been with the Vateson family all their lives. One very old man reminisced about my Uncle Vateson's great-great-grandparents for whom he worked as a child.

February 3rd   This afternoon we went down to Newport Sands and quite by chance there were a great many starfish on the beach. It was a most incredible sight. Crantock coo'ed like a dove every time he touched one. What extraordinary creatures they are! Tybie held one by its points, and when I touched it gently its arm points curled in and feet points curved up. We threw it back into the sea, as we did with each and every one that responded to our touch.

February 5th I have behaved just as I did the other day and I must not do this, truly I must not. My wilful disregard for propriety will end in – in – something awful. I know it. I find it difficult to look anyone in the eye for fear they will guess my secret.

February 6th Snowdrops everywhere – carpeting the park alongside the long drive.

February 7th And crocuses and daisies – *la belle* Margaret, Mama's flowers.

Afternoon. I am on the road to sin and sorrow and rack and ruin and I seem utterly unable to stop myself. I have re-hemmed a pair of trousers to fit me a little better – they are bigger, looser on my legs. I jumped guiltily at every noise, thinking to be caught at my task. What on earth will happen to me? I cannot believe I am behaving in this way.

February 8th This morning I was out in the rain and tucked my trousers into my boots – the boy's boots that Aunt Azenor gave me some weeks past. I walked through every puddle and ford that I could find and did not get my ends wet at all! I have not sneezed even the once from my morning's damping. I am sure I shall be punished in some other way, although neither Aunt Azenor nor the girls ever seem to suffer any after-effects. God has not struck them dead for being manified occasionally.

February 9th A sudden snowfall so I could not go out, yet still I dressed in my trousers and stared at myself in the mirror. My hair was loose and tangled and I looked something like a pirate and I pretended to have a sword and a ferocious scowl – oh, how funny I looked! How silly! Would I be a good pirate or bad? I have never been to sea so perhaps I would be a seasick pirate, which would be very funny indeed.

Later. It is now after dinner and I have put my trousers on again to play in front of the mirror. All day I fancied myself a pirate, but this evening I fancied myself a highwayman – which is too shocking of me, as if I could ever rob someone or shoot them! But what fun it is to pretend. How my Bayard would have adored being a highwayman's horse. He was so fast, so daring.

February 10th   I have committed an even more dreadful sin. What if anyone should ever find out!? I went riding as the boys do and no one must ever know, not ever, or I will never get married. At first all I could think was that I would fall, and I gripped so tightly that my knees are aching and despite my aches – around my hips and in my shoulders and back from the effort of holding on – I feel exhilarated – and that makes it even worse. But I do feel that way – I have never ridden so fast. It was – just imagine how wonderful it must be riding to hounds as the boys do. Oh, what joy and bliss that would be!

February 12th   Still stiff – yesterday I could barely walk. I stayed in bed pretending I had a headache. No more riding as the boys do or I shall do myself a serious injury. There is a good reason for ladies riding side-saddle.

February 16th   I have broken my promise and gone out again – such a crystal-clear morning, perfect for riding. I was more careful this time – not so reckless or fast.

Evening. I have been happy all day and I find that when I am happy I give out kisses. Winnow, who I will admit is my favourite, suffered a great many hugs and kisses from me and kept coming back for more. When I have a son I want him to be just like Winnow.

February 21st   Crantock had an accident three days past and only now can I write of it. For the first two days we thought it possible that he was entirely lost to us, but this morning he briefly opened his eyes. He fell on the steps that go to the river from the Old House, cracking his skull. Thank God he did not fall into the water or he would have – I cannot even bring myself to write it. So many times he has been told not to go there, for the lower steps are dangerously slime-wrapped. All of the children are forbidden. Yet, the more Crantock is told not to do something the more determined he becomes. Wymp and his son saw him fall and managed to get him inside. It seemed an age before the doctor arrived from Dinas Cross, but while we waited we did our best to warm his cold limbs. When the doctor finally came, Crantock hardly seemed to draw breath. My poor Aunt Azenor was so brave and calm, soothing my Uncle Vateson, who paced and paced. And I, not knowing what to do with myself, could only make futile attempts to pray. The doctor's news was not reassuring – if the crack on his head does not take him to God then fever probably will. He was blunt, and has given us little to hope for. We all take turns at his bedside. He remains at the Old House because we are fearful of moving him even a short distance.

February 28th   For the past week our darling has drifted in and out of sleep. He is so pale and frail that it breaks my heart to see him. He is no better, but no worse, and for that I – we – must thank God. When I sit with him I talk quietly of the things I see on my walk from the New House to his bedside. I have told him that the river has burst its banks a little because of all the rain, that more lambs have been born, there are periwinkles in the churchyard, and that the rooks have begun their nest-building. I tell him but I know not if he can hear. I stroke his face as I speak but I do not know if he feels anything at all. I have written to Mama and she says she will come. But what can she do that the rest of us cannot? So I have dissuaded her for the moment.

March 1st   Perhaps I am being punished – for that is what this feels like.
   Early afternoon. I went up to the Carn, I needed to be out, in

the air, away from sickroom worries. As soon as I reached the summit I began to cry and begged God to make Crantock well. I have promised that I will stop behaving in the unnatural ways that I have adopted if only he is allowed to live. I feel better for having taken some air. Thank goodness the winter murk is gradually lifting.

March 2nd   Early this evening our dear one spoke! He looked at me and said my name. I would not have believed it if Corth and Tybie had not heard it as well.

My prayers are answered.

March 3rd   Again he spoke, whispering, Edith, be well, and I have promised him that he will be. Just think, exactly one year ago it was I who was very ill.

March 4th   The doctor remains excessively cautious and concerned, saying that Crantock's forehead wound has yet to be properly assessed. He spoke in complex, puffed-up terms that only Uncle Vateson seemed to understand. I do not believe a word of it. I believe Crantock will be entirely well.

March 5th   The savage daffodils are waiting to burst open and thrust their garish heads into sight of the world. How I hate them!

March 6th   And they have succeeded. I must ignore their ugliness and focus on the beauty – blackbirds, thrushes, violets. A cutting cold frost this morning.

March 7th   More lambs.

March 9th   Blusterous days with the wind bellowing and bullying the clouds from one side of the sky to the other. Occasional flurries of snow.

March 10th   I have escaped for an afternoon – Crantock is

asleep – and it does feel like an escape. I am exhausted and drained. He grows better each day and is a most demanding patient. His head may hurt, but his lungs are most healthy – there is often screaming and shouting and tantrums. We have moved him back to the New House, which is so much easier for us all.

March 11th Early this morning I awoke to find Crantock standing over my bed. I was hardly sleeping – it was more as if I was resting my eyes. Only gradually did I recognise his face staring at me. He whispered, Edith stay. His voice was soft. I closed my eyes but it was some time before he left my side. When I went in to him later he was very quiet and gentle and happily humming to himself.

Later. I have been in tears. Aunt Azenor blamed herself saying she had depended on me too much to share the weight of Crantock's demands and that it has quite worn me out. She said I need more time to myself and added that he loves me. I cried even harder.

March 12th Crantock came to my room again last night and stroked my hair. He spoke only once, to say my name.

March 13th The doctor tells us that Crantock is finally on the mend, as if we could not tell this for ourselves from his growing energy! He is restless and fractious and as stubborn as usual. He is now allowed downstairs, so long as he is accompanied by two of us, as he will suffer light-headedness and possible fainting spells during the coming weeks. And he will always have his forehead scar – it is still an ugly purple thing, the colour of a dark plum, but this will eventually fade. He was very lucky – we were lucky not to lose him.

March 14th Mama is to come for Easter. How wonderful it will be to see her.

March 16th Last night Crantock came to my room again – he crept in without awakening me and unbound and unwound my plait and took the ribbon I used to tie it. When I woke my hair was loose all over the pillow.

Later. It is almost lunchtime; at breakfast Crantock did not once look at me but around his wrist was wrapped my hair ribbon. I passed the morning out walking and slipped into St Brychan's in Nevern just to sit quietly and think. And lovely it is at the moment, although icily cold. The churchyard is bursting with hyacinths and snowdrops and the myrtle has bloomed and there are a great many birds preparing bedding for their babies. And more daffodils desperate to split open their fat heads on the sunshine. As I walked past the yew I dipped my finger into its red ooze, then walked back slowly to Penfeidr, enjoying the chilled air, the horse-chestnuts heftily-budded along the drive, lambs everywhere, and the house in front of me smaze-wreathed from the chimneys. For two hundred and seventy years it has stood so. How I love it. How could I not.

March 19th   Uncle Vateson told a wonderful tale this morning – spun out and out as only he can do. He says that today is the wedding of all the birds in creation, which is why they were silent this morning – and they were! – but this afternoon there would be much joyful singing – and there was!

March 21st   Very tired – an evening up on the Carn.

March 22nd   Mama is not to come after all. She is too busy overseeing the publication of Mr Kingsley's manuscript. Her visit will not be until the summer. Apparently, everyone at Edgarley is well. I feel slightly guilty – I so rarely think of Edgarley these days.

March 23rd   Crantock did not come to my room as has become his habit. I awoke thinking to see him beside me but it was only my imagination and found it hard to fall back to sleep.

March 24th   Again he did not come. I imagine now that he is entirely well he has forgotten me.

March 28th Winnow and Corth saw the first butterfly of the year. We are all agreed that we quite like March.

March 30th My days are passed at the Old House with Crantock and Uncle Vateson working on the Tenth and Eleventh Rooms. I look up references in hefty old volumes and write down what I find.

April 1st In one month I shall be 19 – how very grown-up it sounds.

April 2nd There is something strange in the air today – the gulls shrilled around the house and the sea was in the wind. At sunset the sky was white and the temperature dropped to freezing.

April 3rd I have been awake for most of the night. I cannot explain my unease. The sun rose into a snow-white sky just like the one it sank into. Again it is very cold.

Late afternoon. There is something wrong in the world, on that we are all agreed. Crantock rocks and whimpers and again the gulls screamed around the chimney-tops. The fires are stoked high but barely ward off the creeping coldness.

Later. And again a dead-white sky at sunset.

April 4th Whatever hovered has passed us by. There is now a stillness and a warmth in the air. The world has gone from scarcely a leaf to be seen to small greennesses dotted all over.

Early evening. This afternoon we all gardened, even Uncle Vateson was coaxed out of his bookish-rooms. I weeded and trimmed with the aid of Crantock and Winnow, who gathered my weedings to make a pile to be burnt. They assisted with the utmost seriousness – Winnow pointing out weeds that I missed saying, Edith, look, just as Crantock does. They were the almost-perfect helpers, except for their bouts of squabbling. Poor Crantock still tires very easily – at least the gash on his forehead is less grim, but he will always have a terrific scar.

April 5th A light headache for most of the day from a little too much wine at dinner. Gardening in the soft sunshine with my two boys to assist me.

April 6th Last night Crantock came to my room – he has not done so for two or three weeks. I was still up and he watched as I took down my hair and brushed it and then braided it. When I had done he quite surprised me by undoing the plait, gently brushing my hair, and then rebraiding it. All the while he did not look at me but at my hair. I watched him in the mirror. After he had finished he left – not once did he say a word. How very curious he is, capable of such tenderness.

April 7th Local legend has it that this morning at St Brychan the first cuckoo of spring sings from the top of the Great Cross. I went, just in case, but heard no cuckoo. The swallows are returned for the summer, however.

April 8th Good Friday – too many hot cross buns – feeding the fires with rowan branches – and snow flurries!

April 9th More snow flurries.

April 10th Easter Sunday – the most delicious roast lamb for lunch. Afterwards we sat by the fire sipping hot port.

April 12th I have had a new connexion with Crantock. We were at the Old House. He was not even in the room but it was as if I heard him sigh from the depths of his being. I looked up expecting to see him but did not, although I sensed danger. When I tried to stand my legs took an age to support me and I had to lean on the desk to keep myself upright. Through the window I could see Crantock and the largest black cat imaginable pacing around him in circles. This monstrous animal had four eyes which burned like the fires of Hell, and Crantock stood with one arm over his eyes so as not to see this ugliness and the other outstretched as if to ward off an attack. I screamed and, as I did so, Crantock turned towards me lowering his arms, and the cat leapt at him.

I woke lying on the sofa with Uncle Vateson and Crantock by my side and not a scratch to be seen on Crantock. When I had described what I witnessed, Uncle said the posture in which I saw Crantock is the one that often presages the violent rages towards his own self and that in my vision I had warded it off.

April 13th I have dreamed of the cave. I made my way there in the usual way and came inside where Crantock had knelt at my feet. But this time it was abandoned. I thought, he will return, he knows I am here, and so settled myself to wait for him. In the stillness I heard the lapping waves and the wind humming through the chambers. The sound of the wind grew rough, moaning more and more loudly, so that I put my hands over my ears to bar its noise. But the moaning grew louder still until I thought I would go mad from it, then of a sudden it stopped but the silence was worse than the sound of the wind. I began to weep but felt gentle hands draw me close, hands that stroked the length of my back. I knew it was Crantock although he did not speak and I could not see for crying. And so I was soothed despite the hideous silence ringing in my ears. He held me closer and closer until it was as if we were one.

When I woke I felt at peace but this has quickly faded. I am now very despondent. I have never felt such emptiness in all my life.

April 14th What is this? Like a physical pain deep inside me, and all of today and yesterday the sight and sound of Crantock only made it worse.

April 15th Almost overnight the blossom has appeared – an abundance of scented pink and white. And just to think – I pruned those trees.

April 17th I rode out this morning on my own to the place we went to in winter – the cairn near Pen Cafnau. I rode directly across country at a gallop and the pace seemed to ease the emptiness that I carry inside me. I wore trousers – for the first time in weeks, breaking the promise I made on the Carn during Crantock's illness. Despite the hard ride I was still restless and so rode on, completely losing myself in the pleasure of it, and only when I realised that the sun was high did I turn and retrace my way. But I had to stop, fearing that I had begun my monthly illness, so soaked was my seat. I hid in some trees to check, but it was nothing more than heat-moisture. And I do not know how to write of this – when I put my hand there I was suddenly in pain, a pain that went deep inside me and made me want to cry out. I pressed my hand there harder and harder until the pain stopped and I cried from the release of it. I lay on the ground, crying, and a drowsy peacefulness came over me and then I napped for a while. When I awoke I found a spring to bath my hands and face and then road slowly back.

When I arrived it was after lunch and Aunt Azenor and Corth and Tybie were sewing. They all looked up as I entered. What a sight I must have been – trousers too big for me, twigs in my hair – yet they all behaved as if they had seen me in such a state every day. Aunt Azenor did not even chide me for missing lunch, and all she said was that perhaps I should refresh myself before eating. Goodness knows what she thought of my condition. As I washed, every part of my skin felt tender to my touch. I know not what the pain was between my legs, perhaps something pushed out of place from riding as the boys do and I had pressed it back where it was meant to be. I must be so very careful or I will do myself an injury.

April 19th   Primrose Day and it is Crantock's birthday.

April 29th   A day out collecting marsh marigolds that grow in the heathland above Brynberian. It was quite a long ride. Only Corth, Tybie and I went. It seems an eerie place, haunted, with standing stones and chambered cairns and a family of four children who live in what is little more than a sheepfold. We took food with us for them. I thought they were a family of witches, but Corth said that although they do dabble in witchery it is not of the dark type. Rather they are seers. The boy, who is the eldest, and two girls divine from the shapes and patterns of waterdrops. The youngest, a girl named Cenedlon, is blind. She is perhaps 9 or 10, and with the whitest hair I have ever seen, as white as snow. She is, I am told, the truly gifted one, and despite being blind sees shadows from which she is able to read the future, notably a person's death. She sensed the presence of someone she had not met before and came to stand in front of me, then asked me to walk so that my shadow might fall on her. She spoke in a high-pitched song-like whine, in Welsh, her usual way of speaking. As she spoke she rocked to and fro, reminding me a little of Crantock, and studied the outline of my shadow as if she could really see it. Corth told me what she had said. First, You will know a Love lasting for all of your life but you will never know happiness from this love; and secondly, You will live to a great age and die at Penfeidr mourned by no one, for all those who have loved you will have gone long before.

After we left we spent the rest of the day collecting marsh marigolds – a poor cropping this year, apparently – then rode home in the late afternoon sunshine.

I look at everything differently now that I have been told I shall never leave Penfeidr. But Cenedlon of Brynberian was surely wrong on one point. I shall know happiness quite simply because I am here with Crantock and my Vatesons. I want for nothing more.

May 1st It is my 19th birthday. The sun is bright and warm. I have presents from Mama and Papa. Only the Smallies celebrate birthdays here, but I have asked that we go to Dinas Sands for a picnic lunch.

Last night we observed May Day in the village. Before we left every fire in the house was extinguished, including that in the kitchen, the only time of year that this happens. We wore many layers, as the nights are still cold. On our coats we pinned a cross of rowan twigs made by my Uncle from the trees growing at the Old House. In the village a massive bonfire flared and after it had died down Nectan and Rhun-Owen collected some of the ash, which is for good luck. I remembered the fires on May Day in

Glastonbury when I was a girl and how it seemed as if they were lit especially to celebrate my birthday. Much here seems the same – only held one day early.

Late evening. Tired and sun-warmed, how lovely life can be. I was made a coronet of lilac by Corth and Tybie and then sung to by the Smallies, a song in Welsh they had practised once a day for ten whole days, which is a very long time for a Smallie. After this Nectan and Rhun-Owen lifted me above their shoulders and walked with me into the sea. My dearest Crantock did one of his leaping dances. And then there was cake, cut for me by Ninnon, and wine poured for me by Cleer. My gift, presented to me by Elined, who blushed red to the roots of her hair, is a shawl exquisitely embroidered all over with flag irises amidst a swarm of bees and butterflies, stitched by all the girls. Later, we built a fire on the sands and watched the sunset before riding home.

Truly – truly, I am blessed to be here.

May 3rd Today is the Feast Day of the Empress Helena's Discovery in 326 of the True Cross, which she bought to Wales one year later. We picnicked on the Carn in sweet-smelling sunshine and this evening celebrated with a dinner fit for Her Majesty the Queen herself, so many different dishes and wines were there.

May 15th The days pass quickly – I tend the garden in the morning then in the afternoon either go the Old House or out walking with Uncle Vateson and Crantock. We are mapping the sacred lines linked to the Mansions of the Moon. So far they have mapped two thousand six hundred and fifty-six of them.

May 18th Honeysuckle everywhere, and stout bumblebees, drowsy and drunkenly humming.

May 21st Aunt Azenor has picked posies for every room – a mixture of snapdragons and rose-peonies and tulips in a tumble of pinks and purples.

May 23rd Crantock and I have had one of our moments of connexion. We were out mapping with Uncle Vateson, walking through a field of campion near Soar Hill, when we stopped to listen to the birdsong. Crantock stood near to me, looking at me as he so rarely does, and I felt light as if I were floating and falling, both at the same time. The world slowed and near to my dear one I saw a magnificent butterfly as big as a child's head. It fluttered to rest briefly on his shoulder before moving on and I watched until it had disappeared. Then smiling, I turned to look at Crantock, and so close were our faces that I could feel his breath on my lips. He said my name in the softest whisper I've ever heard, and we stood looking at each other, until the sound of Uncle Vateson's voice calling us broke our reverie.

He is – he is so very dear to me, more dear than anyone ever before. No one has had this place in my heart. No one ever will – it is his place, always.

May 25th   The last two days have passed as if in a dream. Every way I turn I find Crantock watching me, and as soon as I look at him he looks away but nods yes, as if agreeing with me. He knows, he must know – everyone must be able to see what I feel.

May 27th   Out picking blood-coloured rhododendron heads – with Aunt Azenor, Corth, Tybie and Elined – they grow wild up near Gethsemane.

May 29th   It is one whole year since I arrived at Penfeidr. How unhappy I was. Well, I was so very ill, after all. And now I cannot imagine being anywhere else.

June 1st   I have been in tears – at dinner – in front of everyone. I knocked a glass over, spilling wine everywhere. I have become clumsy. I drop things, walk into things – I am so unhappy – I cannot bear the sight of my own face in the mirror. I can feel myself shrivelled inside in the way I used to. I hate to be touched, even by the Smallies. I cannot go on like this.

June 2nd   Last night I dreamt of Crantock. He was happy and so too was I.

Later. All day, every time I turned, his gaze was on me. Now I cannot sleep for thinking of him. I often think over what Cenedlon of Brynberian said – that I would not know happiness with my Love – that my life would be long – that I would die here unloved. How old is old, I wonder?

June 3rd Tired from too little sleep. Every time I began to drift off I thought I heard his voice saying, Edith, and would start awake. Eventually this became unbearable and so I tiptoed to his door but dared not go in. How could I? With what excuse? Of course, I heard nothing, I am sure he was sleeping soundly.

Later. This afternoon we swam at the pond. I looked at all our unclothed bodies, how very different we all are. I wonder what the Vateson girls feel about themselves. Do they feel as I do – do they look at themselves in the mirror – and imagine – imagine – perhaps not. They seem so comfortable, somehow. Only Ninnon is different. She is two years younger than I but carries herself with great awareness. She is womanly and knows it. And Aunt Azenor – Mama would never behave as she does, and if I had been told one year ago that I would feel comfortable in this way, I would never have believed it.

June 5th A sea mist for the last two days. Each morning begins clear and lovely but by noon the light has been suffocated. All the fires have been relit because it is so chilly. Today the wind was so strong that we could see the mist swirling past the windows. Crantock, Rhawin, Haran and Winnow spent the entire afternoon entranced by mist shapes and giving them names.

June 6th Suddenly hot! Clear blazing sky. Most of the day weeding, Crantock and Winnow as my assistants, weeding a little as the mood took them, wheeling the barrow, bickering, squabbling. We all had lunch in the orchard, simple food, bread and cheese and pickles, in the shade of the trees. Then we all drowsed to the sound of Corth reading.

June 7th   Much too hot to do anything at all. We swam this afternoon, most unsatisfactorily for the water was warm and unrefreshing.

June 8th   Hot again – more swimming. Nectan says we are building to a flood storm.

Later. Tonight Crantock amused us all by blowing on our necks to cool us down. When it came to be my turn my body ached in every part from the sheer pleasure. I closed my eyes and when I opened them I looked straight into his eyes – the colour of the sea, the sky – and I watched the room fill with dozen upon dozen of large butterflies in a rainbow of colours, the beat of their wings providing a cooling breeze against my face. When I came to myself Aunt Azenor held a damp cloth to my forehead and Crantock knelt on the floor with his head in my lap and arms clasped around my waist, afraid, no doubt, that he had injured me.

June 9th   Tending the herb garden, cloudy on and off with occasional bursts of rain in which I delighted. Rainwater on my face and hair. The giddy smell of thyme and rosemary in the steaming heat. After one particularly long burst of sun the rain began again more heavily and I ran for cover. Hardly had I reached it when Crantock appeared, dressed as God had made him. I blush hot at this very moment at how I stared, with no modesty at all, at every part of him. How very beautiful he is. Then Winnow appeared and Kew and Keyne, bare bottoms flashing past, squealing like piglets and Crantock giving chase. I watched until they had gone from sight.

Later. I feel very old and sad and – I am going to bed.

June 10th   Still in the downs, I don't know why. What is it about yesterday that has tumbled my moods? We have awoken to Nectan's predicted flood storm, the sky a ferocious bruise, all the lamps were lit as if it were midwinter. There is no thunder or lightning yet, but it cannot be too far off.

June 11th It has poured for most of a day and a night. The river was filled to overflowing and then crept up the lawn towards the Old House before seeming to lose interest and slinking away. Crantock delighted in this savagery, yelping with each crash of thunder, while the rest of us paled at the tremendous amounts of water tipped earthwards. My poor little Winnow-mouse was in traumas and had to be given a sleeping draught and put to bed. I stayed with him the entire time. Our own garden is sopping and stinking. There will be much to attend to in the coming days.

June 12th The coast has taken a battering – a boat ran aground at Cardigan Island and some lives have been lost. I must say I thought often of the witch-children on the moors at Brynberian. How awful that storm must have been in their small sheepfold. I thought they might even have been washed away, and this worried at me until I spoke to Aunt Azenor. She reassured me, saying that when the weather is particularly bad they go into Pontmaenog Forest where they shelter in an abandoned woodsman's hut. She added that over the years they have been offered various homes in return for a small amount of work on farms, but they prefer to stay on the moors and no one can stop them from living as they wish.

June 19th I have hardly had time to draw breath this past week – we lost seven trees in the orchard, four pears, two plums and an apple, and the roses have suffered terribly. It almost broke my heart to see everything looking so forlorn and battered and beaten. It has been very hot but that has not held us back. We rise early and work until lunch, work a little more and then swim, by which time we are all exhausted and so collapse in the shade to wait for dinner. Some nights I have been too tired to eat and gone straight to bed. Not that I am complaining. I would not change my life for the world.

June 20th A day collecting sea-spurge. Aunt Azenor uses it in her tonics. Unfortunately little breeze to speak of, but the fields and the banks, oh my, the fields and the banks are such a picture, inundated with poppies and larkspur and foxgloves.

June 22nd Up to the Carn yesterday where we picnicked and then napped. Uncle Vateson took out his dream-book to record our dreams. How I laughed last year thinking it all so much silliness. How lovely that I have now reached that point of being able to compare with last year.

But my dream was of the cave again. I spent some time running my hands over the surface of the shell-patterns covering the walls and suddenly one wall shifted beneath my fingertips, becoming a doorway that opened into a passageway filled with a golden light. I entered, following a path that led me into the most beautifully decorated room I have ever seen, glowing with an amber light that sparkled upon every surface it touched. I stood near to a long window looking out over the sea. The room itself was high, as if in a tower. I was entranced by the view and stood watching until Crantock's voice said my name. I turned and there he sat on the edge of a bed, holding his hand out towards me. I went to his side, and as I did so I caught sight of myself in a mirror and could see that I was dressed in a flowing gown, such as a mediaeval Lady might wear. I went to him and knelt at his feet and he stretched out his hand to stroke my hair which fell loose about my shoulders and he smiled at me and leaned towards me until our breath mingled. I lifted my hand to touch his face and as I did so I awoke.

I have told Uncle Vateson everything of the dream except the end. I said I awoke when I turned from the window to see my dear one sitting on the bed.

June 23rd A morning picking elderberries, an afternoon swimming, an evening listening to Corth and Tybie and Elined take it in turns to read from Mrs Banks's *Through the Night* – which is no less hair-raising, though this is the fifth time I have heard it. Aunt Azenor was most disappointed at being out-voted in her choice of reading matter. But really, she is as bad as Mama, always ordering books by new writers that no one else has ever heard of. She currently has a bee in her bonnet for an American gentleman called Mr James Henry.

June 24th   Midsummer – blissful long days.

June 25th   A sulk from Crantock – he really is just too spoilt! He grabbed my hat, teasing, expecting me to give chase, but I did not. I was too absorbed in the story Aunt Azenor was reading, a strangely ugly story about a Dr Jekyll. And, oh my, Crantock was annoyed, so cross. When he realised that I really was not going to chase him, he ripped the ribbons off the hat and flung them into the sea. Aunt Azenor was most shocked and said that if he did not stop he would be sent home. At this Crantock went very red in the face and snatched the book from her and tried to tear the pages out. Uncle Vateson intervened and said something too quiet for anyone else to hear but which caused Crantock to sit with his back to us in a sulk. When the boys went off swimming, he at first refused to go until Uncle Vateson had another quiet word with him. When they returned from their swim, Crantock had quite forgotten that he had been in a sulk, but was in a dreadful temper and kept shouting, No, a good many times. Unfortunately, my hat is ruined.

June 27th   The 5th anniversary of Adwen's Resting. I have such vivid memories of last year – of the feeling returning to my hand. Today we decorated her grave and when it came to tell of a favourite thing from last year, I too was included. I spoke briefly of that moment at Dinas Sands when I looked into Crantock's eyes and saw another world. My voice stumbled when I said his name because I very nearly called him my dear one, as I always do to myself, and I felt my face flush hot and bright. At the end we all joined hands and they all sang, Crantock's voice so loud and large and lifting to the heavens. And then he danced, and a most wonderful courtly thing it was, as if from another time. When he had finished he dropped to his knees, resting his head on the flowers at the foot of her grave. He loves her so – it was in his face. Then we all kissed one another on the cheek, squeezing hands. Even the boys kissed me. And when Crantock stood everyone kissed him. I was the last to do so. Hanging back because I felt shy and awkward and clumsy, and when I finally moved forward he too did so all of a sudden and our noses knocked together and I stared deeply into his eyes. There I saw the room of which I have dreamt, with an amber glow warming everything it touched, and the hangings surrounding the bed richly embroidered with butterflies. I saw myself kneel at his feet and his hand reach to stroke my hair. Just as I believed he was about to kiss me I fainted.

He is – so very –

June 28th   A lovely dream last night – I am standing in a forest of apple trees, branches twining over my head and laden with blossoms, the air heavy with their perfume. I am happy just to stand there.

June 29th   Aunt Azenor said to me that surely Mama will want me returned to her at some point. I smiled and replied that she knows I am content, so I am sure she will allow me to stay.

I will never leave – I know that in the very deepest part of myself.

July 3rd   All the Mims run to greet me now and there are three additions, the tiniest kittens, each one the size of my hand.

July 5th   I awoke from a most melancholy dream. I was myself, as I am now, but very old at the same time, my face almost unrecognisable with age. I stood near to the ruined church at Cwm-yr-Eglwys and looked out to sea and then turned to look at a small whitewashed cottage, a fisherman's cottage. And I knew that I would die there, entirely alone and unloved.

Later. A very great sadness oppressing me all day.

July 11th   One week on and that dream still drags at me – festering in my brain – I go over and over the details to no purpose.

July 14th   He –

   I –

How do I write of this – ?

July 15th   I have spent the past day in a daze. Everyone suspects something I am sure. I hardly know whether I am coming or going. I smile all the time like someone who has lost her mind –

   Today my dear one and his papa will go to the Carn to stay for one week.

July 16th   I am terrified of writing down what I feel. What if someone should read it? And yet I need to write. I must. I have no one to speak to – to share my secrets with – and I shall burst if I do not put something down on paper.

   Two days ago – two whole days – my darling kissed me. There! It is written. Two days ago my darling kissed me. And if I am never kissed again in my entire life this memory will be enough.

   It was after lunch. I had gone off to the orchard as has become my habit, to doze on a blanket in the shade of the apple trees. I lay there, tired from the heat and from my morning's activities and sleepy from lunch, drowsily watching the fruit-laden branches shift over my head. I must have drifted off to sleep, for when I awoke Crantock lay beside me, his head propped on one hand, watching me, staring for such a long time that I had to close my eyes again. Then he placed a hand on my stomach and left it to rest there, pressing a little. I shivered though I was not cold. He moved closer to me, so close that his body was moulded into my side and the hand that rested on my stomach took hold of my own, his fingers forcing my fingers apart, interlocking with them, pressing and squeezing so hard that my knuckles ached with pain, to match the pain in my heart. I began to cry and opening my eyes looked at him through my tears. His dearest face, his dearest face, and the words My darling came from my mouth, and hardly had they been said than his lips pressed against mine and forced them open – and – and so many kisses – each one different from the one before. I called him My darling over and again and told him that I would always love him, until his mouth stopped mine from speaking.

For how long we kissed I do not know, but when we heard Ninnon calling my name Crantock moved apart and ran off. I heard my voice say, I am here, I fell asleep. She and I walked back to the house together and I passed the remainder of the afternoon in a daze.

At dinner and afterwards Crantock was his usual self and did not once look at me. Later he came to my room – entering without knocking – and spoke not a word, brushing my already brushed hair, and then leaving. He did not kiss me. I lay awake all night trying to calm myself, forcing myself to stay in bed and not to go to him. Only at cockcrow did I fall into a heavy sleep and I had not awoken when he and his papa left for the Carn.

Every day he is my first and last thought, as well as every moment in between. Yesterday and today I sat beneath our tree remembering every detail as if it were happening anew. Sometimes I turn expecting to see him near to me, almost certain I can hear his voice saying my name, and at these moments I know that he too is thinking of me.

July 18th   Each morning and evening I look up to the Carn knowing that he is there.

July 19th   I look different in the mirror – I almost look pretty. I am glowing, almost – I do believe.

July 20th   A sun-filled day at Dinas Sands. The sea and the sky – both the colour of Crantock's eyes. Only he was not there and I longed for him so – an ache very deep inside my body. On the way back to Penfeidr I asked that we might stop at Cwm-yr-Eglwys and I stood in the same place as I had done in my dream, staring out to sea, before noticing two small white cottages stood where in my dream there had only been one.

July 22nd   They are returned a day early.

Later. A long day – one of the longest I have ever known. When they returned, he did not even look at me. I thought, he has forgotten, and all day felt numb and miserable and dead inside. Then, before dinner, I sought him out. I found him in the long drawing-room and it is just as well that I wished to be kissed, because kissed I was, to the point of suffocation. Then suddenly he stopped and walked away, leaving me to be found by Aunt Azenor, half-fainted.

He loves me still – just as I love him.

July 25th His favourite word is No, which he shouts at every-one. He no longer comes to brush my hair. It is too much for both of us. All his held-in energy – he will be ill – it will be my fault.

July 27th Such hot days, one after another. Every evening there is a broiling black storm to clear the air. And my darling is in such a temper, even with the Smallies, who run off when they see him coming.

July 28th He erupted – it has been building for days – snarling at me, pushing me. I fell, hurting my wrist. He was hateful, his face twisted and angry and ugly.

July 30th I have not seen him for three days, not a glimpse. I do not know where he is gone. I seem to sleepwalk through each day. I cannot focus. I cry at the drop of a hat. Aunt Azenor thinks that I am sickening for Mama. I am so tired.

August 1st Down to the sea with the horses – Crantock was there and behaved as if I did not exist.

August 2nd I will die if this goes on.

August 3rd I am not strong enough –

August 4th It is very early morning – last night I went to him, I could not prevent myself.

I have been day-dreaming out of the window, forgetting to write, watching the heat haze over the treetops. Does it matter if I never write of what has happened? I will always remember and that is enough.

Later. But I want to write of it – I want to – I want to write his name to fill a whole book.

I went to him, it was very late, and he sat by his open window in his nightshirt. His eyes were closed and I thought he slept and so stood watching him – oh, his dear lovely face, the dearest face. His words, Edith, go! were as sharp and sudden as a gunshot. He did not even look at me but remained as he was, eyes closed. I ran to his side saying, No, no, I will not, and took his face in my hands, forcing it towards mine, pressing my lips to his, until he returned my kiss. And he took off his nightshirt and – and what I saw – his beauty – and what I saw – I am not surprised he has been in a terrible temper. He has been in agonies from it. He – I led him to his bed – the feverish heat of his skin burning through my nightdress and he made my hand to touch him where he was swollen and hurting and he cried out from the awfulness of the pain. At first I thought my touch had made him worse, made him bleed, but it was not so. Rather, once the fluid had come out, like pus from a burst boil, the swollenness went down and he rested in my arms, exhausted and peaceful. I thought he slept but each time I shifted a little he asked me to stay, as if thinking I might leave. After a while he began to kiss me and hold me close to him and his pain quickly returned and took longer to release but the fluid finally came out and he was content again. Then we both slept, curled into one another. He woke me with kisses and then I crept back here before the rest of the house awoke.

August 5th   No one seems to have guessed that are hearts are married.

August 6th   I have a great aching pain low down as if I sprained something in our wrestling and tangling last night. And if I put my fingers there and press the ache becomes even greater until I feel quite sick and faint from it.

August 7th   I sleepwalk through the days hardly knowing where they begin and end. Each night I go to Crantock and – and those hours are not long enough for all that we wish to share, while the days are long and drowsy. Soon the grandfather will strike eleven and we shall be together.

August 8th I am exhausted. I can hear Penfeidr breathing and moving, coming to life. Have I slept at all?

August 9th I cannot go on with so little sleep – today I am so heavy, I stumbled through the day. I longed to lie down and did so briefly beneath the shade of the plums, drowsing to the sound of honey-bees, until the ache which comes and goes came again, sending me into a fit of tears and then a very irritable temper for the rest of the day.

August 10th Last night we both slept for the most part. Both very tired. Much refreshed this morning.

August 11th I must find a book about this – about our bodies – Aunt Azenor must have something tucked away. For all I know I may be making Crantock worse with my attentions – last night I attended to him four times and each time he was in as much pain as the first.
    Later. I have been secretly searching all day but could not find any book that tells me what I need to know.

August 12th Last night was different between us. Usually when we are together I keep my nightdress on but last night my darling insisted that it come off – pulling until it tore at the neck. His hands were everywhere on my skin and also his mouth and it was too heavenly, but then the ache came and it was very bad, so bad that I tried to push him away but he would not be pushed away and my hand went there because of the pain and his hand followed mine and he pressed there and wouldn't stop and just as I thought I would scream from the awfulness of it, I fainted. When I came to myself the pain had gone and I felt tired and I cried for a very long time and my darling held me close and was very tender with me for the rest of the night.
    Later. Soon I will go to him – all day the thought of his hand

pressing there. And this makes the ache come back and I feel giddy and hot and breathless and sick. Perhaps there is something wrong with me? If only I could ask Mama or Aunt Azenor.

August 13th   Last night he came to me – for the very first time. He brushed my hair and then took me into my own bed.

August 14th   And again he came to me. It is one month since our first kisses. One whole month.

August 15th   He likes to brush my hair before bed, it pleases him, but last night it made him wrought-up too quickly. I turned and kissed his tip and he came properly into my mouth which was not very comfortable because my mouth is not large – but he liked it very much and later he wanted me to do the same again and so I did. I did wonder if it might make me sick or give me a stomach-ache, but it seems not to have affected me at all.

August 16th   Everyone has noticed a change in my darling – he is very calm and never rocks to and fro and doesn't say no as often as he used to. For the most part he is sweetness and happiness all day every day. Mercifully no one seems to have noticed the change between us – when we are with the others he is very shy and will not look at me.

When we are alone he is quite different, he actually talks to me, in a roundabout fashion, not just saying yes or no, but broken sentences about the things he sees. I have been most taken aback by this – and I do wonder why he is not more like this at other times. It is almost as if he cannot be bothered.

August 17th   I have found a small book that tells me a little of what I need to know about our togetherness. I found it in Aunt Azenor's cottage – an ancient slender thing called *Venus Unwrapt*. It is quite philosophising and I am sure I do not understand half of what it says, but it tells of the male life energy and of how once it is provoked into a storm it must be released otherwise great pain and suffering and illness will be caused. If the fluid does not come out it goes to the brain and the brain ruptures causing paralysis. The book says that it is woman's sacred duty to assist in its release and that is why she was created from Adam's spare rib, because if a man tries to release his own life's energy he will go blind and have fits and become mad. So – I have been behaving in the correct manner after all. The last pages tell of how this fluid causes babies to come into the world – and at the moment I read this I almost fainted. I became hot and cold and hot again at the thought that I might already have a child growing inside me as I have swallowed so much of my dear one's life energy in the past nights. Unfortunately, nowhere did it say how much one has to have before a child is made. So how will I know?

August 20th We are discovered – we overslept . . . Ninnon came to wake me and did so without a word. Oh God. All day I have been mettlesome and fidgety and tense waiting for the storm to break over our heads.

August 21st Last night after dinner, Ninnon walked with me upstairs to my room, she stood at the door and said rather cryptic-ally that we all have our secrets but they are best kept behind locked doors, and then she went to her own room. I do not know what to make of this, but when my darling came I locked the door. How could I not have thought to do so before?

August 22nd I am still heady with nerves. Poor Crantock does not know what to make of it – nor does anyone else. Three times today I shouted at my small sweetheart Winnow and he burst into tears, me following suit.

Later. Cleer and Ninnon have gone off on one of their ex-peditions to collect spring-water specimens and will sleep out for ten days or so. Nothing more has been said so it seems she will keep our secret – for now, at least.

August 23rd Last night I held my darling close and watched him sleep. They could not separate us if they tried – it is gone too far between us for that.

August 24th I am so engrossed in Crantock that it is as if nothing else exists – but Penfeidr goes on with summer life and chores. The fruit trees are laden with apples and pears and plums and greengages and peaches and nectarines. The watermelons are huge and only the boys can lift and cut them. My vase is full of hollyhocks and there are pots of geraniums in every room. The windows are never closed and every now and then the scent of jasmine and honeysuckle will sneak in. I have never known such a hot summer – I wear less than decency allows, two very thin layers, one almost transparent, and even then I push my sleeves high as the boys do. And my face has colour, despite my broad-brimmed sunhat, and my hands are embarrassingly tawny – what on earth would Mama say? Wymp has set up a hammock for me at the Old House so that I might drowse in the afternoon shade. And our work on the Tenth and Eleventh Mansions continues very well indeed.

Sometimes I think of Edgarley, and although I miss my family I cannot imagine what I would be doing if I were there. I cannot imagine it at all.

August 27th Last night was very different. We – he – fits into my body in a way that I would never have dreamed possible. We were playing and tussling and he was rubbing his tip against me in my lower place and suddenly pushed all the way inside. I do not know which of us was the more shocked. He came out of me and then went in again until it seemed as if we were both joined at the hip. I will admit I was afraid – I became very overwrought in a way I have not done before and cried out every time he pushed in and out. I felt as if I might break apart, especially when the ache came and hurt in every part of my body, not just down there. Afterwards we lay unspeaking until we slept.

August 29th There is a moment when we are joining together when I do not believe it possible, I feel unready, uncertain, afraid, but each time I do fit him inside me and there he will rest, kissing me many times, and as much as I want it to end I never want it to end, and when it does he always says my name.

August 30th He is the part of me that was missing.

August 31st Uncle Vateson suspects something – he must do after today. We were at the Old House. I had been drowsing in the hammock and then went to find Crantock and his papa. They were stood on the grass talking together as they often do – my darling is quite the talkative one when he wants to be – and when I walked up to them Crantock put his arm around my waist. At first I thought he would kiss me on the mouth, right in front of his papa, but instead he kissed my cheek. Uncle Vateson looked from Crantock to myself and back again to Crantock with a most bemused expression on his face, but remained silent.

What would they do if they knew – what would they do – the thought makes me feel ill and afraid and – surely they would not separate us?

September 3rd Exactly one month ago tonight!

September 4th Every night is the same yet different.

September 6th Out early to pick mushrooms which we then had for breakfast cooked in butter and parsley and with thick slices of still-warm bread – such a feast.

September 8th He always has something for me, a flower or a stone or a shell or a leaf.

September 10th I yearn to talk of him and do – all the time – with everyone, just to have the taste of his name in my mouth. I think they suspect that I love him – because they always smile in an indulgent sort of way.

September 12th We have argued – I do not remember how or why or what – but he did not come to me last night and when I went to him his door was locked! It is our first night apart. I have not slept at all.

Later. He has ignored me all day, behaving as if I do not exist.

September 13th I will go mad if he does not stop tormenting me. I cannot live this way – I will not – I would rather die.

September 14th I am too tired to get out of bed.

Later. Aunt Azenor came to me. She has guessed that something is wrong between Crantock and me. She has noticed his spite to me during the past days. She said I must not take it to heart, that he does not realise what he is saying, that he does not mean to hurt me. But he does mean it. He wants to punish me. After she left I cried until I was choking sick, and now I cannot sleep.

September 15th I have forced myself out of bed.

Later. I went to the Old House as usual. The leaves have just begun to turn, just slightly, almost unnoticeably. Crantock ignored me, although twice I noticed he almost smiled when I was speaking. At teatime he went into the garden to watch the birds which is one of his favourite things, and I stood at the window watching him, sipping my tea. Uncle Vateson came to stand beside me and although we did not speak some acknowledgment passed between us of my love for Crantock.

When I came up to bed a small feather had been left on my pillow – perhaps he will come.

September 16th He did not come.

September 17th Perhaps he no longer loves me. Perhaps it is as simple as that.

September 18th It is one week since we last lay together. I cannot remember what I said or did not say. It is too long ago. I have lost a little weight but I am well, and I tell everyone so when they ask. I say, I am well, thank you.

He is cruel – his silence is wilful and deliberate.

September 19th He enjoys hurting me – the spite in his face.

September 20th   We have begun picking the fruit.

September 21st   Spider gossamer in the air – floating from heaven it seems.

September 22nd   Another cobweb morning. The Carn last night, no dreams, none at all.

September 23rd   No appetite – I am becoming a little too thin.

September 25th   Two weeks have passed. I awake crying and cry myself to sleep. During the day I console myself that at least I am here, at least I am near to him.

October 1st   It is now October.

October 2nd   Another week gone by.

October 7th   They know of our love. They know everything. What if they try to part us, what then, what will I do, I must think, remain calmness itself.

   Yesterday – yesterday I walked on my own and found a sun-trap corner by the river where I curled up to think of Crantock. At some point I drifted into a world of neither sleep nor wakefulness and dreamed that I was in our special room. The bed with the butterfly hangings had gone and the room was entirely bare and empty. I looked from the window and all was obscured by a thick mist that coiled into shapes and rushed and pushed at the glass so that it bent inwards under the pressure. Yet the glass did not crack and splinter. As I watched, suddenly the mist cleared but the scene I looked upon was one of utter devastation. No tree remained standing, and huge roiling waves tormented the shore where the golden sands had been. I could not believe the desolation I saw where before had been only beauty. Horrified, I turned away to find the room festooned with spiders' webs as thick as curtains, and as I lifted them to pass through I heard a movement as of footsteps near the door – and then I awoke.

   I found myself cold and cramped to the point of pain and enveloped in such a mist that I could barely make out one step forward. But I knew I could not stay where I was. I felt danger around and near to me. I began to follow the river and could hear mist dripping through the trees just like the sound of slow footsteps. Even though I said to myself that it was only the sound of the mist, I walked on more quickly, running sometimes. This continued for what seemed like hours, the river going on and on with no other landmark I could recognise. Eventually, I could go no farther, so tired was I. So I stopped and turned to confront whoever or whatever I feared might approach me. All was silent save for my own chattering teeth. But the mist seemed to come closer, brushing against my face as soft as kisses. I gagged as if to be sick and turned to flee, when suddenly my arms were grabbed and held in a vice. I began to scream and was shaken hard in the grip of someone who turned me to face their way, and it was Uncle Vateson's face I saw. Then there were footsteps again and he was being pushed from me with such violence that he fell to the ground. And I stared into the bluest eyes I have ever seen before my darling pressed his mouth to mine – and in that brief moment in his eyes I saw our room as it had been, the bed, the hangings, and beyond the window a brightly lit world. A land-scape I know and love. And then I fainted and did not come to myself until I was at Penfeidr.

Crantock loves me still – that is all that matters. They cannot separate us – it is impossible.

October 8th Silence again all day – Crantock and Uncle Vateson are gone to the Carn. Aunt Azenor has kept to her room. Nectan and Rhun-Owen are in Fishguard. Elined is hammering in her room. The Smallies are at their lessons with Corth and Tybie. Cleer and Ninnon are who knows where.

And I am here, waiting, waiting.

Later. I have received a note from Uncle Vateson. Tomorrow morning he will see me in the library.

October 9th It is still very early, sun barely awake; a dream of Crantock, I can hear him crying but cannot find him. I have been to his room but his bed has not been slept in. I must remain calm.

Later. Nothing has been said between Uncle Vateson and my-self that I did not suspect. He was most uneasy in his manner of speaking, dillying and dallying with words, faddling and fiddling with his jacket, his cuffs and the objects on his desk, before eventually managing to spit out that he was indeed aware Cran-tock and I had become very close and that this was perhaps inevitable given our special bond. He then spoke at length, saying much with very little meaning. Goodness, how he reminded me of Papa with his endless perambulations. However, occasionally he drew breath and looked at me, allowing me the chance to reply, but I did not, I maintained my silence. He talked on and on and when he had finished we looked at one another, but still I did not speak. Instead I stood and walked to the window and remained there with my back to him. Eventually he came to stand beside me. When I said I loved Crantock, his response was simply to say that we all love him. I replied, my voice strong and clear, using the exact same words Nile had used to describe Win, Crantock is as my Husband. He did not believe me, and so I said, I am as his Wife. At this he recoiled from me. I saw a great many different emotions cross his face before he spoke again – horror and disgust, despair and fear, and sorrow, then an attempt at self-restraint. My dear, he said so very coldly, it cannot be. It never will be so.

I returned to my room and wept.

I am – I do not know what I am. Aunt Azenor will not see me. I dread every sound that passes near to my door. My head is sickly pounding and so is my heart. And the thought of the door opening and Corth standing there, or Tybie, or Elined, come to say that she has come to help me pack . . .

And Crantock – where is he? They are keeping us apart.

Later. I have been to see Aunt Azenor. I forced my way past Tybie and refused to leave. When I tried to take her hand she would not allow it, crying that my dear Mama will never forgive her. I tried to tell her what I had told Uncle Vateson but she only cried harder and put her hands over her ears. Oh, God – what am I to do?

Later again. I insisted on being told where Crantock was and when they said he had gone away with Nectan and Rhun-Owen,

I confess I lost control, crying and screaming that we will never be parted from one another. They cannot stop our love. I am his Wife and he is my Husband.

October 10th Very late last night my darling returned to me of his own free will. They have no choice but to accept our love – if they refuse then I will leave and he will leave with me. I have told them so.

Later. Aunt Azenor has written me a long letter. I read it and wept. She cannot condone my love for Crantock and yet accepts that it shall continue. It is necessary if the great work is to progress. I am essential to his happiness. She has also made it clear that because of my actions she must for ever sever her friendship with Mama. How, she writes, can she look my mother in the face knowing she has betrayed her trust and care of me? And Mama must never again come to Penfeidr. Excuses will be found – I must go to her. Furthermore, Crantock and I are to be moved into the Old House – I am not to come back here under any circumstances. When Crantock does so I am not to accompany him. She says no Church would ever sanction a union between us and our love is something that she can never accept.

I am banished. And yet it feels like freedom! To be with my darling as I wish and as he too wishes. And when there is a child? What then? Will they banish their own grandchild?

Crantock is as he usually is, happy to be with me, understanding that we were separated, but not understanding why. Such comprehension is perhaps beyond him, and never will I say a bad word to him of his mama and papa's behaviour during these recent days. Though, I will admit, that I do not think at all well of them at present, especially Uncle Vateson. It is entirely false of him to behave as if he did not know that a much deeper bond had grown between Crantock and me. Indeed, on so many occasions he encouraged us to be alone together, emphasising our special connexion and how nothing must be allowed to stand in its way, telling me it was God's will that I had come here, that I was chosen to be with Crantock. And he spoke the truth and now I will not allow him to pretend otherwise.

October 11th It is very late. My darling is now asleep in our very own room. We have been given the top two floors of the tower. The uppermost is our bedroom, the next one down our sitting room. The views are quite exceptional. I can see over to Carn Ingli, down to Newport Sands and the estuary, and across country to Gethsemene and beyond. On a very clear day I shall be able to see as far as Dinas Head. Inland to the west I can see for miles past Nevern along the river and up to Constantinople and Pentre Ifan. Wymp, his wife and son will tend to our needs. Wymp's wife, at least, is delighted to have us here and seems not to disapprove of me at all. We cannot speak each other's language but she has a face that expresses her feelings quite plainly.

We shall be happy here – I know it. Cenedlon of Brynberian was wrong – I will know happiness with my great love.

October 12th I like to undress him slowly and only then will I allow him to begin to undress me.

October 13th He has become very silent again, rarely saying much more than my name, but what need have we of words when our bodies are as one.

October 14th I have spent the past three days prettifying our rooms into a little home. I have been given everything I requested and been able to make them colourful and cosy and comfortable. I have hung layer upon layer of curtains and tapestries on the walls to keep in the warmth. I have geraniums in pots in both rooms and many candlesticks for candles and bowls for decoration and my knick-knacks all over.

October 17th I am unused to not having chores in the garden to fill my day – as even that has been forbidden me – and so we spend long hours at the Work because it is all I have to do. I am reading Uncle Vateson's voluminous notes for the past eight years, looking for links between my connexion with Crantock and what had gone before. It is tiring, eye-aching work. It is most fortunate that Wymp's wife takes care of us completely.

Later. I need only to look at his face to know what he is thinking – each tiny expression is worth to me one thousand words.

October 18th   Winnow has gone missing.

Much later. My small sweetheart was found here hiding beneath our bed. He shed a downpour of tears in-between saying he wanted to be here with Crantock and me and would run away again and again if he could not stay. He sat on my lap and cried and talked himself to sleep and then I put him into our bed where he will stay tonight.

Later again. A tantrum from Crantock about Winnow in our bed – I have cajoled and promised that it is for the one night only, but still there were tears. Oh dear, I am tired.

October 19th   I slept squeezed between my two darlings who from the moment of awakening squabbled like hens to be the centre of my attentions. I was exhausted within an hour. My small sweetheart was taken back to the New House by his papa with much noise and kicking of legs and general resistance.

Later. Hardly had we settled down to dinner than a small body hurled itself through the door and into my lap. This time he brought with him the Merry-dog and a pillowcase with just a few of his favourite possessions, saying that tomorrow he would need to collect some more. His papa was only a short way behind. The small one then sat on the floor by the fire and would not be moved, emitting the highest pitched scream whenever he was touched, so that one would have thought he was being tortured upon the rack! When it was suggested that perhaps Winnow might stay one more night and the issue be resolved in the morning, Crantock began to shout No, so many times I lost count. I was quite at the end of my tether and stamped my foot and shouted, Stop, which, surprisingly, he did. I said Winnow could sleep on the sofa and go home tomorrow, and that was that. Winnow cried as if he was heartbroken saying that he wanted to stay with us, and Crantock stormed from the room. I made a nest for Winnow and tucked him into it – and left him crying into his pillow – the dear little heart. Crantock has gone to bed in a sulk and is ignoring me.

And so – it's suddenly peacefully quiet and restful – just the Merry-dog and I.

Goodness knows what Aunt Azenor must think – perhaps, that I am determined to take all her favourite boys from the New House to live with me here.

October 20th Crantock slept with his back to me all night – I was not given a single kiss, not even this morning – how cruel he is to me.

Winnow was very brave and went back to the New House with no tears or tantrums after all. I walked with him and his papa to the gateway and then waved them off. The Merry-dog stayed with me until they were out of sight and then bounded after them.

October 21st A delayed letter from Mama. After endless procrastination she is on her way here. I have managed to send a reply entreating her that we meet at Cardiff, stating that Aunt Azenor is unwell with a fever and it is thought best if I come to her. It is so very typical of her to want to come when it is the least convenient.

How can I leave my darling for even one night?

October 22nd It is one year since my Bayard went to God – I cannot help but feel despondent.

Later. Pleasure – even from bathing together.

October 23rd Winnow visited for a brief while, with Nectan and Rhun-Owen. He flung his arms around me and completely ignored Crantock who was most put out. He is not used to being ignored by anyone.

October 24th A return letter from Mama saying that she will not take me from Aunt Azenor's side while she is ill, but insisting I write more often, so she does not worry. If I miss a day she will come at once – so, a letter every other day it must be.

October 25th   I am too tired to write much here – Crantock is so demanding I barely sleep at night. But – how very lovely he is – and why does what we share have to remain hidden as if it were shameful? Surely it is the most natural thing in the world to love in this way.

October 26th   A very light scattering of snow – in October! Oh the view from our tower!

October 27th   Snow gone – but a very bitter wind. I weeded a little in the sour sunshine, and as I did so I thought of Edgarley and tried to remember the details of the rooms – and found it somewhat hard to do. I was on my knees and sat back on my heels to look around me, to look at my home. This is the life I have chosen. This is the life I want. And my heart swelled with such a hugeness of love, for Crantock, for Penfeidr. There is nowhere else for me to be. I am truly his Wife and always will be. Nothing, no one, will ever change that.

October 28th   The creation of the Tenth and Eleventh Rooms is progressing. Uncle Vateson and I have become close once again and he speaks with me in some detail about what we are and are not achieving, which I try to understand. He knows that I am hurt by Aunt Azenor's silence but he has let slip that she asks after me every day.

October 29th   A very blowy day – the washing on the line flapped so hard that I feared it might be carried away. What a joyous sight – what a little housemaid I am at heart!

October 30th   The Winnow-mouse is wheedling his way into being with Crantock and me more often. He and the Merry-dog spent the entire weekend with us. He came on Friday afternoon and no sooner had he arrived than it began to rain. He must have prayed very hard for it because the heavens opened and have remained thus ever since. He was quietness itself all evening, drawing pictures. I made him a nest on the sofa as I had done before. Yesterday we kept ourselves happy and content with reading and telling stories to each other – by lunch Winnow had forgotten to check whether the rain was continuing and had settled in. Crantock was not too jealous or possessive because I was quick to calm any situation where a tantrum might erupt. Towards the end of the evening, Winnow curled up on Crantock's lap and promptly fell asleep and had to be carried to his nest, where, as I was tucking him in, he peeped, so I knew he had not been sleeping after all. And today was much the same, except Winnow kept to himself. I found him and the Merry-dog in the kitchen with Wymp's wife, helping, so he said, which I took to mean doing a great deal of nothing apart from chatterboxing.

I think – do I dare write it – with Winnow and Merry here it is almost as if we are a little family.

October 31st   Winnow and Merry returned to the New House this afternoon and I do believe Crantock misses him. We had such a lovely time of it this weekend – the four of us.

November 3rd   He sang to me today, just as he often does, but in English, so that I could understand. He sang to me My Love, She's a Venus. I cried when he sang the very last words – My heart, it does love her – but he just laughed at my tears and sang the song again.

November 8th   I am teaching Crantock to dance. He thinks that holding me tight at the waist means doing little more than kissing. I said that there could be no more kisses until he mastered the steps of a waltz and he very quickly did.

November 12th   Yesterday was our first anniversary – one month of being 'married'. I made a cake, or rather Wymp's wife did and I did the icing. I dragged my darling off to bed and we had cake and a glass of wine and lay together watching the flames. For the very first time I realised that if we want to go to bed for all of the afternoon we can, because we are in our very own home. We stayed there until dinner and afterwards returned to our bed.

November 17th The more often we lie together the greater our need for each other becomes, rather than less. He likes to look at me for hours on end, silently, doing little more than gently stroking every part of my skin. Oh, the agony of it, waiting for him to decide to come into me and finish what he started.

November 20th Today I shocked even myself – I refused to wait – I climbed on top of him to take my pleasure. He kept shouting, Stop! but I would not – I could not even if I had wanted to. Afterwards he bit me very hard on the shoulder and so I bit him in return.

November 28th It must be at least one week since we were properly dressed. We have hardly stirred from our bed.

December 11th Our second month together – I now know his body better than my own and yet every day it is as if I discover it anew.

December 13th Bitterly cold days – huge blazing fires day and night. Uncle Vateson has spoken of the solstice and Christmas. We are all to go to the Carn for the solstice – except for Aunt Azenor. At Christmastime I am to have my darling on the Eve, but his Mama will have him for the Day. I will be on my own for the Day – but I am sure I will be fine. I shall find things to keep myself busy until Crantock is back at home again with me.

December 14th The Tenth Room is to be ready after the solstice and the Eleventh is almost complete as well.

December 15th Dark dreams which are disappeared – and I am troubled by their vanishing. I have been in the downs for all of the day for the very first time since my darling and I became married.

December 16th My body feels different – I seem to have put on weight.

December 18th   Startled awake by a cry in the early morning – but Crantock was sleeping soundly. I tiptoed to the window, but cloud obscured any possible light, although I could hear mumbled words, the sound of horses, the clink of bridles. At first I felt unafraid, for if they were ghosts, they seemed peaceable enough. I returned to bed and kissed Crantock's forehead – gently on his scar – and in an instant his eyes opened and stared into mine. He said, They are come for us. Then he was asleep again, as if he had not spoken. I did not sleep again, I could not. I lay watching the door, expecting at any moment for it to burst open upon us. But it did not. All day I have been startled and worried at noises. Most ill at ease.

December 21st   I have washed and trimmed Crantock's hair and kept a thick lock for myself. After I had washed my own, he insisted on assisting Wymp's wife in trimming it likewise. Then we both sat by the fire, heads steaming, eating large bowls of broth. Afterwards we lay by the fire. Tonight we will go to the Carn.

December 22nd   It is late afternoon – rain, firelight, my very own darling. I love and am loved.

Much later. He is finally sleeping; all day he has given me pleasure. As soon as we returned from the Carn we went straight away to bed, remaining there all day. He is so changed from the strange boy I first knew; oh, he still has his shynesses as well as his mute days. But there is little, if anything, we do not share. It is as if our love has healed him in some way.

Last night was much the same as last year – the bonfires, our feather-prayer-sticks. Everyone was welcoming and kissed me most affectionately. My darling and I curled up beneath a mountain of blankets and he held me close and tight and as I fell into sleep I felt his breath against my neck and when the dream came it was as if I was awake and not in a dream at all.

I stood at the head of a path in a churchyard that now as I write seems familiar to me and yet I am not sure how. As I walked along the path, so slowly, that the four seasons seemed to come and go, and spring had returned before I stood at the open door. I walked down the aisle to where I saw Crantock waiting for me –

I recognised him as my Lord and knew that I was his Lady. When I reached his side I knelt in a deep curtsey, remaining there until he held out his hand. I placed mine in his and then I rose to my feet and he lifted my hand to his lips. When he raised his head a jewelled ring shone on my finger where his lips had touched – a thick gold band glittering with stones every colour of the rainbow. I looked deeply into his eyes and saw myself reflected, seeing the lustrous beauty of my gown which was from another age, white and flowing, with on each breast an embroidered winged dragon, and the same repeated around the hem, done in gold. My hair flowed to the ground and was decorated with jewels in the shape of flowers and animals and birds and stars and my neck ached from their weight. All this beauty I could see reflected in my darling's eyes. He said my name and then his lips pressed against mine and drank from my mouth and I did not resist the wave swelling in me. I gave myself up to it, allowing myself to be carried away.

Then Crantock said, they are come for us, and he led me to where twelve horsemen waited, armoured as Knights ready for battle. We mounted too and the Knights formed a circle around us leading us from the church along the coast to a cave. At the cave, we walked into the pitch-black depths before coming to another cave where a banquet had been prepared for us. Here, we ate together. Then we set off once more and came to another cave, where we were refreshed with red wine before again setting off. Eventually we reached another cave, which had paths leading in fourteen directions, but the path Crantock chose led up a set of winding stairs. Up and up and up we walked, until reaching a heavy carved door that opened on to our room with the huge bed with butterfly hangings and the window overlooking the sea. In the distance I could see the church where we had recently stood side by side. In the room were twelve Ladies and I went to them and they unclothed me. I stood entirely as God made me, except for the ring on my finger. In this way I stood before Crantock, who held out his hand to me, and we lay together, joined as is our desire, and at this point I awoke to feel his breath against my neck.

I told Uncle Vateson an incomplete version of my dream – I felt myself grow hot and awkward in the telling and I was thankful he did not press me for details. Crantock refused to communicate his dream – he was in a petulant sulk even with me until we had come home and lain together. He would not even eat before almost carrying me off to bed. He is too spoilt, truly, and it is my very own fault because I cannot say no to him. But I do not want to say no because the pleasure that our bodies share – I cannot write of it. It is a pleasure that goes beyond ordinary words.

December 23rd   I've been shown the Tenth Room. I was anxious beforehand, on account of the secrets I have kept from Uncle Vateson in my dream-tellings. What if something I have withheld should mean that the room is incomplete? But it seems I need not have worried. Crantock stood with his papa as I walked around the room, looking, touching. On the wall was painted the word 'Allgebh' in the simplest of letters. In the centre stood the figures of a lion and a lioness, her stomach swollen with her babies. They faced a double gate fashioned out of wood and painted the colour of ivory. On the wall near to the gate, branches had been placed with fabric blossoms attached, as well as bees and butterflies. Stepping closer I was able to smell that the blossoms had been soaked in some aromatic. I reached out to touch them, and even now the perfume remains on my fingertips, a soft muskiness. Hanging from one of the branches was a silver seal bearing the head of a lion. The room exuded a feeling of love and harmony. I felt such serenity that I lost all track of time, I just stood, breathing in the delicious scent of blossoms, imagining I stood in a spring garden.

I then invited Uncle Vateson to our sitting-room for tea and he accepted. I could tell he found it cosy and comfortable – a blazing fire, while outside the rain thrashed the windows. We spoke of the Tenth Room and of the Eleventh and of how in the spring I will be even more involved in the Work, for when Crantock and his papa go up to the Carn I am to accompany them.

I confess, this all remains somewhat strange to me. I understand so very little. But the Work will continue and I am devoted to its success. One day, some years from now, the Work will be complete and we shall have obtained the twenty-eight keys to the Mansions of the Moon, and this will lead us to the secret hiding place of the Fragment of the True Cross. Then, everything will be explained.

December 24th   Christmas Eve. We have had such a lovely day. We both had a little too much wine. How sweet my Crantock is when this happens! He recited lines from poems as if they were his very own, singing jumbled songs. Then we went to bed, he brushed my hair, and insisted on undressing me, taking an age with each hook and button, but would not let me assist him. Then we lay together for a very long time and when we were joined it was sleepy and gentle and it reminded me of our first times together, which now seem a lifetime ago. We fell asleep together and he is still sleeping.

I am so happy and yet so sad – I long for the day when I am truly his Wife, only then will everything be perfect. And I believe that this day is not too far off. For there is something which I have not written here, a secret that cannot remain a secret for too much longer. Next year – oh my, how my hand is shaking as I write this – next year we shall have our own small one. I shall be a mama. I have missed my monthly illness three, if not four times. Two weeks ago I crept to Aunt Azenor's cottage to find some reading matter on the subject and have been confirmed in my suspicions.

Telling Mama and Papa will be the most difficult of all – but they will understand my happiness, of that I have no doubt. Did Mama not say the very last time I saw her that she wished a love such as Aunt Azenor's for me too?

And when they are told, we shall be married. Sooner rather than later, I do not doubt.

December 25th   Christmas Day. My darling has gone off to the New House. His papa came to collect him. He did not wish to go and only did so because I promised to come in a little while. He kept saying, Edith, come, and pulling at my hand. I was most upset and cried after he had gone.

We exchanged our presents this morning. He gave me a small pendant set with three ruby stones. I gasped when I opened it – who helped him to choose this for me? And my gift to him was so dull in comparison – I feel so unworthy of him at times.

December 26th   It is either very late on Christmas Day or already Monday. My head is splitting apart – I have been sick twice. We have argued as we have not done before. In the late afternoon he returned on his own, about three-ish, surely I remember the clock striking three? I had been trying to keep busy, not to mope, when I heard the door downstairs slam, vibrating through the tower. I ran down to see a soaked-to-the-skin Crantock. He screamed at me, Edith, stay! Over and over again. I still feel sick from the sound of his voice. I have never seen him so furious – his face was plumb-black with rage; when I tried to calm him he became very calm and ran past me to our room where, without a word, he began to smash things. His silence was worse than his screaming. I burst into tears and pleaded with him to stop. Eventually he did, but then he began to rock and to hit his head with his hands the way he has not done for months and months, sobbing. I did not know what to do. I stepped towards him and his voice became higher, more terrifying. Then suddenly his papa and Nectan were there and he stopped his noise and stared at them with such hatred. It was terrifying. He did not look at me, but ran from the room and has now locked himself in the Tenth Room.

Nectan is still here – to make sure that I am safe. It seems that after Crantock arrived at the New House he kept asking when I would come, going to the window to watch for me. He would not eat and insisted on waiting, and then he became distraught and could not be calmed. He went so far as to strike his mama. It is the first time he has ever done this. It is too awful. Poor Aunt Azenor. He then went to my old room, thinking perhaps to find me there, and afterwards he made his way here. He seems to believe he was taken from me deliberately and almost certainly that I colluded in this. He thinks I wanted him to leave, to be taken away from me. He thinks I sent him away. Oh God, I know it! I should never have agreed. It is my fault. We have not been parted for a single moment since we moved here. And the morning had been so wonderful – he was so tender – and I made us tea and jam and bread and then we had our presents. My lovely pendant that he placed around my neck. And when I kissed him he tasted of summer strawberry jam. It was perfect. And now I have ruined it.

December 28th   If there is such a place as hell on earth then this is it. Crantock refuses to know me – he is entirely lost in his own world. It is as if he does not even recognise me, so completely has he withdrawn. This morning I forced him to look at me. I held his face. He did not struggle, but it was as if – I looked deeply into his eyes – and – No. I can hardly write it.

The bond between us is severed. He has gone from me. His love – our love – he no longer loves me. And he doesn't seem unhappy – he just seems – he is like a stranger. Or perhaps I mean he looks at me as if I were a stranger to him. It is a knife in my heart. I am too pained to cry. I feel dead inside – I feel as if I am dead but that my body has forgotten to lie down.

Later. But I am not dead. I am alive. I am having a child, our child. That is what is left to me. I must look after myself for the sake of our child.

1888

January 2nd   Winnow is here. And the Merry-dog. They arrived the day after Christmas and stayed. Every night I tuck Winnow into his nest and each morning I awake to find him curled beside me. They are both with me all day – and if they were not I think I would go mad.

January 3rd   We have been in the garden collecting a basket of dead things – small birds for the most part, downed in last night's storm. Poor frozen things. I've left bread and seed out for the others so they do not starve.

January 4th   Sleep is thick and black. Awaken tired, unrested, craving more sleep. Winnow is beside me – my small sweetheart, how much he resembles Crantock. Our child will have such a face. Soon – soon, I must tell them of this.

January 5th   Winnow holds my hand and sings me songs, his eyes too sad for such a Smallie. He knows. He understands. As does my Merry-dog.

January 6th   Today I realised that I could see Crantock through one of the windows, standing in the place near to where he fell and cracked his skull. Does he remember? He stood there on the dangerous steps watching the water. I watched his beloved face. How I long for you. Do you ever think of me?
   What a question. Of course you do not think of me.

January 7th   Each day passes silently – the noiselessness of being unloved.

January 8th   A dreadful dream, sickening, my own screaming woke me, I can barely stop my shaking – Winnow – I am frightening him. I must be calm.

Later. The dream – the cave, water dripping, puddles slick, a frightening place, a dark dark – and going into this dark, I must find my way, fingers guiding me along wet-slimed walls, walking until I am too tired to walk, asleep on my feet, waking, seeing a dot of light ahead, growing larger as I walk towards it. The last cave. My darling – on his knees, naked. A man whose face I cannot see has his hands pressed over Crantock's ears, rubbing them up and down. I move forward, a four-eyed cat appears in front of me, in each eye a great fire burns. It hisses at me, baring fangs, tail lashing the air, crouching low on its haunches it leaps at me, I hold out my hand screaming, No.

Later still. I have informed Uncle Vateson of the dream – we are in agreement that Crantock is in danger. We do not yet know how to help him. We must go carefully or we could worsen the situation. And I must protect myself and our child. But against what?

January 9th Fell asleep as the world began to lighten. It is now midday. Another dream of the cave – just as I enter the darkness it floods. I try to outrun the deepening water but cannot and just as I reach the last cave the water sucks me down, under. Then I float and am able to see that everything has remained the same, the cat, the man rubbing his hands over Crantock's ears. In a corner I can see my darling's armour, his sword in its scabbard, in the centre of which is a pendant shape decorated with three rubies. Then I awaken.

I know now what I must do.

January 16th It is over. It is done. It is over and done with. One week ago I informed Uncle Vateson of what I wished to do. He did not flinch in assisting me.

Last Tuesday, one week ago tomorrow, I took a very strong sleeping draught and lay on our bed. Sleep overtook me quickly but the dream was not so fast. The plan was for Uncle Vateson to watch at my bedside; I had explained the danger I believed I faced. The room had been made secure, lamps and candles lit in every corner, the fire banked high for warmth, amulets at the windows and doorway to safeguard us.

When finally the dream began, it was as usual – the walk beneath the sea and then up to the cave. I trod carefully, quietly, until I came to the last cave, and there I stood watching as I had watched before. I saw the man covering and rubbing Crantock's ears. The cat slept, all four eyes were closed. In a corner I could see Crantock's sword which I knew I had to reach, but hardly had I taken a step than the cat awoke and noticed me. It did not move but fixed me with its stare, and so afraid was I that I could not move. How long I remained transfixed by the fires of Hell in that animal's eyes, I know not. My voice found itself before my limbs and I cried out – You must stop this Evil. The cat stood and stretched and opened its mouth in a wide yawn so I saw its pointed fangs. Then it sat, gazing at me sleepily, raising its right paw to lick, then using it to clean its whiskers – and all the while fixing me with its fiendish gaze. I felt enraged – such rage and hatred as I have never known – and I screamed and ran for the sword. But the animal reached out its paw and knocked me down. Almost insensible from the blow I remained lying there and watched the cat stand and stretch before it padded to where I lay. With one hand I gripped hold of the pendant I wore at my throat and with the other I slipped from my belt a carving knife which I thrust into the animal's paw. I had no expectation of succeeding with so small a weapon, but I had delivered an unexpected blow, and while the animal recoiled with pain, I moved for the sword. No sooner had I stood and lifted it with both hands than the cat contorted its face, hissing at me, its spittle burning my skin. But it did not pounce. Rather, it teased me, pacing to and fro, spitting, hissing. I realised that it might stay this way for days, until my energy had ebbed and I was too weak to hold the sword. I prayed, saying, Our Father, Who Art In Heaven, Hallowed Be Thy Name, Thy Kingdom Come, Thy Will Be Done, and at these words the cat sat on its haunches and began to purr – huge swelling sounds that grew louder, echoing throughout the cave, so loud that my ears began to throb, painfully, and I longed to cover them, though to do so would mean dropping the sword. Instead, I stopped praying, and in an instant the hideous noise stopped and the cat leapt. I impaled it – or rather it impaled itself, because it had expected me to lift the sword and swing at its neck or head, but I could not lift it that high because of the weight. The cat had destroyed itself by rushing on to the lowered blade. I collapsed on to my knees – weak with fear – weak with the sheer unexpectedness of release. I looked to where Crantock had been and as I did so the dark figure lifted his hands up and away from him and in that movement disappeared entirely, as if he had not existed at all, and with this my darling's body crumpled to the ground. I watched as he fell. I was too late to save him. And as I remained on my knees staring at his lifeless form, knowing that there was nothing more I could do, at the very same time I was watching myself stand and run towards him. I became two separate beings, both of them me. One self I saw go to his side and lift his body to cradle it, rubbing his limbs as if in the hope of bringing them to life, weeping, the tears, my tears, falling on to his face. And my other self I saw stagger to her feet and move to the entrance of the cave, watching, thinking, He is dead, he is gone from me. This 'me' turned away and walked until she found the stairway that led to the door of our room. There she entered, able to see the destruction that time had wrought – the rotted bed-hangings, torn, falling – and went to the window and saw that the tide had gone out farther than ever before, uncovering rocks that held the skeletons of long dead animals and the carcasses of shipwrecks. She opened the window and the breeze that came was sweet and welcoming and she leaned forward into it, and farther forward. Her hand reached up to clasp the pendant at her throat and as her fingers closed around it she heard his voice say, Edith, stay. She closed her eyes and began to weep, and when she opened them found herself back in the cave, cradling his body in her arms, and through her tears thought she saw his lips move, and in that movement saw the shape of her name.

Uncle Vateson tells me that I slept for more than forty hours, and during this time I spoke and stood and paced the room. At one point a livid mark appeared on my face as if I had been struck. He stayed at my side the entire time, vigilant. Towards the end, just before waking, I got up from the bed and opened the window, standing there for some time. When I leaned too far out, Uncle Vateson restrained me, shocked at my strength and the difficulty he found in stopping me fall. When Crantock appeared in the doorway I began to weep and allowed myself to be led back to the bed.

For the next two days I was weak, drifting in and out of sleep, beside me, Crantock, Uncle Vateson, Winnow and Aunt Azenor. Slowly, slowly, it filtered into my heart and soul and mind that he had not left me, that he continued to live, that he was at my side.

January 17th   I have told them of our child to be. Aunt Azenor wept. They agree we must be married, sooner rather than later. I have written to Papa and Mama asking their permission to marry. Uncle Vateson has written as well. I will admit that I am sick with nerves.

Later. Crantock and our child – that is all that matters to me.

The following pages had been torn from elsewhere and tucked inside. They were undated.

What prison is this? I don't remember. The walls are real beneath my fingertips. It is a real place.

Last night you came to me, my darling, just as you have come to me so many times. I awoke & saw your smiling face. Edith, you said, your voice unmistakable – still.

If only –

How many times have I written those words – if only?

Oh, my dearest Crantock – if only.

If only I had known that they were our last weeks together I would have written every detail. I would have written enough words to fill a book about each & every day. But I was too happy being with you. It was warm for late March, for early April, the swathes of bluebells & primroses & wild garlic & the fruit trees so fastly flowering into blossom in the spring sun. Such beauty – the splendrousness of God's handwriting, your papa said to me.

And you – your face & your smile. Your skin near to my skin.

You & only you after all these years.

You & only you –

And I can't remember – can't or won't – can't or won't? I don't know.

I can't write for crying – why did they save me, for what purpose, when I wanted to die? Could they see that to keep me alive was a greater punishment – possibly so – make me live with my loss?

At least – at least – here there is no pretence, no falseness.

I sat drowsing in the sunshine, day-dreaming of our child, of you. I turned, opening my eyes, expecting your face, your lips near to mine, & that feeling of falling, far & fast into the blueness of your eyes. Only it wasn't you – it's – not – I'm on the edge of a cliff & the blue is the horizon where sea & sky merge. Do I know this place? I look inland – yes, I know this place. I know Penfeidr like the back of my hand. I look up to the window where our room is – & I see her standing there. I see myself standing there dressed in black. And this cannot be right because I cannot be there & here at the same time – but I can, because this has happened before, only that time I was asleep and this time I am awake, surely. And I say, No – I shout it – the shout carrying to this woman, myself, who turns her head to look at me.

Looking at me – holding her hands out to me –

And then I'm running, hard & fast, fast & hard, I can hear the wind, or is it the sound of my own breathing? I reach the stairs, ascending, even when I stumble & fall I'm quickly back on my feet. Then – I'm there, stood in the doorway & she – me – I have my back to the room & you are seated in your favourite chair, smiling. I go to you & take your hand but you won't look at me, so I turn your face towards me, but you're tired, too tired, your eyelids are closing, shutting me out, but still I have hold of your hand.

But then hands are pulling me away, so that my hand loses its grip of your hand. They're taking me from you. I'm fighting & shouting & screaming, if I make enough noise you'll hear me, you'll open your eyes, you'll take my hand again. Edith, you'll say, Edith, stay.

But it was you who left me, Crantock – it was you who left me . . .

Cwm-yr-Eglwys, Pembrokeshire

October 1934

The past week's weather had been perfect. Such perfect October days, warm and clear with gossamer floating in through the open windows; leaves yellowing and redding and eddying earthwards. Squirrels rushing up trees and down with the sound of continual birdsong. The world so alive, so happy, as if it were spring. From the top of the Carn Mardie could see clearly in every direction. Staring down at the russeting treetops of Penfeidr she unscrewed the hipflask and took a mouthful of whisky. She understood now why her mother had come back here. After all these years Mardie was finally able to understand. She took another sip and then lifted her face to the sunshine, closing her eyes. During the past days she had driven to all the nearby places her mother had written about, seeing them afresh, seeing them through her eyes.

But Mardie still did not know what to make of the young girl her mother had been. A girl had come here and fallen in love and – and then what? What had happened? She had always considered her mother to be thoroughly cold-hearted and incapable of love. Mardie didn't like her mother's love for Crantock. She preferred to think of her mother as dead inside. Thinking about it too much made Mardie feel anxious, so she kept herself in motion, driving and stopping, driving and stopping, longing for Grand to talk to, knowing all the while the uselessness of such longing.

Half a century had passed and the landscape remained almost unchanged except for the occasional new cottage. While driving she had occupied her mind with banal comparisons – this would have been smaller, this would have been bigger; this would not have been there, nor that. She dithered, along lanes, along pathways. In the places that she stopped, she said their names to herself, tasting them in her mouth. Pen Cafnau, Gethsemene, Nevern, Babylon, Temple Gate, Fynnongroes, Brynberian, Mynydd Preseli, Carn Arthur, Pontfaen, Dinas Cross, Dinas Sands, Dinas Island, Dinas Head, Cwm-yr-Eglwys, Soar Hill, Newport, Newport Sands, Afon Nyfer, Berry Hill Wood, Carn Ingli, Constantinople, Pentre Ifan. As well as all the cwms and cairns and carns and fords and springs and standing stones. As

Mardie listened to the sound of these names spoken in her own voice, she imagined her mother doing the same fifty years ago.

She had not seen her mother for almost two weeks now; she did not want to see her. Yet the first place she had gone after reaching the ending of the diary was to Penfeidr. She had parked outside the gates and walked along the winding drive, her feet crunching conkers, to stop and stare at where the New House had stood for generations before being razed by fire. A fire that had burned for three days, Grand had once told her. Mardie had spent that afternoon wandering the old estate, seeking out the spots that now resonated with the experiences of a girl called Edith. The orchards, which were still tended by her mother, were heavy with fruit awaiting picking. The pond, where the Vateson girls and her mother had swum together naked, was much larger than Mardie had expected. Much deeper, reed-banked on one side, with the water's slow surface gathering a layer of fallen leaves. Azenor Vateson's cottage was locked and shuttered and possibly had been ever since her death. Then there was the Old House itself with which Mardie was already quite familiar, the moat, the bridge, the gatehouse, and across the sweep of lawn the splendid old building, part tower, part hall; but all slightly decrepit now. This was where her mother had lived with Crantock. This was where her mother lived now. Finally she found the chapel, the door grating a little as she opened it, and looked at the wall-paintings and the stone-cold effigies of Brychan ap Brychan and his wife Agnes de Civray, who, sent from the court of Henry III, had come in search of a Fragment of the True and Holy Cross.

What am I supposed to think of such stories? Mardie murmured, frowning. Am I supposed to believe them? She brooded over the instances of what her mother had called her 'connexions' with Crantock. During the last three years she had witnessed her mother's seizures, when she appeared to go into a trance-like state and talk as if in conversation with someone, smiling, even laughing. On some occasions Mardie had felt that her mother could see someone that she could not. Perhaps, just as Mardie herself was able to see and talk with Ben. Only with her mother there was something eerie that left Mardie feeling nervous and ill at ease. It was almost as if her mother came alive only then, whereas the rest of the time she seemed somehow soulless and dead.

In the Vateson Chapel, Mardie stood in front of the memorial stone reading their names. Those Vatesons whom her mother had loved were all gone now, each and every one of them. She stepped into the graveyard, the autumnal sunshine warm on her head, the gossamer drifting to drape itself on her hair and on headstones, on grass and branches. She wandered until she located the one she wanted most to see, the one inscribed: Crantock Vateson, 19th April 1864 – 7th April 1888. Her mother had stood here too. But Mardie could not think of them as the same person. Her mother was not the Edith who had written the diaries.

What happened to you? Mardie startled herself by speaking aloud. She reached out and felt the rough headstone beneath her hand. This was where her mother would want to be buried, she was certain. Suddenly Mardie thought of her father buried thousands of miles away in another country, alone, with no one to tend his grave. Her heart trembled at the idea of her father lying there so very far away. They were all so far apart; father in Japan, Ben on the Isle of Wight and Grand's ashes in India, while Uncle Reggie had been buried beneath the rubble of San Francisco's earthquake. There is nowhere for me to go, she said to herself, to stand and remember. Unlike you, mother, who can, and probably do, come here every day.

Mardie felt the old familiar hatred of her mother rush through her, felt it rush into her mouth with a taste like bile. If her mother had had a child with Crantock Vateson, would Grand have been able to keep such a great secret? Would she really never have told her if that was what had happened? Mardie thought not. So she had written to Uncle Robert requesting that her grandmother's journals be sent to her in the hope of finding some answers to her remaining questions.

Opening the first diary to see her grandmother's handwriting shocked Mardie. She felt giddy, then sick, and sat clutching the book to her stomach. She pushed to her feet, poured a stiff whisky, lifting the glass mouthward with a shaking hand that knocked the glass against her teeth as she drank. She poured herself another, and sat back down, caressing the leather-binding of the diary. She lifted the book to her cheek, stroking the cover as if it were her grandmother's hand. She lost track of the time she sat crying, knowing that she was not crying for her grandmother but for herself. Crying for those years of memories, mourning herself as she had been, because that girl was dead, she had gone with Grand. Mardie believed that when someone died they took you with them; afterwards you were a different person, and could only be different, because they were not there to show you who you were. And she also cried for the woman that she had since become. She was a drunk, she knew that, she saw it every morning in the mirror, in the bloodshot eyes, the puffy face, and in hands that had developed a tremor.

Finally, when she did begin, the diaries were remarkably easy reading, despite her grandmother's elaborate hand. Names were written in capital letters so it was clear when references to Mardie's mother were being made. The curious thing was that there was, after all, so very little mention of Edith or the other children. Each day's entry began with the weather, followed by a lengthy description of the previous night's dreams. Then there were long quotations from books and poems; her grandmother evinced a fascination with death, the more morbid, the more macabre the better. The more personal entries recorded conversations and local news and gossip.

Mardie found the first mention of her mother at the beginning of 1887:

> I have a received a brief letter from EDITH, if such a morsel can be graced with such a name. It is most unfortunate that she lacks any skill in her descriptive powers. I can only imagine this to be from MR PORCH's side, for it certainly does not belong to us BAGEHOTs.

The next was not until late February:

> After some weeks of silence I have finally received another note from EDITH. She implores my presence at Penfeidr. The house is in a confusion because the Idiot Boy has succeeded in cracking his skull open upon some steps. Truly, I cannot help but think that it would be a blessing in disguise if it were the will of God to take the Child to His Own Side. Of course I must go there, to support poor dear AZENOR through her time of trouble, although quite how I am to tear myself away from all that I must do here, I know not. I must take the time to travel, and goodness knows how many days I must be there before returning. This could not have occurred at a more difficult time, but if I must go, I must, and Edgarley must manage without me.

A day later:

> EDITH has written assuring me that my presence is not required after all. The Boy is taking small steps on the path to recovery. I will admit that it is some small measure of relief to me that I do not need to go Penfeidr. When I am a little less occupied in my time I shall do so, and have written to say that I shall visit with them as soon as I am possibly able to.

Then, in an entry in April:

> I continue to be most vexed by the lack of a letter from EDITH. This situation is entirely unsatisfactory and I have been forced to write to her yet again informing her of my vexation. I have written that I find her inability to correspond with her Mother, despite my repeated appeals, not only undutiful but verging on wilful disobedience. Her indocility will not be tolerated. She will not defy or disregard me in such a manner. I have threatened her with removal from Penfeidr if she continues unheedful of my wish for a letter each week.

And:

> As I thought, she has complied, but with such defiance in her words! Who would have thought it of my EDITH?

And:

> EDITH is respecting my request for more regular correspondence and her letters are full of anecdotes attesting to her pleasure in the smallest children. Oh, what a fine Wife and Mother she will become. It hardly seems so long past that I worried daily at her obsession with horses and dogs, fearing that there was something unnatural and unfeminine in her temperament, and that she was too much like her Father. My frettings were unnecessary, it would seem, and I do suspect that my dear AZENOR has played no small part in my child's domestication.

Mardie could not help laughing aloud at this idea of her mother as being domesticated. *What a fine Wife and Mother . . .* Her smile solidified into a grimace. How she had dreaded her mother as a child. The sound of her footsteps approaching had been enough for Mardie to shrink inside herself, to become noiseless and less visible. Her mother's rage and cruelty had ruled the house. Even the servants feared her moods. Mardie could not remember exactly what had occurred during her mother's rages beyond the feeling of nauseated fear they had induced in her. Not even the sound of her father's raised voice beating her mother's voice into eventual submission had helped to ease this anxiety. Now Mardie looked apprehensively towards the door as if her mother might be standing there.

Why did I come here, she asked the empty doorway. There is nothing to know, and if there is, what good can possibly come of knowing it? Father is dead. Knowing why or how he died won't bring him back. Even as she said these words she thought, Yes, people die, but there is much more to it than that. If he hadn't died when I was five and a half, would I be sat here? If he hadn't died then Ben would not have been at school in Cowes and died from meningitis. And Uncle Reggie would not have gone to San Francisco and been killed in the earthquake.

She could clearly remember the last time she had seen her father. He had looked so sad and lonely propped up against a dozen pillows in the middle of the big bed. She had clambered up to sit beside him and, folding her legs beneath her, had sung him the Mary Pickles song that always made him smile. But he had not smiled. He had continued to look at her so gravely that she said that he had been sick for much too long now and it was time to get up. This had brought a little smile to his mouth, and so she had licked her fingers and smoothed both sides of his big thick moustache with spittle, just as she had often done in the past. Even when she heard her mother call her a disgusting child, she had continued licking and smoothing. She was safe from Mummy with Daddy and Uncle Reggie in the room. When finished, she kissed his mouth and cheeks and forehead and asked would they go to Tokyo soon. He had nodded, agreeing, she had thought. But the next day, in tears, Uncle Reggie had taken her on his lap and told her that Daddy was dead. For months afterwards she had continued to ask where he was, how he was, and when was she going to see him? How many years had it taken her to comprehend that dead meant never again? Perhaps, she thought now, I still do not understand, not really.

She looked down at her grandmother's handwriting, feeling the smooth paper beneath her hand. Then she continued to turn the pages, eyes seeking the word Edith, written in capitals, but the only further mentions were cursory. There was very little more until she opened the diary for the following year, 1888, which began abruptly with the word September, but no specific date:

I know not how to write of the past months. I have walked through the Valley of the Shadow of Death and I have feared Evil. Yes, I have feared it and gained no comfort from God. God is not just. God is not merciful. God is not Infinite in His Wisdom. Or how could He allow such suffering to take place?

Earlier in the year my child lost her Reason, much as she did in the Spring of '86. In the last week of April I received an urgent letter from Azenor Vateson. How bitterly do I regret that I ever called her Friend. No, it is even worse than that, for in my heart I considered her as my only Sister and as such entrusted to her the care of my only Daughter. How wrong I was to do so, how very wrong. It can only be with eternal regret that I look back upon the deep affection and esteem with which I regarded Mrs Vateson, for I was entirely mistaken in my judgement of her character, of that there is no doubt.

Her letter requested my immediate presence at Penfeidr. Edith, she wrote, was ill beyond explanation and needed to be removed to a place where she could not be a danger to herself or to anyone else, especially the small Vateson children. Perturbed in my heart and mind by the unfeeling and unfriendly words I encountered in this letter, I went straight away to Penfeidr, with Mr Porch to accompany me. Shockingly, we arrived to find the situation just as it had been described, if not, indeed, worse. Edith's mental condition was extremely and excessively disordered, and her appearance – suffice it to say I barely recognised her as my own child. Her clothes were torn and dirty and she had – oh, how it pains me to write this – she had taken to her hair with a pair of scissors so that the scalp was displayed and on her hands were sores from, from – I cannot write of it – and such vile language she spoke at the sight of her Father and myself. Although I had nursed her through her previous illness, never in all my life have I seen a human being in such a shocking condition, and almost entirely bereft of all dignity. Her poor Father is haunted by what he saw and heard on that day and shall continue to be so for some long while, I do fear.

We were informed by the Vatesons that the balance of my child's mind had been overwhelmed when their child Crantock died of a sudden. This tragedy apparently was caused by a swelling on the brain from a fall the previous year that finally ruptured. When Edith came upon him – for it is she who found him – she at first thought him to be resting. When she attempted to wake him and realised that she could not she became hysterical and would not be consoled. In the days that followed her own state deteriorated daily until we were summoned to remove her.

However, I am convinced that her mind had been gradually weakening for some many months prior to her illness. It transpires that the poor child had come to believe that she and Crantock had an especial method of communication during which he told her of conversations he held with Angels! Alas this belief was actively encouraged by Brychan Vateson, whom I have long considered to be among the most vile men ever to draw breath. So they were permitted to be left alone for hours on end – that idiot child in the care of my daughter, as if she were no more than a nursemaid. I have reread her letters to me from this period, and while there is scant mention of Crantock Vateson, I do not and cannot doubt that she became exceedingly and excessively attached to the boy.

If only I had known. If only I had not been so occupied in the daily events at Edgarley and gone to visit Penfeidr more regularly. But as I know only too well it is worse than futile to wish the past to be different. Nothing is to be gained by dwelling on what might or might not have been, and so I shall not.

We returned home with her, a long and arduous journey assisted by a nurse and a Doctor. Once here, we summoned Doctors eminent in this field from London and even one from Edinburgh. Their prognoses were unrelentingly grim and, as if in concert, they opined that unless she were removed from us and placed in the correct hands there could be very little hope of healing her mind. From the very first suggestion of this, I refused to comply. Instead we took detailed instruction in her care from Dr Longstreete, who has treated many such cases, both here and on the Continent, further agreeing to the necessity of four nurses to assist us.

Since then five months have passed, and even now every part of me revolts at the memory of the torments it was necessary to inflict upon her to aid her mind in healing. These days she is quiet for the most part, except for inexplicable and sudden rages when the foulness of her tongue is shocking. But at least she is no longer tied to her bed and has not been so for eight whole weeks. This is progress indeed. And she is begun this past month to eat of her own accord. The forcing of food was something I could never bear to witness. Only Cousin Louisa was ever brave enough to assist the nurses with this appalling task.

I am no longer the woman I was at the beginning of this year. I could not have continued without my dear Cousins May and Louisa who, even when my own courage failed, persevered. My faithful old Tizzy, what would I have done without her? She has soothed me in her arms since I was a baby, she knows me better than anyone, and it is she who has been my most devoted mainstay. My Husband has suffered as only a man can, with a brave and silent fortitude, but he is become aged in a way I would never have thought to see. I do surmise that he sometimes wishes that our Daughter had died rather than be forced to experience the complete degradation this collapse of her mind has occasioned. He has not said this, but I firmly believe it to be true. The poor man, I would never have thought to pity him so in all my days.

As to the future, I am assured by Dr Longstreete that Edith is on her way to recovery. He sees no reason why she should not eventually be returned to full health. In fact, he has said that a normal life for her as Wife and Mother is to be encouraged, and as soon as possible. But how can this be? What type of man would wish for union with a girl who is as vulnerable and, I shall be blunt, damaged as she? I do not believe her marriageable. A simple and quiet life at Edgarley with her Father and myself is for the best. On some days it is as if the Daughter that I knew and loved is returned. But for the most part she is a stranger to me. At times she sits and whispers, as if in conversation with another, smiling all the while. This is her gentle aspect, whereas her other betrays a capacity for malevolence and malice and physical cruelty that is beyond belief. It is almost as if

There, the entry abruptly ended.

That her mother had gone mad did not surprise Mardie at all. But there was too much missing. What had happened to the child she had been carrying?

Mardie picked up her mother's diary and reread the last few pages. At some point in January 1888, Brychan Vateson and her mother had written to Edgarley asking for consent for her marriage to Crantock. There was no mention at all of this in her grandmither's diary. What then had happened between January and April? Almost four months were unaccounted for.

Sullenly she kicked the fireguard, the jolt dislodging a piece of wood and showering sparks up the chimney. Grand, you've let me down, she said. Do you really expect me to believe that this is all that you wrote during that period? You, who wrote reams every day? She flung her grandmother's diary to the floor. I'm going to ask mother myself, that's what I'm going to do. Then she shivered, immediately drained of bluff and bluster. Please understand, Grand, I need to know what else happened. She shivered again, and caught sight of Ben. It was the first time she had seen him for days. Her voice shook as she said, I have to know, don't you? But he just looked back at her unresponsively with the sad expression he had sometimes. She put on her coat and hat and gloves and then poured several short whiskies, downing them quickly, one after the other. But they did not ease the tightness in her aching chest.

She sat in the motor, uncertain of how she managed to get there. Opening the glove box to remove the small bottle of whisky hurt her hands to such a degree that she had difficulty unscrewing the cap. She looked at her right-hand fingers, afraid that the ring finger was broken, so swollen was it. Nursing this hand tenderly in her lap, she filled her mouth with spirit, only to spit it out of the open door a moment later. She gasped for air, making an animal sound of distress, so intense was the burning pain inside her mouth. Her tongue gingerly probed. At least none of her teeth had been loosened although she could taste blood. She hardly had the time to think I'm going to be sick, before she was, and afterwards leaned back against the seat, feeling too wretched to cry. Uppermost in her mind was getting home and, once there, finding an explanation to offer Mrs Palmer. She sat up, looking into the rear-view mirror. The little smears of blood near her nostrils she wiped at with her licked finger, but the swelling and already bruising cheekbone and eye-socket she could do nothing about. She couldn't focus her mind to think of anything except how desperately she needed to be at home and lying down.

She switched the engine on, careful not to jolt her hand, and set off very slowly, realising that the vision in her right eye was not at all clear. As she drove she thought over what had happened.

On arriving at Penfeidr she had parked in her usual place and then gone in search of her mother, finding her in the orchard, just as she had suspected she would. She stood watching her fill a small basket with pears. On a nearby cart similar baskets stood, filled to the brim. Her mother walked past Mardie without even looking at her, then brusquely asked her what she wanted.

Well, mother, did you have a child with Crantock the idiot boy or not? Mardie's voice had risen with each word. Grandmother never spoke of it, so maybe you made it all up. She told me that you went off your head and that the Vatesons asked her to take you away. Mardie laughed, nervously, savagely. Her mother's expression had not changed at all. Then, without any warning, she turned and struck at Mardie's face with both hands, again and again, before Mardie thought to raise her hands to protect herself. She remembered this from her childhood, her mother's sudden attacks. But then the thought came to her that she wasn't a child any more, she didn't have to stand there. And so she ran. She ran, as she had not been able to as a child because her mother was bigger and faster, and did not stop running until she reached where she had parked the car.

Now, she barely had time to get through her front door before Mrs Palmer appeared in the hall. Why, Miss Carew, she said, you've hurt yourself! She frowned in a way that filled Mardie with loathing before adding, You've not crashed your motor car, have you? Mardie swallowed, still able to taste blood at the back of her throat. No, Mrs Palmer, I took a tumble, on the Carn, and then she rushed past Mrs Palmer to the kitchen, to retch watery bile into the sink. Mrs Palmer was immediately alongside her. You poor woman, you have upset your insides, haven't you? Let's lie you down near the fire, and I'll give your face a tending.

Mardie did as she was told and soon felt the soothing coolness of antiseptic spirits gently dabbed on her fingers and cheekbone. My goodness, Miss Carew, it is a mean bruise that you're going to have there. I dare say it will look as if someone has given you a black eye. Mardie met Mrs Palmer's gaze, but could see no spite reflected there.

Do you know Penfeidr? Mardie asked shortly.

Mrs Palmer smiled, to reveal a fine set of awful false teeth. Of course I know Penfeidr. I worked there as a girl, during the summers and early autumn, just as my brothers and sisters did. Why do you ask? Mardie offered her a half-truth, saying, I'm acquainted with Edith Porch. She used her mother's maiden name as it was how her mother preferred to be known. In fact, Mardie continued, I was going to go to Penfeidr before I slipped on the Carn. Mrs Palmer pursed her lips before asking, Was Miss Edith expecting you? I can very easily get a message to her so that she don't worry about where you are.

Mardie responded quickly, No, no, she wasn't expecting me, not at all. But you know Miss Edith, do you? Oh yes, Mrs Palmer smiled again. I remember Miss Edith from when I was a girl. When she first came to Penfeidr, I was, oh, eleven or twelve. Is she a friend of your family? Mardie shook her head as she replied, Her mother knew my grandmother. Mrs Palmer sat back on her heels. I remember seeing Miss Edith's mother one year when she came, quite a grand English lady she was. Very erect and proper and beautifully dressed. Mrs Palmer stood up. I'll make you a poultice to help take the swelling down and a nice thick coffee, just as you like it, with a topping of whisky, and a sandwich or two, to settle your stomach.

When she eventually returned with the tray, Mardie was ready for something to eat, although her head and face and hand still throbbed. As Mrs Palmer made to leave, Mardie said, Do stay,

Mrs Palmer, I would very much like to hear a little more about Penfeidr. I've heard that it was idyllic. At least that is how Miss Edith has spoken of it. Mardie looked at Mrs Palmer guilelessly. Just imagine, she said, you were there as girl and you saw the New House before it burned down, and you knew the Vatesons. What a fascinating jumble of names they are, and so unusual, those Welsh names, they are so – so romantic. I've heard many of the stories, Mrs Palmer. Of angels on the Carn and the bleeding yew tree in Nevern churchyard and that somewhere nearby is the secret hiding place of a Fragment of the Cross.

Mrs Palmer stood looking down at her. Well, the Vateson family certainly believed it, she said. They searched for it long and hard. All the Vatesons going back and back in time. But they never found it. No one will. It isn't meant to be found. Mardie smiled, saying, Well, perhaps Miss Edith is searching for the hiding place, but she never talks about that. I think that she believes it to be a great Vateson family secret. Mrs Palmer raised her eyebrows. There are not many secrets hereabouts, Miss Carew, she replied.

What then about the rumour that Miss Edith married one of the Vateson boys? Mardie asked, trying to look unconcerned. Mrs Palmer answered immediately. No, no, they were betrothed, but Master Carantock was taken to God before they could be wed.

Why don't you sit down, Mrs Palmer? Mardie urged, looking at her with genuine interest for the first time since they had first met. Mrs Palmer remained standing as Mardie resumed. But wasn't he slightly, shall we say, backward? Surely Miss Edith's family would not allow her to become betrothed to a young man who was so – so afflicted. I mean, after all, Mrs Palmer, Miss Edith came from a very good family, that I do know, so would they have allowed their only daughter to – Mardie paused, looking down and lowering her voice. My grandmother said Miss Edith was carrying his child, so her parents were forced to agree to the marriage.

Oh, Miss Edith was definitely with child, Mrs Palmer said. And she was besotted with Master Carantock, everyone could see that, everyone. Mardie frowned, saying, But, Mrs Palmer,

Crantock Vateson was an imbecile, an idiot, so my grandmother said.

Carantock Vateson were simple, Miss Carew, but not simple enough not to get what he wanted time and time again. He weren't mute, he could speak when it suited him to. He were spoiled, spoiled rotten, indulged and coddled and favoured by his entire family. He had spiritualistic gifts, Miss Carew. He could summon the angels and they left messages with him. He always knew things that were going to happen before they did. And that is why he was let have his own way and run wild and if anyone tried to stop him, well woe betide them, for he could be mighty spiteful and cruel. All we girls were warned to be careful around Master Carantock, by our parents.

But – Mardie started to say, but Mrs Palmer had not finished.

We were warned not to be alone with him and if it so happened that we were, not to look into his eyes, because that was how he caught you: he would stare and once you looked, you couldn't look away. It was like being spell-caught. Mrs Palmer stopped and stood as if lost in thought.

You speak as if it happened to you? Mardie said.

Aye, but I were lucky. His sister Tybie disturbed us and I got away. But my second-cousin Lillas weren't so lucky and had to be married off.

Is that what happened to Miss Edith, Mardie asked, feeling sick in her stomach.

Master Carantock took to Miss Edith right from when she first arrived at Penfeidr, just as she took to him. Everyone saw it happening. And she was lovely, was Miss Edith. I can remember her quite clearly. She weren't that pretty, but she was kind-hearted and gentle. All the small Vateson children wrapped her around their little fingers. And Master Carantock. Well, she were lost in him, followed him around as if she were in a dream. Then when he was taken so sudden – they said his brain had ruptured – Miss Edith went mad with grief. And when her baby was born too early that sent her over the edge. She tried to harm herself, the poor girl, and they sent for her parents to come and take her away.

In the sudden silence the tick of the clock seemed exceptionally loud. Both women looked at it sitting on the mantelpiece and Mrs Palmer seemed to speak there rather than to Mardie. I wasn't surprised when she came back to make her home at the Old House. She's still touched by the grief of it all. You can see it in her. She is more with him than she is in the world of the living. My goodness, how she loved him. It was as plain to see as the nose on her face –

And he loved her, Mardie asked, Crantock loved her?

Mrs Palmer looked at her, smiling slyly. Yes, there's no doubt of that, but that didn't stop him from doing just as he pleased, if you know what I mean. There are more than a couple of folk here in the Preseli Hills that have the Vateson look about them.

Sungei Ujong, Malaya

&

Yokohama, Japan

1889–1896

1889

May 23rd I am married – for almost three weeks. In two days my husband & I sail for Singapore. From there we shall travel on to Sungei Ujong in the Malay Provinces, where he is to be Treasurer to the Resident.

I have had to stop writing for laughing – I caught sight of myself in the mirror – Mrs Walter Hallowell Carew. How I admire her composure. But then she is composed, isn't she – of layer upon layer of lies.

I am at Edgarley. I hardly know this place but I lived here, did I not? I have forgotten when. So long ago, I can scarce remember such a time. Penfeidr is my home. No – do not think of it – do not, must not, cannot – help me – not to – I miss you all so. Tell them, Crantock, my darling. Let them know that in my heart I am there & not here. Which is – where? Where am I – Edgarley, yes, Edgarley, I remember now.

Edgarley, the home of Mr & Mrs Albert Porch, their Sons & Daughter, their eldest child, who was recently married at St John's. She carried azaleas, you know, orange blossom held her veil & trimmed the bodice & train of her gown. Oh, it was such a lovely wedding! Then they honeymooned in Devon & Somerset. How very lovely. Yes, how lovely. But one cannot help thinking, I mean, one should not say it, of course, but what on earth does she see in him? I know, I do know what you mean – it's that revolting moustache, isn't it? Or is it his lips? They are always wet, have you noticed, slug-like, leaving a trail of moisture. Please, please, it does not bear thinking about. And he is huge – those thighs straining at his trousers & that chest – like a bull. How many chins does he have? Did you manage to count? Well, I would hardly call them chins they are just rolls of flesh becoming a neck, do you not agree? Oh yes, definitely, definitely. Love is blind, isn't it? No accounting for taste, now, is there, but surely she could have done better than – well, better than this?

But I have done better. She in the mirror knows that. She

knows that she is the fake. I do not love Walter & he knows – no more than he loves me. He wants a wife, with a small but decent income. He is hardly a catch, & he knows it. He is always ill. Recurring malaria, jaundice, liver problems &, on top of that, when he is a little older he is certainly going to be gouty. You can see it already. He's puffy, from too much heavy food & wine.

But what is she getting out of it then? Who knows, I certainly do not. Although I did hear she loved another & he left her. Aaaaaaah – I see.

No. You do not see at all. You are wrong. He did not leave her. He is with her still & will never leave her. He is her beloved & she is his betrothed.

Oh, my darling Crantock – you & only you. Where are you now? I am listening. Tell me you are with me. You are inside me. A part of me – yes – this I know.

And her? I look in the mirror. She is smiling a little. It softens her face which as a rule seems cold, superior, aloof. But her mind is elsewhere. Her mind is on her packing. She is leaving this place. She is escaping to the other side of the world. She is smiling. You knew that smile, Crantock. Oh, she has looked up, she has caught my eye. She loves you, Crantock, just as I love you, although there is not a clue of this in her face. Not a hint of what she feels. There never will be. She is no more than what she seems – a recent bride preoccupied with her upcoming ocean voyage. She is Mrs Walter Hallowell Carew. She is not Edith any more. She never will be again. Edith is at Penfeidr.

June 1st This is a prison – nowhere to escape to – every day the same – breakfast, morning coffee, luncheon, afternoon tea, sherry, dinner, more drinks. And in between, walking, bow to stern, port to starboard, walk, walk, walk off the food, walk of the rest-lessness, a caged animal, walking, pacing, no escape, nowhere quiet, no green secret places to hide & hold hands & tangle my fingers in your hair, your smile like sunlight, your laughter in my mouth. Just the boiled sea, swelling, heaving.

If only I could be seasick, at least then I could be alone.

And he loves it. But then, he would. The perpetual eating,

gorging himself meal after meal. Where does he put it? No wonder he is such a large fellow. Large! Large! He is immense – that stomach, like something swollen, about to burst open. Quite frankly, I think he is revolting. But she seems to be enjoying herself. I keep catching sight of her in windows & mirrors. She is always smiling, always charming, keeping the conversation flowing. She is lovely. She is, isn't she? She does not even seem to mind the bad weather. Out walking in the wind & rain & when not she is a treasure with the old girls, reading to them, or making up the extra place at Bridge. They always tell her how nice she looks. What a pretty dress! What a smart hat! And her hair, what a lovely colour, such a soft brown with flecks of gold in the sunlight. Where is Mrs Carew, they will ask, even if she is only five minutes late. And someone will say, Well, they are newlyweds, you know, & they will blush at memories of their own younger selves. If only they had known then what they have come to know now. If only – but one would not really want to go back, would one? I mean – after all. But here she is. Here is Mrs Carew & oh, oh, how lovely she looks as she sits & listens carefully, attentively, always asking the right question in exactly the right place.

June 2nd   There is no silence here – the wind rustling the seawater & washing out my ears – but it is better than their voices, anything is better than that today. Mrs Carew will not be up today – dear, dear, we do hope she is all right, that it is nothing too serious. No, she is merely a trifle under the weather. Well, do give her our regards. We hope to see her tomorrow. They whisper together, discreetly. Perhaps, already, you know, could be, it certainly could be, I had my first almost nine months to the day after the wedding, you know. But, I have heard – What, what? – that they do not share a cabin. No. Really? No, I must say that is news to me & I think I would have heard. But he has been ill. He is in the colonial service & was invalided home. Something to do with his liver, I think she said. Well, all I can say is lucky her. I mean, not having to, you know. Having her own cabin, being able to shut the door & sleep in peace.

June 3rd Oh, do look, here is Mrs Carew – as right as rain this morning, a little pale, but back with us. Make a space for her, my dear. My dear, how are you, are you well? We did miss you yesterday.

Crantock – what happened yesterday, your skin was so cold, like marble, and your skin is always so warm, almost feverish, beneath my fingers? What is it, my darling, tell me what is wrong, please tell me?

June 4th Every morning the shock of water, stretched & stretching between my Crantock & me. How many waves away are you now?

June 5th My cheerless heart –

June 6th What a tease she is – she can almost see them laughing at her although she does not look their way. The men like her. She is married, she is safe. She is not going to take their little flirtations to heart. She knows that it is just a game to idle away the time, to make one feel better, to stop thinking about all that seawater beneath one & being smack in the middle of it with no land in sight. And it does seem unnatural. Truly, legs were made to be on land and not like this. Although it is terribly safe, every-one says so, unless one falls, of course, slips between the railings or over them. She can see their expressions as she leans just a little too far over the side, hears their voices caution her.

But I will not let her fall – I will never allow it. Oh no. When I die I will be buried at Penfeidr. Crantock is waiting there for me. I cannot imagine it will be too long. There is nothing to live for. So I lean over the edge of the railing until the wind grabs my hat. Just the way you did that day – flinging it into the sea – & oh, I am laughing at the memory, the wind bringing tears to my eyes, spilling over & down my cheeks. At least that is what they will think & I shall allow them to do so.

As if it is any of their business anyway.

June 7th Sometimes it washes over me that this is it, this is my life, & I want to go home. I want our room & our bed & the sheets smelling of your skin. And you – are you looking for me? I am there waiting for you, for your mouth & your hands –

I feel dazed. Have I been dreaming?

June 8th The orchard at this time of year – fruits ripening together in the heat, to fill our mouths, their sugar-sweetness nothing to compare to your sweet-talk filling my ears.

June 9th It is beyond belief that I am married to this man. It is the little things that thoroughly wound me – the hair on the back of his hands, the way his ears stick out from the sides of his head, the way he nods, his chin disappearing into his neck. You revolt me, Walter. Everything about you offends me. And your ludicrous pride at being The Admiral's Grandson, telling everyone that the sea is in your blood. Do you not notice how their eyes glaze over when you begin to tell a story? You are such a bore, Walter, & I am not the only person to think so. Yes, I can see the stifled yawns, the furtive glances at watches, the discreet communications between lifted eyebrows, fingers tapping on tablecloth, sending messages. I see this & I goad you on, appearing absorbed by what you say, encouraging you, fuelling your endless dull drear narratives.

She is a New Bride after all, their looks say. She will get over it, you mark my words. By this time next year, she will be yawning, glancing at her watch, cutting him short & standing to leave the table.

June 10th Is this sky the same sky that I watched at Penfeidr? Is this the sun that smiles down on my little sweetheart Winnow, & on the Merry-dog, & on all my dear Vatesons. I think not – for this sun does not warm my bones. I feel as cold as death.

June 11th Every day My Husband becomes more and more of an authority on the sea – courtesy of being The Admiral's Grandson. At dinner he spoke at great & tedious length on waterspouts – citing his grandfather. I felt myself ageing – becoming greyer by the minute.

She is patience itself, isn't she? Do you think she has heard it all before? I do hope not for her sake, otherwise she is in for a long tedious life. Poor thing, what does she see in him? I imagine he is second choice, don't you? Well, obviously she does not love him. What? Have you heard something? Not at all, but she never looks at him, never. She always looks beyond him, never addresses him to his face. No? I must say I had not noticed. What is she doing married to the likes of Carew? He is a nonentity, fit for nothing but the lower echelons of the colonial service. I have seen his type before. One sees dozens of them in this part of the world, doesn't one?

June 12th   Yesterday I fainted. Someone shouted, Edith, look! It did not in the least resemble your voice, but it was as if I had been struck down. I stayed in bed for the rest of the day.

You & only you – never another. I remember everything – long, thick tendrils of memory – every word, every look, every touch.

June 13th   Out in the moonlight – God's Bright Beacon providing a pathway back to the land. If only I could walk on water I would run across the sea to Penfeidr.

June 14th   I tell lies with a smile on my face. Do white lies matter? I lied to you sometimes, early on, before I knew that you loved me. I would pretend – is pretending being lie-ish – I said that you did not interest me, that I was indifferent. And I would be pleased, yes pleased, when I saw the hurt on your face. I would pretend not to hear you no matter how loudly you said, Edith, look!

Oh, my dearest – & now all I do is lie & it is so easy to tell people what they want to hear, because they so desperately want to believe what one says.

June 15th   Blissful two days – the foul weather outdid itself & everyone has been seasick – even The Admiral's Grandson has kept to his cabin. I have had the entire ship to myself & spent the days gawping at the waves from the safety of the lounge. How easy it would be to sink. But how far is it to the bottom? And then what is there? The seabed & seaweed & a pathway to a cave, where Crantock is waiting.

June 16th   By now there will be the smell of roses saturating the air – almost a taste – even the grass seemed soaked with their scent. And the warm night air through the window.

June 17th   I gave you everything you wanted & still you left me. Once I remember chasing after you, thinking I will never be happier than this – running barefoot in the grass, skirts lifted high. And you laughing for no reason other than happiness, & running ahead of me, teasing, & me trying to catch you up, & doing so.

I will never be older than I am at this moment – my heart is an ancient thing –

June 18th   No, that is not true, my heart is not ancient for it was smashed to pieces. I left it lying there. I am heartless now.

June 19th   Out of sorts.

June 20th   Oh what a grand and glorious mistake I have made in marrying this man! He is fifteen years older than I & in permanent ill health. I can only hope that he will not live to a great age.

And I did it to spite you both, Mother & Father, because you rejoiced at my loss. You gloated. I heard you do so. With Walter I saw my chance for revenge & I took it & so very sweet it was to see the expression on your faces when I told you. Your reply was exactly as I expected, that it was too soon after my illness, that life as wife to a fellow in the colonial services was not suitable for a young woman with my precarious health. But I will marry him anyway, I said, just after my 21st birthday, and without permission if necessary. It will be a marriage of convenience. Walter is in need of a wife of independent means, which I will become on my birthday. How you laughed, Father, saying, Why then doesn't he marry a real heiress? So, I told you why – & only once before have I seen you look so sickened, only once have I seen more hatred and disgust on your face. Mother had never heard the word before, so had no idea what it meant. But you, Father, would have liked to strike me, just as you did that January day at Penfeidr, when you disowned me, saying that I was no longer your daughter, that I was dead to you both, dead to my brothers, dead to my entire family. But you did not dare strike me as you did on that day. So, I said, as a Fallen Woman who had become Pregnant with my love's child, neither I nor my parents can afford to be choosy. Given my history, there might never be another offer of marriage. What is the alternative, I asked? To remain at Edgarley with people whom I despise? Then I left the room. Five weeks later I became Mrs Carew.

And so here I am. It won't be so terrible when we are ashore. It cannot be. At least in Sungei Ujong I shall have a house & servants to look after. I shall get a horse. Perhaps start a garden of my own. I can get through this, I know I can.

June 21st   The pleasingness of twilight.

June 22nd   Last night they would have gone to the Carn. Did they think of me? Of never-returning times?

I do not dream any more. I go to sleep with the aid of laudanum. I wake up with the aid of a pot of strong coffee.

June 23rd   In the space of twenty-four hours a child has been taken ill, has died & been buried at sea. His poor mother is devastated. No one knows what on earth happened, just that at one moment the little fellow was escaping his nanny & under everyone's feet & the next he was complaining of a stomach-ache & dying in agony a short while later. The doctor believes it was some sort of internal rupture. The poor woman! I locked myself in here & have wept buckets. How fragile life is! Of course I thought of my own small one that died. A miscarriage – what does that mean? It was a real child to me. If it had lived I would have stayed at Penfeidr. They would have wanted me

to stay. I think that they were glad for me to be taken away. Perhaps they wanted it. Perhaps that is why they do not respond to my letters.

June 24th   I have changed so, my dear Crantock. Would you recognise me? Tomorrow we land in Singapore & the day has been taken up with farewells & the exchange of addresses. I have spent the time talking drivel. Not that long ago I could never have carried it off. But now it seems like a game – of charades, perhaps. I will pretend to be polite if you pretend to be interested.

June 27th   Three days in Singapore – I have very little to say about the place. It is hot & humid & overcast & noisy & smelling & oh dear, I just cannot be bothered with it.

June 28th   I wrote eleven times saying, I am well again. May I come? But there was not one single reply. They have stopped loving me. That is why I am here.

June 29th   We are arrived at Sungei Ujong, in Rassa, where we are to live. There was a Welcoming Committee – I quite forgot they knew Walter already. But he has returned with a New Wife, so the proprieties must be strictly adhered to. We are to be given a Celebratory Welcoming Dinner. How awful it all is! How long will it take for me to believe that this is the reality of my life?

Our house is on stilts, the rooms square, clean, simple. The servants speak a little English –

June 30th   Ten cards were left this afternoon – dear God, the boredom of what lies ahead. These people & their petty lives. The endless round of visiting & being visited.

I do not want to be here, Crantock. Please come & take me away.

August 3rd   More than one whole month has passed – I am never left to myself. I am tired. Seeing shadows. The Admiral's Grandson is sick – he is confined to bed. Dr Knelman comes twice a day. And I can barely keep anything down. The smells here trouble me. The air of something rank & the heat, the heat, & having to be corseted as the other women are. And huge cockroaches & centipedes & spiders larger than my hand that jump at one, as well as the endless mosquitoes & bats. The incessant noise, the servants' gibberish, the pouring rain, birds screeching, dogs barking all night. I long so for silence. God help me, I can't even find a decent horse to ride.

August 8th Awake to screams in the night – one of the women literally tearing her hair out with fear, utterly inconsolable. From what I can gather she heard a banshee, something the locals call a *langsuyar* – a white lady. The woman has left & refuses to return & the remaining servants are skittish, although in agreement that they heard nothing. Walter slept through the entire rumpus.

August 9th The rest of the servants went in the night – we awoke to find them gone.

Later. Barely was I dressed than Mrs Boyce-Guthrie was on the doorstep having heard of our plight, with a boy & two girls to help make do. She was kindness itself, but I have met her type before, an incurable busybody & gossip. She nosed her way into every room, including Walter's. She said that the locals have got it into their heads that the house is *rumah hantu* – haunted – & we might want to consider having the place exorcised in order to be able to keep servants. She stayed until lunch organising everyone & everything – I thought she would never go.

August 30th Three weeks since I last wrote here. I have had nothing to write. I give orders to the servants. I greet my husband's guests cordially. I am unfailingly polite. I listen to & to & to their talking. Then, after they are gone, I retire to bed with a large glass of arrack – which is stronger & less expensive than the cheapest brandy – & I lie beneath the mosquito net & think of you. The only way I can sleep is to imagine that when I open my eyes you will be beside me. Your dear sweet face near to mine.

September 2nd   Everywhere one looks there is something disgusting – at the moment we are plagued by bullfrogs. They sound as if they are being slowly choked.

September 3rd   I have been bitten on my hand. It is swollen & agonisingly itchy, but if I scratch the pain returns tenfold. Perhaps I shall die in this place. Perhaps I shall be buried in the Foreigners' Cemetery.

September 8th   Last night I lost my head – such screaming, such shouting. I didn't know I had it in me. Truly they must have heard me in every corner of Rassa. I told The Admiral's Grandson exactly what I thought of Him & then what I thought of Rassa in Sungei Ujong in the Protected States of Malaya. Protected from what? I screamed over & again. Certainly not protected from bumptious fools like Him & Mrs Boyce-Guthrie & Her Ilk! He said not a word – but walked away, quietly closing the door behind him. And then – I am smiling now with pleasure – & then I smashed the china service that His Mother gave us for our wedding. Every single piece crashed & dashed to death on the floor. I left the shards where they fell – what else are those lazy servants for but to clean up after me?

September 11th   I do as I please. In the early morning I go into Serembang & kill time in the Chinese shops. What a ludicrous idea, being able to kill time. If only one could. I return home for lunch & then keep to my room until the early evening. It is the only way I can get away with wearing as little as possible in this awful heat. Then, I go to the Club, because it is expected that I do so, & drink much too much gin & bitters, which is not expected of me, & then dinner & bed & another day is over and done with.

How long am I going to live like this? Is it possible to drink oneself to death? How long would it take?

September 13th   Yesterday it so turns out was Walter's 36th birthday. Did I know or was it that I could not be bothered to remember? There were drinks & then a dinner at the Residence. At least it didn't drag on for half the night.

September 15th   Last night I dreamt of Penfeidr – it is the first dream I can remember having since I left. I was in the orchard, and there was a very low ground mist teasing the grass. All the trees were heavy with fruit, just as they would be now. I reached my hand up to pick an apple but it would not be plucked. So I stretched my other hand up & grabbed the apple with both hands & pulled so hard that I pulled the entire tree down on top of me. I lay there beneath apples & leaves & branches. And then I became a bird – small & able to push myself though the leaves & escape. I flew into cloud – no matter how high I went a smoke-like cloud embraced me. I flew still higher, until I was up on the Carn & looking down into a white world – the landscape, Penfeidr, all indistinguishable. I thought, I will close my eyes & wait for the cloud to clear & I did & I slept. When I awoke I was here.

I feel very at peace – for the present I am meant to be here, but one day I will return to my home.

September 16th   Last night there was a dinner at the Residency. Usually I loathe these events & attend with ill humour. However, last night I still carried my dream with me & it was as if the dinner had become the dream. It was in the presence of the Raja who heads the Government, & there were many important Malays & Chinese present. All the food was from the sea – crab, lobster, prawns, octopi, shrimps, calamaries, local vegetables & fruits, washed down with copious amounts of wine. And all the ladies had made an especial effort in their dress – even I took care for the first time, feeling as if I was dressing for you. On the drive home I watched clouds like skyboats drifting overhead to another place of destination, perhaps even to Penfeidr.

I felt you very close to me. I thought how much you would love it here, how your curiosity, your wonder, would transform this foreign place into a place of enchantment for both of us.

Later. Lost in a dream for most of the day. This morning, as I sat at my writing-desk, I heard you, I'm sure of it. Edith, you said to me, so soft.

September 17th Last night I cried until my eyes swelled shut then I slept deeply. When I awoke I felt warm, rested, as if you had been beside me all night.

September 18th You have found me – I heard you. Perhaps I can be happy now.

September 19th All I could see today was the exotic beauty surrounding me – the colours of market-stalls, the spring flowers everywhere, so flamboyant, so show-offy & impressively so, each & every one.

Spring – & at Penfeidr it's autumn, the air smelling of wood-smoke mixed with raindrops.

September 20th A dream – I'm swimming, seaweed brushing along my body, just as your gentle fingers used to. Awaken to my own pleasure rippling through me. I cried afterwards, longing –

September 21st Dream – your lips near to mine, your smile touching my own.

September 23rd The Admiral's Grandson is unwell. Poor Walter, he really does suffer.

September 25th The better part of three days at Walter's bed-side – lost in Crantock-thoughts all the while.

Later. This afternoon I was forced to go out on errands for Walter – I was stopped by a number of people, most of whom I have no recollection of at all. One acknowledged a thank-you note I had sent after dining with them. Do I know these people? But why am I surprised? Surely I remember so little of them, because there is so little I want to remember.

September 26th Today I sat in front of the mirror – just to convince myself that I am here, in this room in Rassa. Mrs Walter Hallowell Carew. Still I am not convinced. At one point I closed my eyes, drifting. It was almost as if I could feel your hands undressing me. I came to myself half unclothed & on the bed with my hand down there. I wept. Such a sorrow & emptiness I cannot even begin to describe.

September 27th   Heavy, lethargic, in bed all day.

September 28th   Almost mad with yearning – an empty ache as if a part of me had been cut-out.

September 29th   Airless sun & still only spring. Oh, for a Welsh drizzling day.

October 14th   An astonishing couple of weeks – I hardly know where to begin – it started when a Malay boy, of about the age of thirteen or so, went wild in the market in Serembang. In the few minutes that it took to restrain him he had managed to injure Cecil Harvey & to kill three natives, stabbing them all with a *kris*, the knife that they all seem to carry. Apparently such sudden frenzies are not uncommon & happen a handful of times a year – although it is exceptionally rare for a white person to be injured. The local term for this occurrence is 'running amok'. The boy, who had obviously lost his wits, was tried the next day & executed the day after that by having a *kris* driven into his heart through the collar-bone pit. Anyway – Mr Harvey was recovering very well, & that seemed to be that, but then Mrs Harvey was found hanged at their home, apparently by her own hand! It is all a terrible tragedy & one hardly knows for whom to feel more sorry. It turns out the native boy was actually Mr Harvey's son by a native woman with whom he also has five other children. Mrs Harvey had married into the situation un-knowingly about five years ago & only found out later. The truly dreadful thing is that none of us cared much for her as she talked endless piffle about herself & her children & never listened to a word one said. Mr Harvey has been forced to retire his position

& four children under the age of four have been left motherless. They all sailed for England two days ago. Walter says that a good man's career has been ruined because of his wife's selfish act & that if she found the situation unacceptable then she should have returned home with the children rather than ruin their lives. He says that these things happen in the foreign settlements & that they just have to be adjusted to. Needless to say gossip is rife & a good deal of it completely contradictory &, I dare say, untrue.

October 20th This time two years ago my darling & I lived together in the tower of the Old House. How long ago it seems, almost another life, yet one I still inhabit. Cenedlon of Brynberian said that I would not know happiness from my Love – & she was right. But she also said that I would die at Penfeidr. If this too is true then I know I will return. This I must believe otherwise my life has no meaning.

November 11th Walter is unwell again. Dr K told me sternly that my Husband will die unless I convince him to leave for a more suitable climate. I replied – I actually said it to his face – My Husband & I barely speak, so how can I possibly convince him to leave? Such a look of revulsion he gave me, red-faced with disgust! My dear Woman, he said, the private life of a married couple is not my province. I am a Doctor of Medicine, your Husband's health is my sole concern & it is your Duty as his Wife to ensure that he is well. I could have struck him – I felt sick with rage. Why shouldn't Walter die if that is what he wants?

November 12th Dr K on at me again about My Wifely Duty & the Unsuitability of the Climate. Does the fellow actually know what Walter's illness is?

November 13th I've done it – I stood at Walter's bedside & said exactly what I had been told to say – adding that I had been informed it was My Wifely Duty to do so & that he should not take my comments as an expression of my personal interest. How he laughed.

I wanted to ask him, does Dr K know that you have an Unmentionable – but for some reason I couldn't bring myself to.

November 16th Walter has grown stronger during the past days. Dr K was very approving of my behaviour & delighted in telling me that Walter said that he has no intention of leaving me a forlorn young widow just yet. What a perfect pair of old bores Dr K & Walter make.

December 1st It is so hot here – if only I could peel off all my clothes & swim as God made me.

December 13th I've shocked Walter & the servants, who think I'm dabbling in witchery & spells. I built a small fire in the yard, made myself a feather-prayer-stick & held my own celebration. Unfortunately there was no breeze to waft my prayers upwards so I shall just have to believe that they reached listening ears.

December 14th Went out this morning to find that Walter had removed my feather-prayer-stick and we have had the most almighty row. I flung a book – and hit him. I have informed him that I shall do as I please & if he does not like it I shall leave.

December 27th Three nightmarish days – Christmas in the broiling heat. I play the charade of Mrs Walter Hallowell Carew much too successfully. The women really cannot see that I am in any way different from them & persist in forcing their friendship upon me.

Is it not a fine thing that I can lie so very well, so very easily?

1890

January 1st Not only a new year but an entirely new decade. Ten years ago I was a little girl still living at the Abbey House. I hardly knew Crantock except as a strange boy who always held tight to Aunt Azenor's hand – rocking to & fro, his shy face & smile. Even then he loved me & I didn't realise at all. What would my life be like now if I hadn't gone to Penfeidr? What would the girl that I was say to the woman that I have become?

January 2nd Walter is ill again – I am certain it has nothing whatsoever to do with the prodigious amounts of food he gorged on during the Christmas period!

January 3rd Walter still bedridden. I am refusing all invitations. I do not care what they think or say about me.

February 1st One month gone already – each day passes the same as the day before. Walter is unwell most of the time, and even when he is better he still has a complaint of some sort or other. It does now seem as though we might have to leave because of his health. The sultry heat is only making him worse. I will not miss it – neither place nor people interest me at all. But where would we go? He has friends in Singapore & Japan, so they are possibilities. He is adamantly against returning to England.

I live with a perpetual sense of unreality. I cannot believe that I will never awaken in our room again. It cannot be true, there must be a mistake. If only I had not lost our child! How different my life would have been. But I must not to think of it. I must push such thoughts away or I will be ill.

End March I have had malaria – it came on me of a sudden, aching bones, headache, fever, sweats. And while I was immersed in the fever I had such dreams & visions of my love that I believed him to be with me and myself returned to Penfeidr. Luckily, Walter recognised the symptoms & I was treated correctly quite quickly. The bout was not severe, but I must take quinine before breakfast & after dinner, otherwise it will recur.

April 4th We are to leave Rassa in June for Yokohama in Japan. Quite what Walter will do there remains to be seen.

April 19th My very own darling – today is your birthday. I have been in tears since I awoke. Oh, I wish & I wish – keeping the secret – your heart locked in my own.

If only I could kill myself – but then we would be for ever separated. No. No matter how much I think of it, I must wait to return home.

April 20th I even know how I would do it.

April 21st An elaborate plan to free myself – it would even appear accidental.

April 30th I've been in bed for days with a temperature – my dear one near to me the entire time.

May 1st My birthday – I am 22. I am undecided if that seems terribly young or old. How many more years? I will not celebrate – Walter has not remembered, if he ever knew. The last birthday that mattered was three years ago – a picnic on Dinas Sands – I am wearing the shawl that was given me then. Who would have thought that I would wear it on a wet autumn day oceans away from them all.

May 4th I am a Wife of one year. How stupid that sounds. Walter did not remember, thank goodness. I watched him over breakfast. How he revolts me & that is why I married him. Every inch of him reminds me all the more of the beauty I have lost. He is entirely commonplace. One sees so many of his type out here – burnt dry by the sun, bloated from too much heavy food & alcohol & too little exercise. He is here because there is no place for him in England. In England his failure would be writ large.

Some of the men are ambitious, but most are like Walter and just want to get through with as little fuss as possible. When we leave he will, in effect, be retiring due to ill health. He is washed-up at the age of 36. Imagine that. He must have had dreams as a boy. Surely he did not expect this type of life, although he never seems disappointed with his lot. He never complains. But my money isn't going to keep us, so he is going to have to find something to fill his days in Yokohama.

May 5th I've started a notebook on Penfeidr – something to keep me sane – I'm recounting every single detail that I can recall, describing each room of both the Old House & the New House in detail – &, oh, the memories that are rushing back. I was never so happy as then & I never expected such happiness. That was the wondrous thing –

I remember the way we fitted together, you fitting into me, my other half. Is it any wonder that I wander day after day & night after night feeling incomplete? In every movement I make I am able to feel everything that I am not.

May 6th Today, purely as a bit of a lark, I played the Thirty-Six Animals lottery – and I won! All the locals are absolutely addicted to it. The Chinese seem to control it. I placed one dollar & won thirty. Thomas, our houseboy, laid my bet & collected my winnings & for his silence I gave to him one-tenth, which I am certain is much too much. But – everyone here is very against the game & says it is most corrupting & where a goodly portion of the crime stems from. I am delighted to be secretly doing something of which they all disapprove.

May 7th Played again – five dollars this time – & lost. Thomas was much amused. He plays almost every day, never betting a great deal – ten cents or so – & places his stake according to his previous night's dream, & if he doesn't dream he doesn't play.

May 8th Another lost five dollars. We are much caught up in leaving. There is to be a dinner at the Residence to Honour

Walter's Leaving. When he told me, he obviously saw my look of amusement & pointed out the he is Retiring, after all. It is the end of his career. There will even be a speech.

How queer, the idea of honouring Walter. So second-rate, so insignificant.

May 9th Another lost five dollars – is this what is called a losing streak? I must say I do enjoy it though & I enjoy so little these days.

We are to leave in one month exactly – I cannot wait to see the last of the place.

May 21st I am numb – something so horrific – I want to close my eyes & never open them again. I want all this to be a terrible dream. I have taken a large dose of laudanum but it has not helped at all. I am defiled & will never be clean again. I fought him – he has the scratches to prove it. If I had had a knife to hand . . . I will kill him if he ever comes near me again – I have told him so.

May 22nd The Pig is full of bluff & bravado, but afraid of me. I have nothing to lose & he knows this. Is it possible for him to pass on to me his filthy disease?

May 28th We have not spoken a word since – since – I hiss when he comes into the same room.

June 6th During the past weeks I have lost nearly five hundred dollars playing at Thirty-Six Animals & won only two hundred. I am out of pocket by three hundred dollars. Hey ho! But what good fun it is!

June 10th We are on our way to Singapore where we will connect with the P&O for Yokohama. Our last day was curiously melancholy, although there is not a single thing I shall miss about Rassa & Serembang, except, perhaps, playing Thirty-Six Animals. Everyone was so sad to see The Pig go. I really had not guessed at his popularity, or of the affection people feel for him. They were all kindness & generosity. And the speeches that were given in his honour & the dinner & dancing! They pushed the boat out & spared no expense to make a special event for him. And I look at him & just see a hulking, beefy, red-faced man who bulges out of his clothes – & has succeeded at nothing.

How bizarre it is – those amiables creating a little England so far from home & enjoying it, thriving on it. At home they would be Nobodies – even the Resident. Mrs Boyce-Guthrie & Her Ilk shall end their days in retirement in some small villa in Bourne-mouth or Eastbourne recalling their glory days Out There. What none of them could get over was that I was not interested in any of the sights. As if I could be interested in the Jungul, or coffee-plantations, or rice fields, or tin-mines, or wild beasts. The truly dreadful thing is that they've all promised to come & see us in Yokohama. What could I do but smile & say how lovely, you really must come, I shall hold you to that, you know.

As if I could possibly be serious.

June 16th　We have been on the P&O for a day now. I have been sick for the past couple of mornings – too much gin & bitters in the evening, perhaps. We had hardly boarded at Singapore before The Pig started on about being The Admiral's Grandson. Dear God! At the moment they still find him charming – but they will be bored to death with him before too long.

June 18th　I am keeping to my cabin for the rest of the trip. There is a couple on board, newlyweds, utterly besotted with each other. He is my age, she a little younger. I hate them both. I hate them for having what has gone from me for ever & I wish them sorrow & misery & despair. I wish one of them death & the other a long life. Each time I saw them together I felt pain in my womb, as if I had been stabbed, & I crept away to bed – aching to be touched, remembering our pleasure together. I feel so dead inside. Such love will never be mine again.

July 17th　Here for over almost a month – it's all terribly English, a very tightly-knit community. Walter is to run the Yokohama

United Club & it suits him, given his revolting conviviality. Luckily, we barely see each other. The house – which is on the Bluff – is huge, too big really, a family house & quite new, only twenty or so years old. But the views are splendid, down over the Bay. When we arrived the garden was bursting with irises, hydrangeas & three magnificent flowering trees called magnolias. The rainy season has just finished so everywhere is impossibly lush & verdant, & the heat, the stickiness is incredible – very different from that in Rassa. When the weather permits – there have been thunderstorms most afternoons that last for hours – I scout for furnishings. There are some exquisite pieces in the Chinese Quarter – well beyond my purse, however.

So far I have been able to avoid socialising – the house is my excuse – but we are accumulating invitations that, so far, The Pig has been responding to alone. Every time our paths cross we argue about my lack of interest. Here, I do not have to pretend to be interested in anyone or their events. I am no longer the Treasurer's Wife. I am nobody but the Club Manager's Wife. I have no public role, other than the one I choose to take. It is a marriage of convenience, after all, & I do not find socialising convenient.

July 23rd   What I have feared & dreaded is true – I am pregnant from that one ghastly night in Rassa when He forced himself on me. And Crantock & I were together so many times, dozens, a hundred. And this – this – monstrosity! What am I to do? Dear God –

Dear God why, why – ?

July 25th   I am recuperating – I threw myself down the stairs after drinking a bottle of gin – I only succeeded in spraining my wrist. The Thing inside me clings on.

Dr Hanscombe informed The Pig about the Thing. After Dr H had left, I then had to endure a speech about how he hopes this will bring us together as a Married Couple. I would sooner be dead, I told him. Dead.

July 27th   This is wrong – the entire thing is wrong.

July 28th I tried again but only succeeded in making myself horrifically ill. I actually vomited blood. How hard can it be to kill oneself?

August 3rd I have tried to tell Dr H about The Pig's Disease. He looked at me as if I had gone mad and refused to listen.

August 5th Walter & I – such an argument – he is drunk – so afraid I have locked myself in my room. Dr H has told him what I said. Dr H did not know – Walter sees a specialist for His Disease.

August 8th Experienced my first earthquake – although apparently there have been others since our arrival & I slept through them! I don't know how to describe it – perhaps like a mammoth grinding its teeth somewhere deep underground so that the entire house shook! It was all over in a matter of seconds. I am told that there are hundreds of such tremors a year & one is not to worry about them at all.

Perhaps there will be a strong enough tremor to bring the house down on top of me and then it would all be over and done with.

August 12th We are invited to spend a week by the sea near Zushi with a friend of The Pig's, Mr William Bradley & His Wife. Mr Bradley works in Shipping & Export, I believe. They have been in Yokohama for about a decade & are very happy & have, in fact, done very well for themselves. They have four children, whom Mrs Bradley has refused to send back home to school. So she spends part of her day teaching them herself.

I am not very keen on going, I must say, but unfortunately there seems to be no escape from this engagement.

August 15th We have been in Zushi for two days &, lovely though the landscape is, I feel very in the downs. The sea reminds me of Dinas & everything that I have lost. Mrs Bradley is pleasant, as are her children, but I just cannot be interested. We drove down from Yokohama through Kamakura & stopped to look at a Great Seated Buddha which must be almost fifty feet tall. We passed a good many Japanese pilgrims all wearing white on their way to the dozens of shrines & temples in the area. What a curious people they are and yet they do not seem strange to me. Not as the natives in Sungei Ujong did. Mrs Bradley said the Japanese all look alike to her & I do understand what she means. They all have the same features & colouring, black hair, slanting dark eyes & are physically small & slender. But there is a special beauty to them – certainly to the women & the children – & their dress is exceptionally lovely. We English are all so very different. I wonder what it must be like to look almost exactly like everyone else.

Much later. They are very bemused that we do not share a room. Let them gossip, the little parochials. How shocked she would be if I said, Walter & I married because I am a Fallen Woman and He has an Unmentionable.

September 18th Day after day of torrential rain and violent winds. There has been minor flooding and mud landslides all over Yokohama. The locals seem to take it in their stride – but I have not been out of the house for what seems like weeks; all I do is sit at the window watching the weather and brooding about the disgusting condition I am in.

November 6th God knows what the servants think of the goings on in this house.

November 10th I had to get out & so went to Kamakura with the Bradleys and some others to view the autumn leaves. It is a great tradition to do so. The colours were quite spectacular – massed reds and yellows glowing in the sunshine. But even more eye-catching were all the Japanese women in their formal gowns, which appear tremendously rich and luxurious, and are called kimonos. These gowns are worn with wide sashes at the waist that hold all the different layers together. On their feet they wear wooden slippers secured by slender straps. These look most un-comfortable & the women can only walk with tiny footsteps. They never smile, but are forever ducking their heads at each other, and making little bows. They remind me somewhat of starlings – the way they gather and move around together.

I have decided that I want to have a kimono – just for the sheer beauty of the fabric. When I am not – in this condition – I shall find one.

November 12th   Walter is staying at the Club for a few days. We are both agreed that it is for the best.

November 23rd   I spend my days rereading my diaries & thinking about Crantock. All the little details I never wrote down that I now put in my Penfeidr notebooks. Sometimes I just sit & look at my photographs of you. I sit & stare, just as I used to. I touch your face & occasionally it is almost as if you smile. Penfeidr seems so long ago – how many years am I going to live this death?

December 8th   I am sure that today is Winnow's birthday. He would be – what? – eleven or twelve, perhaps. I wonder if he remembers me, my reserve husband. Perhaps he is waiting for me to come back. I hope so.

I clearly remember the day that I asked him to be our ring-bearer, explaining the importance of his role, and he refused me! Unless, that is, he too had a ring and could be a Husband. And so serious was he – his dear-hearted little face was so very serious. After much thought and consideration I agreed, making it sound very complex and difficult and time-consuming and telling him that a Husband, even a reserve husband, had to do a great many chores and was scolded if he did not do them. He refused to believe me, saying, But my papa does not do chores –

If only I could be there.

December 18th   There has been a letter from Edgarley – Walter wrote informing them of my condition, about which they are delighted. They are nothing to me – I have not written to them once since leaving. Why should I do so now?

December 21st   I've hidden a feather-prayer-stick in the garden where no one will find it.

1891

January   Cold. Very little rain. I like to sit by the window watching the fishing-junks in the Bay, day-dreaming. How different this would all be if it were our child inside me – a part of you & me, together.

February   I caught sight of myself yesterday in the long looking-glass – waddling, a swollen grotesquery.

March   It is done – horrific & agonising & over. The Pig has a daughter, born March 1st, whom he has named Marjorie. She looks like him – the same beefy red face. The poor ugly thing has none of me in her at all. She will grow into a chubby ungainly child & become a dumpy cumbrous woman. How strange to think that I am the Mother of an Ugly Daughter. I will have as little to do with her as possible & so we have employed a wet-nurse & a nanny.

    All I can think of is the child I lost. How loved he would have been. How beautiful, with your face.

April 5th   Pink cherry blossom everywhere – reminding me of the orchards at home. I went to Kamakura with Mrs Bradley & some of her friends. The main sight is a wide and long walkway, of almost one mile, that is lined with hundreds of cherry trees. The trees form an arch overhead comprised entirely of cherry blossom & oh, the perfume, with a vague breeze drifting the petals down upon us occasionally. The place was thronged with flower-viewing parties but not even the crowds could spoil the beauty of the day.

    The Japanese ladies were as marvellously turned-out as usual & it has served to remind me that I too want a kimono.

April 11th   Today the child was christened – a huge crowd of people at the church, none of whom I really know. They are The

Pig's friends & acquaintances. Why do people like him? The child was positively cooed over. If she were pretty & delicate I could understand, but she is not. So it just goes to show what liars people are. And what do they see when they look at me? A perfectly normal Wife & Mother, I imagine. I should be in their amateur theatricals too!

This is my life. That thing is my daughter. I will never love it. I know that. Every time I look at it I see The Pig. Will it realise how much it disgusts me? What will its life be like? Mine seemed a promising one. I was a happy child – I was a normal little girl. I thought that when I grew up I would fall in love & marry & have children. And I did fall in love & it was so much more than I ever expected. It was a Great Thing, a Great Love, such as one reads about. I carried his child. Then – a darkness that I still cannot find my way through. I let go of his hand. And now this – and none of this is real. You are not real to me Marjorie Carew. I am not your mother. I know that if I close my eyes for long enough I shall open them & be in our room at the top of the tower – I will be happy & loved & not caught in this nightmare.

Perhaps I am ill – perhaps I have gone mad – is that what this is all about?

April 19th   Crantock's birthday – I have taken to my bed – sick in my heart. Why could I not die in childbirth? So many women do, so why not me? I would much rather lie underground with you, the earth as our covering to keep us warm.

May 1st   My 23rd birthday – I have been given a horse for doing my duty & breeding. I cannot think of a name – except Horse. I rode this morning for the first time since getting married. I am very stiff & out of condition & I must lose weight – I have three rolls of fat on my stomach. I do not want it to look as if being fat is the Carew trademark.

May 13th   And my birthday present to myself – I found the loveliest kimono, much, much too expensive, but I bought it anyway. It is all silk, lined red inside, and the outside is white and embroidered all-over with twining flowers, in red & gold & green. And the sash, which is called an *obi*, is in gold & green. I have not yet put it on – it is too beautiful. Instead, it is laid out on my bed, so that I may feast my eyes on it.

June 1st   I have hung my kimono so that it is the first thing I see every morning. I have not yet worn it, but I like to touch the fabric & hold it to my cheek. For some reason doing this soothes me.

June 12th   It drizzles much more here than it ever did in Wales.

June 23rd   I have been here for one whole year. I wish – if only I could appreciate the beauty that surrounds me – at the moment there are luscious magnolias in bloom everywhere I look.

I never see Walter – thank goodness – not even in passing. He goes out before I am up & returns after I have retired.

August 1st   At home they will be taking all the horses down to the sea – here it has poured with rain every day. I have spent the past month making myself more public & visible – The Pig insisted. People were beginning to talk because they rarely saw me. So, I have been out on Horse every morning & in the afternoons pasted a smile on my face & socialised, trying hard to remember their names. There is no shortage of things to do – & I am trying to make the best of it. I have developed a passion for shopping. I take the train into Tokyo & I shop & take lunch & shop again & then return here laden with parcels. I have enough hats & gloves & shawls & beads & brooches to dress a half-dozen women, at the very least. Shopping for frippery is what Wives do & so it is what I have done – next month The Pig will complain when the bills are sent in to be paid. But that is his problem.

September 7th   We have fought – viciously. I struck him & drew blood.

September 21st   He is building to something, I can tell.

September 25th   He would not dare touch me – not after last time.

October 2nd   Three nights of – of – I am battered & bruised & my body . . . I am His Wife, he said, why should He go elsewhere for what is At Home. It is a marriage of convenience & I am Convenient, he said. I begged Him to be reasonable. I begged Him not to. Not one of the servants came to my aid. Nanny Mackie resigned without taking her pay – she would not look me in the eye, she could not.

October 3rd   I have been to see a lawyer. I told him everything. When I had finished, he said the best that he could suggest was that I return to my parents. When I explained why this was not possible, he replied that he was unable to help me.

October 4th   Another lawyer and a minor variation on what I was told yesterday. Where The Pig is, I do not know – skulking at the Club, I dare say. He'll show up, without doubt.

October 5th   Another lawyer – they are worse than useless. As soon as I say 'a marriage of convenience' they look at me as if I had invented the phrase. I give up – for now.
  Nanny Johns will arrive tomorrow morning.

October 8th   The Pig washed down too many pills while he was drunk and almost succeeded in killing himself. It's such a shame that Yori found him so soon. Another couple of hours & I would have been a widow.

October 10th   He wept & begged my forgiveness.

1892

January 21st I am to breed again.

February 1st An End. This year.

Later. I told The Pig that next year I shall go home for a few months – by which I mean that I shall deposit the children at Edgarley & go on alone to Penfeidr. I gave him no choice in the matter. I cannot & will not live this way.

February 16th Spotting & dreadful cramps – terrible lower-back ache. I remember this pain from another time – another child – a wanted child. This time next year –

And if the Vatesons do not want me – if they turn me away? What then?

February 27th A letter from Edgarley saying that they will be delighted to see us next year. They positively gushed over the photograph of the child. So ridiculous – it is obvious that she is plain & tubby. Her likeness to The Pig is quite remarkable. At present she is into everything within arm's reach & laughing all the time, fat cheeks quivering, one of which I pinched the other day until she bawled. I could not help myself. It would have been quite funny except for the racket & ructions that ensued.

March 1st Today The Piglet turned one year old. I call her this to everyone, who think it most affectionate & endearing. She is still virtually bald. Her first word was her own name, in a manner of speaking – Mardie – not Marjorie, & so Mardie she is become – & hardly surprising given how selfish she is. She adores being the centre of attention & will cry until she has the entire room looking at her. Needless to say The Big Pig is besotted with his Baby Pig – always dandling her, always in the nursery, playing & singing, concocting rhymes, which she then attempts to repeat *ad nauseum*. What a repulsive pair of specimens.

The only thing that keeps me going is the swathes & swathes of camellias all along one side of the house. My one great pleasure in life is cutting a bunch of them every morning, which I keep on my writing desk.

April 19th   You – if I close my eyes I am back there.

May 1st   My birthday – but I cannot remember which one it is.

May 3rd   The Pig is sick again. But he is always ill. I just wish he would get on with it & die.

June 1st   The Pig has been very ill – he looks old & worn & haggard. But then he is old, almost 40. The doctor has insisted that we go to Zushi for the summer. Luckily, the Club is going to keep him on on a small retainer. Goodness knows how we would manage otherwise.

June 20th   Tiring journey – servants will do nothing unless made to, as if they are unable to think for themselves. And I am coping with an invalid & The Piglet & Nanny Johns, in my condition. At least it is cool here – so much more fresh, with the breeze coming in off the sea.

July 3rd   I miss my dreams – the rich vivid dreams I used to have.

August 8th   Number Two arrived four days ago – a boy – to be named Benjamin, after The Pig's Admiral Grandfather. When I first held him all I could think about was the ugliness from which he was created, the poor little fellow. He is small but long, with a wrinkled face, almost like a little old man. But there is also something of him that reminds me just a little of Reggie when he was a baby.

September 9th   We are to stay in Zushi for another month or two – The Pig is not quite back on his trotters yet. Ben is very quiet & easy, unlike Mardie who is all noise. Thank goodness for Nanny Johns, who has turned out to be a gem. I walk every day, for miles on my own, lost in thoughts of Crantock & Penfeidr for the most part.

October 11th   Astounding storms sweeping in from the sea, day after day – lightning lighting the entire sky, & the rain positively cascading down.

November 20th   How strange to be back in Yokohama. The crows on the Bluff, I have not missed at all. Har har har har – jeering at me, undoubtedly.

December 1st   I have begun making plans to leave by mid-February. I want to be in Penfeidr for my dear one's birthday.

December 13th   I must take extra care – I have worked myself into such a state of excited nerves about leaving that I have been sick. I must calm down.

December 24th   Ben's christening – he is a sweet child, huge eyes, so placid, so unlike his swagbellied sister.

1893

January 2nd I think of nothing but my departure. I cannot remember what happened yesterday, or the day before, or the day before that.

Later. None of the dresses I came out with fit me any more! My bosom is a size larger, my waist almost as wide as my hips – that is what breeding does – or at least has done to me. I don't remember Aunt Azenor having rolls of flesh. I actually need to wear a corset at the moment to hold it all in the right place. I must lose weight. I can't return to Penfeidr looking like this.

January 23rd Four weeks more – everything washes over me – it is such a shame that I have to take the children. Still, I must look on the bright side, they are my excuse for escaping. I am taking them back to show them off to the Grandparents.

January 28th Terrible bout of nerves, shaking hands, I can hardly speak, my voice keeps catching with excitement.

March 1st Everything ruined by illness – my malaria recurred, not badly, but enough to delay sailing. I will not be at home for Crantock's birthday. I cannot believe that I am still here. The only good thing to come out of it is that I have shed pounds.

Later. Completely forgot that today was The Piglet's 2nd birthday. I did not even have a present. I rummaged through her toybox & hauled a stuffed tiger from the bottom, wrapped it & gave it to her again. She said, But, mama, I have one of those. I insisted that she did not & made her go & search her toy-box & then come back & apologise to me when it could not be found. Needless to say, The Pig spoilt her silly as he always does & bought a large rocking horse & a locket on a chain in which she is to carry a photograph of her papa back to England.

March 2nd Our new passage has been booked for April 5th.

We should reach England by Sunday 23rd – then straight on to Edgarley. And I'll have to be there for two weeks, I imagine, before making my excuses & heading off. So I shall not get to Penfeidr until mid-May, at the earliest. All the fields will be flowering & there will be water-lilies in the moat at the Old House & early honeysuckle & perhaps late apple blossom. It is still winter there now – blazing fires, hot soup, the wind attacking the budded branches, & the rain, that endless Welsh rain dropping from the clouds.

I have been in floods of tears – I am going home at last. I can hardly believe it.

April 1st Full Moon – the very same man in the moon is watching Penfeidr.

April 2nd The cherry blossom is about to burst.

April 5th We sailed four hours ago – I waved at The Pig with such happiness; never to see him again – oh, what joy! He, of course, made a spectacle of himself by weeping & this sent The Piglet into such a bawling tantrum that I could have slapped her. Instead, Nanny Johns hauled her away kicking & screaming & I was left to hold Ben, who calmly sucked his fist throughout the entire rumpus. He is such a peaceable little chap – I can't but like him for that.

But here I am – on my way –

April 9th I spend my days pacing – I can settle to nothing. I just want to be home. Thank goodness there is no one on the boat from Rassa or Serembang – I was half-dreading there would be.

April 12th Exhausted to the point of dropping! Nanny Johns down with seasickness, as a good many are – we hit storms a couple of days ago – & I have been left holding the children. And what a beast The Piglet is: her favourite words are No & Will Not & Shan't & if forced to do something she will throw herself on the floor & bellow until she is blue in the face. I lost my temper yesterday & spanked her legs thoroughly. It is difficult to say who was the more shocked, she or I.

April 13th   Nanny Johns up & about & to the rescue & it's just as well, for I fear there might have been a Piglet thrown overboard otherwise.

April 19th   Your birthday & I am nearly there, nearly back with you – I love you so.

April 28th   I am in my old room at Edgarley. We arrived yesterday afternoon. I was greeted like a Visiting Dignitary or some type of Honourable or Minor Royalty. He – Father – came to the station wearing his Mayoral Robes & Chains, & Mother had also Dressed Up. The Station had been festooned with streamers. And I just felt embarrassed – I do so hate show-offy-ness – & then we drove to Edgarley. Everyone was outside to greet me & how lovely it was to see Tizzy & Woodsie looking just as they did when I left them. If I care for anyone here, it is them. My parents & I have nothing whatsoever to say to each other but they are already besotted with their grandchildren, especially The Piglet. Ben is still too small to do anything more than gaze at whomever is in front of him & smile adoringly.

Edgarley itself is so much smaller than I remember. My bedroom is unchanged, as if I had never been away. So many memories are here. And who would have thought that this is the person I would become – how very strange & terrible & tragic life is.

April 29th   I insisted on having the day to myself. I went to the Abbey House. The woman who lives there knows Father & so allowed me to see my old bedroom. I stood at the window & looked to the spot where I used to see King Arthur & I was swept with such an anguish & longing for Crantock that I thought I would faint – but I managed to control myself. Then I walked up to the Tor, & there among the ruins I wept. Looking down on Edgarley, looking down upon my past & all my memories, I wept. Not for the past, but for a future that will never be mine.

Five years ago I died. Now I must wait for my body to catch up with my heart.

Later. How often as a girl I sat at this window looking up at the Tor wondering who my husband would be, wondering about our home, our children. It is perhaps as well that we do not know the future –

April 30th   Everyone arrived today to celebrate my quarter century. By everyone, I mean Cecil, who was 20 in January & must be the biggest pomposity who ever grew whiskers. He is at the Royal Military College & very full of himself & his achievements. Robert, who is the family brainbox & Oxford-bound, and dear Reggie who is still the naughtiest boy ever to be born. I am told he fails his exams terrifically every year. But what a loveable chap! He is only 17, but I imagine he cuts quite a swathe through the girls at the Hunt & County Balls. And then there is Edward, 13 & obsessed with India, just like Mother. Cousin May is here too. I always thought of her as old – but she isn't at all. She is only in her mid-40s – I have not seen her since – really, I do not know when. But apart from Reggie & Cousin May, my parents & brothers are all as dull as ditchwater.

The Pig's parents arrived quite latish, thank goodness. How tedious they are! His mother went on & on, wanting to know every single detail of our time in Rassa & Yokohama. At one point she exasperated me so thoroughly that I said that perhaps she might like me to send my diaries to her, as they are stuffed full of such details. She actually thought me serious & became very animated, saying, Oh, my dear, how very kind, how very generous, I would be delighted. So I promised that I would send them. Just imagine if I did!

May 1st   My quarter-century, for what it is worth.

Much later. An incredibly long day, beginning with a family breakfast & then guests for lunch, but no one I know. And then an At Home that lasted for hours, with people calling, friends of my parents for the most part, so that it hardly seemed a birthday celebration at all. Dear God, the same questions & comments a

hundred times over. The Piglet won the day, wrapping everyone around her plump little trotters. How does the ghastly child succeed so? And Ben, smiling like a Buddha.

The Streets came, none of them changed. None of the girls is married. Amelia & Alexander eloped – how many years ago now? If they felt a small amount of what Crantock & I felt then they surely did the right thing. If only I had been as lucky as they.

All day I wanted to say, I am not going back. I have left and I am going home to Penfeidr. But of course I did not. Instead I did my best to seem as pleased as punch to be here, telling & retelling umpteen dozen anecdotes & charming tales of Life Out There, using a lot of native terms, which I then had to explain. I smiled until my face ached. And even then I kept on smiling.

May 2nd   I will go mad if I do not get away from here soon. I have told Mother that I have to go to London to shop for things to be sent out to Yokohama. The stupid woman wanted to accompany me. I refused. I told her that I have neither forgotten nor forgiven her behaviour of five years ago. I never shall do either.

How shocked they will be when I do not return.

May 3rd   I shall leave at the weekend. Dreadful nerves – shivery, terrified that my malaria will return.

May 4th   Today I had the strange sensation that someone was standing behind me. Just as I turned I heard a cough. Crantock is with me! He knows I am returned & on my way to him.

May 5th   Mother has guessed my plan and forbade me to go. I told her that as I am a married woman I shall do as I please. She threatened to tell Father. I would have liked to strike her and she saw this in my face and recoiled. Mother fears me a little, I do believe.

May 6th   In an hour I shall leave. I am ready.

Penfeidr

May 15th It is very late. I have been at home for a little over a week. I am in our sitting-room. I have picked bunches of lilac for every vase & their smell is as overpowering as a sudden peal of bells. Today I passed in the garden sowing cabbages & beans. Tomorrow morning I will pick unripe gooseberries for Wymp's wife to make a tart. I seem to remember that it is my Winnowmouse's favourite.

I remember this silence. I know it. As well as it knows me.

Yes.

I am Edith.

May 16th Eight mornings ago, at daybreak, I left Fishguard. At the time, I felt no sorrow or grief, but was instead light-headed and breathless with anticipation. I borrowed a horse & rode steadily, took my breakfast on Dinas Sands – our sands, where my darling & I found one another. Then I rode inland, taking the short cuts that I once took so many times, riding up to Carn Ingli. There I sat, looking down to Penfeidr, feeling such joy as I recalled all the times I had sat there looking down. I rode at a gallop, pelting along & barely able to see where I was going, giving the mare her head. The gates were unlocked as always & I entered, but did not follow the drive because I wanted to approach the house from the side through the orchard. I wanted to see the house before the house saw me. So, instead I crossed the grass & tethered the mare.

Giddy on the scent of apple blossom & pear & plum, I continued along the path until I came to – oh, how to write of what I saw – I came to the house. But where there should have been a house was a terrible ruin! All I could do was stand in rooms that are now open to the sky, in rooms overrun with ivy & grass into every nook & cranny. I stood & walked & stood & walked – putting my hands on sun-warmed stone – looking up the stairway rising skyward. I sat on the stairs, to breathe, to think, trying to ease the terrible pain in my heart, & an aged bee stumbled about my lap, blind perhaps, mistaking the scent of my skirts for that of a flower. I sat there for an age wondering at the catastrophe, fearing the worst. Then I realised that, of course, they must all be at the Old House, and so, my heart rising with every step, I walked on, sometimes running, following the spidery track, over the moat-bridge & through the gatehouse & then I was there.

It was just as I remembered it. I thought: I have been mistaken. Five years have not passed since I last stood here. Inside is Crantock & I shall go in & kiss him & he will pretend to be asleep so that I shall kiss him again, & I shall say, oh, my dear one, I had a terrible dream, I dreamt that I let go of your hand. I looked up at our room & I thought I saw myself there, standing at the window, staring seaward, wearing black. So thin I was – so awfully thin – & I watched as I opened the window & heard the words, Edith, jump – I wanted to shout them out, but before I could speak, a Welsh voice said, So you are returned & I turned to see Wymp's son standing there. Where are they, I asked, feeling sick with fear. Gone, he replied. But to where? To Him, he replied, pointing heavenward. Yet still I did not want to understand. They have gone to be with young master Crantock, he said. Come, I will show you.

He led the way to the chapel and in through the door, to a slab of marble inscribed with the word Vateson, and underneath was just one single date of death, followed by fourteen names: Brychan, Azenor, Nectan, Rhun-Owen, Corth, Tybie, Elined, Cleer, Ninnon, Rhawin, Haran, Winnow, Kew, Keyne. In disbelief my fingers traced the outline of each carved name while Wymp's son told me of the fire at the New House in September 1889 that had taken all their lives. A fire that had lasted for three nights before it finally burned out.

How can I write of what I felt at hearing what he said? I cannot. The words do not exist to describe my emotions.

Desolate, I went from the chapel to where Adwen rests, knowing that I would find another lying beside her. I stood & stared at the simple headstone carved with my darling's name, but in my heart I knew that he was not really there.

With Wymp's son I returned to the ruins of the New House, to

stand in dearly remembered places. My beloved Vatesons were of
this earth, their ash mingled with the soil. The bark of a dog
broke my reverie, a dog coming towards me, as fast as its old
Merry-dog legs would allow. If he could, he would have leapt on
me. I bent to him, & holding him close I cried into his dear old
dog-skin smell. And when I looked up he was standing there –
yes! Crantock stood there – his faced turned away, rocking. There
had been a terrible mistake! All this time & all this sorrow & all
our time apart & here he was, after all. I managed to say his name
and then I fainted. When I came to myself he & the Merry-dog
had gone & Wymp's son was knelt beside me. Crantock is not
dead, I said, I knew he was not. I knew he would never leave me.

But of course it was not Crantock that I saw. It was Winnow.
His name had been prematurely inscribed on the marble slab.
They had found him, or rather Merry had found him, three weeks
after the fire, asleep in the tower. He was half-starved. Where he
had been for those three weeks no one knows. Nor how he escaped, or how the fire began. He refuses to speak of it. He has
not spoken one word since he was found. Winnow. Rocking, just
as Crantock used to.

We, Wymp's son & I, returned to the Old House. Every room
remained just as if I had left it yesterday. When I came to our
rooms I stumbled round, tripping over my own feet, my skirts
impeding me. I touched my hairbrush on the dressing-table – my
things, my darling's, ours. I whispered your name and closed my
eyes. When I opened them I expected to see you there, but of
course I did not.

That first evening, I ate in the kitchen with Wymp, his wife &
son, & Winnow. He rocked the entire time, backwards and for-
wards, looking down, never at anyone or anywhere, the Merry-
dog's snout in his lap. Afterwards, Wymp's son put him to bed.
When I went to his bedside, he slept like the Smallie I remembered – one who took up the whole of the bed because sleep had
flattened him into the shape of a star. In the candlelight I could
see Crantock in his face. I thought, yes, this is who I have come
back for. In the past days he has not made one single sound or
noise – he takes himself off during the day accompanied by the

Merry-dog & returns late in the afternoon. He eats with us & then he sleeps. Every day is the same. He seems not to know me.

Later. I have been staring through the window, down along the river to Newport Sands and out to sea. I am too empty to cry, I am numb beyond any feeling. During the past days I have spent hours in walking, trying to think, trying to understand what I have returned to. And there is one question that keeps arising, which is why was I not told of this? My parents must have known – and yet, silence. She – Mother – could easily have written to me. But she did not. How she sickens me. If only it had been Edgarley, with my parents inside, that was razed to the ground.

May 18th Sometimes, when I wake in the morning, I see her standing at the window – myself in black – staring out to sea. Twice I have got out of bed and gone to stand behind her to look where she watches.

May 23rd Peaceful days –

May 27th Awake to the sound of my name.

May 28th This morning, your voice – Edith, Love.

Very late. A clear sky pied with stars. We are making headway in the orchard – my hands are becoming gnarly, they are no longer the hands of a girl but those of a woman.

Winnow – how did he escape, if only he would speak to us, tell us. He has taken to following me during the day, but he keeps to himself, rocking, picking a blade of grass or a leaf or a flower & examining it for hours. The Merry-dog is ever present at his side. How it hurts me to see him like this, but there is nothing I can do. He was such a lively little boy, so very loving.

May 29th I found Mr Breton's *Prognostications* – &, oh, the memories that came flooding back of those shared mornings before Crantock & I moved down here. When one of us would read a line at breakfast & how that line would become like a

285

prayer for that day, or a song endlessly repeated. All of my dear ones held this book, each and every one of them.

Later. I feel very alone here. Everyone is dead. There is no one left but Winnow & I & Merry.

May 30th All I can see is what has passed and will never be real again. All that I am not and shall never become. Every day for the past five years I have longed to return & what I did not realise was that when I did, I would be different from the girl who left.

June 1st I went to your grave. I stood silently. I have not the heart to speak or to sing. One day I will find you, unchanged, unchanging. But what if you do not know me? What if you cannot see your Edith in the woman I am become? What then? What if it is all too long ago?

June 3rd I am resting in bed – I cried all day Thursday & had to be given a sleeping draught. Yesterday was no better.

June 4th Winnow at my bedside, rocking to & fro, to & fro. Winnow's hair needs a bath, I must tell Wymp's wife.

Later. And my darling Crantock, I wonder if Wymp's wife washed his hair before he died. I have a lock of it somewhere, I think, or is it Winnow's hair? Is it Winnow's hair? Oh God, Winnow isn't dead too, is he? I cannot remember at the moment. I cannot but I must. I am sure I shall, but I am too tired presently.

Very much later. Cannot sleep – perhaps never again – oh, the sleep of the dead, such peace it must be & I want it – but there is no sleep for me –

June 5th I have looked & looked but they have taken the lock of Winnow's hair. One of the Wymps is a thief & I have said so. I have said that I am going to have it back. They are so bloody to me, taking his hair. Even if it is dirty I want it, it is all that I have. How can they not understand? How can they not understand?

July 1st I have been unwell. Wymp's wife has nursed me. I am become very thin.

July 28th   The days pass in total peace. I garden in the mornings & in the afternoons I walk or ride to Dinas Sands & swim, with Winnow & the Merry-dog always at my side.

August 1st   I insisted that we take the horses to Newport Sands. I wore trousers for the first time since – I cannot remember when. I felt my Vatesons all around me.

August 8th   I have had a letter from Edgarley. Walter's child is sick, I am needed there. I could of course pretend that I have not received the letter.

August 9th   Is there really no one else to sit at the child's bedside & mop her brow?

August 10th   I have written that I shall return this weekend. The sooner I get there, the sooner I can return here. I have a few things I want to say to Mr & Mrs Porch of Edgarley House.

August 15th   Edgarley. I have been here for one day. The child really is quite ill. She is no longer a fat cheeked Piglet. Tears crept down her cheeks when I entered the room. I bathed her face & hands & rearranged the pillows & shocked everyone by throwing the windows wide open to air the room. The poor little thing, I can't bring myself to be angry although it is her illness that has forced my return. She is only a little girl. It is not her fault that I cannot love her. When I return to Penfeidr she will be motherless – surely I can be kind to her for this short period of time?

August 17th   She is here – come with me from Penfeidr. I saw her standing at the window looking up at the Tor. What is she doing here? Why has she come? She does not belong here.

 August 21st   I have never known such hatred as lives in me today.
   I spoke of Separation, citing Walter's Illness as the reason. Unlike last time, I did not say the dreaded word, although Father

flinched, afraid that I would. The children, I added, can either stay at Edgarley or return to their father. And Father said that I was unwell again & needed to be made better & that he knew of such a suitable place where that would be possible. When I said, I am not unwell but merely wish to be free from a marriage in which there is no happiness, he replied, But, my dear child, it was a marriage of your own choosing.

He and Mother have already spoken of my behaviour with Dr Longstreete. He, I am told, is in agreement that my current state of mind is very much a cause for concern. The good doctor will assist in whatever way necessary to help me recover my health and furthermore knows a most suitable place where I will be taken great care of. So, this is the choice – Marriage to Walter or a home for lunatics.

I will return to Yokohama – immediately. And I will have my Separation. I will put Walter in such a position that he will be glad to be rid of me! Then I shall return to Penfeidr. Now I know why she has come with me. She will help me to free myself.

August 22nd   I have managed to book a passage to Yokohama in ten days' time. Until I leave I shall take my meals in my room. These people are no longer my family. They are dead to me. I have written to Wymp's son informing him that I must return to Yokohama but that I shall be home as soon as possible.

Later. I have been sick from crying. I would kill myself but then they will have won & that I will never allow. They would like to destroy me. I must remain strong.

August 26th   I managed to catch Mother unaccompanied. She fears being alone with me & tries to avoid the possibility. When I most politely asked why I had not been informed of the fire at Penfeidr, she declined to tell me. I did not even raise my voice but I refused to leave her alone until I was told. She became hysterical, repeatedly pulling the bell & crying out for someone to help her. She later said that I had physically threatened her. She is a stupid ridiculous ghastly hideous hideous hideous old woman, and I told her so.

They think I am mad. I can see it in their faces. But I am not. How it would please them to lock me away. I will not give them the satisfaction. Never.

August 29th We are packed & ready to leave. I shall never return to this house. I never wish to see these people again.

September 1st We sailed an hour ago. They insisted on accompanying us to Southampton – to ensure we sailed, I presume. I refused to say goodbye. Father's last words were that one day I will thank him for all this.

September 10th I keep to myself entirely. In my heart I am at Penfeidr. She is here also. I occasionally see her from the corner of my eye.

Nanny Johns sees to the children for the most part. I have told The Piglet, who is completely recovered, that if she does not mind herself I shall throw her overboard to the sea monsters. The little beast laughed at me. What could I do but laugh too.

I find it so hard to believe that she and Ben are my children. But since leaving Penfeidr I do find it difficult to ignore them as I did before. They did not ask to be born. It is not their fault that I long for another life. They are Smallies after all, and if I cannot love them, then I must at least treat them with kindness and some compassion.

September 23rd Have I really only been back in Yokohama for three days? Walter is ill again. There is no question of a Separation. He has refused point blank. But by the time I have finished with him he will be begging for me to go! If of course His Disease does not account for him first.

She will think of something – that is why she is here.

September 30th A letter from Wymp's son has finally arrived. He has the most astoundingly elaborate handwriting I have ever seen – all flourishes & hooks & swoops – & his sentences are dreadfully laborious to read. But thank goodness Uncle Vateson insisted on his receiving some schooling from Nectan & Rhun-Owen. He has promised to proceed as if he expected me returned tomorrow, & I believe him. Winnow has taken to sleeping in our room. He is definitely aware that I am not there & seems to look for me at times. And that is all he writes. The letter is signed Ol Wymp. Ol. Did I ever before know his first name? To me he will only ever be Wymp's son.

1894

February 17th I have been ill now for months. No sooner do I recover from one bout of malaria than another is upon me. My hands are permanently scoured with an itchy red rash & I have taken to wearing gloves all the time. The slightest noise jangles every nerve-ending in my head. I must leave this place. I will die if I stay.

April 19th Crantock's birthday.

May 1st There was once a girl called Maiden May. She is now old & turning grey.

June 5th The Pig has offered my services to a Japanese woman to help improve her English. It's all quite convoluted. The husband, a Mr Yoshitsune, has lived abroad & speaks impeccable English, while his wife has only a smattering & needs conversation to become more fluent. He is a business-trader of some sort & The Pig seems to think that there might be something in it for him – some type of business opportunity. And I have agreed to do what I can because I must get out of this house more or I will – I will . . . I continuously see Her from the corner of my eye. She wants something from me, I know it. I thought She had come with me to help me. But I now think She hates me & would kill me if She could.

June 19th I took the train to the Yoshitsunes'. They have an exquisite house in the hills in Kamakura – I was shown into a drawing-room filled with French antiques. He has lived in France & Holland & travelled very widely, but she has never left Japan. They both wear Western clothes & have very refined manners. There is something alluring about both of them. I am to go for one afternoon a week. Mrs Yoshitsune's English is much better than I was led to believe – she is just very hesitant in her way of speaking, a little lacking in confidence. She is rather lovely, about my age, and very delicate and precise in all her gestures. When I first arrived she bowed to me many times; I felt rather embarrassed & not quite sure how to respond. I managed not to remove my gloves during the entire visit & I'm sure she thought this most strange, but my hands are still in a dreadful state.

August 4th We are come to Zushi for the summer. My afternoon visit to the Yoshitsunes' has become a high point in the week & it shall be resumed in mid-September. Their four boys are exceptionally well behaved & do not speak unless spoken to. So different from the rabble with whom I live. Ben has developed a sullen temper & The Piglet seems not to have a single redeeming feature. I never see Walter. Even the façade of dining together in the evenings stopped months ago. Neither of us cares what the servants might think or what gossip they might spread.

August 14th She blames me that She is here. But what would She have me do? If She does not help me –

September 25th The Yoshitsunes' today. I arrived early to join her for luncheon. It was a feast – & quite awe-inspiring. The meal went on for hours & comprised at least twenty courses, presented one after the other. I did my best. There was soup & all manner of raw fish & vegetables – in the tiniest portions – & served in exquisite porcelain bowls. Mrs Yoshitsune used chopsticks but I wisely stayed with cutlery. I drank a little too much rice wine, which is tremendously potent, & had to go to bed as soon as I returned.

September 29th There has been a tremendous storm for the past two days – the Bay was like a steaming, stewing cauldron & the Ships & Junks were thrown about like toys. It was quite thrilling. There is flotsam & jetsam everywhere.

October 17th Another special event at the Yoshitsunes'. We took tea in their autumn pavilion which overlooks a pond with orange carp & very small turtles – or are they tortoises – & the flowering trees surrounding us were winter cherry. After tea we walked back to the house & Mrs Yoshitsune showed me many hidden corners of their gardens. There is a stream that becomes a waterfall, flowing into a series of seven pools that are crossed by stepping stones & small bridges, & at the bottom of their shallow waters stones of all shapes & sizes can be seen. This eventually leads to an enclosed garden that is made entirely from raked gravel, at the centre of which stands an enormous rock. Mrs Yoshitsune said that it is a sacred stone and pointed out to me a dent in the top, which she described as a cup, & from there she gathers rainwater to drink. She said to me that until one understood the character of such a stone one could not understand life. She then told me of a miraculous stone at the nearby Temple of Hachiman – which she has suggested I visit with her. All her talk of sacred stones reminded me greatly of Uncle Vateson.

October 18th   I have not seen Her for weeks now – not even a glimpse out of the corner of my eye. She is up to something – plotting – I hope it may be something helpful.

November 8th   I have been crying & come to my bed. A letter from Wymp's son with a photograph of Winnow & the Merry-dog. Winnow is looking away, with his hands in his pockets, & Merry is looking up at him with his mouth wide as if in a yawn. My goodness, what a dear old stouty he has become! It was taken by a travelling photographer who was in Dinas Cross making portraits.

November 11th   I am ill again – blinding headaches, & nerve pain in my face & ears & hands, nausea & exhaustion.

November 12th   Hands scoured, raw, bleeding, can't help scratching –

November 14th   Yesterday Nanny Johns smeared my hands with cream. I almost fainted from the pain. I could do nothing afterwards but sit with mangled hands upon my lap. What on earth does she think of us? This house is about as cheerful as a mausoleum.

December 3rd   When I returned home from the Yoshistunes' She was here – pacing up & down, Her face black with rage. I watched Her pacing, terrified. She is so thin & gaunt, I couldn't bear it any longer and begged Her to stop, stop, & She did. She stared at me, boring Her dead empty eyes into mine, Her voice in my head, saying, whore. You betray Crantock every day by continuing to be here. I thought She would attack me – I tried to turn away but wherever I turned She was there, taunting me, until I collapsed on the bed weeping.

What would She have me do?

December 15th   She is always here. She hates me because of the life I live. And She is right to call me whore. Every day I am here is a betrayal.

December 22nd   She wants me to kill him – but I will not – not even to be free. Murder, I said, murder? What do you imagine me capable of?

December 25th   She's plotting & pacing.

December 26th   How I despise Her. How She disgusts me. And I told Her so today. You kill him, I said, if you think it is so easy & then I can return to Penfeidr.

But She will not do it. She cannot. She has no stomach for it. She is a coward in Her black of deepest mourning for Her husband Crantock.

December 27th   She – if She does not succeed in killing him, She will surely kill me.

December 28th   A small amount. Too small. Stupid woman. Bloody stupid woman.

1895

January 1st   How many times can Walter be at death's door without actually going through it?

January 15th   They can go to Hell for all that I care. Every single one of them.

February 4th   She follows me everywhere. She thinks I can't see Her. It did not work last time why should it work this time?

February 14th   I am worn out with remembering.

April 19th   The only way out is death, I am sure of it. Last night I dreamt that we were together – the first such dream for months and months and months.

May 1st   I am 27.

August 9th   I have been ill these past months and almost succeeded in killing myself. I am told that I ceased breathing. They all think it was an accident. They need not know the truth. It is hardly important.
   She has finally gone from me. She failed me. Not even She could return me to Penfeidr.

August 20th   Numb – something to help me sleep, something to wake me up, something to help me stay up on my feet.

August 27th   During the past couple of weeks I have watched Walter carefully. He is not quite as stupid as he likes to imply. He plays at being the amiable fool, allowing others to win at whatever game they are playing in order to be liked. He wants them to think that they are faster than him, slightly smarter – & because of this they all consider him a jovial fellow & a good sport when losing, & so they push things his way – little deals to give him extra cash. I found some papers that he had left lying around & he is involved in a variety of schemes, all above-board, I presume. How could I have not seen this before? But what, may I ask, does he do with the extra money?

Later. I had a rummage through his desk & most of it is put aside for the children, little investments here & there, all adding up to something quite comfortable. And there was I imagining he might be spending it on the Geishas!

September 14th Overhear a conversation on the train between three impeccably dressed women – all obviously quite well-to-do. One, slightly older, perhaps in her forties, was giving advice – My dear, she said, if you want a Divorce then you must give your Husband a reason to insist upon one. So long as he is fearful of public humiliation, you will get your own way.

If I were to pretend to have an affair & then threaten to make it public –

But how? I so rarely leave the house.

October 2nd The most surprising of surprises today – a letter from dear Reggie who asks if he might come & stay with us next year. It is a hazy maze of a letter & I cannot quite make my way to understanding it. But I have replied that of course he must come to us. Perhaps he is being sent to spy on me – to make a report to Edgarley.

October 5th The Piglet comes to me every evening just before her bedtime & talks to me about life in her small world. She is a tremendously affectionate child – she likes to hold my hand while talking to me. Sometimes she will pat my cheek and say, Sad mummy. One day, when she is older, I will tell her of Crantock and Penfeidr. Then she will understand why I have been sad.

October 20th A letter from Wymp's son – my Merry-dog has gone – Winnow is bereft, & I too.

How can then be more real than now?

November 25th I am trying to keep busy – another letter from Reggie, full of humour and light-heartedness.

December 26th Christmas done – children giddy, I allowed them to run wild – they ate what they wished & went to bed when they had exhausted themselves.

I have no doubt that by this time next year I shall be returned to my real home.

December 27th She is returned. This morning I awoke & there She was, standing by the bed, rocking to & fro. She looks different. Not so thin, not so gaunt. I said, You look well, where have You been? She laughed – her teeth are rotting, black, Her breath, the stench of Her breath, dear God. I tried to turn my face away but She wouldn't let me, Her hand shot out & She forced me to look at her. Look, she hissed at me, Edith, look!

1896

January 1st Every day the same – She wants me to do it & if I do not She will kill him Herself.

January 15th The seething rage on Her face makes my blood run cold – She had swept through my room like a typhoon & while I tidied I had to endure Her pacing. She said, there are so many opportunities – how can you not see how easy it is?

January 20th She attacked me – I fought – but have small cuts, on my arms & legs. She says it does not hurt, dying does not hurt. It is either him or me & I must choose. She said black does not show the blood.

February 9th She stands beside him. How can he be oblivious to Her hatred? She knocks things down & he thinks it accidental. Sometimes the violence is expressed on Her face.

March 23rd Reggie arrived a couple of days ago – very much the young man, & what a breath of fresh air he is! He has The Piglet & Ben eating out of his hand & gets on famously with Walter. He has been sent out due to a bit of a scandal – he became overly friendly with a married woman whose husband threatened to blow his brains out – Reggie's as well as his own – apparently there were the most awful scenes. Reggie says he was just whiling away the time. He likes flirting, it cheers him. He had not meant anything by it & did not realise that the lady in question was taking it seriously until he received a letter from her husband. Anyway, he is quite happy to be sent away – he is desperate to travel & have adventures & make his fortune.

He seems to know nothing of my experiences, only that I had been 'unwell'. This was the word he used.

March 25th I must be more careful. Reggie noticed some

scratches on my wrists. I could hardly tell him it was Her, so I made up some story. Goodness knows if he believed me.

April 7th It is eight years since my darling left me. Eight whole years.

Later. Today I had a thorough look at myself in the mirror. I put on my kimono for the very first time – & oh, how soft it was against my skin – but it does not suit me. I looked ridiculous. I then held up the photograph of myself with Crantock, comparing her with what I have become. I look so – is that really me – was I ever so young? Definitely not a beauty, but something in my face, love & happiness is what it was, I think. And my dear one standing beside me – even now he wears the same face, wherever he is.

But I feel as if I am a ghost. I did not clearly understand before now that I too died, on that day eight years ago. I look in the mirror & I do not know that woman. The real me is at Penfeidr, with you. When I return I will find my name carved beneath yours, Edith May Vateson, 1868–1888, wife of Crantock, most beloved wife. I am dead & this is Hell. Finally I understand.

April 8th No – I am mistaken. This is not Hell. I am dead and this is death.

April 19th She tried to cut my hair off. I managed to get the scissors from Her but not soon enough.

May 1st My 28th birthday – dear Reggie took me into Tokyo for the day. What a high old time I pretended to have – just to please him. But it was a relief to get away from the House & Her, even for a short while.

May 2nd I said to Her, you cannot kill me, I am dead already. My how I laughed at the expression on Her face.

May 3rd She has promised that She will get me away from here – She says I must trust Her.

May 4th   She has found the right fellow – a chap called Dickinson. She says that he will lose his head over me, She can tell already, & then I shall have my Separation, if Walter does not want A Scandal. All I have to do is Play The Game. How very clever She is. So I have been going to the Club with Reggie – socialising in a way I previously refused to. Everyone is most surprised – Walter's Wife is Charming & Her Brother is Such a Wag.

However, Dickinson – yes, well. As if I could ever be interested in the likes of him, but he will do well enough to compromise Walter.

June 7th   Dickinson has really taken the bait.

July 11th   Under the weather – I cannot be ill, not now when everything is falling into place.

August 9th   Dickinson, Dickinson, Dickinson – what a fool the fellow is.

September 18th   She is angry again. She has had enough of me trying to push Dickinson further along and decided to take matters into Her own hands. And She will do it. There is no doubting that. Oh yes.

September 30th   She has started
   Slow & steady
   Slow & steady wins
   Slow & steady wins the race

October 1st   And again

October 2nd   And again

October 3rd   And once more

October 4th   Walter is unwell, the poor dear.

October 5th   House is revolving around Walter & his illness.

October 6th   She

October 7th   All I can do is watch. Watch out for Her. Watch that Her hand is steady.

October 8th   That fool Dickinson putting his nose in where it is not wanted & I told him so.

October 9th   She is very peaceful, very serene. She hums to Herself & rocks as She does so.

October 10th   This shall be no more

October 11th   Twilight – the calmness of it in a sickroom

October 12th   Reggie sits by him every morning & reads aloud from the newspaper. What a dear fellow he is. He does not have to, I said so. He should be out having adventures, exploring. But he is very fond of Walter and is quite worried & upset by his condition. I told both Reggie & the Doctor that Walter has been taking arsenic for years, as well as strychnine & goodness knows what other concoctions & potions & pills. From long, long before I knew him. Yes, years & years. And it is bound to build up in his system & affect him. Reggie said, The poor old chap, I hope he is going to pull through.

October 13th   In all our years of marriage I have never known Walter to be so ill.

October 14th   She cannot keep the smile from Her face.

October 19th   Dreadful days. Awful seeing him suffer so.

October 20th   He is in great pain. He can't last much longer like this, surely.

October 21st He seemed quite rational & clear-headed today & saw both Mardie & Ben. Mardie sang to him – Reggie cried.

Later. It's all just – it's just too – he can't really be dying. He can't. He's been at death's door so many times. He'll pull through, I'm sure of it, I said so to Reggie. Walter will be fine, I said, he's such a big fellow, sturdy, strong, he will outlive us all, you'll see.

October 22nd Walter left us at almost 4.30 this afternoon. I was at his side & so was She. Poor dear Reggie is devastated.

October 23rd Spend most of the afternoon being fitted for mourning clothes. She & I, both wearing black. It suits Her better, I do not have the colour for it. Nanny Johns is looking after the children – goodness knows what she has told them.

October 24th A packed funeral. Shocked faces, stunned, paleness surrounding me, & tears of course. He was much loved. I always knew that to be so. I am so very sorry – I heard myself saying over & over again – comforting everyone.

The crows in the trees that surrounded the cemetery – har, har, har, har. I wanted to say, har, har, your bloody selves.

She had the good sense not to come.

October 25th I have told Reggie that I will return to England – there is nothing to hold me here.

October 26th I am in a bit of a state about the Inquest, but She assures me that there is nothing to worry about. He took arsenic for years – his Doctors can verify that.

November 1st When the Inquest is finished I shall go home. I can hardly believe it. Oh God, to be at Penfeidr again.

November 2nd This just seems such a waste of time. Still it must be done, it must be sat through, graciously, grievingly – the young widow sat.

November 3rd Dickinson came up in court. And the letters. They seem so tawdry. How can I explain that I did not mean a word of them, that I just wanted a Separation? As if I would ever be interested in a Dickinson. What type of woman do they take me for? The boy is nobody – even worse than Walter – he is a bank clerk, for goodness' sake. Am I to be held responsible for his gullibility?

November 4th According to My Counsel, I must allow them to drag my name through the mud but I am forbidden to say that Walter had Syphilis. The Good Name of the Dead Man must not be Slandered. I said, it is not Slander, it is Truth. Ask his Doctors. And so they did – but not a single one of them would confirm this fact. I have been made to look like a liar & I am not.

I must be strong – I must not lose my head.

November 5th She is with me. I see Her watching the Inquest proceedings. She achieved what She wanted & I must trust Her. She knows what She is doing.

1897

December   walled-in, moisty walls
   prison number four
   prisoner number X19

I am called Nineteen, by Turner the wardress, Edith does not exist.

From next month I am allowed one letter a month, one visitor, I have said there is no one I wish to see

I will not be here long – the Porch & Carew lawyers are working to free me – soon soon

I have begun the Penfeidr notebooks again – difficult though it is in this half-light, or rather, half-darkness better describes

Cwm-yr-Eglwys, Pembrokeshire

October 1934

Mardie had sat barely moving for the better part of the morning. Occasionally she lit a cigarette that would burn down between her fingers, entirely forgotten. Sometimes she would take a sip of whisky or just stare into the liquid. She felt at peace with herself, calmed by the muted domesticity of the drifting day, the clock gently marking time. Through the open window came the shush of the sea, and now and then the wail of a gull, accompanied by a surprising warmth for the time of year, but laden with Octobery smells, wood-smoke in particular.

For some reason, unknown even to herself, she looked at her hands, examining her palms, wondering what she might know of her life, if only she could read the lines. She studied their shape, large and broad, with long fleshy fingers and square blunt finger-nails. Her hands were those of a man. Perhaps very much like her father's.

She had learned, in reading her mother's diaries, that everything she had always believed of her parents' marriage was horribly true. In addition she had discovered that her parents had never loved one another. From the beginning the marriage had been a façade, a fake, a sham. Apparently, her father had had syphilis. And her mother was mad. Yet Mardie almost did not care. During the past days she had periodically said aloud: You killed him. You, mother, are guilty. But she could not make the words carry any real meaning. It seemed to Mardie that there was no such thing as the truth, although it was what she had thought to find. And if not the truth, then some answers to the tragedy of her father's death and her mother's life. But there was no tragedy. There was only life with all its familial tedium. Her mother's story. Sad. Pathetic. Deluded. With such words, Mardie tried to stir herself to either anger or sorrow. Instead, she felt emptied of all emotion.

Her father had died accidentally. This was what everyone had believed, or chosen to believe. Her father had been ill for years, dying slowly but surely, taking arsenic in ever-increasing quantities with little regard for the harm it was doing. That he had, in effect,

307

done himself in, was what Mardie had been told about his death when she had reached an age capable of understanding. At one time, she had overheard her father's mother say that such was her dear boy's pain it was possible he had taken more arsenic than he needed to in the hope of ending his own suffering.

But the British Consular Court had thought differently, and found her mother guilty of murder and condemned her to death. Instead, she had been reprieved and sentenced to life in an English prison. How different would my life have been if mother had been hanged as a murderess? Mardie asked the bottom of her empty whisky glass. All our lives revolved around Grand's monthly visits to you in Aylesbury, as well as the Porch and Carew lawyers' annual attempts to have you pardoned and freed. Petitions to Their Majesties that were repeatedly declined.

Aylesbury. No one ever said the word prison. Not even once. Edith is in Aylesbury, they would say. Mother is in Aylesbury at the moment, we expect her to be home by the end of the year. In this way, they had lived for nearly fifteen years, until her mother's release in 1910. It would have been easier if you had been hanged, Mardie thought. At least then I could have mourned you. At least then you would have been dead and buried. Instead, I knew that one day you would return.

Mardie could remember asking Grand when her mother was coming back, to which she would always reply, soon. But when is soon, Mardie would ask, fearful that it might be that very afternoon. I didn't miss you, she muttered, I pretended to, but I didn't. My childhood at Edgarley was happy. I had Grand and Ben and grandfather and letters from Uncle Reggie. I was loved and spoiled and although I missed father, I was not unhappy.

Then, in 1906, Ben died, followed just a few weeks later by the news that Uncle Reggie was missing and presumed killed in the San Francisco earthquake. I was fifteen. For the very first time in my life I encountered the reality and meaning of loss. People went away and never came back. They died and one never saw them again. All that could be done was to go on living and create a space around oneself comprised of days becoming weeks and months and then years. One year after their deaths, two, three, four, five, ten, fifteen, twenty. As if time could matter, as if time healed. I finally understood that all those years previously father had died and that you were in Aylesbury because of his death. Ben and Uncle Reggie's deaths opened the door of questions about what had happened to him. What, where, when, why and how? Grand did not know, or did not want to know, and you would not answer the letters I wrote. Even after you were released you refused to tell me anything. So how could I have believed that my coming here would change anything between us?

Mardie sighed. She touched her cheekbone with tentative fingertips. The swelling where her mother had struck her had gone down, leaving behind a tender, curdled bruise.

I have no wish to see you again, mother, she said aloud. What would be the point? There is nothing between us. There never was. You should never have been allowed to marry. Poor father, didn't he know you were sick? Did my grandparents really not tell him?

As the days passed the mild weather continued, the light, soft and mellow. Each day Mardie walked around the headland to eat at the fishermen's shack near Dinas Sands. During her return she invariably stopped at the same point on the headland to watch the surge and swell and shape of the sea. I am leaving soon, she always said.

The twenty minutes or so of sea-watching was the highlight of her day. For the most part she felt numb. She would arrive home and stare at herself in the mirror and smile at a face that seemed to hesitate before returning her smile. Then she would lift her hand to touch her cheek, seeking reassurance that her skin was warm, that she hadn't died and not noticed, after all. It's as if I'm a ghost, she said to her reflection. It doesn't even hurt if I pinch myself. She looked for Ben, but did not see him or hear his voice. But even this did not surprise her. Why should he come, she thought, when there is nothing left to say?

She caught sight of her mother approaching on the Dinas headland path, coming from the direction of the Cwm. Her energetic step was easily recognisable. She occasionally took this path, Mardie knew, but this was only the third time in as many years that they had accidentally encountered each other. Mardie stopped, waiting for her mother to draw level, and when she did so they looked at each other silently.

I'm leaving, mother, Mardie finally said. I've had a letter from Uncle Edward. I'm to go to Calcutta for as long as I wish. Her mother didn't respond. I shall, of course, return your books before I go, she continued. Her mother looked at her blankly. This woman gave birth to me, Mardie thought. But the fact seemed irrelevant. She looked at her mother, seeing an old woman who might live another ten or twenty or thirty years. Father was forty-three when he died, the very same age I am now. Mardie spoke these words aloud, clearly, plainly. And the sound of her own voice suddenly took her back to that time she had last seen her father. That huge fellow propped against a welter of pillows; her own father, dying. This woman had been his wife. She had been there at his bedside, mixing his medicines, smoothing the covers. This woman had poisoned him. He had known that, surely? Mardie frowned, the light on the sea sharply catching the corner of one eye so that it watered.

Do you think father doesn't know you poisoned him, she said, her voice flat, not expecting a reply. Of course he knows. And he watches you. I'm sure of it. He walks around with you, like a shadow, watching and waiting. My father is dead. You killed him. And he knows. Mardie heard her mother's sharp intake of breath as she continued, When you die he'll be waiting to see you. He will be the first person you see, not your darling Crantock, not your bloody Vatesons, but my father.

Her mother hissed something inaudible and moved to turn away. But Mardie was quick enough to stop her, grabbing her mother's wrist and tightening her grip when she tried to wrench her arm free. As her mother continued to struggle Mardie squeezed her fingers more and more tightly. Then she let go, at the same time pushing her mother away with considerable force.

Mardie watched as her mother stumbled backwards trying to get her footing, but failing, falling; then came the thud of her head as it hit the ground.

In prison, in prison, don't tell Mother, find Reggie, Reggie knows, and Nanny Johns, they need to be told, I don't want Mother, You yes you I want, You you you you are time and Yesterday is not past, not here, You can forget, you love me, yes, and you're right, you've seen remembrance, and only you, even here, you'll find me, you'll know me by your thoughts, you left me, you left me Crantock, you love you said, you'll find me, maiden May, then came fair Edith May, the fairest maid on Dinas Sands, at Penfeidr, at the New House, at the Old House, in the orchard, you taught me this, here, here you said you are sure, and I waited in the sun's bright rays, and you'll know me as you know yourself, and you danced your leaping dance, here, just here, and I looked on, your spirit, your wish, your talk talking into me, taking my life into your voice, talking me into a destiny, talking and taking, Yes and I freely grant thee my life, my virgin-place is yours, falling asleep I touch you, I gave myself to you and you are gone now and Winnow, do you remember Winnow? he died, you will always live but he did not, another dead child, another dead child, I can't hear you muttering, can't you, but why, why, you loved me, you've come to comfort me, you are all together, all, and I am alive, I breathe, I cannot see how but I do, how slow life is, I can't die, how many times I tried, never within my reach, never . . .

Mardie stood beside the hospital bed next to the two doctors. Apart from the bump on her mother's head there was little wrong with her. As far as the doctors could ascertain Mrs Porch Carew was, in their opinion, in better physical health than most sixty-six-year-olds. What was cause for concern was the state of her mind.

Yes, Mardie said, my mother has had periods of nervous agitation ever since she was a girl.

No, she has never needed to be hospitalised for it.

Yes, she has lived alone for years and always been entirely capable of caring for herself.

No, I do not agree that my mother is unstable and I take offence at the use of that word.

At this Mardie glared at both doctors, neither of whom would meet her eye. She did not like their officious manners or their slicked-down hair. But although her tone and expression dismissed them and their words, they persistently refused to release her mother from hospital due to what they called her questionable mental condition.

And so the three of them stood at the bedside looking at her mother propped against the pillows, her hands resting on the top of blanket and sheets. Mardie tried not to stare at the place where her mother's thick grey hair had been shaved to reveal the sickeningly white skull and a bump the size of a plover's egg, with a blood-black line along it, crossed in four places by heavy black stitches. Instead Mardie focused on her mother's lips. Mardie had often seen her mother in this state. To her such behaviour was not unusual. But in the eyes of the doctors her mother appeared incoherent and mentally unbalanced.

Well, Miss Carew, while there is no physical problem to keep your mother here . . . we cannot possibly release her . . . She does, after all, live alone . . . And as far as we can see . . . your mother requires full-time care . . . As I am sure you can appreciate . . . in her condition . . . Unfortunately . . . Fortunately . . . Yes, there is a very good . . . Yes, a private nursing home . . . at Haverfordwest . . . that has the facilities to care for your mother . . . In her somewhat unfortunate . . . Yes, quite so, quite so . . . her unfortunate condition.

They both looked at Mardie, smiling benignly; the matter had been decided between them and they expected her acquiescence. She looked at them, lowering her eyelids in disdain, dismissing them, just as she knew Grand would have done. The loony-bin, she said, her voice brusque, cold, hard. They tsked in unison as if to a child creating a nuisance and seen dragging its heels in public.

Mardie looked at her mother. Four days ago she had stood over her unconscious body on the path on Dinas Head. At that moment elation had coursed through her at the thought, Mother is finally dead. Then she had fled, turning to run towards the

Cwm is search of help. It had seemed only a short while later that she was pacing the waiting-room in Fishguard Hospital, smoking, drinking from her hip-flask. Her mother was not dead, that much she did know.

Eventually the matron came to inform her that her mother would be kept in overnight. Her skull was not fractured. The bump had just required four stitches. She was sleeping now and it was best not to disturb her. Presented with forms, Mardie filled them in, diligently. The matron with her thick Welsh accent made her nervous. Never before had she been in a hospital. Doctors treated Porchs at home in their own beds where they were nursed by family. Everyone had died at home in their own beds, her father, Ben, grandfather, Grand. It was even possible that Uncle Reggie had been at home, if not in bed, when the earthquake had hit. Somehow, it did not seem at all possible that her mother would die here in this hospital, Mardie thought with a sour resentment.

On her way back to the Cwm she drove with the windows down in an attempt to shake the hospital smell from her hair and coat. She took corners recklessly, her mind focused on the idea of a very strong whisky, or two. At the house she slammed the door. Mrs Palmer took her coat, saying, I'll bring through a coffee with whisky, just as you like it; and when she did, she politely asked after Miss Edith. Mardie looked at her, wondering how much she really knew. My mother is going to be fine, thank you, Mrs Palmer, she replied. And Mrs Palmer smiled, nodded and left the room.

She looked at her mother lying in the hospital bed. Why shouldn't she go into a nursing home? It hardly matters to me where she is, Mardie thought. She looked at the doctors to find them intently watching her. She had not liked their hectoring tones and had no intention of consenting to their wishes. Not just yet. So she murmured, I must think about it a little further, and then left.

That evening she decided to telephone Uncle Robert, although she put off doing so as late as she possibly could and sat nuzzling a whisky glass and staring into the fire. The later the hour became the more she looked forward to telephoning, delighting in the idea of disturbing his evening. Mardie did not like her Uncle Robert. She never had. Not from when she had first encountered him at Edgarley when she was almost six. Nor had he liked her. He had tried to bully her and she had resisted, had said no straight to his face, and he had smacked her, fast and hard around her legs. It was the only time he had done that, because she had informed her grandmother, who had berated him. As she had grown older, she had come to consider him as little more than a pompous ass. He was a schoolmaster. At every word he spoke he would pause as if to dot his i's and cross his t's, making even the most basic attempt at conversation a laborious chore. Even Grand had found him tedious, saying on more than one occasion that the poor fellow was dusty, don't you think?

Mardie listened as the clock chimed nine. If she put off telephoning much longer he would be in bed and that would not do. She dialled, counting each ring at the other end. She knew he would pick up on the fifth ring, he always did, and she was not disappointed. Clearly, concisely, she told him what had happened, the accident, the hospital, and the doctors' insistence on the nursing home. In between her words she could hear his slightly wheezy breathing and she shivered in disgust. Hardly had she finished than he began to speak, his voice ponderous, relentless.

Of course it is not acceptable for your mother to go into a nursing home. Even when she was unwell, when I was a boy, she was looked after at home. Despite the inconvenience to the entire family, Mother insisted on caring for her. Mother did her duty. We all did. Just as Mother did her duty by taking you and your brother in, even though it would have been far better for you both to have gone to your father's family. But no, instead she inconvenienced herself and her entire family to provide a home for you both. And now it is incumbent upon you to care for your mother for as long as she needs to be cared for. He spoke on and on, repeating himself: moral obligation; acceptance of one's responsibilities; what must be done; duty, dutiful, duteous, duty-bound.

Tired of this and wanting another whisky she spoke over him, saying, Well, thank you for that, Uncle Robert, I'll sleep on it. Cheerio. And she hung up the receiver before he could say any more. For a moment she stood there looking at the telephone, expecting it to ring, but it didn't. He had not said anything that she had not expected him to say. Refilling her glass with whisky, she took a large gulp, panting breathlessly as it burned down her throat, before taking another. She moved to stand by the fire, positioned so that she could see herself in the mirror. Periodically she lifted the glass to her lips, sip-sipping, all the while watching her father's face. This face, her face, her father's face; there was nothing of her mother there at all. Or Grand for that matter.

Duty: was Grand doing her duty with herself and Ben? Mardie did not think so. Grand had loved her. Grand had loved Ben. Just as she had loved her daughter Edith and this was why she had nursed her during her illness. And there lay the difference. Mardie did not love her mother. Her mother was responsible for her father's death. Why should she take it upon herself to take her into her own home and care for her? But even as she thought the question she knew the answer. She would take it upon herself because it was what Grand would have wanted. Mardie owed that much at least to her grandmother. She knew that. But this obligation was not called duty, it was something more profound. She continued to love her grandmother and could not bear the idea of her disapproval although she was dead.

The following afternoon, she helped her mother into the back seat of the motor car and arranged a rug over her knees. The doctors disapproved of what she was doing. She had had to ask Uncle Robert to telephone and have a word with them. As she started the engine she stared at her mother in the rear-view mirror, asking, Are you comfortable, mother? but her mother remained oblivious.

Mardie took the coast road that led up towards Dinas Cross, occasionally glancing in the mirror at her mother, who stared out through the window, rocking a little, murmuring indecipherably to herself. Mardie felt uneasy and tried to assuage her unease by thinking that it wasn't as if she didn't have good reason to feel this way. At the top of the hill the view opened out to provide a panorama of Fishguard Bay and farther out one could see along to St George's Channel. Mardie slowed almost to a stop as she always did at this point, to gaze out over the water stretching as far as the eye could reach. She watched her mother smile, the lips lifting and parting to reveal slightly protruding teeth. Mardie felt a savage pain in her chest. Tears burned her eyes. She crashed the gears and stalled twice in an attempt to get the motor moving. Through gritted teeth she muttered, I don't want Grand's smile on your face. You killed my father, you bloody bitch. But just as suddenly as the rage had surfaced it drained from her completely. From the back seat she heard her mother ask in a peevish tone, Does Crantock know where I am? This was followed a short while later by the question, What day is today? Mardie responded, It's Thursday, mother. But her mother gave no appearance of hearing so she said more loudly, It's Thursday, mother, the first of November. Still her mother gave no sign of having heard, she rocked sideways, then stopped to change direction, rocking to and fro, all the while murmuring, murmuring. I can't hear a bloody word you're saying, mother, Mardie shouted, flaring into an irritated rage, thinking, Dear God, why didn't you die? Why don't you die? When will you die? Her mother's eyes caught her own in the mirror and briefly she smiled the smile of Mardie's grandmother before saying, It is now November. She looked back out of the window, and began her sideways rocking, whispering loudly, as if to a child in a game, November, November, it is now November, after all.

Mardie listened to her mother's voice as she drove onward past Dinas Cross, and farther onward before sharply braking to take a left turn on to a narrow road where the hedgerows caught and scratched at the windows, down past Soar Hill, and Cotti Clyd, and further down to Cwm-yr-Eglwys, where she stopped at the white cottage that looked out to sea. She opened the car door, extending her hand to help her mother alight, and waited as she stood staring, first at the cottage and then at the sea beyond the sea wall and along to the ruined church with its tip-tilted headstones, where the wild cyclamen were already in flower.

She turned to Mardie, I know this place, she said, I have been here before.

As Mardie unlatched the gate, Mrs Palmer opened the front door and stepped out to meet them. Mardie could see that she had dressed as if for a special occasion. There was warmth and affection on her face and in her voice as she said, Oh, Miss Edith, it's Maivey, Maivey Owen as you'd remember me. I were at Penfeidr, so many years back now. Do you remember? I were with you and Master Carantock, and I haven't forgotten, not a one of you. How could I forget, Mister and Missuss Vateson, and Corth and Tybie and Elined and . . .

Mardie listened to the litany of names continue as she looked at her mother, who had stopped in the middle of the path when the door had opened. Her mother, wearing a headscarf to protect her injury, and a coat that was much too heavy for the mildness of the day, and stockings that rumpled and caught around her ankles, while in front of her she clutched an incredibly old and odd-looking bag, her hands all knuckles and bone. She watched as Mrs Palmer took her mother's arm, saying, Let's get you inside, Miss Edith, and out of that coat, and after I've settled you by the fire, I'll make some tea for you, and a coffee for Miss Mardie, just as I know she likes it. As her mother allowed herself to be led up the garden path and in through the open door Mardie heard her ask, Does Crantock know that I am here?

Mardie clicked the latch on the gate behind her but remained standing where she was. She looked at her hands, so thick and broad and fleshy. I have my father's hands, she said, and his face, so why shouldn't she have her mother's smile. Ben's voice responded, Because you hate her. Yes, Mardie replied, I do hate her, but it is even too late for that. What is the point of hating someone to whom I mean nothing? And revenge would make me no better than her. I can do this, I know it. When she is recovered, in two or three weeks, then I will go to India. Uncle Edward wants me there, he said so. No one wants her. She will be alone. But I will leave her behind and start afresh, far away from here and far away from her.

Mardie turned to look at the cottage, squinting a little as she gazed up at the chimneys, sniffing the wood-smoke that curled upwards reaching for the clouds. Yes, she said nodding, as she walked up the garden path and towards the open door.

End Note

For the next twenty-four years Edith and Mardie lived together in the white cottage at Cwm-yr-Eglwys.

On 27th June 1958, Edith died at home, aged 90 years. She was cremated at Swansea Crematorium and her ashes were scattered there in the Garden of Remembrance.

Mardie survived her mother by twenty years, dying, aged 86, on 9th February 1978.

This novel is the first of three on the subject of Victorian murderesses. The second will concern the story of Florence Maybrick (1862–1941), who was found guilty of poisoning her husband, James Maybrick, in what appears to have been a miscarriage of justice. The third novel will bring Edith Carew and Florence Maybrick together; both served their terms of imprisonment at Aylesbury Prison where, it is said, they became good friends.

I would like to express my gratitude to the librarians of the Society for Psychical Research in London and Cambridge for responding to my questions and queries with patience and politeness. This novel was written over a number of years, and in a great many places, and owes much to the generosity and kindness of others. For this I would like to thank the late Dr Robert Woof and Pamela Woof, of Grasmere, Cumbria; Ian and Shelagh Shipley, for tolerating my extensive stays at their London home when I needed to do library research; Angela Lee-Foster and her family for my relaxing and restorative visits to Suffolk; and similarly to Michael Morley and Vera McKechnie Morley. Last, but not least, thank you to Tina Usher and Simon Morley for their love and support.